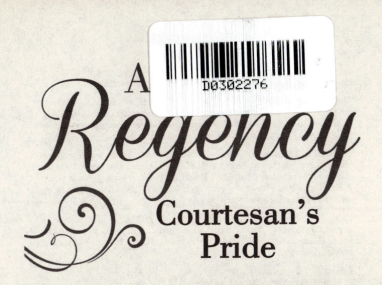

A Regency

Courtesan's Pride

ANN LETHBRIDGE

MILLS & BOON

Published in Great Britain 2015
by Mills & Boon, an imprint of Harlequin (UK) Limited,
Eton House, 18-24 Paradise Road, Richmond, Surrey, TW9 1SR

A REGENCY COURTESAN'S PRIDE © 2015 Harlequin Books S.A.

More Than a Mistress © 2011 Michele Ann Young
The Rake's Inherited Courtesan © 2009 Michele Ann Young

ISBN: 978-0-263-91762-8

052-1015

More Than a Mistress

ANN LETHBRIDGE

In her youth, award-winning author **Ann Lethbridge** reimagined the Regency romances she read and now she loves writing her own. Now living in Canada, Ann visits Britain every year, where family members understand, so they say, her need to poke around every antiquity within a hundred miles. Learn more about Ann or contact her at www.annlethbridge.com. She loves hearing from readers.

Chapter One

January 1820

Only a man dedicated to duty travelled to Yorkshire in January. Hunkered against the cold, high on his curricle, Charles Henry Beltane Mountford, Marquis of Tonbridge, couldn't miss the irony in his father's proud words. What choice was there for Charlie, other than duty, if Robert was to be accepted back into the family? If he was found. No. Not if. When he was found.

Face stinging and ears buffeted by the wind, he lifted his gaze from the road to the leaden sky and bleak stretch of moors ahead. Three years and not one word from his wayward twin. While on some deep level, he knew his brother hadn't come to physical harm, every time he recalled Robert's face as he left, Charlie's gut twisted with guilt.

He should not have said what he did, imposed his own sense of duty on his brother. They might look alike, but there the similarities ended. Their lives had followed different paths and each had their own roles to play.

Finally, after three years of arguing and pleading, he had

sold his soul to bring his brother home. He would visit Lady Allison and begin the courtship his father demanded. The weight of duty settled more heavily on his shoulders. The chill in his chest spread outwards.

Damnation, what in Hades was the matter with him? Lady Allison was a modestly behaved, perfectly acceptable, young woman of good family. She'd make a fine duchess. Marriage was a small sacrifice to bring Robert home and banish the sadness from his mother's face. Sadness he'd helped cause.

He urged his tired team over the brow of the hill, eager to reach the inn at Skepton before dark.

What the hell? A phaeton. Sideways on. Blocking the road. Its wheels hung over the left-hand ditch, its horses rearing and out of control. Coolly, Charlie pulled his ribbons hard right. The team plunged. The curricle tilted on one wheel, dropped and swung parallel to the obstruction. It halted inches from catastrophe, inches from a slight young man in a caped driving coat bent over the traces of the panicked animals of the other equipage, unaware of the danger.

Damn. What a mess. Charlie leaped down. Nowhere to tie his horses. He clenched the bridle in his fist. 'Need help?' he yelled against the wind.

The young man spun around. 'By gum, you scared me.'

Not a man. A woman. Charlie stared, felt his jaw drop and could do nothing to stop it. Her eyes were bright blue, all the more startling beneath jet brows. Her cheeks were pink from the wind and black ropes of hair flew around her oval face in disgraceful disorder.

A voice in his head said *perfect*.

Her arched brows drew together, creasing the white high forehead. 'Don't just stand there, you gormless lump. If you've a knife, help me cut the bloody traces.' She hopped over the poles and began sawing at the leathers on the other side with what looked like little more than a penknife.

Charlie snapped his mouth shut, pulled the dagger from the top of his boot and slashed the traces on his side. 'Here, use this.' He passed her his knife, handle first.

She grabbed it, cut the last strap and proceeded to untangle the horse's legs with very little care for life and limb.

Charlie grabbed the bridle of her horses while hanging on to his own.

The young woman straightened. She was tall, he realised, her bright sapphire eyes level with his mouth. 'Thank you.' She dragged strands of hair back from her face and grinned. 'The damned axle snapped. I must have been going too fast.'

Another Letty Lade, with her coachman-style language. 'You were lucky I managed to stop.' He glanced around. 'Where is your groom?' No gently bred female travelled alone.

'Pshaw.' She waved a dismissive hand. 'I only went to Skepton. I don't need a groom for such a short journey.'

Reckless, as well as a menace on the road. 'It seems on this occasion you do.' He huffed out a breath. He couldn't leave her stranded on the side of the road with night falling. 'A broken axle, you say?' It might be a strap, in which case he might be able to fix it. 'Hold the horses for a moment, please.'

With a confidence in her abilities he didn't usually feel around females, he left her holding the horses and went to the back of her carriage. He crouched down beside the wheel and parted the long yellowed grass on the verge.

Blast. No fixing that. The axle had snapped clean in two near the offside wheel. She must have hit the verge at speed to do so much damage.

He returned to her. 'No hope of a makeshift repair, I'm afraid. I'll drive you home.'

'That's reet kind of you,' she said, her Yorkshire accent stronger than ever. Then she smiled.

It was as if he'd looked straight at the sun. The smile on her lips warmed him from the inside out. *Lovely.*

A distraction he did not need.

He glared at her. 'Where do you live?' His tone sounded begrudging. And so it should. The careless wench could have killed them both, or damaged some very fine horses. She'd been lucky. And she should not be driving around the countryside without a groom.

Her smile disappeared. She cocked her head on one side. 'No need to trouble. I'll ride.' She jerked her chin towards her team.

'One is lame. And the other is so nervous, it is sweating and likely to bolt. It is my duty to see you safely home.'

And his pleasure, apparently, from the stirring in his blood.

Damn it.

He looked up at the sky, took in the fading light. He'd be finding his way to Skepton in the dark if they didn't get started. 'I insist.'

'Do you, by gum?' She laughed, probably at the displeasure on his face. 'I'll not deny you your way, if you'll tie these beasts on behind.'

Kind of her to oblige him.

Leaving her with his horses, grateful they were tired enough not to protest a stranger's hand, he led her team to the back of the curricle and jury-rigged a leading string.

Returning to the girl, he shouted over the rising wind, 'I'm going to push your vehicle further off the road.'

He strode to her wrecked equipage, put his shoulder to the footboard and pushed. The phaeton, already teetering on the brink of the shallow ditch, slid down the bank, its poles tilted to the sky. No one would run into it in the dark.

'Strong lad,' she yelled.

Good God, he almost felt like preening. He suppressed an urge to grin, climbed up on to his box and steadied his team. The perfectly matched bays shifted restlessly. Probably feeling the chill, as well as the panic of the other horses.

'Can you climb up by yourself?' he asked, controlling the beasts through the reins.

She hopped up nimbly. He caught a brief glimpse of sensible leather ankle boots and a silk stocking-clad calf amid the fur lining her driving coat before she settled herself on the seat.

A very neatly turned calf, slender and sweetly curved.

Bloody hell. 'Which way?'

'You'll have to turn around. I was on my way home from Skepton.'

Skepton was at least five miles on. A mill town. Not a place a respectable female went without a groom. Just what sort of woman was she? Not gently bred obviously, despite the fine clothes. Apparently, he was soon to find out. He manoeuvred his carriage around in the road, the prospect of a warm fire any time soon receding.

He cast her a sidelong glance. She was as lovely in profile as she was full face. She had a small straight nose and full kissable lips. If Robert was in his place, he'd be enjoying himself by now, making love to her.

But he, Charlie, was a dull dog according to his last mistress. A prosy bore. Robert's parting shot rang in his ears. *Try to have a bit of fun, for once.*

That was all right for Robert. He wasn't the ducal heir with hundreds of people relying on his every decision. Hades, the last time he'd done as he pleased it had ended in disaster. For everyone, including Robert. Never again.

He'd do well to keep this woman firmly at a distance.

Mindful of the lame horse following behind, Charlie walked his team. He raised his voice to be heard over the wind's howl. 'As travelling companions, I believe introductions are in order. Tonbridge, at your service.'

'Honor Meredith Draycott,' she said. 'Call me Merry. Thank you for stopping.'

As if he'd had a choice.

'Tonbridge,' she said. 'That's a place.'

He felt slightly affronted, as if she'd accused him of lying. 'It is also my name.'

She considered this in silence for a second, perhaps two. 'You are an of.'

He blinked. 'Of?'

'Something *of* Tonbridge. Duke or earl or some such.'

He grinned. Couldn't help it. 'Marquis of,' he said.

'Oh, my.'

The first thing she'd said that hadn't surprised him, he realised. Which in and of itself was surprising.

'What are you doing in these parts?' she asked.

'I'm going to Durn.'

'Mountford's estate. Oh, you are that marquis. You still have a long way to go.'

'I do. I plan to put up in Skepton for the night.'

They reached the top of hill and the road flattened out. The clouds seemed closer to earth up here, the wind stronger, more raw, more determined to find a way beneath his coat.

She inhaled deeply. 'It's going to snow.'

Charlie glanced up at the sky. The clouds looked no more threatening than they had when he set out earlier in the day. 'How can you tell?'

'I've lived on these moors all my life. I can smell it.'

He tried not to smile. He must not have succeeded because

she huffed. 'You'll see,' she said. 'I can smell when it's going to rain, too, or feel it on my skin. You have to feel the weather or you can get into trouble out here on the moors.'

He chuckled under his breath. 'Like running off the road?'

'That was not my fault,' she said haughtily. She glanced back over her shoulder at her horses. 'I think his limp is getting worse.'

Charlie didn't much fancy leaving the horse out here, but he might be forced to do so if the animal became too lame to walk. He slowed his team down a fraction. 'How much further?'

'Two miles. Turn right at the crossroads.'

At this rate it was going to be midnight before he reached the next town. Blasted woman wandering around the countryside alone.

'You can leave me at the corner,' she said.

Had she read his mind? More likely she'd seen the disgruntlement on his face. Clearly, he needed to be more careful about letting his thoughts show. 'I will see you to your door, Miss Draycott.'

'Pigheaded man,' she muttered.

Definitely not a lady. Most likely bourgeoisie, with lots of money and no refinement.

As they turned at the crossroads, white flakes drifted down and settled on the horses' backs where they melted and on Charlie's coat where they did not.

'See,' she said.

He shot her a glance and realised that she didn't look all that happy about being proved right. 'Should we expect a significant amount?'

She shrugged. 'Up here on the high moors? Like as not. The wind will drift it, too.'

Hardly comforting. The few flakes turned into a flurry, and pretty soon he was having trouble making out the road at all. Only the roughness at the verge gave him any clue he was still on track since there were no trees or hedges. Even that faint guide wouldn't last long. There was already a half-inch of pure white blanketing everything in sight. In the growing dusk, he was beginning not to trust his vision.

She gave a shiver and hunched deeper in her coat.

The cold was biting at his toes and fingers, too. If it came to a choice between the lame horse and the two people in the carriage, he was going to have to choose the people, even if he valued the horses more.

'There,' she said, pointing.

A brief break in the wind allowed him to see the outline of a square lump of a house. A monstrous ugly house. Not what he'd been expecting. Though he should have, given the expensive clothes, the fashionable phaeton and the mode of speech.

'Good,' he said. He glanced back. The lame horse didn't seem any worse though it made him wince to see how the animal favoured his right front leg. 'I assume you have some-one who can care for that animal?'

'Yes.' She turned in her seat, her knees bumping slightly against his and sending every nerve in his body jangling.

Her eyes widened as if she, too, felt the shock.

It was the cold. It couldn't be anything else.

'You will stay the night, of course,' she said.

He opened his mouth to refuse.

'Don't be an ass,' she said. 'You won't find your way back to the main road.'

He raised his gaze. All sign of the house was gone. The snow was blowing in his face and it seemed a whole lot darker than it had a minute or two before.

'It looks as if we will not find your house after all.'

'Let the horses have their heads. They will keep to the road. Since I'm expected, someone is sure to be waiting at the gate with a lantern.'

They should not have let her drive out alone, and he intended to tell them so, but he did as she suggested. It felt odd, handing control of their lives to a couple of dumb beasts, but their ears pricked forwards as if they knew where they were going when he let the reins hang slack. After only a minute or two, he saw a light swinging ahead of them, a faint twinkle rocking back and forth. Within moments a wizened man in a coachman's caped coat was leading them between the shadowy forms of a pillared gate. They rounded a turn in the drive and more lights glowed through the swirling snow. They pulled up at a magnificent portico.

Two more men rushed out of the dark with lanterns.

'We'll see to the horses,' the coachman bellowed over the wind. 'Get yourselves inside afore ye perish, Miss Draycott.'

One of the grooms helped her down.

Charlie jumped down on his side.

'This way,' Miss Draycott called, hurrying up the steps.

Charlie followed. The blast of heat as the front door opened let him know just how cold he'd become.

Merry stripped off her coat and handed it to Gribble, whose smile expressed his relief.

'We were beginning to worry,' he said.

'Gribble, this is the Marquis of Tonbridge.' She gestured towards the stern dark man who was looking around him with narrowed eyes. She suppressed a chuckle. Grandfather's idea of the style of a wealthy industrialist was a sight to behold. 'My rescuer will need a room for the night.'

Tonbridge's gaze shot to her face, dropped to her bosom as he took in the low-necked green muslin gown. It barely covered her nipples. She'd worn it quite deliberately today. Clearly her guest did not approve, for his firm lips tightened, before his gaze rose to her face again.

She cast him a flirtatious sideways glance. 'You don't have a choice, my lord.'

'The green chamber is ready, Miss Draycott,' Gribble said. 'I'll have Brian bring up your valise, my lord. He will serve as your valet while you are here. May I take your coat?'

Still frowning, Tonbridge shrugged out of his fashionably caped driving coat and handed it over, along with his hat and gloves. The lack of a coat didn't make him look any less imposing. His black morning coat clung to his shoulders as if it had been moulded to his body, an altogether pleasing sight. Or it would be if she cared about that sort of thing. Without his hat, his jaw looked squarer, more rugged, but the smooth wide forehead and piercing dark eyes surprisingly spoke of intelligence. She doubted their veracity, because although his thick brown hair looked neat rather than fashionable, his cravat was tied with obvious flare. It must take his valet hours to turn out such perfection.

Merry knew his sort. An idle nobleman with nothing to do but adorn his frame. And there was plenty of frame to adorn. A good six feet of it, she judged. Tall for a woman, she still had to look up to meet his gaze. But she'd known that already. He'd loomed over her out there on the moors. And made her heart beat far too fast.

And the odd thing was, it was beating a little too fast now, too. And grasshoppers in hobnail boots were marching around in her stomach.

Surely she wasn't afraid of him?

Or was it simply a reaction to the events of the past few

hours? The disappointment at the mill owners' intransigence, followed by the accident. It had not been a good day. She straightened her shoulders. She wasn't beaten yet.

She needed to talk to Caroline. 'Where is Mrs Falkner, Gribble?'

'In the drawing room,' the butler replied. 'Awaiting dinner.'

Blast. She'd have to change, which meant no time to talk over what had happened with Caroline until later. She turned to Lord Tonbridge. 'Gribble will see you to your room. When you are ready, please join us in the drawing room.'

She ran lightly up the stairs. Dandies took hours at their toilette. She stopped and turned. Tonbridge was watching her with an unreadable expression.

'Dinner is in one hour. Please do not be late.'

His slackened jaw made her want to laugh. He must think her completely rag-mannered. And so she was.

She continued up the stairs to her chamber. If she was quick, she could speak to Caroline before their guest arrived downstairs.

A frown gathered beneath the chestnut curls on Caro's brow. Her hazel eyes filled with sadness. 'There is no help from that quarter, then,' she said, at the end of Merry's swiftly delivered report.

No matter how drably Caro dressed—tonight she'd chosen a dark blue merino wool with a high neck and no ornament— or how serious the expression on her heart-shaped face, the petite woman was always devastatingly lovely.

'None at all, I believe,' replied Merry, who always felt like a giant next to her friend. 'Do not worry, the women can stay here for as long as is needed.'

She paced the length of the drawing room and came back to face Caro. 'I'm so sorry I could not convince them.'

Caro gently touched her friend's gloved hand. 'It is not your fault. We will find another way.'

'I wish I knew how.'

'We will think of something. What is our visitor like?'

A generous change of topic given Caro's disappointment. Merry filled her lungs with air. 'Tonbridge? Handsome, I suppose. Rather disapproving of me, I'm afraid.'

'That's because he doesn't know you.'

If he knew her, he'd be more disapproving than ever. She sat beside her friend. 'I hope he doesn't take too long. I'm starving.' She looked at the clock. In one minute the hour would be up.

Tonbridge stepped through the door. He had shaved and changed from his driving clothes into a form-fitting blue evening coat, starched white cravat and ivory waistcoat. His tight buff pantaloons fitted like a second skin over muscle and bone. One would never guess from his languidly fashionable form he had recently heaved a wrecked carriage off the road single-handed.

He'd looked magnificent, like Atlas supporting the world.

'Come in, Lord Tonbridge,' Merry said. 'Let me introduce you to my dear friend and companion, Mrs Caroline Falkner.'

'I am pleased to meet you, Mrs Falkner.' Tonbridge made his bows, gracious, elegant and formal. Coolly distant. The highborn nobleman meeting the unwashed masses. No wonder Caroline looked thoroughly uncomfortable.

'I hope my unexpected arrival is not a dreadful inconvenience,' he said, moving to stand beside the fire.

Polite blankness hid Caroline's thoughts. She sounded calm

enough when she spoke. 'I am so grateful you were on hand to help Miss Draycott.' She rose to her feet. 'I hope the servants took good care of you?' She went to the console on the far side of the room.

'Excellent care,' he said.

'And your quarters are to your liking?' Merry asked.

'Indeed.'

A consummate liar. Merry hid her smile. Like the rest of the house, the green guest chamber was a nightmare of ostentation.

'Let me pour you a libation to warm you after your ordeal,' Caroline said. 'Sherry for you, Merry?' She turned to look at Tonbridge. 'A brandy, my lord?'

Tonbridge was looking at Caroline with a frown of puzzlement. And no wonder. Caro's ladylike airs and modest appearance would seem at odds with this house of gross opulence.

Oppressive scarlet velvet curtains, gilt scattered with abandon, garish fabrics on the floors and wildly patterned silk on the walls—she could almost see Tonbridge wince as he looked around.

Grandfather had wanted no one to underestimate his wealth.

'Takes a lot of brass to fill a room like this,' she said.

His gaze came back to her face. 'Beauty needs no adornment.' Mischief gleamed in his eyes. Not the reaction she'd expected. The man had a sense of humour lurking beneath that haughty lift of his deeply cleft chin.

Dash it. She did not want to like him. It would only lead to embarrassment. He was simply being polite. A gentleman. No doubt when he joined his friends, he would have a mocking tale to tell.

Oh, how she'd like to peel off the polite veneer and reveal

his true nature. Prove she was right and stop her foolish heart's flutters every time he sent that cool dark glance her way.

'A pox on your sherry,' Merry said with a quick laugh. ''Tis brandy for me. I vow I am still chilled to the bone. Perhaps *you* would prefer a dish of tea, my lord?'

As she'd expected, Tonbridge turned with a frown. Clearly she'd shocked him with her teasing. Blasted nobility. They thought everyone who didn't conform to their idea of polite society to be beneath them. While they gambled away their fortunes, men like her grandfather accumulated great wealth by hard work. He could look down his nose all he liked, she wasn't ashamed of her background.

A small smile curved his lips, a brief softening of his harsh features and her heart gave a lurch, the kind that hurt and felt good at the same time. Not a feeling to have around such a powerful man. If he sensed it, he would see it as weakness.

'Brandy would be equally welcome to me, Miss Draycott,' he said.

Did nothing put him out, or did he just never show it? Too well bred. Too reserved. 'Call me Merry,' she said, as she had on the moors, an inner wildness overcoming good sense. 'Everyone does. I hate formality, don't you?'

He looked more than a little startled at that, which gave her a moment of satisfaction.

He responded cheerfully enough. 'As you wish, Merry.' He didn't offer his own first name. She guessed he'd already placed their relative stations in life and knew he was far above their touch.

Caroline poured the brandy. Merry took both glasses and handed one to Tonbridge. 'To my knight in shining armour,' she toasted boldly and tossed off the fiery liquid. It burned its way to her stomach.

She really didn't need any more heat. The proximity of this man made her skin glow. She cocked a challenging brow.

He raised his glass, a smile curving his finely drawn mouth. 'To a lovely maiden in distress.'

More devastating charm. He must practise in front of the mirror, the way the girls practised simpering before the glass at school.

He took a cautious sip and then nodded. 'Excellent.' He swallowed a mouthful.

'My grandfather kept a very fine cellar,' she said, not without a little pride. Grandfather might have lacked town bronze, as the *ton* called it, but he knew quality. Unfortunately, he had no sense of style. Hence the costly but dreadful décor.

Gribble opened the door. 'Dinner is served, miss.'

Tonbridge held out both arms. 'Ladies?'

Gribble's grey brows shot up, wrinkling his forehead.

Speechless, Merry looked at Caroline, who lifted her shoulders in a slight shrug. As usual her hazel eyes gave nothing away. Merry had found Caroline serving at an inn in York and had instantly seen her predicament. A well-bred lady brought low. She'd offered her the position of companion on the spot. But Caroline never talked about her past. And she rarely offered an opinion.

Not that Merry relied on anyone else's judgement. Grandfather would never allow it. She made her own decisions.

She placed her hand on his right forearm and Caroline did the same on his left. As they walked, she glanced at his face and saw nothing but bland politeness. And that made her nervous. Because politeness hid lies and knives in the back.

She had a strategy for dealing with practised deceit, developed after years of misery. Frontal attack.

Chapter Two

'Is this your first visit to Yorkshire, my lord?' Caroline asked when the food was served and the butler had withdrawn.

Tonbridge paused in his carving of the roast duck and smiled politely. 'Not at all. I came here often in my youth with my family. It has been some years since my last visit, I must say.'

'Lucky for me you chose today,' Merry said, fluttering her eyelashes in a fair emulation of the girls she'd despised at school.

Caroline cast her a startled look.

Tonbridge continued carving. 'It seems we were both lucky. I doubt I would have made it to Skepton in the snow and I would never have found hospitality on so grand a scale else-where in the wilds of the moors.'

Grand meaning horribly bourgeois, no doubt.

'May I help you to some of this fine bird, Mrs Falkner?' he asked.

'Thank you,' Caroline said.

'Not for me,' Merry said, then waved her fork and the carrot on its tines airily at the picture behind her. 'That is my grandfather, Josiah Draycott. He rose from shepherd boy to owning one of the largest wool mills in Yorkshire.'

'Impressive,' Tonbridge said. He put the best slices of the bird on Caroline's plate and took the remainder for himself.

Merry wasn't sure if he referred to the portrait in which her grandfather, with his full-bottomed wig and eagle-eyed stare, looked as if he could eat small boys for breakfast, or his accomplishments. Strangely enough she had the impression it was the latter when she'd expected the former.

She cut her roast beef into bite-sized pieces. 'He left it all to me.'

He stilled, his duck-laden fork hovering before parted lips. Lovely full lips. The kind of lips that would cushion a girl's mouth. No awkward clashing of teeth for him, she felt sure.

His eyes widened. 'You are a mill owner?' he asked.

Hah! She'd managed to surprise him. At least he'd managed not to sneer. 'Owner of Draycott's Mills.'

His gaze met hers. 'I recognised the name, of course. I just didn't expect...'

'A woman in charge?'

'We sell Durn's wool to Draycott's,' he said, neatly sidestepping her question. He put the duck in his mouth and chewed. How could anyone look so scrumptious, just chewing?

She dragged her gaze from his mouth. 'And very fine wool it is.'

'The best,' he agreed.

'But not producing as much in recent years.'

He blinked and she felt a little glow of satisfaction. She wasn't just a mill owner, a reaper of profits. While she rarely visited the mill because the blunt Yorkshire men felt uncomfortable around their female employer, she received weekly reports, statements and accountings. She knew her business. Grandfather had insisted.

'We've seen revenues fall off,' Tonbridge admitted. 'One reason for my visit.'

One reason? What would be the others?

He turned to Caroline. 'Are you also involved in Draycott's, Mrs Falkner?'

For a man of such an exalted position, he had exquisite manners. Merry found herself warming at the way he included Caroline in the conversation. But he'd not get carrot juice out of that turnip.

Caroline shook her head. 'Oh, no.'

'I don't know what I would do without Caroline's companionship,' Merry said on her friend's behalf.

Caroline smiled at her with gratitude.

Tonbridge's dark eyes looked from one to the other. A question entered his gaze, a dark thought that caused a slight tightening at the corners of his mouth. More disapproval? 'You are lucky to have such a good friend,' he said quietly. The words seemed to hold more meaning than she could work out.

What on earth was he thinking? She found she couldn't hazard a guess and that was annoying. Accompanying her grandfather on his business dealings had taught her how to read men very well. This one, however, was a bit of a mystery. A challenge.

'What do you do when you are not visiting the outposts of the Mountford empire?' she asked.

He laughed. 'You are nothing if you are not direct, Merry.' He held up a hand when she began to apologise. 'I like it. It is refreshing.'

Refreshing meant naïve. Ignorant of the social niceties. She flashed him a sultry smile. 'I'm glad you find it stimulating, my lord.'

Glints of amber danced in his eyes. 'You have no idea.'

Oh, but she did, because her blood was stirring and her

pulse fluttering in places she shouldn't be aware of in polite company. She felt more alive than she had for months, perhaps years. For the first time since her fall into disgrace, she felt her body tingle with interest and excitement.

Lust.

Thank goodness she knew it for what it was and could resist it.

Caroline cast her warning glance, an admonition that the flirtation was getting out of hand.

What did it matter if she flirted a little? It wasn't as if she could be ruined. And this man with his icy reserve deserved a little shaking up. Pretending not to notice Caroline's unspoken message, she raised a brow. 'Well, Lord Tonbridge? You didn't answer my question. Perhaps you are a gambler or a rake?'

'Both,' he said, his expression suddenly darker. 'Have you a wish to test my skills?'

Caroline coughed and picked up her water. 'My throat is dry,' she muttered after a sip.

Merry only knew one way to deal with a man of his sort. Call his bluff. 'La, sir, where would we start? With a wager? Or a seduction?'

Dark eyes observed her intently, then flicked to Caroline, who was bright pink and looking mortified. 'I bow to your wishes,' he said, his deep voice a silky caress on her ears.

Her stomach did a long slow lazy roll that left her breathless. And speechless. Blast him, he didn't scare easily. Most of the noblemen she'd met in the past would be running a mile by now at the thought of an entanglement with Merry Draycott.

Gribble entered quietly with his minion at his heels to clear the table for the remove, affording her the opportunity to marshal her defences.

'Do you plan a long stay at Durn, my lord?' Caroline asked,

covering an awkward silence as the servants went about their business.

'I'm not sure,' he said, looking at Merry. 'It depends on several factors.'

Merry really didn't like the thrill that rippled through her at the thought that she might be a factor. Did she? He might be the handsomest man she'd ever seen, but he had an arrogance about him, a sense of entitlement, put there by wealth and position. There was also a coldness. It wafted from him like a chill wind. He'd judged her instantly and sensed his superiority. Perhaps he thought she should be honoured to fall at his feet. The thought jangled her pride. A need to take the wind out of his sails was pushing her into outrageous behaviour she could not seem to stop.

Finished with their tasks, the servants withdrew.

'Can I offer you some of this very fine aspic, Mrs Falkner?' he asked.

Caroline inclined her head. 'Yes, please, my lord.'

He raised his gaze to her face. 'Merry?'

She should not have given him permission to use her first name. It put her at a distinct disadvantage. 'A small amount. Thank you.'

He served Caroline first. He had large strong hands. The fingers were elegant, yet not at all limp or fluttery. Grandfather always knew a man's nature from the way he shook hands. Most of the time, men bowed over hers, so she never got the opportunity to judge their grip. She'd found other ways to assess their worth.

The way a man handled his knife and fork and the business of eating told her a great deal. This one used his implements with casual ease and ate with firm elegance and a pleasing economy of movement. The Marquis of Tonbridge exceeded all her standards.

He'd been good with the horses, too, she recalled, firm, yet gentle. Not once had he pulled on their delicate mouths while keeping firm control.

Was she letting her biases lead her astray in regard to this man? Was he merely following her lead out of politeness? If she truly believed so, she should simply bid him goodnight after dinner and retire. It would not be difficult to declare a headache or weariness from the day's events.

But she didn't believe he was just being polite for a minute. He wanted to put her in her place. She could see it in his eyes.

'You haven't answered my question,' he said, raising a brow.

Clearly, he needed a lesson in humility. 'Why don't we start with a wager?'

He raised a brow. 'Cards? Or do you prefer dice?'

'Billiards,' she said. 'If you play?'

He nodded. 'Billiards it is.'

The conversation passed on to more mundane topics and it was not long before Caroline was making her excuses, leaving Merry to deal with the fruits of her challenge.

The billiard room was, without a doubt, the most comfortable room Charlie had entered so far. Linen-fold panelled walls of oak provided a warm background for comfortably heavy wooden furniture dating back to the last century. An equally impressive green baize-covered slate table stood in the centre of a red-and-green-patterned rug.

Not a scrap of velvet or gilt in sight. A relief to his weary eyes. The only glitter beneath the overhead light was Miss Draycott herself. Merry. What an apt name for such an unusual female.

She eyed the balls, running her palm up and down her cue.

Her fingers were long and fine and the action brought other images to mind. Sensual images.

The simmering arousal he'd been fighting all evening made itself known with a disgruntled jolt.

He'd never before felt such instant attraction for such a—how did one describe this woman? Statuesque, certainly. Gloriously so. She didn't have to crane her neck to see his face. He'd thought he liked his women small and delicate. Until now.

He certainly wouldn't worry about hurting her when romping around in a bed. His body stirred in approval. He tamped down his desire. The last thing he needed was a distraction like Merry Draycott.

For an unprotected woman, she was far too bold for her own good. Many men would have no qualms about taking advantage. He had to admit he found the prospect tempting.

Her behaviour had him thoroughly off kilter, too. On occasion, her manner of speech left much to be desired. At other times she seemed almost genteel. She confused him. And, unfortunately, intrigued him.

For an instant at dinner, he'd suspected the two women of being more than platonic friends, that they might worship at the altar of Sappho, but as the meal progressed he had not sensed anything warmer than friendship.

Not that he was averse to the special friendships some women preferred. It just put those particular women out of reach, and, in her case, he'd felt disappointed.

The truth was, he wanted her. He couldn't remember the last time he'd felt so urgent about having a woman. He fought to control the impulse to seduce her. As her guest, good manners required he accommodate his hostess's wishes. A part of him wished those desires included more than a high-stakes game of billiards. The undercurrents swirling around them suggested they might. And no matter what he thought, his baser male nature wanted to oblige.

A man about to become betrothed did not enter into an entanglement with another woman. Hell, he'd just got rid of his long-term mistress for that very reason.

Meeting this particular woman on the road was, without a doubt, a confounded nuisance.

She played a damned fine game of billiards, too. She'd won the first game, mostly because he had been focusing too much on her sweet little bottom when she'd leaned over the table. A quite deliberate ploy on her part, no doubt. Not unlike a Captain Sharp plying his mark with gin.

He watched her saunter around the table with a jaunty swing of her hips and clenched his jaw. She was deliberately tormenting him with a gown that skimmed her breasts and revealed every curve when she walked. While her gown wasn't any more provocative than many respectable married ladies of the *ton* wore to a drum or a rout, on her, it seemed positively decadent.

The woman was a menace. Teasing a man came with consequences she might not like. Perhaps she needed a lesson in acceptable behaviour. A warning.

He covered his mouth and yawned widely. 'Excuse me. It's been a long day. I think I am ready to retire.'

She frowned. 'Afraid you will lose again?'

'Not at all,' he drawled. 'My interest is waning. I'm afraid I need more of a challenge.'

She eyed him suspiciously. 'Fifty guineas a point and a hundred for a win is reasonably challenging.'

'I'm not trying to fleece you, Merry, but I think both of us can lose a few hundred guineas in a night and not turn a hair.'

Her eyes widened a fraction. 'Do you want to make it thousands?'

He grinned and leaned on his cue. 'That is more of the same, isn't it?' Oh God, he was going to hell for this. 'In this next game, how about for each point we lose, we remove an article of clothing?'

It was the kind of thing he would have proposed during his misspent youth, before his stint in the army. Before he became duller than ditchwater, more sedate than a spinster walking a pug. The sharp voice of his handsomely paid-off mistress rang in his head.

Merry was staring at him wide-eyed, shocked to her toes.

A rueful smile tugged at his lips as he waited for her to retreat in disarray and leave him to take his brandy to his empty bed.

'An article of clothing per point?' she said, a little breathlessly, her cheeks flushing pink, but her shoulders straightening.

A breath caught in his throat. By thunder, she wasn't going to back down. The naughty minx. Someone ought to put her over their knee. He drew on every ounce of control, the kind a man needed going into battle.

Clearly there was only one way to teach this young woman not to play with fire. Singe her eyebrows.

'Anything on your person,' he said as if the whole topic bored him.

'Including jewellery? Because it seems to me I have far less clothing than you do.'

'Certainly.'

She boldly ran her gaze down his body as if considering whether seeing him disrobed would be worth the risk. He pretended not to notice the heat of desire flaring in the depths of her summer-blue eyes and let her look her fill.

She parted her lips and his body hardened to granite. He forced himself not to shift to find ease for his confined flesh.

Some women found him too large, too overpowering physically, when the fashion was for lisping mincing dandies. In her case the thought of doing a bit of overpowering made the prospect all the sweeter.

If she dared take his challenge.

She drew in a deep breath. 'All right,' she said. 'Fifty guineas and an article of clothing per point to twelve points. The hundred guineas for the win remains unchanged.'

She expected to win. It was writ large on her face. He took a slow inward breath, controlling the surge of heat at the thought of seeing her naked. 'That sounds fair,' he said coolly.

And then she laughed. A low chuckle in the back of her throat. 'Perhaps I should ask Gribble to have the fire stoked before we start. So no one catches a chill.'

'I don't think that will be necessary. Our blushes will keep us warm.'

Her shoulders tensed. 'Your blushes, you mean.'

What a surprise, this woman—the first who had dared challenge him for years. They usually simpered and flattered. If he was any kind of gentleman he would stop this right now, but he wouldn't. Not if his life depended on it. He was having too much fun. He smiled at her, a sweet, but slightly devilish grin. 'It seems you are first, my dear Merry.'

She missed her first shot. Nerves. Not as blasé as she pretended.

'Bad luck,' he said. 'A one-point penalty.'

She removed the pearls at her throat and placed them on a side table with a little toss of her head. 'You will not be so lucky in future.'

He eyed the board, and played his shot carefully. His ball missed hers and came to rest temptingly close to the pocket.

'You missed. One point for me,' she said.

He bowed and removed his coat and draped it over a chair back, while she walked around the table, looking at the balls from all angles.

He waited, leaning nonchalantly on his cue.

With a small smile of triumph she lay across the table and eyed the balls. An easy shot. Just as he'd planned. He and Robert had actually orchestrated one of these games with a couple of the village tarts at Durn. It was all coming back.

The sweet curve of her bottom as she stretched over the table tempted unbearably. From this angle, the draping fabric left little to the imagination and put her at just the right angle to receive his attentions. Two steps closer and he could slide his hands over the soft flesh and press his groin against the full roundness of her buttocks.

He drew in a swift breath. Brought his body under control. Passion, strong passions, led to nowhere but disaster. And even if she was wriggling that little posterior on purpose, she was doing it as a distraction, a way of putting him off his own shot.

She knocked the white ball with a swift jerk of her elbow. It caromed off the red and hit his ball with a crack, sending it into the corner pocket.

He smiled. 'Good shot.'

She lowered her feet gracefully to the floor. She cast him a glance over her shoulder. 'I know.'

He grinned.

She raised her brows.

He removed the diamond pin from his cravat, adding it to her pearls, then unknotted and slowly unwound his cravat. She looked highly pleased with herself, but he couldn't help wondering if it was because she wanted to see more of him, or because she'd won. The former, he evilly hoped. He had no qualms about removing his clothes before a woman, despite the scar.

He draped the long strip of cloth over his coat. He glanced down at himself. 'What next, do you think? Ah, yes.' He toed off his shoes and, standing first on one leg, then the other, divested himself of his stockings. He did not miss her sidelong glance at his feet and bare calves, or the quick swipe of her lips with her tongue.

Heat flowed to his groin.

Ignoring his burgeoning arousal, he sauntered around the table, replacing the balls, while he felt the touch of sparkling eyes on his body.

'How many pieces of clothing do you think you are wearing?' she asked.

'Less than the number of points required to finish the game,' he said, instantly guessing the direction of her thoughts.

'Good,' she said, but there was an undercurrent of nervousness behind her bold front. An unease. Unless he wanted her to be better than she appeared? Surely not?

'You didn't tell me you were an expert at this game,' he said, rubbing the end of his cue with chalk.

Her gaze flew from the cue tip to his face. 'I used to play with my grandfather all the time. It passed the long winter evenings and while we played he taught me about the mill.'

'He sounds like a grand old gentleman.'

'He was. A darling.' Her face brightened. It was as if she'd lit a candle inside, she became so dazzling. The brightness wasn't true, he realised. It flickered and wavered as if a sharp gust of wind would blow it out. But why would he care? He had enough baggage to shoulder of his own without delving into hers. She'd made it quite clear from the beginning of the evening that she was interested in a dalliance. The idea became more attractive as the evening wore on. He didn't remember the last time he'd felt quite so enlivened.

Her ball was easily accessible. His guarded the red. She played her next shot with consummate skill, knocking his aside and giving her access to the red ball.

He leaned in for his shot. A flick of the wrist and he struck the red and white in quick succession. They fired off into the centre pockets. 'Seven points,' he said calmly, straightening.

Her mouth dropped open. Her blue eyes were wide with shock, staring at the table. 'You cheated.'

He folded his arms across his chest. 'Oh?' He raised a brow and stared down his nose. His ducal-heir-look, Robert always called it.

She flushed. 'I mean, you pretended you were not very good at this game. Only an expert can make a shot like that.'

'Are you wishing to forfeit the game?'

She stiffened, her gaze meeting his with blue sparks of anger. 'Certainly not.'

As he'd suspected, Merry Draycott did not back down from a fight. The small qualm of contrition for goading her wasn't strong enough to make him concede. 'Seven items, then, Merry.'

She tugged three hair ornaments from her artfully arranged curls. Long black silky tresses fell to her exquisite sloping white shoulders. She placed the ornaments on the table with her pearls. Her bracelet followed. Her wince said that was the last of her jewellery.

She sent him a resentful glance and he tipped his head on one side as if completely unaware of her concern.

She glanced at his bare feet, sat down on a chair and started untying the ribbons around her ankles. Her hair fell forwards as black as a raven's wing, hiding her face.

'Do you need any help?' he asked.

Chapter Three

Merry felt a blush crawl up her face. 'I can manage.' She ducked her head, untied the bow at the back of her ankle and slipped the shoe off.

Oh Lord, seven points, he only needed four to win. And what would she have left to remove if he won another seven points? She should never have let him convince her to play such a shocking game. He had cheated. He had let her think he was a hopeless player.

And then, when he'd offered her a chance to forfeit, she'd let her pride speak instead of common sense. But a Draycott never backed down, be it in a bargain or a game.

The ribbon snagged. She tugged at it. The knot drew tighter.

His bare toes appeared within her vision, which was restricted to her feet, the hem of her gown and the carpet. He dropped to his knees. 'May I help?' he asked again.

The sound of his voice was like a taste of hot chocolate, warm and rich and wickedly tempting.

'I can manage.'

He sat back on his heels. Sweeping her hair back, she

glanced up at his face. His gaze remained fixed on her foot, on the knot. She let go a huff of impatience. 'Very well. See if you can untie it.'

She couldn't breathe. She had a huge fluttery lump stuck in her throat. Her mouth dried.

The wretch grasped her ankle and lifted her foot to rest on one knee. The heat of his hand, the feel of those long strong fingers taking the weight of her leg, sent ripples of pleasure through her body. She swallowed a gasp.

'Such a pretty ankle,' he murmured as he worked at the ribbon.

A melting sensation weakened her limbs. Oh, dear. If he made her feel this way with a touch on her extremity, how would she feel if he wanted to help her with her garter? She could not, nay, would not let him undo her like this. 'La, thank you, sir,' she said and was infuriated by the breathy note in her voice.

He glanced up at her face with a smile. 'No need to thank me. I speak only the truth.'

The man was impossibly handsome when he smiled like that. A dark inscrutable devil with the expression of an angel. In her heart she knew it for what it was, an act, a flirtation, but he played his part so well he almost had her convinced.

She pointed at her foot. 'The slipper, my lord.'

He bent his dark head to the task. His dark brown hair fell in thick luxurious chocolate-brown waves. She had the urge to touch it, to feel its texture. She gripped the chair arm instead.

He untied the ribbon around her ankle and slid the shoe from her foot, his palm caressing the arch. Delicious. Intoxicating. She wanted to wriggle her toes. She kept a bright smile fixed on her face. Bright and teasing, when inside she wanted to weep at the tenderness in his touch.

Gently he placed her foot on the ground. She wished she had a fan close at hand instead of a cue. She was glowing from the inside out. How could this be? She wasn't some innocent schoolgirl to have her head turned by a handsome man. Particularly not one with a title. And yet she wanted to melt into this man's arms. Feel that broad chest pressed against her breasts. Run her fingers through his hair and feel his strength beneath her fingers. Utter foolishness.

'I don't need your help with the garter.' Her voice sounded strangled.

His head snapped up. 'You disappoint me.'

She managed a quick calming breath and a light laugh. 'Intentionally, sir. To allow such familiarity would be more reward than you have earned. Turn around.'

He stood. His rueful gaze made her heart beat just a little too fast. 'Saving your life is worth so little, then?'

'Unfair,' she cried, laughing a little herself at the neat way he'd tried make her feel guilty. Oh, this man was a rake indeed and she was a fool to continue their game. 'Am I not feeding you and giving you lodging as well as helping you wile away the hours before bed?'

His lips twitched, but he bowed and turned his back.

The clock on the mantel struck midnight. She glanced at it to make sure. She could not believe so much time had passed so quickly.

She leaped out of her chair, turned her back, in case he should decide to peek, and untied her garter, a pretty thing made of the finest lace from Nottingham she'd bought on a visit to look at their mills. She walked to the chair and laid it on top of his cravat. The rug felt odd under her stockinged feet, the silk no barrier to the rougher nap of the woollen tufts.

'Let us finish our game,' she said, trying to sound as if it didn't matter that one of her stockings was slowly sliding down her calf, or that the heat inside her seemed to have reached the temperature of a furnace. He'd been right when he said their blushes would keep them warm.

Or her, anyway. He seemed remarkably unaffected.

'It is my turn.'

He bowed and gestured for her to continue.

She inhaled a deep breath, forcing her unruly thoughts back in control. She needed seven points to have any hope of winning this game. She had done it in the past. Not often. And not for a very long time. She looked at the table, the balls back in position. It would not be an easy shot.

She steadied herself against the table and lined up her cue. Her mouth felt terribly dry and her hands were shaking. The hit on the red was clean, it cracked nicely and shot across the table spinning, while her cue ball downed his ball in the nearby corner. The red ball hovered at the edge of the centre pocket…and stopped.

It stopped. Surely it would topple over. She stared at it. Willing it to move. A fraction.

She could not believe it.

'Oh, too bad,' he said and sounded sincere.

She shrugged. 'I won four points.' She'd wanted seven.

'We could take it as potted. It is so close.'

Her back stiffened. 'I'm not a child, sir. I haven't lost yet.' She brushed her hair back from her shoulders. 'You have four items to remove, remember?'

He smiled and shrugged. He took off his waistcoat and watch, then slowly released the buttons of his shirt, all the while keeping his gaze on her face.

Heat blazed in her cheeks. She was having trouble breathing and she couldn't look away.

He tugged the shirt free of his waistband and pulled it off over his head, tossing it on his growing pile of clothing.

He was beautiful. 'Oh, my,' she whispered.

Merry had never seen such a virile gorgeous male. Not out in the fields at haymaking or in the mills, where the men often discarded most of their clothing in the heat of the summer. And certainly Jeremy had looked nothing like this. Although she'd been fascinated at the sight of his body, she'd not been in awe.

The lean and heavily muscled Tonbridge, with his skin of pale gold as if he sometimes exposed it to the sun, left her breathless. The scar, puckered and white, ravaging tight sculpted flesh from breast to hip, emphasised the perfection of his form.

She felt a strange urge to touch the scar, to run her fingers along its length, to press her lips to it as if somehow she could make it disappear. A little shiver ran down her spine. Pleasure. Lust. She knew it for what it was, but had it firmly under control. Didn't she?

She raised her eyes once more to his face. He was watching her closely as if trying to read her reaction. Perhaps other women were repulsed by the sight of his ruined flesh. A tension that had not been there before invaded the room.

Oh, there had been tension, between them. The sort of electricity one felt before thunderstorms as they fenced verbally. She had found it quite exciting. This, however, felt more like the undercurrent in a fast-flowing river. An irresistible tug of unseen emotions.

She forced a bright smile. 'What will you remove next?'

He chuckled. A deep sound in his lovely broad chest. 'Not much left for either of us.'

And it was his turn to play. This was going to be very embarrassing. Four points would be bad enough. Seven would have her completely disrobed.

'Do you want to stop here?' he asked.

Why did he have to be so gentlemanly? And yet there was a knowing look in his eyes as if he guessed she would never forfeit a game. 'That would be cowardly,' she managed.

Her gaze darted from his face to his chest. 'What happened to you?'

'A sabre.'

'Duelling?'

'Something like that.'

'I think duelling is a foolish pastime,' she said, frowning at the scar. 'Real men resolve their problems without hacking each other to pieces.'

The hobnail-booted grasshoppers had returned. This time they were running around in a frenzy. Out of self-defence she turned her attention to the table. It didn't help, because he walked around retrieving the balls from her last shot, his upper arms bulging and stretching as he replaced them on the table.

She took a deep breath and realised with horror her hands were shaking and damp.

He leaned a hip against the edge of the table. 'My shot.'

His shot. This was going to be a disaster.

He leaned over the table and his elbow slid smoothly forwards, but he dropped his shoulder. His ball missed the red by such a small fraction, for a moment she was sure he was about to get another seven.

Relief flooded through her body in a hot wave.

He stood staring at the table as if he didn't quite believe it himself. 'By Jove,' he said, frowning.

'You lowered your shoulder at the last minute,' she said.

He grimaced and removed his signet ring. It tinkled against the other jewellery as he set it down with a snap.

He took a deep breath and the underlying bones in his chest expanded, drawing attention to the narrowness of his waist and lean hips, though she tried her best not to let him see she had noticed.

She was going to win. He had almost nothing left to remove. She wiped her hands on her gown. She ought to stop now. She really ought to.

But he needed taking down a peg or two.

And she wasn't going to look when he removed the last of his clothes.

Not one peek. He would remove them and leave.

'Your turn, Merry.'

For some reason, she loved the way he said her name. It was as if he savoured each syllable and consonant. As if he tasted them on his tongue.

'Yes,' she said. Her hands trembled. She didn't need to do anything fancy. Put his ball in the corner pocket.

'Whenever you are ready,' he said quietly.

She jumped. Desperate to have this over and done she took her shot quickly, neatly caroming off the red, the ball ricocheting into the pocket at the end of the table.

He made a sound like a laugh quickly stifled.

A second later she realised why. She'd downed her own ball.

'Hell,' she said.

'Oh, dear. I believe that is three points to me.'

'I know that,' she said, staring at the table where his ball happily rested to the right of the red. Blast. She hadn't made a mistake like that since she'd been a young girl.

She looked up at his face and saw his broad grin. Damn it. The sight of him half-naked had scattered her wits.

A smile pinned on her face, she let her eyes sparkle and fluttered her lashes. 'Might I ask if you have a preference?'

His look of astonishment, quickly followed by a flare of

heat in those dark eyes, was all the reward she needed for her daring.

Her satisfaction didn't last long, because he was eyeing her like dinner had finally arrived. What on earth had made her give him the choice?

'The other garter, I think, and both stockings. And then it is my turn to shoot.'

And she would be the one who was naked. Her stomach dipped down to her feet.

'I will forgo the rest of the game,' he said, his eyes gleaming wickedly, 'if you will permit me to remove those items.'

Her stomach sank even further, dropping away in a rush. As if she'd fallen from a high place, or dropped into a well.

He raised his brows.

Dash it all. It was the only way to retain a shred of propriety and honour. Letting him take off her stockings and feeling those wonderfully strong warm hands on her naked flesh all the way to her knee sounded dreadful. Dreadfully delicious.

And not nearly as awful as being required to undress, should he down his next shot. He had missed once. He might miss again. Her mind went back to that odd drop of his shoulder, when usually he moved with such elegant grace and surety. He'd done it on purpose. Missed his shot. To give her a chance to win. And she'd muffed it.

No wonder he'd laughed.

She closed her eyes briefly. Then he deserved his reward. Her insides quivered. Excitement. Anticipation. Wicked. She was nothing but wicked.

She nodded.

She sat on the nearest chair. 'Your hands must go no further than the top of my knee, nor your gaze.'

The corners of his mouth curled in a sensual smile. 'Do you play the part of Portia, now?'

She lifted her chin. 'And will you play the part of fair Antonio or be the lesser man?'

'A hit,' he said and bowed. 'I will abide by your rule most cheerfully.'

She carefully arranged her skirt so that no more than the top of her left stocking showed below the hem. It had slid below her knee.

He dropped to his knees in front of her and sat back on his heels. 'A delectable sight.'

'I trust you to keep your word.'

She could not see his face, but his shoulders shook a little as if he was trying not to laugh. She saw no humour in the situation, for he had cheated. She was sure of it.

Her skin tingled with the anticipation of his touch. She bit her lip as he hooked one finger into the fine silk and rolled it down over her ankle. He eased it over her heel and off. 'That is one.'

There. Not so bad. No caresses or touches driving her mad.

His fingers went to the hem of her gown, gathering up the fine material until he reached her knee. She tried not to look, or to guess at his reaction. A rake like him would have seen lots of ladies' limbs. Her legs were long and well muscled from striding about her property like a man, when she wasn't conducting business, also like a man. He would find no feminine softness beneath her skirts. He'd probably find her unappealing.

She stared at the wall opposite and gritted her teeth.

The tug on the bow of her garter was like a tug at her centre. Wicked sensations pulsed in her core. She felt naked, exposed, yet when she glanced down to watch, her hem had risen only on one side and not a fraction above the edge of her stocking. But he knelt so close, concentrated on his task with such focus, she could feel his warm breath brush her thigh through the layers of gown and chemise. It tickled unbearably.

He pulled the garter free and dangled it before her face. 'Two,' he said.

She swallowed. Resisted the urge to pull down her skirts. Ignored the fire she could feel burning on her face. She did not fear him doing anything she did not permit. She feared she might permit him to take liberties. But she would not be so cowardly as to go back on her word, not after his generosity. 'Well, go on.'

He cast a swift glance upwards. 'Your wish is my command.'

Oh, how she wanted to hit him. She rolled her eyes to the ceiling and yawned instead. But as soon as he returned to his task, she lowered her lashes, pretending to close her eyes, and watched as he ran a finger beneath the edge of her stocking. A second finger joined the first. He made great play of stretching the fabric over her knee. Her insides turned liquid as if they had melted. Her limbs grew languid. She hauled in a deep breath.

He leaned down and placed a kiss on the bared skin. A swift brush of warm dry lips.

She gasped and gripped the chair arms tighter. 'You go too far.'

'Such beauty deserves worship.'

'You tease me, sirrah.'

He looked up, his eyelids heavy, his lips sensual. 'Not about something as lovely as this.'

A warm glow suffused her skin. Her body clamoured for more than a whisper of touch. She must not succumb to him. She'd sworn never to let a man take her for a fool. She was her own woman. Now and always. Only with him she seemed reckless. Dangerously so.

Was it reckless to keep one's word?

She bit her lip. 'Continue.'

He rolled the stocking, as neatly as any maid would, careful not to damage the cobwebby silk. Another inch of skin, another kiss. Thrills coursed through her blood. She held herself rigid against their temptation, but she couldn't stop watching.

He continued to roll and kiss every inch until the stocking reached her ankle. He shaped her calf with his palm, lingering there as if he'd exposed a treasure. Her insides tightened with desire and longing.

He sighed, a waft of warm gentle air against her skin, then pulled the stocking off. He rubbed the ball of her foot with his thumb. Her body hummed with pleasure. He massaged her arch. She wanted to purr like a cat. Her back stretched. Her shoulders loosened. Dazed, she stared down at his broad naked shoulders, the curve of his back, the movement of muscle beneath. He was lovely.

She yearned to touch him. If only she dared.

Gently he lowered her hem, and rose to his full height, smiling down at her. Clearly waiting for sign from her as to where they would go next.

When she said nothing, he gave a slight nod. 'I think it is time I bid you goodnight.' He put on his ring, tucked the rest of his jewellery in his coat pocket and slung his discarded clothing over his shoulder.

He looked just like a pirate carrying off his booty.

She half-wished the booty included her.

Her heart knocked against her ribs. Her body trembled with the urge to join him in his chamber. To enjoy his beautiful body and the pleasure he would give.

It had been a long time since she'd known the pleasure of a man. But she never expected to be attracted to a man like him, a nobleman who no doubt would mock her in his clubs and to his friends. Blast it. Pricked by her pride, she'd let him push her too far and been tempted by his beautiful body. What a fool.

Thank goodness he'd be gone in the morning and leave her in peace.

'I'll collect the rest of my winnings tomorrow,' he murmured.

Her heart lurched.

Money. He meant the money. 'It will be waiting for you,' she said with a calm she did not feel.

She acknowledged his sweeping bow with an inclination of her head.

He closed the door softly behind him. She sat still, imagining him climbing the stairs. Would he walk slowly? Lingering, hoping she might follow? Or would he run, glad of his escape? Or had it all been one great joke?

Did he know she was his for the taking had he persisted? Did he know she'd lie awake all night, reliving his touch on her flesh?

Shame sent more heat to her face. Her stomach fell away. Would she never learn? She inhaled a deep breath, pushed to her feet and looked up at Grandfather's portrait beside the hearth. A gentler one than that in the other room. 'I certainly made a pig's ear of that, didn't I?' No doubt more scandal would attach to her name when he gossiped to his friends.

Thank God, he would be gone in the morning.

Chapter Four

Voices. Female voices. As consciousness returned, Charlie lay still, eyes closed, his cold naked body rigid. One movement would be his downfall. A laugh chilled his soul.

'Do you think he tupped the missus?'

'Why else would she bring him home?'

Odd. Charlie cracked an eyelid. Peered at the two women at the end of a monstrous four-poster bed and remembered. He was in Yorkshire, not a war-torn field in Europe. He let go of his breath, relaxing his body.

The women were dressed modestly, like chambermaids, one a chubby young blonde with an inquisitive expression, the other a sallow-faced brunette past the first blush of youth. Their eyes perused his body as boldly as a farmer sizing up a bull at the market.

Flipping the sheet over his groin, Charlie sat up and smiled. 'Good morning, ladies.'

The blonde one squeaked. The other put her hands on her hips. 'Sorry, your lordship. We didn't mean to wake you. Your fire is made up and we stopped to admire the view.'

'You should draw t'curtain,' the younger one said defensively, 'if you don't want us looking.'

He choked back a laugh. Miss Draycott had the most unusual of staff. But then there was nothing about Merry Draycott that was usual.

The dark one lowered her lashes a fraction and her gaze to the sheet, which hid little of the evidence of his morning arousal. 'I could help you out with that for a shilling.'

'I wouldn't charge you at all,' the blonde said, licking her lips and smiling. 'I'd bounce on that any day of t'week.'

Good God, what sort of house was this? Charlie tried to keep his jaw off his chest. 'Thank you, but no.'

The hopeful smile faded. 'You won't say nowt to missus, will you? About us waking you. We are supposed to be quiet.'

With a sense of unreality, Charlie shook his head. 'Thank you for the fire.'

The older of the two narrowed her gaze. 'How come you left all the candles burning? Not scared of the dark, are you?'

Scared didn't come close to describing the insidious panic he felt in the hours before dawn. He grinned. 'I fell asleep reading.' He gestured to the book on the night table, placed there in case of such questions.

'Waste of good beeswax, that is,' she muttered and flounced out of the room.

The other girl followed, lugging the coal bucket and a dustpan and brush.

Charlie collapsed against the pillows and let out a laugh. There was no mistaking the sort of fires those women preferred to light and it had nothing to do with hearths and coals.

He should have guessed from the style of Merry's dress and her lapses of speech that the damned woman was a brothel keeper.

An abbess. And one with enemies? Overnight he'd been thinking about that broken axle.

Another look at her carriage was required, but this latest piece of information added to his suspicions about her supposed accident. It wasn't one.

He glanced around the room. The candles augmented by light from the window illuminated a carved and tapestry-hung nightmare of a room in every shade of green. It looked worse than it had the previous evening.

He threw back the covers and slipped from the bed. He strode to the window. He'd left the curtains open, too, as well as the bed curtains. Unending white accounted for the unnatural light. He frowned at the sky. While the clouds seemed less lowering, he doubted the roads would be passable.

And he was stuck in a house of ill repute. A joke Robert would have loved. Charlie didn't find it in the least bit humorous. She should have told him last night instead of her pretending to be respectable—well, almost respectable.

A vision of Merry's lovely slender leg in his hand popped into his brain. The arousal that had tormented him the previous evening, and upon awakening, started anew. He cursed. He'd behaved like a perfect gentleman with a woman who kept a bawdy house. What a quixotic fool she must have thought him.

He turned away from the window at the sound of the chamber door opening. Brian with boots in hand. The lad bowed deeply. 'Good morning, my lord. Mr Gribble said to tell you the snow on the moors is really deep.'

'I guessed as much. You don't need to stay. I can manage.'

The lad looked so crestfallen at the dismissal, Charlie relented. 'Brush my claret-coloured coat and then iron my cravat, if you wouldn't mind.'

The lad touched his forelock. 'Reet gladly, my lord.'

* * *

In less than an hour, Charlie was hunching his shoulders against a wind stronger than the previous evening and holding fast to his hat brim. The drifting snow came close to the top of his boots as he slogged down a hill to the stables. Set around three sides of a square courtyard, the building offered welcome shelter from the gale. He entered through the first door he came to and almost bumped into a fellow coming out. Not a groom. Of course not. It was Miss Draycott in a man's low-crowned hat and her mannish driving coat.

Charlie raised his hat and smiled. 'Good morning. I didn't expect to see you up and about at this early hour.'

After the startled look faded from her expression, she frowned. Not pleased to see him. 'I didn't think London dandies rose from their bed before noon.'

'Mr Brummell has given us all a very bad reputation,' Charlie said mournfully. He knocked the snow off his boots against the door frame. 'I came to see how the horses were doing.' No sense in alarming her, when he had nothing but vague suspicions.

'Don't you trust my servants to take proper care of your animals, my lord?'

My, her temper was ill today. 'If I didn't trust your servants, Miss Draycott, I would have come out here last night.'

She acknowledged the hit with a slight nod.

'I also wondered about your team. How is that foreleg?'

Her shoulders slumped. 'Not good. Jed poulticed it, but it is badly swollen.'

'Do you mind if I look?'

'Not at all.' She sounded quite doubtful. Probably thought he wouldn't know one end of the beast from the other. Nor would he indicate otherwise. The fact that he liked working with horses was no one's business but his own.

They walked along the stable block. A single row of stalls built along each back wall, nice drainage, fresh straw and a surprising number of mounts, both riding and draught. He nodded his approval.

The carriage horses were in the middle block. The wrinkled wizened man who'd met them with the lantern the previous evening stood leaning on a broom, watching the injured horse eat.

'Jed, this is Lord Tonbridge,' Merry said.

He knuckled his forehead. 'Aah. Yours are reet fine animals, yer lordship. Two stalls down they are.'

'Thank you. Miss Draycott is concerned about this one. May I see?'

The old fellow ran a knowing eye down his person. 'Well, if you don't mind mucking in the midden, you're reet welcome.'

Charlie inched in beside the horse and sank down on his haunches. The groom had packed a mixture of warm mash and liniment around the injured foreleg. 'How bad do you think it is?'

'No more'n a strain, I reckon.'

'He got hooked up in the traces,' Miss Draycott said. 'I hope he didn't do any permanent damage.'

So, she'd followed him back. That was going to make his questioning of the head groom difficult.

'Have you tried packing it with snow?' Charlie asked.

Jed scratched at the grey stubble on his chin. 'Never heard of that for a strain.'

Charlie grinned. 'Nor I. My groom discovered it takes the swelling down faster than warm mash, if you want to try it. Little else to be done apart from plenty of rest.'

'It wouldn't hurt to try, would it, Jed?' Merry said quietly.

'I feel so badly. Not once in my life have I ever injured one of my horses.'

She sounded dreadfully guilty. Charlie wanted to put an arm around her shoulders and offer her comfort, then press her up against the stable wall and offer a bit more than that, she looked so starkly beautiful with her hair tucked up under her ridiculous hat.

"T'was my fault,' Jed said. 'I should have seen somat were up wi'carriage. I should never have let you drive alone.'

'No, you should not,' Charlie said. 'The carriage could have turned over. The horse's legs might have been broken rather than strained. Not to mention Miss Draycott's safety.'

The groom's wrinkled face looked grim. 'Aye.'

'It was not Jed's fault,' Miss Draycott said. 'And it is beside the point. That poor creature is in pain.'

'Nowt to worry your head about, missy.'

'I'll check again later,' she said, rubbing her upper arms.

He hadn't thought her so sentimental a woman. Yet on their drive she had kept turning back to look at the injured beast. Perhaps, beneath her hard brittle shell, she'd a soft centre. Hopefully, the head groom wouldn't let her rampage around the countryside alone in future. He'd have a word with him in private. Later. When Merry left.

'You'd be better off staying warm by the fire,' the groom said.

'I'll take a look at my cattle while I'm here, Jed.'

'Sixteen mile an hour tits, I'm thinkin', my lord,' Jed said.

'On a smooth road downhill.' Charlie patted the injured horse's rump and exited the stall. He exited further along the stable block.

'I was going too fast,' Merry said, following him. 'I was

angry and hurrying because of the weather. I must have hit a rut.'

He'd seen no signs of a rut large enough to damage an axle. 'Fretting won't change it.'

Her chin quivered. 'No. It won't. But that horse is in pain. I can see it in his eyes.'

Charlie didn't quite know what to say, so said nothing. He strode along the block until he found his team. They huffed a greeting. He spent a moment or two going over their hooves and their limbs. Someone had brushed them and their brown coats shone.

'You have a good man in Jed,' he said.

'He worked for my grandfather.' She spoke as if the words answered all.

They walked side by side along the alley in front of the stalls.

'It seems you are to be burdened by my company for a while longer,' he said.

'It is no burden,' she said absently as if she had something else on her mind. 'It won't be the first time we are snowed in for a few days.'

'Thank you for your hospitality.'

His voice must have sounded just a little dry, because her head turned, her eyes meeting his gaze.

She gave a rueful smile. 'Did I sound dreadfully rude? I apologise. I meant to say that it will be an honour to have you stay as long as you wish.'

Somehow he preferred the earlier offhand invitation to this lavish courtesy, because the first was pure Merry and the second *pro forma*.

'You must allow me to perform some service for you while I am here,' he said just a little mischievously, thinking to test the waters.

Her eyes widened just a fraction as she considered his words. 'What might you have in mind?'

He grinned, and the sparks were once more hovering in the air. Attraction and interest. Not the searing fire of the previous evening, but it wouldn't take much to set it ablaze.

'How about a sleigh ride?' He pointed to the equipage stored behind her phaeton.

'In this weather?' She glanced out into the courtyard.

'When it clears.'

'All right.'

He hesitated. 'Merry, I conversed with some unusual young women this morning. In my chamber.'

She frowned. And then gasped. 'Beth and Jane.'

'I didn't get their names. However, they seemed very… obliging.'

'They didn't…' She covered her mouth with her hand.

His lips wanted to smile. He held them in check. 'No. They didn't.' But they would have, and she knew it.

'Oh. Oh, dear. I must apologise. They are…housemaids in training. I should have told them to leave your room to Brian.'

Housemaids in training. A new twist on an old profession. She must have seen the disbelief in his face. 'I will speak to them,' she said stiffly. 'And if the weather breaks, we will go for a sleigh ride. In the meantime, I have some business affairs needing attention.'

He imagined she did—but which business?

'In the meantime,' she said breathlessly, 'please make free of the library where you will find books and a nice warm fire.'

They stood in the doorway, looking out at the world turned into a white desert, the house barely visible in a sudden flurry of snow. He inhaled. She was right, snow did have a scent all of its own. Why had he never noticed?

He took off his muffler and wrapped it around her neck and up over her mouth and nose. 'Then at least let me escort you safely back to the house.'

Over the top of the scarf laughter spilled from her blue eyes. She looked like some Far Eastern princess, saucily peeping out from behind a veil. Or she would, if not for the manly driving coat and the man's felt hat.

He grabbed her hand, tucked it beneath his arm and they began the trek up the hill. He liked the feel of her leaning on him for support. She wasn't a fragile flower of a woman, but there was absolutely no denying her femininity.

And today she was acting with the propriety of a duchess. He had the strong urge to unravel the puzzle he'd found. And part of that was learning who might want to cause her harm.

He barely noticed the icy fingers of wind tearing at his coat, or the snow cold and wet on his face, because for the first time in a long time he was doing exactly as he pleased.

Chapter Five

Merry hurried along the corridor. She knew why she was hurrying. It had nothing to do with talking to the women and everything to do with escape. From him.

Not because she was attracted to him, because that part she could handle. Indeed, it was rather pleasant being looked at with desire. But it was the other part that caused her unease. Every now and then, when he looked at her with those intense dark eyes, she had the feeling he could see her innermost thoughts, whereas he seemed to hold himself very much at a distance because he really didn't approve.

The sooner he was gone the better.

She pulled the key from her pocket and unlocked the door to what had once been the nursery. Voices from an open door let her know where she would find Caro and her charges. She entered the day room. Caro faced the two women sitting at desks along with Thomas, Caro's six-year-old son, writing his letters on a slate. The women each held a book. Beth was reading, slowly sounding out the words. She stopped the moment Merry entered.

Looking at the two women, one would never guess their

original profession. Their faces shone with good health and
cleanliness. They wore the modest practical clothing of the
women who worked at the mills.

'Good morning, ladies,' Merry said smiling.

'Good morning, Miss Draycott,' they chorused.

'Good morning,' Caroline said. Her gaze held curiosity.
Wondering about last night, no doubt.

'If I could have your attention,' Merry said, to the room at
large. 'Because of the snow, we have a guest at Draycott House.
I gather you ladies met him this morning. I think it would be
best if you remained in this wing until his departure.'

Beth giggled.

Jane frowned. 'Ashamed of us, then, are you? Is that how
it's to be?'

Heat stung Merry's cheeks. Jane was not the easiest woman
to deal with, despite the fact that she'd sought out Caro's help
on her own account. Jane had come north from London and
was far more worldly than Beth, or the other girls they had
rescued. And she'd appointed herself as their leader. The other
girls had fled after the fire—Jane and Beth were all that were
left of the soiled doves they'd been trying to help.

'I am not ashamed,' Merry said firmly. 'It is for your protection. I don't know this gentleman very well and I do not
want any misunderstanding.'

Jane curled her lips. 'She wants to keep him all to herself,
that's what it is.'

'Enough, Jane,' Caro said.

Jane sniffed. 'I don't care about no fancy man. What I wants
to know is when do we get a proper job, instead of cleaning
your grates?'

In other words, was her meeting successful? The townspeople had called the house in town Draycott's whorehouse and
had thrown bricks and stones through the windows. Finally

a torch had been thrown, starting a fire and forcing them to flee. The meeting yesterday had been supposed to bring the other mill owners over to her side.

The two women looked at her hopefully. 'It's bloody awful here,' Jane said. 'No shops. Nought to do 'cept readin'.'

'I like it,' Beth said stoutly. She'd grown up in the country. Most of the other girls they'd rescued were town girls, daughters of shopkeepers and millworkers who had taken a wrong turn and been cast out on to the streets to make their way as best they could. All had turned to the oldest profession known to women.

When Caro, who had narrowly missed turning to the same calling out of desperation, had proposed Merry use her money and her influence to help some of these women, Merry had readily agreed. She hadn't expected the resentment of the community. They seemed to believe the presence of these women would taint them and their families.

They'd driven the girls off.

She glanced over at Caro, who looked sad, but offered a supporting smile. 'I wasn't able to meet with them yesterday.'

Jane's mouth turned sullen. 'Too busy enjoying yerself with yer fancy man.'

'He is a gentleman,' Merry said. 'He provided me assistance on the road and he will be leaving as soon as the snow is passable.'

'Gentlemen are the best,' Beth said, as if repeating a lesson by rote. 'They's polite and don't have no pox.'

''Course they do,' Jane said.

Caroline rapped on her desk with her ruler. 'Ladies, please. This kind of talk is not helpful.' She glanced at Thomas, who had stopped writing and was listening with a furrow between his fair brows. 'Miss Draycott will find you work and a place to live as soon as she is able. In the meantime, you are being paid to learn to read and write.'

A groan from Beth made Merry smile.

None of the girls had found the concept of reading and writing particularly relevant. Only by offering them a wage had she been able to convince them to try when they'd moved into the house in Skepton. They'd been making great strides until forced to run for their lives. Caro insisted these two continue while they stayed with Merry. If nothing else, they would be able to read a newspaper and their employment contract before they signed it.

If they could find jobs.

'What about the grocer's in the High Street?' Beth asked. Her father had owned a shop, but when he found out she was pregnant, he'd turned her out. The boy had run away to sea and left her to fend for herself. If she couldn't support herself respectably, she would never get her child back from the orphanage. 'He's got a sign in the winder for a shop assistant.'

No one in Skepton seemed willing to risk employing Draycott's whores, no matter how clean they were or how well behaved. The townspeople claimed they would be a bad influence on the men as well as the women.

Merry pressed her lips together. 'I told him of your experience, but he said he'd changed his mind.' She'd even threatened to stop purchasing from him, but then he told her his fear of the mob tearing his shop apart. What could she say?

Jane's lip curled. 'See. I told you it was all a farradiddle.'

'They think we'll steal them blind,' Beth said.

It was an outbreak of burglaries that had turned the townspeople violent, even after Caro told the constable she could account for all her girls at the time of the crimes.

'I'm leaving at the end of t'month,' Jane said. 'There's good money to be made in London. Abbesses always looking for new blood. Once the weather breaks, I can walk there in a fortnight.'

'How much does a girl make in Lunnon?' Beth asked.

'A fortune if you finds the right man,' Jane said. 'Dripping with jewels and furs, some of the girls are.'

Beth's eyes grew round.

'It is not quite like that,' Caro said. 'Very few girls meet that kind of man. And often they cast them off, the way they throw out old clothes.'

'What would you know about it?' Jane sneered.

Caroline coloured. 'I have eyes.'

Merry didn't care much for Jane. Gribble had found her slipping a silver teaspoon in her pocket. Caro had reminded her that she might have done the same, if she had been in Jane's situation.

Damn it. If Merry didn't do something soon, these two women would slip back into their old ways.

A feeling of inadequacy swamped her. Grandfather would have been able to deal with the mill owners and the shopkeepers. He wouldn't have been locked out of the meeting.

Because he was a man.

If only Prentice would stand up to them.

As a manager, Prentice had very little clout. He could speak on her behalf, but even though he was the manager of the largest mill in Yorkshire, he wasn't the owner.

The only way she would ever have a voice in those meetings was if she was married. And then that voice would go to her husband.

Which brought her right back to the mad idea she'd had this morning—and rejected before it was fully formed. How she could have let such an idea creep into her mind, she didn't know.

'I'll find a way to bring them around,' she said. 'Don't worry.' But how?

* * *

Merry squeezed her eyes shut, then looked at the document, forcing herself to read the figures again. The mill was in trouble.

How had it happened so quickly?

The door opened and Caro glided in as if she walked on air. Even on a good day, Merry galumphed around, as Grandfather always said.

But then Caro was as small and delicate as Merry was tall and big boned.

She smiled at her friend. 'Lessons over?'

'Yes. I've left them with some needlework. There are sheets in need of turning.'

'They really don't have to work for their board, you know.'

'I know.' Caro clasped her hands together. 'But it does them good to keep occupied as well as giving them a feeling of worth. They are not bad women. Only misguided.'

'Of course.'

'Although I'm a bit worried about Jane. I think she'd sell her grandmother for a shilling.'

'Probably less.'

They laughed.

'How soon can we rebuild the house?' Caroline asked. 'Is it possible?'

'Not until the snow clears, I'm afraid.'

'I suppose Mr Prentice did his best?' Caro sounded doubtful.

'I'm sure he did. Although he doesn't feel as strongly about finding the girls work as we do, he has always followed my instructions.'

'As far as you know.'

'Your biases are showing.'

'He's too nice. Too friendly.'

Merry sighed. 'He's young. He tries too hard and I wish Grandfather's old manager had stayed on. He was crusty, but he knew everything there was to know about wool. He would have known how to handle the other mill owners.'

'Did he retire?'

All the old anger returned in a hot rush. Her hands curled into fists. 'He didn't want to work for a woman. Said if I got married he'd be happy to come back.' She'd been terribly hurt.

'Oh, Merry. That is ridiculous.'

'I know.' She sighed. 'Sometimes I wonder if I'm making a mistake.'

'Why should you give up something you've worked so hard at all these years?'

'Grandfather always used to say I was just as good as a son. But honestly...'

Caroline winced. 'You are as good. Clearly you are.'

It wasn't the first time they'd discussed the appropriate roles for men and women, and in the past they'd been in accord. Merry glanced down at the figures in her book. Was she wrong after all?

'We will find a way,' Caro said. 'I didn't have a chance to ask you how your game of billiards went. You were in high form last night.'

Merry felt heat creep up the back of her neck. 'He won.'

'Then I suppose you will be wanting a rematch this evening?'

Hardly. 'Perhaps you'd care to join us for a game of cards.'

'You need four for cards,' Caro said.

'We could ask Jane.'

Caroline giggled. 'Poor Tonbridge. He wouldn't know what hit him.'

Jane had fleeced the other girls of their pin money the first night she arrived at the house in town. Merry had the feeling she would not succeed with his lordship, but was not going to put her theory to the test.

'Perhaps I'll ask him to play chess.' And there would be no removal of garments either. Her insides fluttered pleasurably as the image of his naked chest popped into her mind. Perhaps she should go straight to bed.

She almost groaned at the unfortunate thoughts that idea conjured. It would be better if she'd never known the pleasures a man could bring to a woman.

'You will join us for dinner, though?' Merry asked. 'I can hardly entertain him alone.'

'Naturally. I will see you in the drawing room at six as usual.'

Caro glided silently out of the room and Merry turned back to her accounts. It was only to be expected that the mill wouldn't be as profitable as it had been under her grandfather. The army no longer needed the number of uniforms they'd required during the wars and the clothiers had cut back on the quantities of cloth they bought from the mill. If things didn't improve, soon, she'd have to cut back on the number of workers she employed. With the price of bread continually rising, even those fully employed were barely surviving.

Nothing but problems, no matter which way she turned.

She began adding the column of figures again. The door opened. With a sigh, she looked up.

Tonbridge. The aristocratic lines of his face stark in the cold light from the window. Gorgeous. She blinked.

'Ready for our sleigh ride?' he asked. 'I have taken the liberty of requesting the horses put to.'

Oh, she had promised, hadn't she? She glanced out of the window. No help from the weather. It looked like a perfect afternoon.

'It would be good to get some fresh air,' he said, seeing her hesitation. 'I want to take a look at your phaeton. Make sure it isn't a hazard to other travellers.'

'Oh, no, really. You did enough yesterday.' The image of him heaving the carriage out of the way returned. One would never guess he hid such strength beneath the dark burgundy superfine of his coat. Why did she have to think about that now? 'Jed will see to it.'

His gaze drifted to the papers. He hesitated a fraction, then gave her a boyish grin. The kind of grin that no doubt made ladies of the *ton* swoon. And didn't do such a bad job on her either. 'All work and no play makes Jill a dull girl.'

Her heart gave a small thud of excitement. Her knees had the consistency of mashed turnip as the force of his charming smile hit her full on. Escaping from her account books sounded terribly tempting. Temptation seemed to personify this man.

'All right. Why not?' Decision made, she leaped to her feet. 'But the sleigh hasn't been used for years.'

A vague impression of the sharp bite of the wind on her cheeks and the feel of her parents' large, warm bodies on either side of her teased at her mind.

And laughter. So much laughter.

'It's been well maintained, like everything else in your stables,' he said.

'Jed wouldn't have it any other way. I know he is mortified by that axle.'

A shadow flickered over his face. 'It can happen to the best-maintained equipages, as he well knows, and so I will assure him if you wish. Would Mrs Falkner care to accompany us? The sleigh easily holds four.'

'I will ask her.'

She suddenly felt lighter, as if the problems looming over her these past few days had disappeared, or at least become less monstrous. 'It will be fun.'

Chapter Six

Cloaked in a fur-lined rug, with a hot brick at her feet and Tonbridge's large form beside her, Merry felt toasty and warm. She curled her fingers in her swansdown muff and breathed in the crisp clear air.

The snow glinted and sparkled like fairy dust. 'This was a good idea,' she said, glancing at Tonbridge.

Once he'd manoeuvred the horses between the gates, he smiled at her. 'It's a long time since I drove a sleigh.'

She'd been surprised when Tonbridge insisted on driving them, and then decided it was just as well that his hands were kept busy with the reins, since the seats were not very wide and the thought of his hands on her body was keeping her far too warm. Just feeling him alongside her sent delicious tingles over her skin.

Not surprisingly, Caro had refused to accompany them on their jaunt and Merry had blithely said a groom would go with them. So much for decorum.

The day was too lovely for such thoughts. She wanted to absorb the warmth of the sun in through her skin. Feast on the brilliance of a cerulean sky and rolling hills of pristine white.

The vastness shrank her problems to nothing. She leaned back with the muffled thud of the horses' hooves and the jingle of the bridles filling her ears.

'The Yorkshire countryside is magnificent,' he murmured.

'Most days I'm too busy to notice,' she admitted. Too wrapped up in business matters.

He tipped his head back to look up into the sky, his eyes creasing at the corners as he squinted at the light. 'An eagle,' he said. 'See it?'

She looked up and saw the bird, wings outstretched to catch the wind, wheeling high above them. 'It will be lucky to find any prey with so much snow on the ground.'

'Oh, he'll find a vole or a mouse or two. Did you know one of my ancestors was responsible for the King's mews? Back in Tudor times?'

'Mine probably cleaned up the droppings.'

They laughed and the horses' ears twitched.

The tension flowed from Merry's shoulders. He'd made her feel comfortable. She didn't feel the need to hide the smile curving her lips or to say something blunt to keep him at a distance. She could be herself. She let go a sigh. 'I wish every day was like this.'

'Me, too.'

He turned at the crossroads, entering the main road. No tracks marred the snow. No vehicles had passed this way since the previous evening. The wrecked phaeton soon came into view. Snow had drifted around it, but the shafts sticking straight up reminded her of a sunken wreck.

It looked sad and lonely. 'I hope it can be repaired,' Merry said.

He frowned. 'You know, you really shouldn't be driving around the countryside without a groom. Footpads are not unheard of in this part of the country. And there are rumours of Luddites again.'

'I know everyone in the Riding.'

He shot her a look from beneath his brows that said he thought she was a stubborn foolish woman. She glared back.

He drew the horses to a halt and handed her the reins. 'I'll just be a moment.'

'You surely aren't thinking of pulling it out of the ditch?'

'No. I want to look at the axle.' His frown deepened.

'Leave it to Jed.'

He didn't reply, just climbed down and trudged through the snow. Stubborn man.

It was ridiculous. The snow had drifted well up the wheels. There was nothing to see. And what was the point of him getting soaked and cold? He was spoiling the afternoon.

She had a good mind to drive off and leave him there.

He headed back, stepping in the tracks he'd left. He went around to the back of the sleigh and grabbed a shovel.

'Leave it be.'

He ignored her. Blast the man. Merry wound the reins around a strut and jumped down. She followed in his footsteps, the snow clumping on the skirts of her coat, making it hard to walk. By the time she reached his side, she was sodden. He had one of the wheels cleared of snow.

'This is foolishness,' she said.

'Is it?' He crouched down. 'It is just as I thought.' He looked up at her, his face solemn. 'This was no accident.'

She put her hands on her hips. 'Do you suppose I drove off the road on purpose?'

'No. Look at that axle. It's been sawn halfway through from below. The rest of it snapped, but it wasn't an accident.'

Her stomach fell away. 'Why?'

He rose to his feet. 'Yes, Merry, why? Who would want to cause you serious harm? You could have been thrown from the carriage and killed, or died in the snowstorm.'

Her heart stopped. Bile rose in her throat as she stared into the concern on his face. The world seemed to spin around her head as she tried to breathe.

Slowly her heartbeat picked up again. She managed to take a breath. 'I can't think of anyone…' Her voice tailed off as she remembered the mill owners' faces at the guild hall. Angry red faces. And one very worried-looking Mr Prentice. 'Oh, dear.'

Was it possible one of them hated her so much he wanted her dead? Or all of them? Men she'd known all her life? The backs of her eyes burned. Her chest hurt. She wanted to bury her face against Tonbridge's shoulder and weep like a child.

'Who, Merry?' he demanded, his voice almost a growl. 'Who wants to hurt you?'

She turned her face from his irate gaze. 'You are mistaken,' she said dully. 'It must be an accident.'

'The evidence is clear and it seems to me you *know* who did this.'

The urge to unburden herself ached in her throat. She bit her lip against its allure and felt the chill of the air on her teeth. 'There are several people who don't like me very much at the moment.'

'People?'

He wasn't going to let it rest. 'Other mill owners. Town councillors. But, honestly, I don't think any of them would have done such a dastardly thing. They are all respectable men. Pillars of Skepton.'

'Is anyone else angry at you?'

Her teeth started to chatter. Cold. Shock. Damn it, fear, too. 'Certainly not. Next you will be telling me this is my fault.'

She spun away from him. 'This is none of your concern, my lord,' she called back as she stomped away. 'Let us return home before we freeze to death.'

'Merry, wait.'

She kept walking. She couldn't stop, because if she did, she might fall down, her knees felt so weak. Because if she stopped, she might truly believe someone had deliberately tried to end her life.

He caught her by the arm and pulled her around to face him. 'Oh, hell,' he said. 'I'm sorry.' He wiped her cheek with his gloved thumb. 'I didn't mean to scare you.'

Her breath stuck in her throat at the gentle concern in his face and the softness in his dark brown eyes. 'Of course you didn't scare me. The wind brought tears to my eyes.'

He chuckled, a soft low warm sound that comforted rather than mocked. He pulled his hand from his glove and placed his palm against her cheek. Warmth infused her skin, not just where he touched her, but all over, as if he had the power to heat the blood in her veins from her head to her feet.

'You are cold,' he said. 'You should have stayed in the sleigh.'

Her teeth chattered and her body shook. 'No, I shouldn't.'

He swept her up in his arms as if she were nothing but a half-bolt of cloth. 'My dear Merry, allow me to help you back to the carriage.'

'Put me down.' But the words were half-hearted and mumbled against his coat. Somehow her arms had gone around his neck and he was walking. Beneath his hat, his dark hair curled against his temple. His ear was very nicely formed, she decided, not too large, nor did it stick out from his head. In profile against the bright blue sky, his nose was a little crooked. A very small imperfection, scarcely noticeable unless you looked closely. Somehow it made him seem less of a god and more human.

Her heart tumbled over.

Oh Lord, she really did like him. She loved the feel of being in his arms, of being held close to his chest, like something precious. She felt feminine. Cared for. Protected.

He glanced down with a smile. 'Ready?'

Dash it, they were back at the sleigh already. He lifted her up on to the seat and walked around to the other side and climbed up. He arranged the rug over her knees and tucked it up under her chin. 'Is there any warmth left in that brick?'

'A little,' she said. She had no idea, her toes were too cold.

'But not enough, I am sure.' He put his hand under her chin, turned her face towards him. 'Tell me, Merry.'

The strength of command in his voice shivered all the way down to her toes. The intensity in his dark brown gaze trapped her.

'Who would want to do you harm?'

His hands cupped both sides of her face. She looked at the firm set of his mouth, anything not to have to gaze into his searching eyes.

'You do know,' he said. 'You foolish female.' He lifted her face, then those wonderful lips descended on hers, gentle, comforting. 'Tell me, Merry,' he whispered against her mouth. 'Let me help you.'

Then his mouth firmed, it wooed and tormented until she could no longer think of anything but the delicious sensations ravaging her body. Her insides quivered with the joy of it, her heart thundered and she angled her head for better access to those wonderful lips. She pulled her hands from her muff and put them on those powerful shoulders.

His tongue traced the seam of her mouth, not demanding,

sweetly requesting. Resistance had no place in her mind; the joy filling her took up every inch of space. Trembling deep inside she granted him entry and he swept her up on a tide of passion.

She clung to him, and let her senses drift where they would. Delightful waves of desire washed over her, thrilling and beautiful.

Slowly he drew back, his brown eyes smoky beneath half-lowered lids, his breathing as ragged as her own. 'Tell me.'

The man had no mercy. And she had no will. Never had she felt so weak. So vulnerable. Not since the day her parents died and she'd learned love was a fleeting thing. She shivered.

'Damn,' he said under his breath. 'You are still cold. I need to get you back to the house.' He paused, his dark gaze hardening. 'But I will have the truth of this.'

She briefly closed her eyes against the pull of the insidious weakness. Brushed his demand away with a half-laugh. 'You make mountains from molehills, my lord.' She sounded breathless. And, God help her, afraid. The moment he released her, the bone-chilling fear had returned. Someone had tried to do her harm. A warning, or had they actually intended her death?

It didn't bear thinking of.

He picked up the reins. 'Call me Charlie. Make no mistake, Merry, I will not let this rest. You will let me help you.'

The heir to a dukedom was used to getting his own way. And he wanted to shoulder her burdens. It felt good. For once having a man want to protect her felt freeing rather than constraining.

'Very well,' she said, the words spoken before she really had time to think. 'There is one thing you could do for me.'

Chapter Seven

Years of dodging matchmaking mamas sent Charlie's hackles rising. He hadn't expected such a trick from a woman who seemed so straightforward in all her dealings. Inwardly, he cursed. He had held her to comfort her obvious distress. And let their mutual attraction flame out of control. Idiot.

She must have guessed at his thoughts because the smile on her lovely lips died.

Outwardly, he smiled calmly, as he had on so many other occasions when a female tried to net the heir of a dukedom. 'You flatter me.'

She rearranged her expression into one of polite dismissal and shrugged. 'I didn't mean it the way it sounded.'

He urged the horses on with a click of his tongue. 'Then what did you mean?' He shouldn't ask. He should let it go. This ground was as dangerous as the quicksand in the Wash, but knowing her life was in danger, he could not walk away. Not until he knew she was safe. Once he knew who was behind this cowardly attack, he would bring all the power of a dukedom to bear on the blackguard.

The vehemence of his reaction took him by surprise.

'I meant we could pretend an engagement,' she said carelessly, but there was an undercurrent of something in her voice he didn't quite understand.

Oh, Father would really like that. And Robert, poor Robert, would continue to be left out in the cold. 'How would that help?'

'I think some of the other mill owners are angry at me,' she said quietly. 'They are opposed to my idea of providing an asylum for women who have led less than respectable lives.'

'You mean the ladybirds I met this morning,' he said, smiling at the memory.

'Yes. They need a place from which they can find suitable work.' She winced. 'Perhaps meet husbands. I asked the local mill owners to give them employment.'

'And because they are not in favour of the idea, they decided to damage your carriage?' He couldn't quite keep the incredulity out of his voice.

'Caro and I opened a house in Skepton. They called it a bawdy house. Men came one night and attacked the girls and set fire to the house.'

'Which is why they are living with you.'

'Only two of them. The rest disappeared. We need to find them. Give them a home.'

'I still don't see how a pretend engagement resolves the problem.'

She turned in her seat, a furrow in her brow, her eyes focused somewhere in the distance, as if she could see the future playing out before her.

He wanted to kiss her.

God, he ached for far more than that. If he hadn't broken free of her a few minutes ago, he might have laid the blankets down in the snow and made love to her right there in the open. And he would have been forced to accept her proposal of marriage.

Such an error of judgement would be the final straw for the duke. The disgrace at Waterloo and then Robert's scandal had been bad enough, but for his heir to marry beneath him might well kill the old man. His father had looked ill for weeks after Robert's scandal broke. Another such event would likely cause him an apoplexy, not to mention it would certainly end all possibility of Robert's return to the family fold.

'Because I am a woman, the other mill owners will not admit me to their meetings at the guild hall,' she said stiffly, as if the admission stirred more anger than she wanted to admit. 'They would listen to you, if they thought you were my future husband.'

The slight bitter edge to her words gave him pause. How would it feel to be successful, as she so clearly was, and yet ignored by one's peers?

'If you pretended to be my fiancé for a few days,' she continued. 'If you put your name behind my plan, they would be forced to give in. Then you would cry off.'

'A business arrangement,' he said. Irrationally he felt a sense of disgruntlement. An odd reaction, when he'd been ready to flee at the word *marriage*. He shook his head to clear it of such stupid thoughts.

It had taken weeks of argument to convince the duke to accept Charlie's promise to make a suitable marriage in exchange for Robert's forgiveness. To go back on his word would be cruel to his mother as well as dishonourable. He had to be practical.

Guilt weighed him down. No matter how much he wanted to help Merry, this was not the way.

Not because he couldn't see himself married to Merry, he acknowledged with surprise, but because of what it would mean for his family if he broke his agreement with the duke.

She nibbled her bottom lip and then let go a long breath with a shake of her head. 'It would never work anyway.'

'Why not?'

'No one would believe a man of your station would stoop to wed me. Not unless you were in desperate financial straits.'

He raised a brow, considering her words.

'Well, they wouldn't,' she said. 'Look at the way *you* reacted.'

He felt insulted by her quick dismissal. But she was right. He'd instantly hunkered down behind his defensive walls. Yet he could not leave any woman defenceless, especially not this one, not now when his suspicions of foul play were confirmed.

He turned the sleigh in through the gates of Draycott House—the carved words on the pillar announced the name. Beneath the name was a coat of arms. A kingly red deer surrounded by ivy. It looked vaguely familiar.

'I will speak to these mill owners on your behalf.'

She gave a small shake of her head, a wry smile twisting her lips. 'As my friend, or even as the son of a duke, you would have no real influence. They will meet you individually, agree with everything you say, but behind closed doors, they will do as they please.'

How she must hate the exclusion. 'Then I will speak to the constable. And the magistrate.'

'You are most kind.'

She couldn't have sounded more unconvinced. He wanted to throttle her pretty little neck. Or kiss her pursed lips. Neither one of which would help matters.

'Don't underestimate the force of the Mountford name.'

'Oh, I won't.'

The dryness in her voice grated. He had the feeling she felt let down, but she really didn't know the power he wielded as heir to a dukedom.

'Oh, my word!' she exclaimed, sounding shocked and amused.

Charlie followed the direction of her gaze. In front of the house, on an expanse of snow-covered lawn interrupted only by the odd ancient elm and cypress, several figures darted about with cloaks flying. Snowballs flew through the air. The sound of laughter and shrieks of joy pierced the quiet. There was a smaller figure, too. A child?

'Your ladies are out on a spree,' he said.

'I suppose Caro decided they needed some exercise in the fresh air.'

'They look like any other young women when faced with sunshine and an unexpected fall of snow.'

'I know,' she said. 'Hard to imagine how awful their lives must have been before.'

For a moment, Charlie tried to imagine what it must be like, selling your body to live. Hell, wasn't that what his father wanted him to do when he married Lady Allison in order to expand the Mountford influence? The thought left a sour taste in his mouth.

One of the women collapsed in a heap of giggles on a snow bank. Another dropped a snowball on her face. Mrs Falkner— Charlie could make her out quite clearly now dressed in dark grey—called to the small boy.

All the women were laughing and giggling. He guessed there were few times in their lives when they'd been as happy as they appeared this afternoon. Something about it felt right and good. One of them picked up the boy and whirled him around.

'Do you think they would like a sleigh ride? Around the lawn?'

Merry's face broke into a smile. 'They would love it. And it would be a terrible shame to waste all the work of harnessing the team.'

Her obvious pleasure put warmth back in a day that had grown cool after their kiss. He walked the horses across towards the small group. One girl came running when she saw the horses approach. The thin sallow-faced one hung back.

He doffed his hat and bowed. 'Ladies.'

The round-faced one giggled as she had this morning. She covered her mouth with her hand when she saw him looking at her.

He grinned.

Merry threw off the blanket and jumped down. No waiting for help for Miss Draycott; it didn't surprise him in the least.

'Clydesdales,' the giggly girl said, stroking the off-side horse's nose. 'They are beauties.'

The horse nuzzled at her hip. 'I don't have anything for you,' she said with obvious dismay.

'I do,' Merry said and pulled a lump of sugar from her pocket.

The girl's face lit up, making her look terribly young. No more than eighteen, Charlie was sure. Too fresh-faced for the kind of life she'd fallen into. The freshness would fade all too quickly in her line of work.

The other woman stayed well clear, obviously unused to such large animals.

'Lord Tonbridge offered to take the girls for a drive,' Merry said to Mrs Falkner.

Mrs Falkner eyed him a little askance.

'I won't take them out of sight of the house,' Charlie hastened to assure her. 'A couple of spins around the lawn.'

The girl petting the horse turned a hopeful expression in Mrs Falkner's direction.

'Of course,' she said. 'Thank you, Lord Tonbridge.'

'Don't thank me, it is Miss Draycott's rig.'

'Let me introduce you to the girls,' Merry said. She pointed to the giggly one. 'Ladies, this is Lord Tonbridge. This is Beth and that is Jane.'

Jane lifted her chin as if daring him to say anything about their earlier meeting.

'What about the lad?' Charlie asked. 'Would he like to go, too?'

'That is Thomas,' Merry said. 'Mrs Falkner's son.'

Charlie touched his hat. The boy bowed with a grace many men would envy.

An anxious expression crossed Mrs Falkner's face.

'Please, Mama,' the boy said.

'Tonbridge is a very good driver,' Merry said. 'I can assure you, Tommy will be perfectly safe.'

The boy looked pleadingly at his mother.

'Very well,' Mrs Falkner said. 'Stay close to Beth, Thomas.'

Charlie jumped down to help the ladies aboard, handing Beth up first into the back seat. An eager Thomas waited his turn.

'You can sit next to me,' Charlie said and lifted the boy up into the front seat, ignoring Mrs Falkner's frown. The boy's happy smile clearly prevented her from remonstrating. He pretended to notice nothing amiss and held out a hand for Jane.

She shook her head with an ingratiating smile. 'Not me, thank you very kindly, my lord. I need a good walk after being shut up in t'house for days, if it's all right with you, missus?'

Mrs Falkner nodded. 'When you return, come to the day parlour. I will ask Gribble to send up hot chocolate. I doubt his lordship will be long.'

A warning to Charlie. The woman was a proper mother hen. He hid the urge to grin.

Jane nodded and trudged along the tracks left by the sleigh, heading for the gates. Mrs Falkner watched her go with a frown.

Merry released the horses' heads and stood back. Not that the team really needed holding—Charlie had never driven more placid obliging beasts.

He flicked his whip over their heads, jingled the bridles and they lumbered forward. He glanced down at the bright-eyed boy beside him. 'Would you like to hold the reins?'

The boy stared up at him. 'Will you teach me how to do that thing with the whip?'

'Get used to guiding these beasts first,' he said. He turned and looked over his shoulder. 'Everything all right, Beth?'

'Oh, yes,' she breathed, her eyes shining.

The sleigh glided off.

Merry stood beside Caroline and watched the sleigh draw away. 'How kind of him.'

'Very,' Caroline said. 'What is he after?'

'Not me, sadly.' Dash it. Was she speaking the truth?

'Merry!' Caroline sounded shocked.

'He offered to help me with the mill owners, that is all.'

Caro frowned. 'Won't that look rather odd?'

Merry stiffened. Another person who viewed her as beneath a marquis's touch. 'Do you think so?'

'Merry, can't you see? If a man like Tonbridge takes an

interest in your affairs, might they not make assumptions about why? Why does he want to help?'

'Out of friendship. Gratitude.'

Even to Merry's ears it sounded rather weak. Nothing but the truth would do. 'He thinks someone tampered with the carriage.'

Caro pulled her gaze from the slowly diminishing sleigh, her wide eyes searching Merry's face. 'Oh, no. Surely not?'

'I think someone wanted to give me a warning, but Tonbridge is taking it more seriously.'

'This must stop.' Caroline clasped her gloved hands together. 'First a fire. And now this. We will set up the house somewhere else. I will not endanger your life.'

'Do you think it will be different elsewhere?'

'I won't have your death, or your injury, on my conscience.'

'It is not your decision.'

Fists clenched, Caroline spun away. 'I will have nothing to do with it.' It was the first time they had ever argued. Merry felt quite adrift, as if she'd lost her friend.

'Caro, we can't just give up.'

Caro turned around slowly. 'Why not?'

'A Draycott never admits defeat.'

'Never is a long time. Please, Merry. We will find another way. We certainly don't need to involve a man like Tonbridge in our affairs.'

Merry stared at her friend. Perhaps she was right, but it felt galling to give in to threats.

Caro turned to watch the sleigh in the distance. 'Oh, good Lord, is that Thomas standing up?'

'Yes,' Merry said, nodding. 'Charlie seems to like children, doesn't he?'

'Charlie?'

'We are friends.' Dash it, did she sound too defensive? 'I told him to call me Merry the first day we met.'

The suspicious gleam in Caro's eyes made her skin itch as if she'd done something wrong.

'Be careful, Merry,' Caroline said, shading her eyes with her hand. 'A man with his kind of charm and wealth is used to getting his own way, and it will be for no one's benefit but his own.'

Merry's stomach dipped. Few men did anything out of altruism. He would want something in return. Caro put an arm around her shoulder. It was an unusual display of affection. 'Tell him you don't need his help. Like all men, he'll want to take control. We don't need a man to solve our problems. We will deal with it.'

Caro was right. Of course she was. What on earth had she been thinking? She'd never needed anyone's help since Grandfather's death, despite her mother's family trying to insert themselves into her business. She would tell him not to bother with the councillors or the magistrate, that she was giving up her plan. She'd wait until he left before she tackled the problem.

She and Caro would manage.

All through the dinner Caro kept looking from Merry to Charlie, acting the chaperon. Looking for signs of misconduct on Tonbridge's part, no doubt. Merry sighed. With no opportunity to tell Lord Tonbridge her decision since returning from the drive, Merry kept her discourse so carefully light that her head ached.

'Shall we take tea in the drawing room?' she said brightly, after Gribble cleared the table of all but a decanter of port. 'You could bring your port there, Lord Tonbridge, unless you prefer drinking in solitary state. I am sorry we have no other gentlemen visiting to keep you amused.'

'You do yourself a disservice, Miss Draycott. Your conversation keeps me well entertained.'

'I am a chatterbox, in other words.' She almost poked out her tongue at him, but remembered not to just in time. 'Will you join us, too, my dear Mrs Falkner?'

Caroline looked torn. 'I really should see Thomas to bed. He likes me to read a story,' she explained to Lord Tonbridge, 'before I tuck him in for the night.'

'You are truly a devoted mother,' Tonbridge said. 'Don't worry about us. I will take Miss Draycott up on her offer of conversation in the drawing room.'

A look of relief crossed Caro's face. She turned her gaze on Merry, an intent gaze, reminding Merry of her promise. She rose and curtsied. 'Then I will bid you both goodnight.'

Tonbridge's eyes narrowed, but he said nothing as she left the room.

Merry popped to her feet. 'No time like the present,' she said, heading for the door.

She hoped they could have their discussion without the tingle of attraction, the incendiary sparks that filled the air.

She strode into the drawing room. The tea tray awaited them, just as she'd arranged with Gribble. She had no wish to end up playing billiards again.

She sat in front of the tray 'Tea for you, my lord, or will you stick to port?'

He looked down into his almost-empty glass. 'A cup of tea will do very well, Merry.'

He sat on the sofa opposite her. She poured the tea. 'Milk and sugar?'

'Yes, please,' he said. He crossed one ankle over the other.

He looked every inch the dandy tonight. The deep blue coat hugged his form. The high cravat was tied in a complex knot, its creases perfect. How Brian had managed it she didn't know. And his cream waistcoat embroidered with lily of the valley was a work of art.

She handed him a cup.

'So, have you thought further about my offer?' he asked. 'I feel strongly that the person or persons responsible for this crime should not go unpunished. Who leads these mill owners? I will speak to him.'

She smiled politely. 'By gum, I've been doing some thinking since last we talked.'

A frown furrowed his brow. 'Why do you speak like a common labourer when I try to offer a suggestion?'

'Common is what I am. Listen, Charlie, I've been talking things over with Mrs Falkner. We do not need your help.'

His expression darkened. 'Now you really surprise me.'

'Full of surprises,' she said lightly. 'There is no need for you to speak to anyone. We are giving up on the idea.'

A hard intent gaze searched her face. She tried to look calm, unaffected. 'I don't believe you,' he said finally. 'You are not one to give up, Merry.'

The way he made her name sound like a caress caused her breath to catch in her throat. But worse yet was his correct assessment of her nature. It wasn't like her to give up. She made a desperate bid to unscramble her thoughts. 'What I do is nowt of your business, my lord.'

His lips tightened. 'Because I won't engage in trickery.' He curled his lip. 'I am shocked, Merry. Draycott's is known for honest dealing, in word and deed. Would you compromise your good name?'

His accusation struck her on the raw. She held on to her

rising temper, a hot fizz in her chest. 'It is precisely because I treasure my good name that I am refusing your offer.'

He blinked. 'I do not see the connection.'

'I am sure you do not.' And she wasn't going to tell him. 'Let us be quite clear on your position: while the Draycott name may be known for honest dealing, I certainly understand why it is not good enough to be linked with that of Mountford.'

'Blast it, Merry, I didn't mean that.'

But he did. She could see it in his eyes. Rich Merry Draycott. Low class and unacceptable, unless someone wanted her money. She folded her hands together in her lap and tried not to show the ache in her heart. 'You are leaving tomorrow. None of this is your concern.'

He got up and threw a log on the fire. The scent of burning apple-wood filled the room. 'So you are refusing my aid?'

'Yes.' She put up her hand, when he opened his mouth to speak. 'The matter is closed.'

He turned to face her, his eyes hard. 'You expect me to walk away when your life is in danger.'

'Do you think that words falling from your lips will change that? You faffing in my business will only make things worse. I will speak to the constable and the magistrate myself.'

She didn't see fit to add that the local magistrate was also a mill owner or that his wife had been among the most vociferous in her objections to the house in town.

He clearly wanted to distance himself from her and she'd offered him the perfect way out. She certainly had no reason to feel hurt by his rejection. He owed her nothing.

Nor did she need his approval. She didn't need anyone's approval.

'Let us not talk about this any more. It is a storm in a teacup. Would you like me to play for you?'

Without waiting for an answer she went to the pianoforte and lifted the lid. She arranged her skirts around her on the seat and began to play.

A look of frustration passed over his face.

Well, it would. He could scarcely interrupt her. It would be very rude indeed. The one benefit of attending a select academy for young women was that she knew all the rules of polite society. Grandfather had been so proud of her accomplishments. If he'd any idea how she had suffered in that place, it would have broken his heart.

As well as teaching her social niceties, to paint and play the pianoforte and the harp, her time there had taught her to survive all the meanness the world could toss her way. She'd also learned something about men.

Charlie wanted to strangle her as she played one piece after another. The moment he began to applaud a piece, she started another. Her playing was excellent. Not a single note did she miss, and she played without music. The pieces were all about lost love. Positively heart-wrenching, if one had a heart to wrench.

An hour had passed and the punishment continued. Though what he had done, he couldn't imagine. Unless it was his sensible alternative to her madcap plan.

Clearly the headstrong wench was too used to getting her own way. And while he could see a kind of logic in her devious plan, it put him in a hell of an awkward position, when he was on his way to make overtures to Lady Allison.

Not to mention that the men she planned on duping, if they didn't want her blood now, would once they realised her trick. If she refused to accept his offer of help, there was little he could do. He'd have to accept her decision, much as it went against the grain.

He leaned back in his chair and let his mind drift. She looked beautiful tonight and completely different from the previous evening. Her modestly cut gown only hinted at the lush figure beneath. Her black hair, pulled back severely from her face, showed off her high cheekbones, vivid blue eyes and unblemished milky skin. It also revealed the faint blue lines at her temple and tracing down her long elegant throat. If anything, she looked more alluring than she had in her seductive attire. Unattainable and therefore utterly desirable.

Beautiful. Cool and closed off. And brittle. The tension from their earlier kisses vibrated in the air. Whatever was happening, he feared if it went on any longer, she might shatter.

The closing notes of the piece she was playing brought him to his feet. He clapped loudly at the same time as he strode to the piano. He took her hand and kissed the back before she could start again.

'That was lovely, Miss Draycott; however, I think it is time I retired.'

She glanced at the clock. 'Eleven already? I had no idea. Still, I am sure that is not all that late for a man such as you.'

Ah, still angry then. He smiled wolfishly. 'And what sort of man would that be?'

Her lips parted. Her face flushed. 'A man who spends his time in London, I suppose.'

'Have you ever been to London?'

The blush deepened. 'I visited once. As a child.'

'Perhaps it is time you visited again. And when you do, let me know, and I will be delighted to show you the sights.' He took her hand again, held it in his and had the urge to bring her to her feet and kiss her again, recapture that moment of blissful mindlessness in the sleigh. The moment before she made her outrageous proposal, which now hung over them like a storm cloud. Kissing her would be a mistake. She would think his resolve was weakening.

He would not be twisted around any woman's finger.

He raised her hand to his lips one more time and dropped the tiniest of kisses on the back of it, felt the tremor in her fingers in response and his body clenched.

He released her hand. 'I bid you goodnight.' He bowed and strode for the door before he changed his mind.

Why did doing the right thing feel so completely wrong?

Merry paced her chamber; her nightdress swirled around her ankles each time she turned and the rug was rough beneath her bare feet. Two hours has passed and she still couldn't settle. She just wished she could clearly see a path.

Caro *was* right. She was. They must find a way to accomplish their goals and vanquish their opponents. She certainly didn't need the help of a husband. Not even a pretend one. A woman with a husband wasn't a person. She had no rights. No freedom of choice or of decision. Until Caro came, she had never thought of it that way. She'd always thought that one day she would have a husband and children. Men married for money and power. A man would absorb her money, wield her power, without consultation. Grandfather had trusted her enough to leave her his hard-earned business; she would never hand it over in exchange for a ring. Or companionship in bed.

She kicked her gown out of the way and turned. Tonbridge had no place in her life.

The thought left her with a deep sense of loss. Because her body was yearning for the pleasure it knew could be hers? Was that the reason she felt restless? On edge. She kept remembering his beauty as he left the drawing room. Virile, powerful and unbelievably handsome.

And that was the problem. She glared at her empty rumpled bed. The flare of heat in his gaze and the intensity of his kiss this afternoon had called to long-repressed desires and longings.

It had been years since she felt the warmth of a man. And this one knew how to seduce a woman's senses. When his mouth had plied her lips, her body had been overjoyed.

She missed it.

She clenched her fists until they stung from lack of blood and lifted her gaze to the portrait above the mantel. Her mother. Daughter of an earl, beloved wife of her father—what would she think of the wicked thoughts going through her daughter's mind, the hot fires of lust burning in her loins?

They burned within him, too.

Merry turned away from the gentle face looking down. No doubt her mother would be ashamed of her along with the rest of the fashionable world.

Tonbridge lay nearby alone in his bed and she would lie alone in hers. This was her future. She and Caro would live together, helping each other while she remained a spinster in name, if not in truth, forever.

Why not take advantage of the chance that brought him into her house? a voice whispered in her mind. *Why not?* A night of pleasure they would both enjoy. It would only be one night. No ties. No obligations. No tit for tat.

She'd kept him at a distance this evening, despite the way her body hummed each time he came close. Was still humming with the after-effects of his kiss this afternoon. Oh Lord, and the pleasure of his touch last night.

In spite of her coldness toward him tonight, there was no doubt of his desire when he kissed her hand. She rubbed the back of her hand as if she could erase the feel of his lips against her skin.

Lust.

Unrequited passion.

What if he rejected her? But if she didn't ask, how would she know?

Chapter Eight

Tired! Hah! Charlie hadn't felt less tired in his life.

Used to awakening in the smallest hours of the night, he always kept the candles alight to ward off the hated sensation of suffocation brought on by total darkness.

At home, when it got really bad, he'd go for a ride. His servants were used to his odd ways. But here, there would be questions he wasn't prepared to answer.

He rarely had trouble falling asleep. Only when the dreams started did he feel the need for escape. Tonight was different. He tossed off the brandy he had poured. It added to the heat in his blood, increased the thud of his heart.

Desire for Merry.

An urgent pressing lust.

Never had he felt like this about a woman. Naked, with the fire almost dead, he didn't feel the least bit cold. The vaguest thought of the woman had his blood running hot, had him rousing.

She'd certainly taken him by surprise this afternoon, asking him to pretend to be her betrothed. God, he'd like to pretend to be her husband.

His shaft jerked with pleasure at the thought. He could bring himself to release. A youth's trick, something he'd given up long ago in favour of control. If a man couldn't control his own base urges, what hope did he have of controlling his life? Or his bloody dreams?

He got up and strode to the window, thrusting back heavy brocade curtains glinting with gold bullion knots and twists. The cold permeating through the casement seared his over-heated skin. He breathed in the smell of old wood and frost on the windowpane.

He placed his palm on the glass and thawed the ice.

The world outside looked ghostly. Snow glittered where the moon cast its path. Here and there, dark patches ruined the purity. A thaw well under way. Tomorrow he would leave.

Drive away from temptation.

Slowly, painfully slowly, his erection subsided, chilled by the cold air, or the thought of departure.

It didn't matter which.

Sure he would now sleep, he let the curtain fall and returned to the bed. The candles had hours of life left. They would last until dawn.

Stretched out on top of the covers, he closed his eyes, kept his mind deliberately blank and breathed deeply.

A sound by the door.

A mere whisper of noise. His gut clenched.

Nothing. It was his mind playing tricks. He forced himself to ignore it, the way he had ignored far worse indignities after Waterloo. He would sleep. He must.

He resisted the urge to toss and turn. Forced his limbs to remain quiet and once more emptied his mind.

More rustling.

The bed sank in one corner.

Heart drumming, he shot upright, staring wide-eyed at the foot of his bed.

Merry? 'What the hell are you doing here?' He scrubbed a hand over his face. 'I beg your pardon.' God damn it, he was naked. He flipped the edge of the counterpane over his hips.

Her gaze remained on his face, but she must have seen, when she walked in, that he was stark naked. Once more, blood headed for his groin. Damn the woman. 'What did you want?'

'I couldn't sleep.'

That made two of them. 'So you thought you'd wake me to share in your lack of rest. Hand me my robe.' It lay beside her across the foot of the bed.

She bit her lip and handed it to him. 'I'm sorry.' She slid off the bed and walked to the hearth, looking down at the fire, while he pulled the banyan around him.

She spun around as he finished tying the knot. 'I did not intend to disturb you.'

Disturb. Hah! He couldn't be more pleased. Or at least one part of him couldn't. The rest of him wasn't so sure. He waved off her apology. 'How can I be of service?' A bad choice of words. The low thrum in his blood had become a steady pounding beat. He could smell her, the scent of lavender and soap, and a woman fresh from her bed. He wanted to carry her to his. He wanted to lay her down amid his sheets. He wanted all she would give. But only if she gave it freely.

She looked at him, her head tilted on one side, her full lips parted. Lips he longed to take with his own. He clenched his jaw.

'I came to apologise,' she said and pressed those full lips together as if trying to decide what to say next. She clasped her hands at her waist. The firelight behind her shone through the flimsy nightgown and wrap. Outlined in the faint glow, her legs were long and slender, the dark triangle at their apex more imagined than seen. Black as night to match her hair, no doubt, and a delightful contrast to her pale skin.

His teeth ground together. He picked up a candle. 'Let me escort you back to your room.'

She backed away, thankfully into the shadows beside the hearth. She looked nervous. 'You cannot deny the attraction between us.'

The clenching of his groin anticipated what might come next, but at what price? 'I won't change my mind, Merry, whatever coin you use.'

She flinched. A mere flicker of an eyelash, a minute tightening of her jaw. He'd hurt her. He wanted to apologise and grant her wish. He couldn't. It had taken all of his powers of persuasion to convince Father to let Robert return. One misstep and all would be ruined.

Yet she did not retire in defeat. It wasn't in her to give up. Her gaze did not shift away. Instead her bright blue eyes held his gaze boldly. She licked her top lip, leaving it moist and pink. It held his attention as she spoke again.

'It has nothing to do with…' she gestured vaguely with one hand '…that. No one would believe you would offer for me anyway.'

Truth was a bitter brew. He wished she wasn't right. But if she wasn't here to convince him to follow her plan, then why had she come after her coolness this evening? A bubble of something light and airy restricted his breathing. Hope. Damn it. When he should really be turning her around and sending her out of the door, he nodded for her to go on.

'I enjoyed our kiss today. I would like to repeat the experience.'

His groin gave a pulse of approval. Why not, indeed? The urge to say yes filled his throat.

He walked to the window, before the words left his mouth. Before he did something he'd regret. 'You are a beautiful woman. I cannot deny I find you alluring, but I no longer believe the impression you gave me on my first night here. Or my conclusion this morning that you might be an abbess.'

She gasped.

He turned with a smile. 'Finding two very bold females in my bedroom this morning led me astray.'

A small smile of acknowledgement touched her lips. 'I see how it might happen.'

He forced himself to say the next words. 'I certainly recognise the spark of attraction between us, it was there from the first, but you are unmarried and therefore out of bounds. I'm sorry.'

Hades. How utterly priggish he sounded. But it was the right thing to do.

Her fingers played with the tie at her waist.

Bloody hell, if she didn't take him at his word and leave he'd have that small knot untied and the whisper of silk covering her form puddled at her feet.

Randy bastard.

She glanced at him from beneath half-lowered lashes. 'You are indeed a gentleman. But we are both adults, are we not? Both experienced in the ways of the world and capable of making our own decisions. Why should we not have one night of pleasure before you leave?'

He strode to face her toe to toe. She didn't flinch. Her gaze didn't drop from his as he held her chin between forefinger and thumb, tilting her face up, bringing her lovely mouth within reach of his own.

He wanted her.

More than he wanted to give her aid, he wanted her in his bed. Had wanted her since the moment she gazed at him on the road.

And here she was offering herself to him. Not a virgin, the kind of woman he must marry, but a bold sensual woman who knew what she wanted.

A groan rose in his throat. He forced it to silence. Closed his eyes briefly against the urges riding him hard and forced himself to speak. 'Are you sure?'

'Yes,' she whispered, her body swaying towards him, her lavender perfume rising like incense to his senses, sweet and heavy.

He bent his head and claimed her mouth.

Merry sank into his embrace, clutched at the front of his robe with desperate fingers in case she collapsed to the floor on legs weak with relief.

She let her senses drift on the pleasure of his kiss, the lovely feel of his body hard against hers, the intruding thigh between her legs, the large hands roaming her body at will.

Ever since he had caressed her feet in the billiard room, her body had been on fire, her mind a senseless mess of conflicting and confusing thoughts. She wanted this, even if she was beyond the pale to him except in this most basic of passions.

Tonight she would have her desires fulfilled and out of the way, so she could plan how next to proceed without regret for what might have been.

His tongue licked her lips and pressed against the seam of her mouth. She opened to him, tasted brandy smoky on her tongue.

Her breasts felt heavy and full, the place between her thighs moist and tingling; she tilted her hips, increasing the pressure of his thigh and was rewarded by his brief indrawn breath.

She uncurled her fingers from the fabric of his robe and slipped them beneath, to run her hands over his broad expanse of chest.

She'd seen much of him in the billiard room and again as he lay naked on his bed with his eyes closed.

She'd been surprised but grateful for the candles' revealing light. His body was gorgeous, his male member thick and large; she could feel it now pressing against her lower abdomen as his hand brushed up from the indentation at her waist to cover her breast.

She let go a long sigh of pleasure and a satisfied sound of male approval rumbled in his chest.

It sent a shiver down her spine.

Her fingers splayed across the warm silken skin of his chest, felt the roughness of hair and the puckered skin of his scar.

She longed to touch it with her tongue, taste it with her lips, but right now his mouth was taking her senses to new heights of arousal. She slipped her hands up to his shoulders and thrust her tongue in his mouth.

He groaned and swept her up in his arms, breaking the kiss. She looked up into his face.

'My bed or yours?' he asked.

'Yours.' She laughed. 'It is closer.'

'A sensible woman indeed,' he murmured, his dark eyes hazy with passion and glinting with amusement.

He was so bloody handsome. It wasn't fair.

But he was hers for now. And she would make the most of the one night he'd granted.

He frowned.

Had he sensed her regrets?

She smiled and licked her lips. 'What now, you great gormless statue?'

At that he threw back his head and laughed out loud. He

strode for the bed, pressing her back against the mattress, and gazed into her face. 'Did I tell you how much I adore that tongue of yours?'

'For what it says?' she asked, fluttering her lashes. 'Or what it can do?'

'Hades,' he muttered under his breath and swooped down for a kiss. Their mouths melded, blissfully fitting together. Her thoughts scattered as he plundered her mouth and she clasped her hands around the back of his neck, holding him tight, as she devoured the slick silkiness of his tongue in her mouth. She sucked.

He stilled.

Had she been too bold? Gone too far? Would he think her completely wanton? Her heart beat hard against her chest as he broke the kiss. She let her hands fall away as he drew back, his low-lidded gaze sweeping her body, his lips curving in a sensual smile of approval. 'You are a feast for the senses.'

The words struck a chord low in her belly. Flutters tormented her feminine core. What was he waiting for? Suddenly shy, she twisted her fingers in the curls falling over her shoulder, staring at the strong column of throat emerging from his robe, at the rise of his angular cheekbones. In daylight they made his face look hard and stern, but now they made him look like a fallen angel.

Her angel. For one night. A yearning she did not expect pulled at her heart. Such yearning had no place in her life. She pushed it away and opened her arms to him.

He untied the cord at his hips, and discarded his robe in one easy movement. The scar across his chest gleamed white in the candlelight. It crossed sculpted muscle and striated ribs, missed his navel by an inch where it sliced a path across a stomach ridged with tight muscle to come to rest at his hipbone.

And below, the evidence of his desire, the engorged member jutting from wiry black curls, a dark tip. Proud and very male.

She sucked in a breath and raised her gaze to his face. His expression was dark, harsh and full of seduction.

She reached up and traced a finger down the scar's length, from just above his left nipple to his right hip, where the skin jumped beneath her touch.

'Ticklish?' she asked.

Mischief gleamed in his dark eyes. 'If so, be prepared for repayment in kind.'

Her skin tingled as his hot gaze seared every inch of her body. In a moment of weakness, a slight edge of fear that this dark angel would steal more than she was prepared to give, she covered herself, her breasts, her groin.

His brows lowered. 'Unlike you to be shy, sweet Merry.'

What could she say? She hid behind rough words, yet none came to her tongue. She felt weak with yearning.

'Will you stand there all night looking, then?' Perhaps not completely undone. She brought her arms up, stretched like a cat, feeling the peaks of her breasts against the soft muslin of her nightgown.

He grinned. 'Ah, sweet tormenting witch.' Leaning over her, a hand each side of her head, he brought one knee up on to the bed, a tall man, with no need for the step. He nudged his knee between hers, a gentle insistent pressure of warm skin and hard bone.

No going back. She opened her thighs. Gave him room. Gave him leave. Her breath left her in a rush of anticipation.

Half-on, half-off the bed, he hung over her, his dark eyes searching hers, seeking assurance? Permission? She raised her hands, cupped his cheeks, felt the roughness of beard and drew him down.

Blissful kisses rained from his lips, a touch on her mouth, her chin, her cheekbone, her eyelids, between her brows. Each kiss fired heat low between her legs, her body ached to feel him within her, her breasts longed for his touch and all the while featherlight kisses seared her face.

'Lovely, Merry,' he murmured in a low growl at her ear. His tongue traced the swirls. Her skin thrilled and her insides shivered. Never had kisses felt so sweet, yet the brush of his lips promised so much more.

Panting, she tugged at his shoulders, wanting him closer, hard against her, his bulk weighing her down. She ached.

The strength in his shoulders resisted her feeble attempts to drag him on top of her. She raised herself up to press against him, feeling the prod of his erection against the softness of her belly, the press of his chest against her breasts. 'Charlie,' she moaned.

'Yes, love?'

The amusement in his voice flared her temper. She struck at him with her fist and fell back against the pillows. She glared up at him. The muscles in his upper arms bulged with the effort of holding his weight. She shoved at his arm. 'Don't tease.'

Dark lashes swept down and rose again, revealing wicked laughter in their depths. His mouth curved in a smile so sensual her insides tightened beyond bearing. 'What, Merry? Is this to be naught but a hurried encounter, a quick nibble, when I would savour the banquet before me?'

'Sometimes,' she whispered in sultry tones, 'the table is cleared before you can taste.'

'A threat, Merry? Are you playing the tease?'

The edge to his tone gave her pause. This was not a man she could manipulate. He liked to be the one in charge as much as she did. Mayhap more.

If she wanted him, she would have to take what he offered.

She clawed her fingers through the rough hair on his chest and tugged. His jaw flickered. Curving her lips in what she hoped was a smile as seductive as his own, she peeped up at him from beneath lowered lids. 'This is a banquet for two, is it not?' She lightly pinched his nipple between her fingernails.

His eyes glazed. His chest expanded on a quick breath. 'It is.' His voice sounded ragged.

'Then I would taste, too.' She let her hands wander over the smooth contour of his shoulders, felt the slight tremble deep in his bones as he held himself still, looking down at her face. Desire warmed his eyes, while restrained power tensed his jaw. Control.

A man with a will of iron.

Her fingers traced the contours of the arms bracketing her head against the pillows; her palms warmed to the heat of his blood beneath the satiny smoothness of his skin. A pulse beat in his strong neck, a hard beating throb that echoed in her own veins.

Once more she raised herself up, but not to take, to give. She licked along the artery. Blue blood for the son of a duke. She nuzzled against his neck, sweeping her tongue across the salty skin, sucking and nipping. His breathing roughened. Not so much in control as he would have her think.

She nibbled his earlobe and breathed into his ear.

He groaned and pressed closer, encouraging her tongue deep into the orifice. Controlling again. Demanding.

She pulled away.

'Witch,' he muttered. 'Will you torment me?'

'No more than you torment me,' she whispered.

He took her mouth in a hungry plundering kiss.

Strength surrounded her, his body a wall she could see

nothing beyond. It filled her vision, and her mind. He was powerful male. Beside him, she seemed feeble.

Vulnerable. Her heart picked up speed. Trickles of fear rose up from her belly. Her wanton yearnings had almost destroyed her once; she should not let it happen again. Even so, the kiss overwhelmed her senses, carried her upwards on currents of air, rising in twisting strands of pleasure and the pain of need.

A hand, large and firm, cupped her buttocks, caressed the curve. A finger dipped lightly into the crease. A titillating sensation through the fabric. She gasped into his mouth.

He squeezed and kneaded her bottom, while his erection pressed against her.

The teasing fingers travelled down her thigh to her knee. They bunched the gown, easing it upwards. Yes. Now they stroked the bare flesh above her knee, little circles travelling up her thigh, bringing her gown higher, while his kisses numbed her mind to all but his touch.

The fresh scent of his soap and the musk of male arousal dizzied her senses. The longing to submit to his greater will made her limbs languid and heavy. She was pliant in his arms, a shadow of herself. Overpowered by his skill.

His to mould and to shape. It felt lovely.

Chapter Nine

Charlie longed to see her naked. The fine lawn of her shift, the satin of her robe, hid little, yet veiled enough to send his imagination wild. The torment of not possessing her left a growl low in his throat.

He slipped the robe off her shoulders and down her arms. Long, slender, white-skinned arms. He kissed the inside of her elbows, one at a time, smelled the scent she'd placed there earlier, lavender, inhaled it to the depths of his lungs, knowing he would never smell that scent again and not think of Merry.

Eyes half-closed, she lay with her black hair spread over the pillow. He lifted her hand, kissed each finger. The pulse in her throat beat hard and fast. Her breathing quickened.

So sensual. So feminine. So desirable.

He tugged the hem of her nightrail free and she raised her arms to help him lift it off. Her breasts, full and round and high, left him in awe. He filled his hands with their bounty, marvelled at the whiteness of her skin and the firmness of the beautiful flesh.

Beautiful. Rounded. Firm and proud. The peaks were dark,

a soft shade of brown, puckered and tight from the exposure to cool air.

He puffed out a breath.

She wriggled.

'Not yet,' he said. 'I have been waiting to see these all night.'

He swirled his tongue around first one tightly budded nipple and then the other.

She moaned.

He felt her dampness on his thigh pressed between hers. Oh, yes, she wanted him as much as he wanted her. Desire shone like a bright flame between them, glowing on their skin and heating their blood. The pulse at the base of her throat urged him on, yet he was loath to let it flare and all too soon die.

He suckled.

She speared her hands in his hair, pressing his mouth to her breast. He caught her by one shoulder, supporting himself and holding her trapped, teasing her other breast with a flicking thumb.

She cried out her pleasure. The shudder of her body as the shocks of pleasure held her in their grip drove him beyond control and into the darkness of his own urgent need.

He widened his knees, opening her thighs. Her dark curls were damp. He guided himself to her entrance.

'Merry,' he commanded. 'Look at me.'

She lifted her eyelids. Her full lips smiled. There was yet one more thing he needed. One thing he needed to know.

'Say my name.'

She licked her lips. 'Charlie,' she breathed.

He slid deep inside her. Knew her as only a lover could know a woman.

Her heat closed around him in welcoming warmth. He kissed her mouth, probed with his tongue as he moved his hips. She clutched at his shoulders, digging her nails into his skin, tilting her hips, rising to meet his every thrust as he stroked her insides. He watched her submit to the pleasure.

The urge to drive into her, to bury himself deep and simply let go, jolted through him.

He fought for command. Battled for the will to lead her from one little death to the next without taking his own. He was known for it. Anything else was unacceptable.

He slowed his breathing.

Clung to control by a thread with each warm slide into her depths, each slow lingering withdrawal.

He breathed deep and slow, the body and the mind in perfect harmony. Energy building to peaks, then rippling away in muscle and bone.

'Charlie?' She ran her fingers over his chest, tweaked his nipples, raised herself to suckle.

His breathing faltered, distracted by the sight of her glorious black tresses against the whiteness of her shoulders and the generous exploration of his body.

Her touch felt wonderful. Not giving or taking, but delightfully shared.

She lifted her legs high and took him deeper.

The pleasure hit him hard and fast. A breath caught in his throat. Breathe, damn it. He twisted his hips, grinding himself hard against the yielding heated flesh.

'Oh, Charlie.'

The sound of his name on her lips, the feel of her luscious body around him, her legs tight at his waist, sent him over the edge. He succumbed to the urges beating in his blood.

He pounded into her. Mindless. Feral.

The climax built. Hit him hard. 'I can't… Merry you have to…' He pumped his hips and caressed with his thumb.

Her eyes widened. Her body trembled. Her inner muscles

tightened around him. Gripped him, as her fingers gripped his shoulders. He gazed into her face, saw the strain and the reach. Her eyes opened wide. She let out a cry as she fell apart.

Undone by the glory of the utter bliss on her face, unable to contain his own race to the finish, he pulled clear and spilled against the covers.

Oh, what did she do to him? He felt like an inexperienced lad. Vulnerable. Without control instead of bringing her to greater heights, keeping her in a state of ever-increasing arousal, until he decided to let her go.

Dear God, he'd almost spilled inside her body.

Aware of her laboured breathing, he turned on to his side and gazed into a face dreamy with satiation. Eyes closed, she lay utterly relaxed, her face still flushed; the scent of their lovemaking perfumed the air.

Her eyes drifted open. 'Mmmm,' she murmured, her chest still rising and falling. 'That was…good.'

Bloody hell. He was leaving in the morning and one night with Merry was not nearly enough.

'You are glorious,' he said and pulled her into the cradle of his arm, let her head rest on his shoulder. His pounding heart slowly quieted, her breath tickled his chest and his own breathing slowed to match hers.

Cosy and warm and deliciously replete, Merry woke to light filtering through her eyelids. It must be morning.

Time to get up. She opened her eyes.

The room was ablaze with candles. They burned on the tables each side of the bed. And on the mantel. Beside her the sound of another's deep breathing. The gentle inhale and exhale from Charlie. She glanced over at the window. Still dark outside.

The last thing she remembered was him saying he wanted to

watch her sleep when she suggested they snuff the lights. Carefully, she eased on to her side and gazed at the man sprawled beside her on top of the covers. He lay on his stomach, his flanks and broad back gilded by candlelight. She reached out to run a hand over the beautiful skin, then whipped it back, touching her lips with a fingertip. He looked so relaxed, it seemed a shame to disturb him. Even if the little flutters low in her abdomen suggested he might very well like it.

She glanced at his face, at the full lips, relaxed in sleep, the dark crescent of eyelashes, the slash of brow, the rugged features.

Delicious. A gorgeous man.

She raised up on her elbow. He looked younger in sleep. Less world weary. Less drawn. Less severe. Closer to her own age than she'd thought.

The clock on the mantel struck the quarter hour. She glanced over and saw it was past five o'clock. Very soon Brian would come to make up the fire and find her here. She'd asked him to take over the task from Beth and Jane. She didn't want Tonbridge propositioned again. Not by them, anyway. She quelled a small smile.

Nor did she want to start any gossip.

The ripple of concern over the bourgeois Miss Draycott and her brief girlish love affair in those long-ago schooldays would be nothing to the scandal of being caught in a marquis's bed.

Her first indiscretion had been with a boy. Charlie was a man. A beautiful, wonderful man who knew how to please a woman.

She stretched. She really should return to her own room.

Their mutual passion had been nectar from the gods to her, but might have seemed passing ordinary to him. A sow's ear, rather than the silk purse in her mind. Hopefully, Tonbridge wouldn't betray her indiscretion. He was much too much the gentleman.

What did it matter? After today, she would never see him again. A pang beneath her ribs halted her breath.

Sadness, when she should be feeling nothing but sated. A longing for what could never be. How futile. How unlike her since she'd grown up.

She retrieved her robe from the floor beside the bed.

Charlie sighed, but didn't waken. Just as well. He only had to look at her with those dark eyes and sweep away any semblance of reason.

She slipped on her nightgown, thrust her arms into the sleeves of her robe and knotted the tie. She glanced around the room. It was dangerous to leave candles burning unattended. The thought of a fire made her skin crawl. The house in Skepton had taken but minutes to burn. The girls had been lucky to escape with their lives. She took the snuffer from the mantel and tiptoed around the room, quickly extinguishing them all.

Unfortunately, Charlie didn't seem to notice her departure. With a rueful smile at her continuing feeling of regret, she opened the door and peeped out into the corridor. All quiet. And dark. With no sound from her bare feet on the runner, she ran lightly back to her own room at the end of the hall.

She jumped between the cold sheets and shivered.

It would have been nice to stay next to Charlie. For them to wake up together. Like husband and wife.

The faint memory of sitting on her parents' bed in the early mornings, drinking chocolate like a real grown-up lady slid into her thoughts. They'd been so happy. Before the fever had struck.

Afterwards, everything had changed. Poor Grandfather had been so sad, so worried about what to do with her.

She snuggled deeper beneath the sheets and closed her eyes. If only things could have been different. If only she could have been a lady like her mother, as Grandfather had hoped, Charlie might have gone along with her proposal. Betrothed to a marquis. Merry Draycott. What a thing. She couldn't help but chuckle beneath her breath. She hugged her arms around her body. Imagine meeting such a gorgeous man on the road across the moors.

The vision of her phaeton, shafts upright in the ditch, brought her upright. Deliberately damaged.

Her stomach roiled. Her heart raced, rising in her throat to shorten her breathing. Fear.

Saints above, she'd never sleep now. She couldn't go back to Charlie, admit her terror. He'd use the knowledge to impose his will.

Shivering, she got up and lit a candle to keep the dark thoughts at bay. She stared at the flickering flame. Was that why Charlie kept his candles alight when he slept? To keep away evil?

It would have to be something terrible to trouble such a powerful man.

Numbers were her escape. She picked up the accounts ledger she'd put aside earlier in the evening. It would either put her to sleep, or she would get her morning's work done before first light. She must find a way to increase production, or she would have to let employees go.

Why was everything going wrong now? Were all the nay-sayers who had wrung their hands in horror at her inheritance of the mill right after all? Was it impossible for a woman to run such a large enterprise as Draycott's? Should she have abided by her uncle Chepstow's wishes and put everything in his hands?

She sighed. Grandfather would have solved the problem

in an instant. *Look out for t'coppers* was his motto. Was that what she was doing wrong? Looking out for the pounds?

Dash it all, she would not be beaten.

She opened the ledger at the beginning. The answer had to be here.

Cold. Alone. Charlie opened his eyes.

Darkness assaulted his gaze. Silence his ears. A band tightened around his chest, cutting off air. Sweat trickled down his back. His heart thundered. He lay rigid. Still. Suffocating.

In a bed?

Why the hell was it dark?

The candles must have gone out. Darkness had woken him. He threw back the covers and drew back the curtains from the window. It didn't help.

He gathered the supply of candles he'd left ready with shaking hands. He brought down the candelabra and struck the flint. A candle flared. He inhaled a deep calming breath.

He held the flame to the candelabra. Its candles hadn't burned down, they'd been snuffed. Some time ago by their length.

He glanced at the rumpled bed. Merry must have doused them when she left.

Why hadn't he awoken then? He had slept through her departure. Were the nightmares finally gone?

He rubbed at his breastbone and stared at the window. A faint trace of grey in the darkness of the room. He wanted to cheer. He felt rested. For the first time in years, energy coursed through his veins at the thought of a new day.

He'd made love to Merry, wonderful passionate wild love, and fallen asleep. God, he'd lost complete control with her, behaved like a green boy with his first woman.

She had climaxed deliciously. He hardened, wanting her again.

It wouldn't happen.

Their lovemaking hadn't changed her decision. The two things were not connected. She wanted him gone. He was to drive away and leave her to face the danger alone. Impossible. Yet what choice did he have…unless he agreed to her suggestion that he pose as her future husband.

He groaned. If his father ever learned of this new adventure of his, Robert would be outcast forever. But leaving Merry in danger was out of the question. He already had enough guilt to carry. What he'd done to Robert. His failure at Waterloo.

He would not fail Merry.

He stilled. Was he once more being reckless, endangering others to satisfy his own ego as his commanding officer had accused?

He went hot, then cold. Damn it all, what else could he do? If he left and something happened to Merry, he would never forgive himself.

A knock sounded at the door. He grabbed for his banyan as Brian stepped in, carrying hot water in a jug. 'Ready for your shave and a bath, my lord?'

Ready? Yes, indeed. Because he needed to see Merry as soon as possible. Not that he expected the conversation to be easy.

Chapter Ten

The account books didn't look any better now than they had in the early hours of the morning. One thing was obvious—while costs were rising at the mill, income was falling. Clearly, she would have to deal with the other mill owners' enmity quickly or face ruin.

Merry raised her gaze from the rows of numbers and stared out of the window. No blue skies today. The moor looked particularly bleak, a wasteland of white patches amid the brown grass.

A brief knock and the door opened to admit Charlie. He looked wonderful. Refreshed. And, damn him, more handsome than ever.

An odd feeling of shyness tensed her stomach. Warmth stung her cheeks. He'd think her such a naïve fool for blushing after her wantonness in the night. She kept her smile cool. 'Good morning, my lord. Ready to leave?'

He grinned. 'Forgotten my name so soon, my sweet? How are you, Merry? Did you sleep well?' He strode to the desk, gathered her hands in turn and kissed each palm. 'You look beautiful.'

Right, beautiful in her plain brown gown and ragged grey wool shawl. Her working clothes. The man was a flirt. 'I am well, thank you, *Charlie*. Is your carriage at the door? I will come and bid you farewell.'

He wandered around the room, looking at the neat rows of ledgers on the shelves lining one wall, each one neatly dated. 'So this is where you spend most of your time?'

'Yes.' She pulled her old shawl closer around her, not because she was cold, but because having him prowling around her office seemed to make the room smaller.

'I'm not leaving,' he said.

'What?' Her mouth fell open.

'I'm not leaving while your life is in danger.'

Why did men always think they were the only ones able to solve problems? 'I don't need your help.'

He sat down in the chair opposite the desk. His jaw set in a stubborn line. 'Yes. You do.'

She squeezed her eyes shut. 'Do you know what they will think if you run around town standing up for me? They will think I am your mistress.'

His dark eyes gleamed, but his face remained deadly serious. 'After last night, you are.'

'Well, it won't matter what you say in that case. They will listen politely and once you leave they will do as they wish. As my...my...'

'Lover,' he said, raising a brow.

'Very well. As my lover, you will have no influence at all. And my reputation will be ruined into the bargain. I have to deal with these men every day. I need their respect. This will only garner ridicule.'

He leaned back in the chair, kicked out his legs and folded his arms across his chest. 'Not if I pose as your fiancé.'

She stared at him. 'Why? You were vehemently opposed to this idea barely a few hours ago.'

'I won't leave you to face this alone. It wouldn't be right.'

She blushed. 'You owe me nothing. No. I don't need your help. Caro and I can manage this for ourselves.'

He shrugged a shoulder. 'Your choices are fiancé or lover. Either way I will speak to them today.'

Blackmail. *Brass makes t'wheels turn.* Only he didn't lack for money, and, unless she was completely deranged, he still wanted her.

'It's a mickle for a muckle, then,' she said.

He stared at her blankly.

'Is't not plain as the nose on your face? I'll be your mistress while you play the fiancé. 'Tis a fair bargain and when it is done, there's no obligation on either side.'

His eyes flashed. 'There you are with the outrageous statements in that dialect again. I'm not looking for damned payment. What kind of man do you think I am?'

She glared at him. 'What? Is it beneath you to make an honest bargain? Smell too much of the shop?'

A blank look crossed his face. He took a deep breath. 'It's a matter of honour, Merry. Surely you understand?'

Unfortunately she did. A man who thought his honour was at stake would never give in. Her heartbeat quickened. Her pulse raced. The thought of him remaining here for days, no doubt. The temptation of having him close by.

Caro would be furious.

She glared at him. 'You said you were in Yorkshire on business. I suggest you continue on your way.'

A dark brow flicked up. 'Suggest all you want, I am speaking to these men and that is final.'

He meant it. This man was as stubborn as she was. And if he succeeded, she would be beholden to him. *Every good turn deserves a reward.* Asking him to tie his name to hers deserved a far greater reward than one night in her bed.

'And you won't accept payment.'

A muscle flickered in his jaw. Anger. Pride. Well, she had her pride, too.

'But you won't turn me away if I come to your bed of my own free will.'

He closed his eyes briefly as if he battled demons of his own.

She half-expected him to back down. The other half waited desperately for his answer. Because if he rejected this offer, she would know he despised her indeed and his offer of help was out of the question.

A long sigh escaped him. 'No, I would not turn you away if you came to me of your own free will. I'm damned well not made of stone.'

She let go a breath of her own. She'd actually been holding it while she waited for his answer. 'Then we have a bargain.'

Dear God, what would Caro say? She'd be angry, and disappointed, but she'd have to admit, eventually, it was the best solution. She'd have to forgive her, eventually.

Her insides trembled. He was staying. He would be hers tonight and tomorrow and into the future. The pen dropped from fingers weak at the thought of nights in his arms.

He leaned forwards, elbows on his knees, gazing at her intently. 'Now that is settled, let us start with who you think might have tried to damage your carriage.'

Merry could quite happily drown in those dark brown eyes.

Concentrate, Merry. She shook her head. 'I've gone over and over it in my mind. I know some of the mill owners and clothiers hate dealing with a woman, but they were Grandfather's good friends. I can't believe any of them would do me harm.'

'Businessmen are notoriously ruthless,' he said reasonably.

She rose to her feet. 'But they are not murderers. I won't believe it. I've known these men all my life.'

He held out a hand. She walked around the desk and took it, feeling its strength. He enclosed her hand in warmth. 'You can't let soft emotions cloud your thinking.'

'I'm not one of your sentimental women who doesn't know about harsh realities.' She pulled at her hand. He gave it a tug and somehow she ended up sitting on his knee, enfolded in his arm, resting against his chest. It was so easy to lean against him.

He placed a warm hand on her thigh. His heat scorched her leg through the wool. 'Merry, listen to me. Someone tried to kill you, no matter how you look at it.'

'But why? I've done no one any harm.'

A finger toyed with the fine hairs at her nape. A shiver ran through her, not cold, searing hot. Her insides turned to liquid.

His voice was a gentle murmur when he spoke as if he, too, felt the rise of passion. 'Let us think it through together. What is the reason behind their dislike of the asylum you established? It is not unusual for towns to help those less fortunate. Indeed, every parish is obliged to help their poor.'

'It might be their wives egging them on. Because of the kind of women we sought to help.'

'Ah,' he said.

'What do you mean, "Ah!"?' Indignant, she pulled away.

He hauled her back against his chest. His chuckle vibrated against her shoulder. 'Nothing like an angry woman to move a man to action.'

His hand caressed the underside of her breast. Oh, heaven help her, was that his…his erection against her thigh? Desire flooded through her. She turned her face up. His dark eyes were glimmering with light, yet his expression contained concern. For her. As if he cared.

The door burst open.

Merry tried to jump to her feet. She found herself restrained as she looked into the startled face of her manager. 'Mr Prentice?'

The short stocky man reared back as his pale blue eyes took in the scene. His ruddy face flushed a deeper shade.

'Miss Draycott,' he gasped, shock writ large on his face.

Merry winced. More grist for the gossip mill. She pried Charlie's hand free and stood up. 'Mr Prentice, let me introduce you to the Marquis of Tonbridge, my betrothed. My lord, this is Albert Prentice, my manager.'

Charlie rose easily to his feet. He stuck out a hand. 'Prentice,' he said easily, with just the right amount of friendliness and condescension that would put the man at ease without being effusive.

Prentice's eyes goggled. His jaw worked, then somehow he managed to take Charlie's hand and bow. 'My lord. A pleasure.' He turned his eyes to Merry. 'I'm sorry for interrupting. I wasn't expecting…'

'I am glad to see you. I hope you had no trouble on the roads?'

'I…no. I came along just as they were removing your carriage from the ditch. For a moment I thought… Jed said you had an accident. Are you all right?'

She saw Charlie narrow his eyes, watching Prentice's reaction. Good Lord, the man suspected her manager.

'I'm fine,' Merry said quickly. 'Luckily his lordship arrived in time to rescue me.' She shot him a look. 'Although I had things well in hand.'

Prentice's gaze swivelled to Charlie. 'I didn't know you were expecting company.'

'No reason why you should, is there, old fellow?' Charlie asked.

Merry's gaze flew to his face. His expression was dark. Stern. Questioning.

'Mr Prentice is my trusted adviser in all aspects of Draycott's,' she said quickly. 'I wasn't sure his lordship would come so early in the New Year, Mr Prentice, but negotiations regarding our betrothal have been under way for some time.'

Prentice swallowed and tugged at his neckcloth. 'Oh, aye.'

'You have no cause for concern, Mr Prentice,' Merry said firmly. 'Nothing at Draycott's will change.'

'Except my assistance with Miss Draycott's problems,' Charlie said in rather a dangerous-sounding voice. It was almost as if he mistrusted the man. Dash it. She wouldn't have him upsetting her manager.

She smiled at the young man. 'Albert, Lord Tonbridge is going to help with our plans for the Skepton Asylum. He and I are going to speak to the other mill owners. Who do you think we should approach first?'

Prentice twisted his hat in his hand; expressions chased across his face: chagrin, worry, doubt. He forced a smile. 'Mr Broadoaks would be best, Miss Draycott.' He took a deep breath. 'All t'other owners listen to him.'

'Is he married?' Charlie asked.

'Aye. Got four sons and three daughters, too.'

Charlie gave her a significant look. 'I suppose the sons are out of leading strings?'

'Aye. Two of them already help their Pa at t'mill.'

'Benjamin Broadoaks was Grandfather's best friend,' Merry added. 'He has been the most receptive to my ideas. He will help us.'

Prentice looked unconvinced. 'Shall I speak to him?'

'No,' Charlie said, before Merry could answer. 'Mr Broadoaks will receive a visit from me.'

Merry bridled at the tone of command. 'From us,' she said. 'Mr Prentice, I have here a list of instructions for the mill. I think it will reduce production costs appreciably. Would you see to it, please?'

Prentice ran his eye down the notes she had made. 'It might help,' he said. 'I'll take it right away.' He hesitated. 'You are sure you were not harmed yesterday?' His gaze darted to Charlie. 'You were lucky out there on the moors with a snowstorm coming on.'

'Very lucky,' Charlie said.

'I am fine, Mr Prentice. Thank you for your concern. Please give my regards to your mother.'

A muscle in Prentice's jaw flickered at the obvious dismissal. 'Mother will be most glad to know of your kind wishes, Miss Draycott.' He bowed and went out, closing the door behind him.

'Shifty-eyed bastard,' Charlie said. 'I don't like the look of him.'

Merry blinked.

'Bursting in here as if he had the right,' he continued.

'He's a friend and an employee.'

Charlie rose to his feet. 'You may think of him as a friend, but do not be surprised if he has other designs.'

Had she been too friendly? Let the young man jump to conclusions? 'Nonsense,' she muttered. Dash it. Yet another problem to resolve. She couldn't afford Prentice going off in a huff.

'Time to visit Mr Broadoaks,' Charlie said.

'Not without me.'

He grinned. 'Now why would I miss an opportunity to drive a lovely young woman out in my curricle?'

She wrinkled her nose. 'I have a better idea. We'll take the closed carriage. More private. And warmer.'

He smiled. 'Why, my dear Merry, you are a naughty puss.'

She hadn't been expelled from school for misbehaving with a gardener's boy without learning a thing or two about taking chances when they came along. She cast him a sideways glance. 'You don't know the half of it.'

'Regretfully, I must decline.'

Dumbfounded, she stared at him.

'My horses need exercise.' It was a lie. She could see it in his face. But why? She tried not to care, not to feel rejected, but it didn't seem to be working.

They were admitted into the courtyard of Broadoaks Mill, at the edge of town, by a child of about ten with a runny nose and a ragged jacket covered in white fluff.

There but for the grace of God, Charlie thought. Only an accident of birth separated him from the masses. He certainly didn't believe in divine right. Charlie tied his horses to a post.

'Master's in t'office.' The boy pointed to a set of wooden steps up the outside of the building.

Charlie gestured for Merry to go ahead and enjoyed the view of her shapely ankles and the sway of that deliciously curved bottom as she climbed. No wonder men had invented this bit of courtesy. Ready to catch them if they fell, indeed. It was all about the view.

To his chagrin, his body responded with enthusiasm. He

hadn't expected her to offer to be his mistress, and he'd had the devil of a time refusing. Not that she'd listened. The determination had been clear on her face. And damn him, he was looking forward to tonight with impatience.

He ought to be ashamed.

When they reached the wooden landing at the top, Charlie rapped his knuckles on the peeling green paint on the door on the narrow landing.

'Come,' a deep voice said.

Charlie ushered Merry inside. The room overlooked the mill floor on one side and the courtyard on the other. The elderly man behind the desk with red cheeks, a nose covered in broken veins and a full beard sprinkled with grey covering most of his lower face, hauled his bulk to his feet. 'By gum, Miss Draycott. I weren't expecting you! Not so soon after the meeting.'

If ever again, Charlie thought, searching the other man's face for signs of guilt or disappointment. He looked genuine pleased to see them.

'Come in, lass. What can I do for you? My word, young lady, don't know when I've seen you looking more gradely.'

Bliss had that effect. She glowed with it. Charlie felt more than a little pride, though he kept his face completely expressionless as the mill owner turned to him with curiosity in his gaze. 'I don't think we've had t'pleasure, sir.'

'Tonbridge,' Charlie said. He put out a hand.

The older man's eyes widened. 'Mountford's heir, if I'm not mistaken.' Curiosity deepened in the muddy brown eyes.

'Miss Draycott has done me the honour of accepting my offer,' he said. Not a complete lie. The offer was merely not the one this man would expect.

He hoped. He was none too sure what the townspeople

thought of Merry Draycott. He wasn't quite sure what he thought of her himself.

'By gum, lass,' Broadoaks said, grinning. 'Your grandfather would be in alt. My heartiest congratulations.' He took Merry's hand in his big rough one and patted it. Charlie had the urge to snatch it away, but held still. Finally the elderly merchant stuck out his hand to Charlie. 'By thunder. A Mountford. Congratulations.'

Beneath the older man's assessing gaze, Charlie felt a bit like a prize Arabian stallion. It wasn't the first time he'd been accorded that kind of inspection, but usually it was the mothers who looked at him that way.

He managed a grim smile and shook the meaty paw. 'Thank you, sir.'

'Ah, you are a Mountford, all reet. By gum, a chip off the same block as your father.' He rubbed his hands together. 'I'll wager Chepstow is crowing from the rooftops about this.'

A cold weight settled in Charlie's gut at the sound of the familiar name. He glanced at Merry.

She winced and shook her head.

Charlie's bad feeling travelled up to his chest. 'Chepstow?'

'The earl. From over York way,' Broadoaks said, oblivious to the chill sweeping the room. 'The Purtefoy family are her ma's family. Not pleased with the marriage they weren't. Always was a thorn in your grandpa's side, lass, the way they treated your poor ma. But you showed them.'

'You are related to the Earl of Chepstow?' Charlie asked, hearing the growl in his voice, the building anger, but didn't care to hide it. The earl was a crony of his father's. A man with political clout of his own. And Lady Allison's father.

'He's my uncle,' Merry said, looking decidedly uncomfortable. Guilty.

Charlie's anger rose from his chest to the skin at the back of his neck. Had she played him for some sort of dupe? The hart in one quadrant on the shield on her gatepost came from Chepstow's coat of arms, he realised. The rest of it, some sort of puffery. Hell. Why hadn't he recogised it?

Broadoaks's bushy eyebrows shot up. 'Something wrong, my lord?'

Charlie stared at him. Wrong? It couldn't be worse.

Merry shot him a pleading look. 'We can talk about this later, Tonbridge. We came to ask Mr Broadoaks a question.'

Charlie gave the old fellow a smile that said he was about to impart a secret. 'If you'd keep the betrothal between us for now, we'd be grateful. The settlements are not yet final.'

'Aye, certainly, my lord. Business comes first.' He winked at Merry. 'Make sure you drive a hard bargain, young lady. Do your grandpa proud.'

Merry blushed, as well she might, the sly little baggage.

Charlie took a deep breath, reining in his temper, tamping down the suspicion he'd been gulled from the first moment they met. If it wasn't for the fact that there was no way she could have known he'd be travelling along that stretch of road two nights ago, he might have thought she'd planned the accident herself.

She couldn't have known.

While some of the glow seemed to have gone out of Broadoaks's smile, he waved expansive hands. 'Even so, this news calls for a celebration. A glass of wine? Some brandy?'

Merry smiled. 'Not this early in the day, Mr Broadoaks.'

Making the decisions again. Ruling the roost. Indicating he was under her thumb. Charlie gritted his teeth. 'Perhaps another time. Our business is pressing.' Not nearly as pressing as the words he had for Merry after this meeting. 'Let me explain.'

Merry looked startled, no doubt surprised he had taken charge of the conversation.

The old man's eyes sharpened. 'Aye. Sit ye down, both of you. Tell me what service Benjamin Broadoaks has in his power.'

Charlie gave Merry a warning glance. 'The matter of a home for women in need.'

Broadoaks's face turned the colour of puce. His gaze swivelled to Merry. 'Now then, lass. The matter was put to rest the day before yesterday.'

'I think not,' Charlie said. 'You know as well as I, Miss Draycott has no intention of letting the matter die. The real question is how did you and the other mill owners plan to stop her if setting light to the house didn't work?'

Broadoaks recoiled. His chair creaked in protest. He stared at Merry. 'That's a terrible thing to say.'

Merry bit her lip. 'Someone put those men up to it.' She looked at Charlie. 'And now—'

'Someone tampered with Miss Draycott's carriage on her way back from her meeting with you and the other mill owners. She was lucky she wasn't killed.'

Broadoaks lunged forwards, his beard stiff with indignation. 'Now wait a minute, your lordship. I won't say I like the idea of a flock of whores setting up shop in the middle of town as bold as brass, but it ain't a matter to kill someone over. Nor did I have owt to do with t'fire. Were some of the lads from the Muddy Duck got fired up about t'women taking their work.'

'They are not whores,' Merry said. 'Not any more. How will they ever get free of that life unless someone gives them a chance?'

'Hmmph,' Benjamin Broadoaks replied. ''Tis same old argument. We don't want them here.'

'Not quite the same,' Charlie said, before Merry could speak again.

Broadoaks eyed him warily. 'Now, young fellow, surely you see the right of this. Miss Draycott here has a soft heart, but we are men of the world. We know—'

'The Durn estate will pay for the rebuilding of the house. The asylum will be named for the duchess. I will act as her agent in this matter and Miss Draycott will head up the Board of Directors.'

Merry's look of gratitude was like a knife to the gut, because it was a bloody lie. He wanted to throttle her. He flashed her a charming smile. 'That is all you want, isn't it, my dear?'

From the way her face stiffened, he was pretty sure she heard the sarcasm in his voice.

Broadoaks didn't seem to notice. He sank back in his chair with the look of a man about to be hung. 'That puts the cat in with the pigeons.'

'You have a problem with the plan, Mr Broadoaks?' he asked quietly.

The old gentleman fought through his beard to tug at his shirt collar. 'No, my lord. The wives won't be best pleased, I'll admit to that, but they'll come round once they know a Mountford's behind it.'

His father would know nothing of the matter. Or at least he wouldn't have known, if Merry wasn't related to the Purtefoys. Now Charlie wasn't quite so sure if he could bring this off without the betrothal becoming common knowledge. He'd been well and truly caught. Just as Robert had. An ironic smile formed on his lips. 'Good.'

'How is Mrs Broadoaks?' Merry asked a little breathlessly. Fearing his wrath now she'd been found out, no doubt. 'Well, I hope?'

Broadoaks's eyes twinkled a little. 'My missus doesn't

change, Miss Draycott, but she is well, thank you for asking.'

Merry grinned.

Charlie glared at her and then at Broadoaks. 'I still want to know who is behind the threat to Miss Draycott's life.'

The old man closed his eyes briefly. 'I know nowt about it. Nor do any of the other owners, I'd vouch my life on it. Aye, no good looking down your nose at me, my lord. Why would we be involved? We had her set to rights. No. You look elsewhere. I've not heard any gossip neither.' He looked at Merry. 'Only you know who might want thee feeding t'worms.'

Right now Charlie wanted to do a bit of worm feeding himself. 'Who *would* know?'

'Beyond me, my lord.' He shook his head. 'I'd try talking to the innkeeper at t'Muddy Duck. He might know what set them off.'

'The Muddy Duck is in the Skepton Town Square,' Merry said.

'Not a place for a woman,' Broadoaks said heavily. 'You know, lass,' Broadoaks went on, 'if you'd put that house of yours on t'other side of town, people might not have been so fratched by the idea.'

Apparently, Merry didn't care who she angered, as long as she got her own way. Damn her. 'Do you have a suggestion, Mr Broadoaks?'

Merry gasped. Charlie shot her a warning glance.

She pressed her lips together. At least sometimes she showed a little sense, because he was in no mood to tolerate an argument.

The elderly gentleman pulled a large handkerchief from his pocket and mopped at his brow. 'There is a house, a small one, over on west side of town. Regular folks live there. It would do for two or three women.'

'To keep the numbers down,' Merry said with a marshal light in her eyes.

'Within reason, I'd say,' Broadoaks said.

'I—'

'We will think about it, Mr Broadoaks,' Charlie said. He smiled at Merry. 'Won't we, my dear? Advice is always appreciated.'

'Well—'

'We won't take up more of your valuable time, Mr Broadoaks. I believe I have business at the Muddy Duck.'

Broadoaks rose to his feet. 'Tell t'innkeeper I said for him to tell you all he knows.'

In those few words, the old man had admitted Charlie to the inner sanctum. The local gentlemen's club. He knew it from the chagrin on Merry's face. He shook hands with the fellow. 'It has been a great pleasure, sir. I hope we meet again soon.'

'Ah, and good luck to you, my lord.' He darted a glance at Merry. 'Needs a strong hand on the bridle, a woman like her do.'

So she might, but that hand wasn't going to be Charlie's. Finally he'd seen right through the scheming little wench and he felt more than a little foolish. Not to mention angry.

He ushered her out of the office and down the steps.

She turned to him. 'I—'

He grabbed her by the arm and pulled her along, not hard enough that anyone would notice, but firmly enough so that she knew he meant business. 'We will talk in the carriage.'

Several times in the past few days, Merry's escort had looked less than pleased. Now he'd withdrawn into a cool remoteness that put the distance of miles between them.

The distance of a duke-to-be from a lesser mortal. She

had no trouble recognising it, since she'd seen the same kind of look on her fellow students' faces at school when she was intemperate or bold enough to express her opinions or join their conversations. The reason she'd sought solace with Jeremy.

She lifted her chin as she'd done in those long-ago days. 'What bee's bustling in tha's bonnet then, lad?'

'Oh, for God's sake, you don't think I'm fooled by that rubbishy accent, do you?'

She stiffened. 'There is nothing wrong with the way I speak.'

'Isn't there? Perhaps the names of Purtefoy and Chepstow might give you a hint as to why it doesn't ring true.'

She shrugged.

Anger flared in his eyes. Anger she could deal with. Better that than indifference. 'My mother's family has nothing what-soever to do with me.'

A muscle flickered in his jaw. His lip curled in derision. 'I'm not green, Miss Draycott. Or wet behind the ears. Nor do I have my mother's milk still on my lips, my dear. I know exactly what you are up to. And it won't wash.'

Inside she shrank from the bitterness in his quiet voice; on the outside she kept her back straight and her expression disdainful. 'Doing it rather brown, Charlie. You forced your way into my business uninvited, you know.'

'You asked me to pretend to be your fiancé.' He said the words as if they tasted of poison.

'For a few days,' she said warily.

'Let us hope Broadoaks is good to his word and keeps a still tongue in his head or Chepstow will be on my father's doorstep tomorrow morning. And won't that stir up an ant's nest?'

What on earth was he raving about? 'The Earl of Chepstow barely acknowledges my existence.'

'Believe me, that will change if this betrothal comes to his ears. He'll care enough to learn I have been living at your house. A house full of prostitutes, no less.'

'They are not prostitutes.'

He raised a cynical brow. 'I know when I am being propositioned.'

She gave him a slit-eyed look. Did he mean her?

'I'm talking about Jane,' he said.

'I told you, I don't think she is going to stay. In fact, I had already decided to talk to Caro about her leaving as soon as we get back.'

'Stop avoiding the issue at hand.' He leaned against the seat back, a hard smile thinning his lips. 'Oh, Merry, I'll admit you are good. Chepstow's niece, for God's sake. All that straightforward honest stuff really had me fooled. But I'm wise to you now. So let's just deal with the business at hand and we can end this farce and go our separate ways.'

Chapter Eleven

It was if a hive of bees had stung her all over. The hot and itchy feeling was swiftly followed by a sweep of cold. She inhaled a few deep breaths through her nose and the cynical twist to his mouth became more pronounced. She wanted to hit him. Scratch his face. She curled her hands inside her muff and bit down on her tongue. The old hurt and misery boiled in her chest, the memory of things she'd never told Grandfather, knowing he would be cut to the quick. Not for himself, but for her.

A burning sensation scoured the backs of her eyes and bile rose in her throat. Damn him. She would not let him make her cry the same tears she had shed as a lonely schoolgirl in the gardener's shed.

There, someone had cared to offer comfort. Here she was on her own.

Glad of his need to focus on his horses as they passed a cart, she forced a smile, even managed a couple of flirtatious bats with her eyelashes and turned in her seat. 'Ah, I see your problem.'

He shot her a quick dark glance.

Her smiled broadened. 'It is all right to seduce a woman of the lower classes, but a noble-born wench requires a different set of rules. Not because she is any better, but because her family has the power to do something about it.'

He stiffened. 'You go too far, madam.'

'Do I? Well, rest your mind easy, your lordship. I wouldn't marry you, if you were the last single man on this earth. What would I want with some useless nobleman, only interested in horses and gambling and the cut of his coat?' She glared at his exquisitely cut driving coat with its layer of capes and gold buttons, at the artfully placed whip points in the lapel, and did a bit of lip curling of her own. 'All right for a bit of fun in bed, but about as much use as tits on a bull, as Grandfather would say.'

His jaw dropped. 'Good God, woman. Your grandfather should have been shot for talking like that to a gently bred female.'

Smile fixed, she straightened in her seat. 'Get it through your thick skull. I am not gently bred just because I am related to the Earl of Chepstow. Draycotts are common hard-working people. My grandfather watched sheep from the age of four until he was ten. My father worked in the mill all his life. If I had been a boy, I would have worked there, too.' Instead of going to Mrs Driver's Academy for the daughters of gentlefolk and finding out exactly how unacceptable she was to the upper classes of England.

'Don't act insulted,' he said stiffly. 'You know you should have told me.'

She pulled all the pieces of her that seemed to have scattered themselves in the air around her—the pride, the hurt, the anger—and settled them back where they belonged with one deep breath. She clenched her hands together inside her muff and willed herself to feel nothing.

'I am not acting insulted,' she said, her voice deadly calm. 'Angry, yes, but since we are almost at the Muddy Duck, I suggest we make our enquiries and then return to Draycott House. You may continue your journey to Durn immediately.'

He frowned. 'You will wait in the carriage. I will make enquiries.'

'Certainly not. If someone is out to harm me, I want to know who it is.'

The curricle pulled under the arch and into the small courtyard. An ostler ran out to take the horses' heads.

'If we are to carry off this *betrothal*,' he spat the word, 'in the eyes of the world, you will remain in the carriage. Any inn laying claim to the sobriquet of the Muddy Duck is no fit place for a respectable woman.'

'I thought we had already agreed I am not the slightest bit respectable,' she said. Blast. That sounded bitter when she had intended it to be simply sarcasm.

Tonbridge frowned at her. 'If you are my fiancée, then you are respectable. Do as I bid, Merry, or I promise I will go right back to Broadoaks, swear it was all a hum, a lie, so that you could get your own way, and leave you to face him and his friends.'

She gasped at his perfidy. 'You wouldn't.'

'Would you care to test that assumption?'

She stared at the granite line of his jaw and into the dark of his eyes. No laughter. No yielding. They'd won the day with regard to the house because of him, because Broadoaks wouldn't risk the enmity of one of the most powerful landowners in England. One word and Tonbridge would ruin it all. It was blackmail.

She would not be blackmailed.

Caro had been right to caution her about involving him in her problems. And now there was no going back without losing all the ground she'd gained on Caro's behalf. She gritted her teeth. There were other ways to show him he wasn't going to push her around. She awarded him a tight smile. 'As you wish.'

'Good.' Charlie jumped down. 'Turn them around,' he called out to the ostler. 'I won't be more than a minute or two.'

Merry watched him disappear inside the inn in a swirl of black coat. A three-storey building built in Tudor times, the inn looked tired, its roofs sagging and covered in moss. The curricle lurched as the man manoeuvred the horses in the tight space.

A hollow feeling filled her chest. Hurt because he assumed the worst.

Drat him. Why would she, a Draycott, wish to marry him, just because he was heir to a dukedom? He was judging her by his own standards.

A pang of realisation turned her stomach over. Naturally it would make him look bad if the betrothal became public. If she cried off, people would wonder why a low-class woman hadn't found him worthy. Was that why he'd been so angry? Or was it because people would believe he had actually asked for her hand?

Her. Common as muck, Merry Draycott.

The latter. Definitely the latter. The emptiness seemed to grow.

The carriage ceased moving and Merry watched the door through which he had entered. Would he find out who had damaged her carriage? Lord, she hoped so, then he would go and leave her in peace. She winced. The locals were unlikely to tell tales to a stranger. Perhaps Prentice would have been a better choice for this task. She'd speak to him the moment he arrived tomorrow with his report on the mill.

He couldn't have done anything with Mr Broadoaks, though. Clearly only a duke or his blasted heir could persuade the wily old mill owner to go against the indomitable Maria Broadoaks.

Minutes had passed. Where was he?

She hated waiting. Hated not knowing what was going on. She grabbed the side of the carriage and jumped down. 'Back in a moment,' she said to the ostler.

The courtyard needed a good sweep. If it was her yard, she'd see it done, too. She glared at the ostler, who appeared not to notice, and picked her way around the dung. The door opened before she could put her hand on the latch.

A frowning Charlie took in her presence. 'I told you to wait in the carriage.'

'You've been gone half an hour.'

He grabbed her elbow. 'That's because it takes time to get questions answered.'

She didn't like the grim note in his voice. 'What did you find out?'

'I'll tell you once we are on the road, as I promised.'

She glared at him.

'Someone ought to have taken a birch twig to you as a child,' he muttered.

Her lip curled. 'What makes you think they didn't?'

His eyes widened. 'Damn it, Merry.'

Now what did that mean?

Back in the curricle and heading back for Draycott House, Charlie couldn't stop wondering who could possibly have beaten Merry. While she was utterly infuriating, and had put him in an impossible position with regard to her family, he really couldn't bear the thought.

'Well?' she said.

The anger simmering beneath the surface of his skin would have to wait. The current problem required all his attention. He formulated what he had learned into some sort of order.

'Don't sweeten the medicine,' she said.

He huffed out a breath. 'The landlord said someone got the men stirred up the night of the fire. A small group of them in the corner were muttering about jobs being lost. Men who haven't worked for a very long time. They blame it on the changes in the mills, the new machines. One moment it was the usual complaints and the next a mob ready for mischief.'

'Did he recognise the ringleader?'

'He said not.'

'Did you believe him?'

Charlie made a wry face. 'I offered him a pony to tell me who led the charge.'

She gasped. 'Twenty-five pounds is a great deal of money,' she said, then she shook her head. 'But Yorkshiremen have their pride. And very stiff necks. I will ask Mr Prentice to talk to him when he comes in the morning.'

Damn. Couldn't she give him any credit? 'He won't get any more information than I did. The man swore he didn't know and looked me straight in the eye. I believed him.'

She pressed her lips together as if to stop herself from saying more. He didn't like that. He preferred her open and honest.

His stomach fell away. He couldn't seem to reconcile the woman he thought she was with the person who had emerged in that meeting. She hadn't been the slightest bit open and honest with him. She'd hidden her noble connections, when most people would have trotted them out to impress. How could he not suspect her motives? And of all people, her uncle had to be Chepstow. The duke's friend. And the father of Charlie's intended betrothed. What a mess.

'I don't think there is any more to be done,' she said. 'Mr Broadoaks will see there is no more trouble and you can be on your way to Durn in the morning.'

'Eager to be rid of me.'

'As eager as you are to be gone.'

He damned well ought to be eager. 'There is the little problem of our publically announced engagement.'

Her mouth fell open. She snapped it shut. 'We agreed. You will cry off as soon as we sorted this out.'

'And what will your relatives have to say about that?'

'They have nothing to say. I am not answerable to them.'

But he was answerable to his father. And he'd gambled Robert's future on a roll in the hay—something Robert would no doubt find humorous and ironic, if he were here to enjoy the joke. It wasn't the slightest bit funny. 'If your family learn of this we will be in the soup.' Especially since he'd proposed to the wrong cousin.

'I can stand the heat.'

Damn her, now she made him sound like a coward. He cursed under his breath. 'I wish you'd told me you were related to an earl. I was blind-sided by Broadoaks back there. And we still don't know who is responsible for the attacks on your person. Until we do, our betrothal must stand.' And the longer it stood, the harder it would be to keep it a secret. As she must have known.

She flashed him a glance of dislike. 'The mill owners have agreed to support the house so there is no reason to continue the pretence. No reason for you to stay.'

He could think of another reason. Not that it was very noble minded. He widened his legs, touching her thighs with his, a simple shift of position that could be interpreted as innocent. 'Perhaps I can convince you otherwise later this evening?'

A low blow. But anger still rode him hard.

She edged away from him, but the narrowness of the seat kept her pinned against his side. 'You, sir, are a blackguard and a scoundrel.'

'So it seems.' They passed beneath the old medieval gate and beyond the cobbled streets of the town. It was colder out here on the moors, the wind fresher. It would have been kinder to bring the closed carriage. And more fun.

The thought of being closed up in such a confined space made his blood run cold. He reached down and pulled the blanket up over her shoulders. 'Warm enough?'

'Perfectly,' she said through gritted teeth. 'Thank you.'

Perhaps it was as well she disliked him. It would make it easier to resist her temptation, make it easier to depart once he discovered who had sawed through that axle. What if the bastard tried again? A woman alone, unprotected, would not stand a chance.

She ought to be married.

His gut twisted at the thought of Merry in another man's arms, even though it was quite clear he was not her first encounter. Why did he give a damn about this aggravating, infuriating woman?

Was it her apparent honesty that had somehow pierced a hole in his wrought armour and continued to do so, even knowing the open gaze hid a devious streak? Or was it her odd blend of strength and vulnerability, which caught him in strangely soft places inside that others had never touched?

'I'm not leaving until I find out who tried to kill you and bring them to justice and that is final.'

A gasp made him smile.

He looked down into her outraged expression, took in the parted lips, and the urge to protect her rose up stronger than ever.

The woman only had to look at him with those bright

sapphire eyes and smile, and his blood ran hot. One thing was clear. He needed to get her out of his blood. And soon. He should have accepted her offer and made her his mistress. Used her desire to impose his will. His body tightened. It wasn't too late.

'The more our engagement becomes common knowledge, the more of an idiot you will look when it is called off,' she said with the attitude of a magician who had conjured a rabbit from a hat.

Quick-witted Merry, fighting a rearguard action. She brought her guns to bear without hesitation. 'I will stand the reckoning,' he said.

Father wouldn't like it, of course, but well…too bad. The heir to a dukedom would never be cast off the way Robert had. Not for the triviality of breaking off an engagement to a nobody. People might assume that the duke's pockets were to let for a while, given Merry's fortune, or assume he couldn't hold his nose and bring the marriage off, which would be all about vilifying Merry, but since she didn't move in London circles, either way the damage would be minimal.

'I don't need your help,' she said.

'I'm staying.'

'Not at my house.'

He laughed at the snap in her voice. 'Are you saying you will throw me out in the snow? Now that doesn't sound like true Yorkshire hospitality.'

'Impossible,' she muttered. She hunched beneath the blanket, glowering at the road, clearly brooding on her next line of attack.

A crack sounded off to the right. A shot.

Instinctively Charlie ducked, flicked his whip and set the horses into a gallop.

Merry grabbed his arm. 'What are you doing?'

'Damn it,' he yelled. 'Let go.' It was already hard enough to manage the careening team.

He risked a glance over his shoulder. Some boulders. Scrubby bush and a flock of sheep streaming across the meadow towards the road in fear.

'What is happening?' Merry yelled, looking around her.

'Someone fired at us.' He steadied his horses and they shot over the brow of the hill out of the shooter's line of fire.

He'd recogised the sound. A Baker rifle. Deadly from a distance in the right hands.

Off to his right, the fleeing sheep veered, climbing on each other's backs in their panic. They'd seen something. Charlie pulled the pistol from under the seat. He scanned the roadside. A man rose to his feet on the other side of the wall.

Charlie fired. A wild shot.

The blackguard staggered, then adjusted his aim.

'Get down,' Charlie shouted, shoving her head down into his lap.

Another crack. A stinging pain in his right arm. Right where her head had been a moment before. He flinched. The offside horse stumbled. He regained control, let the team have their heads and prayed whoever had fired hadn't yet reloaded.

The horses galloped at breakneck speed. With no hope of halting them until they exhausted themselves, all he could do was try to keep them straight on the road. Fear-induced foam flew from their mouths. They ran blindly while Merry clutched the side of the carriage, white-lipped and wide-eyed.

His head floated above his shoulders, while the world moved by at a snail's pace. Loss of blood.

Feeling stunned, Merry looked back over her shoulder. 'I can't see anyone.'

'Good,' he said grimly. 'Hang on, the gates are up ahead.'

Somehow he made the turn into the drive. The winded horses slowed. The carriage ceased to sway.

'I don't think they followed us,' she said.

'Let us hope not,' Charlie said between gritted teeth. He looked terribly pale. He drew the carriage up outside the front door. 'Get inside as quickly as you can.'

Merry saw the blood on his hand. 'You are hurt.'

'Do as I say and get down.' He stumbled out of his seat while she scrambled down on her side.

Jed appeared as Merry climbed down.

Leaning against the side of the carriage, clutching his arm, Charlie called out to the coachman. 'Get the horses inside the stables and bar the door, then bring everyone into the house.'

Startled, Jed nodded. He led the horses away at a run.

'Good man that,' Charlie said. He leaned on her and she helped him up the steps.

Gribble swung the door wide. 'Lock the door behind us,' Charlie ordered. The butler slammed it shut and shot the bolt.

Relieved to be inside, Merry collapsed against the banister.

Caro ran out of the drawing room. 'Merry, what is the matter?'

Merry took a deep breath and gathered her scattered wits. 'We were attacked on the road. We need bandages and basilica powder. His lordship has been shot.'

Caro paled.

Gribble frowned. 'What we need is the constable.'

'Not tonight,' Charlie said. 'No one is going outside the gates before daylight.' Charlie looked at Merry. 'And even then it isn't safe. Who *are* these men?'

'I wish I knew.'

'Luddites?' Caro hazarded.

'Criminals, that's what they are,' Gribble muttered, hurrying off.

Merry turned to Charlie. 'Let me see your wound.'

'It's nothing,' Charlie muttered. 'Give me a brandy and I'll be as right as a trivet in a moment or two.'

She ushered him into the drawing room. He didn't look anywhere near as right as a trivet. Caro rushed to the console and poured a brandy.

He swallowed the glassful in one gulp.

'Let's get you out of that coat,' Merry said.

'Don't fuss. Brian will take care of it.'

Typical male. She hadn't lived with an irascible old gentleman without learning a thing or two. One was to act rather than argue. She attacked the buttons on his greatcoat. First, she pulled it down the uninjured arm. The other side posed more of a problem. It was damp and sticky. 'You've lost a lot of blood.'

'It's a scratch,' he said. 'I've had worse falling off a horse.'

His lips were blue, his face pale.

'Caro, lend me a hand,' Merry said. 'Pull on the cuff while I ease it over the wound.'

Thin-lipped, Caro did as requested. She grabbed the heavy greatcoat as it slipped to the floor and flung it over the chair.

'Now this one,' Merry said, undoing the buttons on his morning coat. She gazed at the sleeve. 'I think it is ruined.'

'I have more,' he said. The coat was so blasted tight she had to pull it over his elbow. His face turned to stone. A hiss of pain escaped his lips.

Her stomach rolled sickeningly as she parted the bloody tear in his shirt. The wound oozed blood.

Caro's face blanched.

'I can't see for all the blood,' Merry said. 'Caro, please request hot water from the kitchen.'

Looking grateful, Caro hurried off.

Merry backed Charlie towards the sofa. 'Sit down.'

He fought her off. 'We don't have time for this. We need weapons. I need to set your men to watch at the windows, front and back.'

She couldn't draw a breath, her chest felt so tight, her stomach roiling at the thought of those men storming her house. 'You think they would dare?'

'I don't know. I am not prepared to take the risk.'

The thought froze her blood. 'Perhaps they want money.'

Charlie stared at her, his eyes dark, his mouth flat and the creases either side deep with pain and with worry. 'Merry, who stands to benefit from your death?'

The breath left her body in a rush. She sank on to the sofa beside him. 'W-what?'

He took her hand in his good one. 'I know this isn't something you want to think about, but we don't have a choice. If you die, who benefits? Do you have a will?'

Her stomach clenched. She shook her head. 'It isn't possible. The townspeople have to be behind this.'

His eyes narrowed, as his grip tightened. 'Tell me, Merry. I need to know.'

'I changed my will in favour of Caro,' she whispered.

'When? What do you know about her?'

'She changed the will the day before the attack on the house in Skepton.' Caro's voice, as cold as ice, came from the doorway. In her hands she had rolls of bandages and a bottle of powders. Her face was as white as the bandages.

She strode into the room followed by Gribble carrying a bowl of hot water. 'Put it there,' she said to the butler.

Gribble deposited his burden and left.

Merry's heart ached at the sight of her friend's distress. 'Caro, I know this is nothing to do with you,' she said softly.

Caro's face was blank, shuttered. 'I will leave tomorrow.'

Charlie narrowed his eyes. 'How convenient.'

Merry glowered at him. 'Be quiet. This is none of your business.'

His dark brows drew together. 'I think it is, fiancée of mine.'

'That is all a hum and you know it.' She picked up one of the bandages, dipped the end in the water and began to clean the nasty gash on his arm. Her hands shook. Not at the sight of blood, but at her fear for Caro. She'd seen how desperate Caro was when they met. For her to go back to that because of his wild accusations would be too much. Kind-hearted Caro wouldn't hurt a fly. She raised her gaze to Caro's tight face. 'Don't worry. I won't let anyone poison me against you. And we are not going to let these people, whoever they are, drive you away. I won't allow it.'

Tears filled Caro's eyes. She blinked them away. 'Your trust means everything,' she said in a low voice. 'I swear, I am not behind these attempts on your life.'

Merry made a 'so-there' face at Charlie. 'I believe you.'

He grimaced.

She stared down at the open wound on his upper arm with a frown. 'You need to see Dr Jessup in Skepton.'

'We are not going back to Skepton,' Charlie said, as she sprinkled the powders over the oozing gash. 'If we are going anywhere, we are going to Durn.'

Merry felt her jaw drop. 'Durn?' Her hand hung suspended over his arm, the powder leaking down in a little pile. 'Oops.' She righted the bottle.

'Yes, Durn. You will be safe there.' He gave Caro a hard

look. Clearly, he wasn't convinced of her innocence, no matter what Merry thought. 'I have men there. And guns. From there all the power of the duke can be brought to bear on these blackguards.'

She began winding the bandage around his wonderfully muscular arm. Please God it didn't turn gangrenous. She pushed the horrid thought aside. 'I've never run from anything or anyone in my life.' Not since she'd run from school, humiliated and mortified. 'You need a doctor.'

'There is a doctor in the village on the Durn estate,' he said with the triumph of a man laying an ace and winning the trick.

'He's right, dear,' Caro said, placing her finger on the knot, so Merry could tie it off nice and tight. 'You will be safer there. His lordship can find out who is behind this. You should go.'

'And leave you here? What if they come back tonight? How will you defend yourself? And Thomas?'

Caro's expression turned fearful. 'If it is you they are after, then we will just let them search the house and then they will leave,' she said with a touch of bravado.

It might work. Merry looked at Charlie, whose pallor seemed worse. He must have lost a lot more blood than she'd realised. He gazed at Caro, then let go a breath. 'They would question you. If you refused them the information, they might hurt you or the child.'

Merry leaped to her feet. 'Then I'm not leaving.' She glared at Charlie. 'That is final.'

'Very well,' he said, the corner of his mouth kicking up in a smile. 'We'll all go.'

'Caro's ladies, too?' She couldn't help sounding suspicious.

He chuckled wryly. 'Oh, yes. Everyone. Even the servants

if you want. But we have to go soon, before these fellows regroup. We have a couple of hours at most. I hurt one of them, but not enough to stop them.'

'You mean leave tonight?'

He nodded.

'How? We can't all fit in the carriage.'

'If I might make a suggestion,' Caro said, 'the ladies and I could travel in the carriage. You and his lordship could take his curricle. We can leave by the back gate. Gribble and Cook can ride on the roof with Jed. Brian can ride in the tiger's seat on his lordship's vehicle. I think Jed has a shotgun for hunting rabbits.'

Merry frowned. Caro seemed very knowledgeable about methods of escape.

'It would be nice if he had more than one,' Charlie said. His voice sounded less strong than it had moments ago.

'All right,' Merry said. 'Durn it is.' A surge of anger rose in her chest. 'But when I find out who is chasing me out of my home...'

Charlie put up a hand, looking just a little green. 'Merry, do you think you can bring that bowl closer?' he leaned forwards, his head between his knees.

She gazed down at him. Oh, no, he was going to... She shoved the bowl between his feet.

Chapter Twelve

It hadn't taken them long to pack and pile Caro, Beth and poor little Tommy inside the carriage. Jane had disappeared. They'd looked all through the house, until Beth finally volunteered she'd gone for a walk earlier in the afternoon and hadn't returned.

They didn't have time to search for her and Caro had no qualms that the woman could look out for herself.

Not all the servants had wanted to come with them. Cook and Gribble preferred to guard the house with an old blunderbuss they'd found in the stables. The stable boy and the other young footman had run home across the fields with some extra coin to make sure of their welcome. They'd promised to come back the next day and check on the house.

There was no more they could do.

Merry looked back, but could see nothing of Jed and the town carriage. Night had fallen and they'd decided against lighting the carriage lamps.

She had insisted on driving and had been surprised when Charlie hadn't argued. He must feel worse than he openly admitted. The vehicle was beautifully sprung and light bodied;

the horses, tired from their earlier race, were docile. Ahead, the rear gate looked extremely narrow.

'I'll get down and walk them through,' she said, slowing the team.

'You'll be fine,' Charlie said. 'Aim for the gap and envisage yourself on the other side.'

His trust in her was quite remarkable. He'd never seen her drive until now.

She took a deep breath, steadied the offside horse, who tended to break step, and shot out into the lane. She made the turn easily. Beside her Charlie relaxed against the seat back. 'Couldn't have done it better myself.'

Brian, riding on the step behind her seat, gave an audible sigh. 'Right gradely, miss.'

She grinned. 'Praise indeed.'

She and Charlie laughed.

'Spring 'em,' he said.

She flicked her whip and the team broke into a nice steady canter. The carriage rocked a little, but held the road beautifully. 'This is as fast as we dare go,' she said, 'or Jed won't keep up.'

Five hours later Merry's fingers were stiff from holding the reins, her feet were numb, the horses were blown. At her side, Charlie looked white around the mouth and he kept shivering. Every time they went over a bump Merry winced, feeling for his pain. A snow squall, one of several they'd encountered, swept in and obliterated the road. Would they never make it to Durn?

'Just around the next bend, you will see the gates,' Charlie said.

'Thank heavens.'

'You did well.'

'It doesn't seem as if we were followed, though it is hard to see. I wonder if they will guess where we went?'

He straightened in the seat. 'Let them.'

'How is your arm?'

'Fine.'

Which probably meant it was hurting like hell.

'There, Miss Draycott,' Brian said from beneath his muffler.

A gatehouse hunched beside imposing wrought-iron gates bearing the ducal coat of arms. Merry pulled the horses up in front of the gates and Brian jumped down to rouse the gatekeeper. An elderly man in homespun hurried out before Brian reached the door.

He rushed to open the gate and stood back as Merry eased the curricle through.

The gatekeeper touched his forehead. 'Welcome, my lord.'

'Wait,' Charlie said to Merry. He leaned over the side of the carriage. 'Good to see you again, Ritson. There is a carriage following—let it through, then lock and bar the gates. No one else is to enter without my permission.'

'I'll see to it, my lord.'

Merry whipped up the tired horses and gamely they managed a trot. The drive was lined with ancient chestnut trees. Bare and limned with snow they looked giant soldiers ready to fight off any intruders. Then the house filled her vision. An enormous castle, all Gothic towers and crenulations. And very gloomy.

'Oh, my word.'

Charlie chuckled softly. 'I know. Dreadful.'

He climbed down from his seat the moment the carriage halted and came around to help her down, while Brian ran to the bridles.

Merry had never felt so stiff or so cold in her life. Her knees creaked when she climbed down.

'Welcome to Durn,' Charlie said wryly.

Light streamed down the steps as the front door swung open. A stiff-looking butler stood framed in the opening, the glow of warm candles behind him. Footmen ran down the steps, taking the horses in hand, pulling down their meagre luggage. Merry stared up at the ducal emblem over the door. Her heart sank.

It was too grand. Too imposing. Coming here was a mistake.

A moment later they were joined by Caro and Beth holding Thomas in her arms. 'Poor little lad,' she said. 'He's fair exhausted.'

Merry knew exactly how he felt.

'Come on,' Charlie said. 'Let's find a warm fire.' He gestured for them to enter.

Behind them, Beth was silent. No doubt equally overwhelmed.

The butler greeted them with a bow. His eyes widened as he took in their party. He recollected himself quickly. 'Welcome home, my lord. We have been expecting you.'

'Days ago, I know, Logan,' Charlie said, striding into the hall. 'I got caught in a snowstorm in Skepton.'

Merry followed him, looking around at medieval armour and weapons, and the banners hanging from enormous ceiling beams. Intimidating.

'What a beautiful home you have,' she said, brightly.

She undid the buttons of her greatcoat, stripped off her gloves and handed them to the waiting footman, as did Charlie and Caro, who then took the sleeping Thomas from Beth.

A footman tried to help Beth with her coat. ''Ere, that's mine, lad. You get your own coat if you needs one.'

'It's all right, Beth, he will hang it up for you and bring it next time you go out,' Caro said.

Beth gave the elderly footman the evil eye. 'Don't lose it.'

The footman whisked the outer raiment away.

'There is a fire in the blue drawing room, my lord,' the butler said. 'And in the library. When would you like dinner?'

'Is there a nursery?' Caro asked. 'Or a schoolroom? I think it would be better if Thomas and I were housed there. Supper on a tray would be all we need.' She gave Charlie a pointed stare.

'Yes, of course,' Charlie said. 'Logan, please make the arrangements.'

Logan snapped his fingers. A footman materialised from the shadows beneath the stairs. 'Escort the ladies up to the schoolroom.' He looked at Beth. 'The maids' quarters are in the other wing.'

'She is the child's nurse,' Caro said swiftly. 'She'll remain with me.' Merry had never heard Caro sound so imperious. It clearly worked because Logan bowed acquiescence and the little party followed the footman up the stairs.

Obviously grappling with curiosity, Logan waited for Charlie's instructions with an expression of polite enquiry.

Charlie drew the butler a little aside and lowered his voice. 'I have given instructions at the gate that no one is to gain entry to the grounds without my express permission. Please pass the word to the other gatekeepers. Have a boy stationed at each entry to warn me of any arrivals and have the gatekeepers arm themselves with a shotgun and a pistol.'

Logan's eyes sharpened. 'Are we expecting trouble, my lord?'

Charlie shook his head. 'Expecting, no. But I would like us to be prepared.' He exuded a quiet confidence. The aura of a man used to commanding and having his orders followed without question. The heir to a dukedom.

The duke would be as horrified as the butler looked, if he learned his son had brought his mistress and her entourage into his home. A cold chill settled on Merry's heart. It was good of Charlie to want to help, but he hadn't thought through the implications.

'That is all, Logan,' Charlie said.

'His lordship needs a doctor,' Merry said quickly. 'He was injured on the road. Please send for one right away. He is to be admitted at once. In the meantime, my lord, you need to get out of your clothes and into a warm bed.'

At Logan's wide-eyed look at his master, she flushed. What must he think of her taking control in such a fashion? Charlie, on the other hand, blast him, was looking rather smug.

Logan visibly gathered himself. 'I'll send Andrew up to you, my lord.'

Charlie's smile broadened, becoming wolfish, and Merry wanted to hit him.

'No need,' he said airily.

Merry held her breath wondering what he would say next. 'Brian, one of Miss Draycott's men, has been serving as my valet these past few days. Have him come up to my chamber.'

Logan's moment of utter stillness gave his disapproval away. 'Yes, my lord.' He stood there irresolute.

'Get on with it, man,' Charlie growled. 'Miss Draycott, your arm if you please.'

Logan hurried off, but Merry could imagine what he was thinking.

Charlie had certainly made it clear that he had been staying with her the past few nights, and by implication that she was his mistress. Revenge for her keeping her noble relatives a secret? Merry shot Charlie a glare as they headed up the stairs, but held her words behind her teeth. There were servants standing at every door and in every hallway. What she had to say required privacy.

At the top of the stairs, a footman opened a chamber door as they left the main landing. Not a chamber, Merry realised, but a gallery running along a windowed wall with a suite of rooms on the other side. Medieval style.

'This place must be very old.'

'Fooled you, did it?' Charlie said, striding past a room with a chair on a dais, a sitting room and a small room with a truckle bed. Finally he stopped at a room with a gold-canopied monstrosity of a bed set on an elevated platform at one end and an enormous carved-stone fireplace at the other.

'My grandfather had it built to replace the ruins that once stood here. Completely outmoded now, of course. And just as draughty as the real thing.'

Only someone of enormous wealth could construct such a folly. 'What is along there?' She pointed to the end of the gallery.

'A water closet. The only modern thing in the place. Hot-and-cold running water. I had it put in last year.' He glanced up. 'Beyond it is your room, I hope you find it to your liking.'

She swung around. The devilish look was back in his eyes. Along with a challenge.

Now was not the time for an argument, not with him look-ing so pale and cold. Their conversation would wait until after the doctor's visit.

He eased one shoulder out of his coat with a wince. She inspected his arm. The bandage showed no evidence of further bleeding, but he was clearly in pain. 'Sit down. Can I get you anything?'

He shivered. 'A brandy, if you please. I find I am quite

chilled.' He pointed to a console of inlayed ivory and teak against the wall beneath a tapestry of a boar hunt. It held a variety of decanters and wines.

'Sit by the hearth.' She poured him a glass of brandy, ministering to him when she should be ripping him to shreds for his outrageous words in front of the butler. She handed him the glass.

He tossed off the liquid and a shudder ran through his large frame. She shook her head. 'I think perhaps we should not have risked such a journey with you in this condition.'

'We didn't have a choice.'

'I cannot stay here. I have a business to run.'

He grabbed her hand and held her fast. 'You are not going anywhere, do you hear me? Not until we find out who those men are and why they are trying to kill you.'

She stiffened. 'I still think it is all a mistake. Besides, you have no right to tell me what to do.'

He laughed, a rather chilling sound to Merry's ears, since she could not break free of his hold. 'Oh, but I do. I'm your betrothed, remember? We announced it this morning.'

The bitterness in his voice stung. 'You didn't make it sound as if we were betrothed down below.'

His gaze darkened. 'Nor did you.'

She pulled at her hand and finally tore free. She stepped back. She did not understand this moodiness. He'd been trying to control her since the day they met, but until now the hand had been light on the reins. It seemed he'd changed to a curbing bit.

'Let us be quite clear. I let you convince me to come here after those men attacked us, but the more I think about it the more sure I am that Broadoaks, or whoever started this, had no time to call off his dogs. That they acted before new orders reached them. By now, everything will have returned to normal. Tomorrow we will return to Draycott House.'

His mouth flattened. 'Is that so?'

'Yes.'

A cough sounded in the gallery just beyond the chamber. 'Who is it?' Charlie snarled.

'Brian, my lord.'

'Good. You are just in time.'

Brian stepped into the room, his face rather stiff. He must have overheard some of their conversation. Merry felt more heat in her face. Drat the man.

'I'm to help you undress, my lord.'

'Yes, you are. But first ring the bell by the fireplace.'

Brian did as instructed, then proceeded to help Charlie out of his waistcoat and cravat.

'I will find my own room now,' Merry said, starting for the gallery.

'You will wait for Logan,' Charlie said. 'He will direct you.'

Imperious beast. If he wasn't so ill, hadn't been wounded helping her, she would have continued on her way. Instead, she went to the window and pulled back the heavy curtains. There was nothing to see. Her ears filled with the sounds of Brian helping Charlie with his clothes, her mind filled with visions of his wonderful body. Her heart picked up speed, her breathing became a little too rapid, her skin too warm. Dash it all, despite his autocratic commands, she felt the need for his strong arms around her. Wanted his body bringing her pleasure, which in turn would silence the fears in her mind.

She ought to be ashamed, knowing she was about to bring shame to the Draycott name again. Grandfather had trusted her with his mill and his fortune, and here she was again proving she was nothing but a weak female as Uncle Chepstow had charged when he learned the terms of her inheritance.

A rather harried Logan strode down the corridor. 'You rang, my lord?'

Charlie sat in a huge armchair beside the fire; his cheeks were flushed, his glittering eyes fixed on her. Dear Lord, he was in the grip of a fever. No wonder he was acting so strangely. Where on earth was the doctor?

He fixed his dark gaze on Merry. 'Logan, I gave an instruction earlier that no one was to enter the grounds without permission?'

'Yes, my lord.'

'No one is to leave, either. Do you understand?'

'Yes, my lord.' Logan's voice held no expression. 'I will bring the doctor up the moment he arrives, my lord.'

'Good. Please show Miss Draycott to her room. Go with him, Merry. You will see that to enter or leave your room, you, or anyone else, must pass by here.' He shot her a dark look. 'We will dine together as soon as the doctor leaves. We have not finished our discussion.' His dark gaze turned to Logan.

Impassivity masked the butler's expression. 'This way, Miss Draycott.'

'Brian will fetch you once the doctor has been.' Charlie's voice followed her down the corridor.

They passed a door. The only one in the suite. The water closet, no doubt. The one new-fangled invention Grandfather had refused to entertain in Draycott House.

The next chamber was a bedroom decorated in the French style. The fire was already lit, along with the candles. Yet no one had passed by Charlie's room. She frowned. 'You surely weren't expecting us?'

Logan glanced back along the corridor and stepped deeper into the room. 'This suite of rooms is made ready when his lordship is expected.' He frowned. 'He has on occasion been accompanied by a...a lady, but not for a long time. Still, we must be prepared.'

'I see.' She wished she hadn't said anything. The thought of being one of many didn't sit well in her stomach. 'Thank you.'

'I'll send one of the maids to attend you, since you only brought a nurse for the child. She'll bring up your valise.'

Merry nodded. 'Where is Mrs Falkner?'

'In another wing. You will have to ask one of the footmen to guide you if you want to see her. Will that be all?'

'Yes, thank you.'

He bowed and left, not back the way he had come, but in the opposite direction. She rushed to see where he went, but the corridor was empty. Charlie was wrong. There wasn't only one way into this suite of rooms. Somewhere a servants' staircase lurked. A secret way in and out.

How could he not know? Because men like him didn't notice servants. They were like furniture, only there to serve him. How they arrived and left was a question that likely never entered his head.

Chapter Thirteen

Charlie suffered the doctor to put his arm in a sling, then he sank into an armchair beside the fire.

'You are lucky, young man,' Dr Wells proclaimed, packing up his instruments. 'The wound is shallow. You should feel as fine as fivepence tomorrow, but to be sure I wish you would allow me bleed you. For sleep, you would be better off with laudanum.'

'Is your patient not co-operating, Doctor?'

Merry's voice. It gave his flagging spirits a lift. He turned his head to watch her glide in. She'd changed from the practical gown in which she'd travelled into something of vivid pink, very low at the neck. Her breasts looked delicious.

He frowned. She was up to something. Damnation, he should not have been so hard on her in front of Logan, wouldn't have been if she didn't fight him every step of the way.

'Is your patient permitted wine, Doctor?' she asked.

'He must suit himself,' the doctor grumbled, buckling his bag. 'He has no interest in my advice, but please do not feed him red meat.'

Charlie leaned back against the cushions, watched her

cross the room to the console. She moved with purpose, her curvaceous body supple yet elegant. He also felt wearier than he wanted to admit. A glass of wine would set him up better than all the doctor's potions and pills. 'I will take a glass of wine, Miss Draycott.'

Merry turned and glared at him.

The doctor's heavy white brows drew together. 'Wine might help you sleep, or it might make the fever worse.' He bowed. 'Good day to you, my lord.' He turned to Merry. 'Whoever saw to his wound in the first place did a fine job.'

She smiled. 'Thank you. I will pass on your praise.'

The doctor bowed. 'Send for me if you feel worse.'

'Thank you. Show the doctor out, Brian,' Charlie said. 'Order dinner to be brought up. I am sure Miss Draycott is in need of sustenance.'

Brian ushered the doctor out.

The servants would never dare gossip and not one word would pass Dr Wells's lips about Merry's presence in the house. The duke paid him a handsome sum to serve the Mountfords on their rare visits to Yorkshire.

But Merry didn't know that. She would no doubt be very angry with him for speaking her name. She deserved it after keeping her ancestry a secret. He was looking forward to sparring with her about her intended departure, too.

Despite her wilfulness, and the awkward situation she'd forced on him, she would remain here as long as he chose. As long as there was any chance she was in danger.

Damn, he wished he didn't feel quite so hot, or so bloody weak. And with his arm in a sling, he felt at a distinct dis-advantage. If she decided to leave, he wasn't sure he had the strength to stop her.

Merry handed him his glass.

He raised it in toast. 'To the beautiful woman in my bed-room. I had far rather she was in my bed.'

An unwilling smile curved her lips. She shook her head. 'You are incorrigible.'

He sipped at the wine. 'I meant what I said, Merry. You are not to leave Durn until we find out just who is behind these attacks.'

She shrugged. 'Why did you not allow the doctor to bleed you?'

A sudden change of subject, even for her. His hackles rose, but he let it pass. For now. 'The wound is fine, thanks to you. I have already lost enough blood for one day.'

'Then you should take the laudanum, it will help you sleep.'

The drug left him open to the dreams. He knew from experience. He stifled a shudder. 'I prefer to keep my wits about me.' He narrowed his eyes. 'Did you think to sneak off in the night?'

A scoffing sound came from her throat. 'Another night without sleep? I can't see Caro agreeing to any such thing.'

All the same, she looked a little disconcerted. She'd given it serious thought, he realised. 'No one will be allowed in or out of Durn tonight.'

She rose and went to the hearth, sipping her wine as she stared down into the flames. Plotting more ways to flout his authority.

'It will be interesting to learn if anyone did try to gain entrance at Draycott House,' she mused.

'Yes, it will.'

'How long do you think we should wait before deciding it is safe for us to return home?'

A fair question. 'I don't know. I will have some investigations undertaken first.'

'And in the meantime, I am here in exactly what guise—your mistress or your betrothed?'

Ah, now they had reached the crux of what bothered her. 'What about both?' he said with a grin.

She swung around, a gleam of anger in her eyes. He liked the way her passions rose so quickly to the surface. All of them.

His body hardened. 'Come here.'

In a few quick strides she crossed the room to his side, remaining just out of reach.

'Closer,' he ordered, the urge to bedevil her strong.

She eyed the distance between them without moving.

'I don't bite.'

'I do,' she muttered. The sensual tension between them flared. Never far below the surface, it rose to the temperature of a blast furnace.

He laughed. 'Oh, Merry, don't tempt me.'

'Once your servants realise the sort of woman Beth is, don't be surprised if they hand in their notice.'

'Is that why you had them serving as chambermaids?'

'Partly. Jane made it worse, though, by trying to lure the housekeeper's husband into her bed.'

The one who had disappeared. 'Do you think her departure is suspect?'

Merry shrugged. 'Not really. She's never really taken to the idea of reform.'

'Nevertheless, a possibility.' He'd set his steward to making enquiries first thing in the morning.

A polite cough heralded the entry of the dinner tray wielded by two footmen in livery. A third pulled out a table from the wall, opened out an extra leaf and placed a chair on each side. In moments, a sumptuous dinner for two was laid out and the men had departed.

He could see Merry was impressed by the widening of her eyes. She thought her grandfather a powerful man, but when it came to a duke, the power was awesome.

He pushed to his feet. 'Shall we?'

She let go a sigh of defeat. 'I could eat a horse.'

Glad to see her practical side win out, he gave her a smile of approval. Female dramatics were such a bore.

'Would you like me to pour you more red wine?' She nodded at his arm in its sling.

'That is kind of you.'

'Sit yourself down, then.' She took their glasses to the console.

Awkwardly, he pulled out her chair and then seated himself on the opposite side of the table. He glanced over when she seemed to take a long time. 'Is there something wrong?'

'I—the stopper is a little tight. There, I have it now.' She turned with a glass in each hand and a smile on her face. A rather strained smile, he thought. Weariness, perhaps.

'Here you are.' She set the glass down beside his plate and settled herself in her chair. She lifted her glass. 'Thank you for your generous welcome and your timely rescue.'

Thank God she'd decided to accept his hospitality instead of fighting him. 'To the loveliest woman of my acquaintance,' he said, raising his glass.

'Very gallant.' She sipped her wine. 'Let us see what culinary delights they have brought us.'

She lifted the cover. A fricasseed breast of chicken, covered in mushroom sauce, filled the room with a delicious aroma.

Charlie took a deep swallow of his wine and set his glass down. He was hungrier than he'd thought. He lifted the cover from his plate and let her help him to some buttered parsnips.

Merry tucked into her food. 'Delicious.'

Charlie tasted from his own plate. The meat was so tender he had no trouble cutting it with his fork. 'You are right. It is excellent, even if there is no red meat.'

'You have a talented chef to prepare this at a moment's notice.'

'Poor fellow, he nearly goes mad stuck here all the time with no one to cook for, except for our annual visit.'

'Why does he stay?'

'Because the duke makes it worth his while.'

'Brass greases the wheels,' she said. She picked up her glass. 'Here's to lots of brass.'

He grinned. 'I love your bluntness, Merry. I really do.' He picked up his glass and tossed back the remainder.

He leaned back to watch her eat, his appetite having already been assuaged. His appetite for food, that was. He also wanted her in his bed.

The question was, having let his fury have free rein, would she now turn him down? Sometimes she made him so angry he spoke and acted without thought. Rashly. A battle it seemed he fought and lost over and over.

He watched her devour her food, her white teeth biting into a morsel of chicken, her throat moving when she swallowed. The red wine staining her lips.

She tilted her head to look at him.

His eyelids drooped. He blinked and forced them open.

'You look sleepy,' she said.

Hell, he didn't feel tired, he felt as if his head was stuffed with wool. A thought pierced the fog slowly building in his mind, a not unfamiliar sensation. He turned his head to look at the wine decanter…and the bottle of laudanum left beside it by the doctor.

'Damn it, Merry,' he said, his tongue thick, 'what did you do?'

'I gave you your medicine,' she said, her voice sounding distant and foggy. Then she was beside him, looming over him, helping him to his feet. 'Time you retired, my lord.'

He staggered to his feet. 'You idiot. You don't know what you've done.'

She put an arm around his waist and helped him to the bed. 'Doctor's orders,' she said. 'That's all.'

He measured his length on the bed. Fought to keep his eyes open, not to descend into the dark wavering at the edge of his vision. He felt the covers slide over his body. He grabbed for her wrist, caught it and held it fast. 'Two things, Merry.'

Her eyes looked huge. She nodded.

'Promise you won't leave in the middle of the night.'

She tugged uselessly at her hand. He gripped it tighter and saw a grimace of pain. She nodded, her lips thin. Angry again. He wanted to laugh.

'I'll take the nod as a yes,' he whispered. 'And hold you to it. Second, light all the bloody candles.'

He couldn't hold on to her any longer. The darkness was winning. His hand went lax. Even as he fell into unwelcome sleep, he heard her move away from the bed.

Blast. He'd trusted her again and once more she'd tricked him.

'Thirsty.'

The voice from the bed sounded hoarse and dry. Merry rose, her back twingeing with the ache of unaccustomed discomfort. A carriage ride and now hours in a chair. She poured a glass of water and went to the bed.

'I can't breathe.' He panted for air and threw the covers back. 'God, it's dark.'

She tried to hold the glass to his lips, but he turned his head away. 'My name is Major Robert Mountford.'

'Charlie,' she said, a trickle of fear running through her stomach.

'Hide. I'll cover us.' He grunted, his head rolling. 'Dear God, the stink.'

His free arm flailed, then he lay still.

A dream. It had to be a dream. Should she ring the bell for help? Try to wake him up? Perhaps the fever was worse. She put a palm to his forehead.

Hot, but not dreadfully so.

He flinched away. 'Lay still. Got to keep still. Will? Talk to me.' He sounded panicked.

'I'm here,' she said.

He quieted. He must have fallen back to sleep.

He stiffened. 'I hear them. They're coming. Why do they come?' He stopped breathing. Terrified, she grasped his arm to feel for a pulse. His limb felt as stiff as a board.

'No. No. Oh God, Will. I'm sorry.'

'Charlie,' she whispered. 'What is the matter?'

'They've gone.' He let go a long breath. 'Will, are you still there?'

'Yes,' she whispered, not sure if it was the right thing to say or not.

'Thrice cursed rain. It has to get light soon. If only I could see.' His chuckle was a horrible gasping sound. 'Can't move. My chest hurts. I'm cold.' He shivered. 'So damnably dark… They are out there. Hear them?'

She couldn't stand it any longer. She shook him hard. 'Charlie, wake up. It is me, Merry.'

'My name is Major Robert Deveril Mountford.'

'Your name is Charles. You are at Durn Castle in Yorkshire.'

His eyes snapped open. He sat bolt upright and put his hand around her throat. 'I will not let you finish me off.'

'Charlie,' she gasped through a throat being squeezed.

His eyes focused.

He let her go and stared at her. He looked around, then back at her face. 'Merry?'

'Yes,' she said, rubbing at her neck.

He glanced around; he was shivering and pale. He clenched his jaw, visibly pulling himself together. 'Did I hurt you?'

'No. I startled you awake. I think you thought I was attacking you.'

He inhaled a deep shuddering breath. 'I remember,' he said. His dark eyes held accusation. 'Laudanum brings bad dreams.'

'I'm sorry. I didn't know.'

He inhaled a deep breath and looked around. 'You couldn't know. Thank you for lighting the candles.'

She nodded. 'What happened to you?'

He stiffened. 'I don't know what you mean?'

'Whatever you were seeing in your sleep has to be real.'

He looked at her for a long moment, then he smiled. 'I thought you'd be on your way back to Draycott House.' He held out his hand and she took it. He tugged her until she fell across the bed.

'Your arm,' she exclaimed. 'Be careful.'

He tipped her chin and briefly brushed her lips with his mouth. 'I know what will make me feel a whole lot better.'

She stared up at him and saw desire in his eyes, but his face was still pale and drawn.

'Not before your arm is healed,' she said.

'But you will stay until then?'

'Yes, I will stay until then.'

He closed his eyes. 'Lie down next to me, Merry, and I am sure I will sleep just fine. I won't be worrying about where you are.'

She settled beside him and he immediately relaxed. Did he think she believed she was the cause of his dream? He probably didn't realise what he had said. Why had he called himself Robert? And what had he feared in the dark?

Blast him, he'd put paid to her questions by falling asleep. She peered into his face. Still flushed, but peaceful. Having given her word, she was trapped. And heaven's above, she was dreadfully tired.

The moment he knew she was sleeping, Charlie slipped out of bed. What the hell had he said? Damned laudanum. They'd given it to him in the army hospital. When he woke all he could remember was the terrible feeling of suffocation, a kind of heart-pounding panic with the stink of human filth and blood fouling his nostrils.

He slipped off the sling, poured water from the ewer into the bowl and washed his hands and face, inhaling the clean scent of soap. His breathing steadied, his head cleared.

Interfering bloody woman. He should have guessed she'd take it upon herself to follow the doctor's orders. He should think himself lucky she hadn't tried to bleed him, too.

Moving quietly, he left the chamber and wandered past her room. He lifted the tapestry and tried the door. Locked.

Logan never let the family down, no matter how much he disapproved.

Beyond the window, the sky showed no sign of dawn, but he'd sleep no more tonight. He went back to his room and settled into the armchair. In the bed, her head pillowed on her hand, her breathing deep and even, Merry looked young and vulnerable. The urge to kiss her awake almost brought him to his feet. He wanted to taste her lips, feel life against his body and lose the presence of death. Lose the horror of his dark dreams within her arms. It wasn't possible, because they weren't dreams—they were memories.

He forced himself to remain where he was. It wouldn't be fair to wake her after such a gruelling day. Only a man lacking control would let such base urges get the better of him. Watching her was all the pleasure he needed tonight.

Would asking her to be his mistress really be the answer to bringing her to heel? Or was reason driven by lust? Whatever it was, he had to find a way to ensure her safety. Tomorrow. He'd deal with it tomorrow.

And with her lovely form tempting him, morning could not come soon enough.

Charlie tossed his reins to the waiting groom in the stable courtyard and strode for the house. His breath hung before his face in a cloud. His cheeks tingled. A ride in the fresh air, despite grey skies, had cleared his head.

The fever of last night had passed. He'd even managed to sleep in the chair until daylight awoke him and he'd carried Merry back to her bed. She'd felt good in his arms. Right. The compulsion to keep her safe as rampant as his desire, which was why he'd gone out riding. To rid himself of lust.

With the light of day, some semblance of rational thought had resurfaced; given his purpose for coming to Yorkshire, the attraction he felt for Merry must be excised.

While it would be impossible to woo Lady Allison with Merry under his roof, the less cause for gossip, the better. If one word of this reached his father, Robert would never be allowed home.

His brother's last piece of advice about having fun was the stupidest thing he'd ever said, because when Charlie had fun everything went to hell.

The sooner he found out who Merry's attackers were, the

sooner he could send her home. He entered the house through the side door. The footman stood to attention.

'Miss Draycott up, yet?'

'In the breakfast room, my lord.'

The thought of Merry eating brought a smile to his lips. He strode along the corridor and met Logan coming the other way.

'My lord?' Logan said, holding out a note. 'A letter arrived from the duke, marked urgent.'

Damn. He might have known he couldn't be away for more than a few days before his father would start checking up on him. No matter how hard he worked or what he did, Father no longer trusted him.

He broke the seal.

His heart sunk as he read the cryptic message in his father's scrawl. *Robert is in London. Return by Saturday.*

'Bad news, my lord?'

'I'm not sure.' He couldn't prevent a grin of relief that Robert was found, even as he realised what the request meant. The duke would expect Charlie to make good on his promise right away.

And the urgent nature of the message meant Robert must be in trouble. Again.

Damn it all. Why now? Right at this moment, after all his months of searching?

Hades, Saturday was three days' hence. He'd have to leave right away. What the hell would he do about Merry in the meantime?

There really was only one choice. And she wasn't going to like it. He opened the breakfast-room door.

A frown creased Merry's brow when she looked up and saw him. 'Thomas is ill,' she said. 'Caro thinks it might be scarlet fever.' Her voice hitched on the last words.

'Send for Dr Wells.'

'Do you mind? I will pay his bills, of course, but I could not bear for anything to happen to the child.'

Charlie went to the sideboard and filled his plate with eggs and ham and a thick slice of bacon. 'I, too, have news.'

He sat down. Merry eyed his plate askance and returned to spreading marmalade on her single piece of toast.

He frowned. 'You should eat more than that.'

She gave him a wan smile. 'I'm too worried about Thomas.'

'The boy will be fine,' Charlie said. 'I am sure it is no more than a touch of ague after the long journey. Children come down with them all the time.' He hesitated. 'It would, however, be best if you didn't take him on another journey while he is unwell.'

'Do you think so?' She clung to his words as if they were a life line.

This might work in his favour. 'Positive, he said. 'It happened with my younger brothers and sisters all the time.'

Her tension eased and he felt unaccountably glad he had set her mind at rest.

'What is your news?' she asked.

He glanced down at the letter beside his plate. 'Urgent family business. I am needed in Town.'

'Oh.'

He saw the idea in her head the moment the expression crossed her face. She'd decided to leave.

'You cannot go back to Draycott House.' He spoke more sternly than he intended and she bridled.

'Damn it, Merry, all I am thinking about is your safety, but this urgent business calls me away. You will stay until I return.'

'Will I? Sir, you go too far. I choose where and when I go.'

He wanted to hit something. He kept the frustration out of his face, curled his lip a little. 'Think of the child.'

Her shoulders slumped. He held back a triumphant smile.

She stared at her toast and then glanced up at him. 'How long will you be gone?'

'Six days at the most.'

She stared at him. 'You will scarcely have time to get there and back.'

'My business will not take long. My curricle is built for racing and there are fresh horses in the stable. I've done it in less.'

'Not in the middle of winter.'

'All right, give me two weeks.'

She rose and went to look out of the window. 'Two weeks is a long time to be away from Draycott's. No one knows where I am, except Gribble, and we swore him to silence.'

'Write to your manager.'

'What am I supposed to do here for two weeks? I hate being idle.'

'Ride. Read. Help Mrs Falkner with Thomas. Continue teaching your young…er…lady to read. There are all kinds of things to be done, but promise me one thing?'

She swung around, a refusal on her lips and in her flashing eyes.

He grinned. 'Promise me you won't play billiards until I return.'

Shaking her head, she laughed. A smile stayed on her lovely mouth as she gazed at him. 'My mill needs me.'

If only he could make her want to stay. Perhaps there was one thing that would keep her here. The only kind of promise he could make.

He got to his feet, came to stand next to her. Her perfume rose around him. He dropped a kiss on the place where her pale shoulder met the elegant column of her neck. He put his hands on her waist, lowered his voice. 'I want you here when I get back.'

Desire darkened the clear blue of her eyes to misty dusk. Her eyes closed for a moment, her long black lashes hiding her thoughts. Deliberately cutting him off. She took a shaky breath. 'Don't do this.'

He tipped her chin, searching her beautiful face for some sign she would yield. And deep in her gaze he saw secrets. Painful secrets. He didn't have time to find out what they were and reach London in time. But he needed her to stay.

'Merry, I beg you, please do not venture off the property while I am away. Before I leave I will speak to my steward. He will undertake some investigations on your behalf. We will find out what is going on when I get back. I promise.' He put every ounce of persuasion he had in his voice.

It wasn't enough. He could see it in her stiff shoulders and her restless hands.

'It is so very awkward for me to remain here under your roof in your absence. No matter how powerful your father, you will not stop the gossip.'

Was this the true reason behind her reluctance? 'I thought you cared naught for gossip.'

She stepped away and waved an airy hand. 'I don't care for myself,' she said. ''Tis your reputation, my lord.'

He looked at her grimly. 'No one will censure me. You are grasping at straws.'

She flushed.

Charlie pulled her close and smiled down into her face, willing her to listen, to hear him. 'Wait for me.' He kissed her lips, then took her mouth and kissed her hard.

The kiss deepened to something far more sensual, an erotic tangling of tongues and breath, the feel of her soft curves against him, her encouraging moans. A kind of desperation overtook him, the need to keep her safe, to know she would be here waiting when he returned.

He pressed one thigh between her legs and heard her intake of breath, a hiss of pleasure that heightened his arousal. He pressed her back against the wall, cradling her face in his hand, pressing against her, until she cried out with longing.

He wanted her in the most primal way. To possess her, to bend her to his will. Roughly he lifted her skirts, slid his hand up the satiny flesh of her inner thigh and found the warmth and dampness of her centre. Lust. She wanted him as much as he desired her.

He stroked her soft feminine flesh, felt her tremble and pant, her desire flaming instantly to his touch.

She arched her neck, her head falling back. He kissed the hollow of her throat, licking and nipping his way to the rise of her breast. He cupped her buttocks, lifting her, pressing her against his erection. He growled low in his throat at the torment.

Her eyes flew open. 'Charlie, your wound.'

'My shoulder is not what aches.'

'What if someone comes in?'

'I'll murder them.'

Her laugh was low and husky. It thrummed a response low in his belly.

He lifted her, supporting her back against the wall, one hand beneath her luscious bottom. She brought her legs around his hips, clinging tight to his shoulder, nuzzling and licking at his ear, nipping the lobe until he thought he might lose his mind.

Fingers tearing at the buttons, he unfastened his falls and guided his shaft into her heated depths.

With a sigh she sank down on to him.

Hot and tight, she enveloped his engorged flesh. He drove into her, hard, again and again, hearing her muffled cries of pleasure against his neck, her fingers digging into his shoulders as he pounded her against the wall.

She was his woman. She might deny it, and resist his will, flaunt her independence, but in this he was her master.

Her fingers ran through his hair, tugging with painful intensity. She flattened her palms against his jaw, lifting his face, and she took his mouth, delving her tongue, tasting him, as if she, too, wanted to stake a claim. Slowly she withdrew her tongue, and when he followed her retreat, probing the hot sweet depths of her mouth, she sucked.

The sensation drove him to the brink. He would not go over without her.

Desperate, he sought her centre with his hand, teased her with his thumb, felt her shiver and tremble and he drove home one last time.

Not her master. She was his equal. The climax rode him hard and as she fell apart, against everything he wanted, he jerked from her body and finished within the tails of his shirt.

Shuddering and gasping, they leaned against the wall, forehead to forehead, her legs lax around his waist. 'You will wait for me,' he ground out.

She nodded.

Slowly, he lowered her to the ground.

She leaned back against the wall, her eyes closed, her lovely mouth rosy from kisses, her delicate cheeks reddened by his stubble.

'Oh, my,' she said. 'I'm going to miss these encounters of

ours.' She laughed. But there was heartache in the sound. It touched a soft place in his chest, a tender place that had no place in his life.

'Only two weeks,' he whispered and pressed a kiss to her chin.

He fastened his falls and led her to the nearest chair, pulling her down to sit on his lap. She snuggled down to rest her head on his shoulder. They sat quietly, their breathing slowing, the heat of bliss gradually fading.

'Now give me your promise in words,' he said. 'Two weeks is all I ask.' He kissed her temple.

Eyes smoky, the lids half-lowered, she smiled. 'I will be here when you return.'

He trusted her to keep her word. 'I will return sooner if I can.' Slowly, he lifted her to her feet and rose beside her. He kissed her deeply, savoured her soft pliant body against his. He broke the kiss and left the room, before he lost the strength to leave her at all.

The journey to London had been hell. Merry had been right about travelling at this time of year and Charlie had pushed the horses far too hard, changing them at every posting house and travelling without stopping. He'd made it as far as Hampstead, then one of his hacks threw a shoe and left him walking two miles to the nearest tavern.

But he'd done the journey in two days. Only to arrive at Mountford House and be met with the news that the family was at church…for his brother's wedding. Not only was Robert found, but he was getting married. Today.

He still hadn't absorbed the news.

He scrubbed at a chin covered in two days' growth of beard. His Grace would not be pleased to see his heir looking so disreputable, but what couldn't be cured, must be endured.

The hackney carriage drew up a short distance from St George's, Hanover Square.

'Can't get no closer than this, gov,' the hackney driver called out. 'Some nob getting married. I hear he's caught himself an heiress.'

Charlie's heart sank. If Robert was getting leg-shackled for money, things must be desperate indeed. He leaped from the hackney and tossed the man his fare. 'I'll walk the rest of the way.'

An odd feeling emptied his chest as he strode through the throng of people on the footpath. Robert home and getting married after years of no word—how could that be?

If Charlie had stood up against his father, Robert would never be in this fix. Perhaps he could stop it.

He broke into a run past the carriages lined up and well-dressed folk mingling with London's riff-raff, all hoping for a glimpse of the couple.

Charlie pushed through them and received some dirty looks. He paused at the bottom of the church steps as the bells began pealing. A joyful sound. He was too late.

The doors swung open. The people around him pressed forwards. A man and his bride walked out into the chilly London air.

Robert. He looked well, if a little weathered. Indeed, he looked as dark as a gypsy, as if he'd spent a great deal of the past three years out of doors.

Charlie had feared seeing his brother starving and gaunt. Instead he looked…happy, even overjoyed, as he gazed into the eyes of the bride at his side.

Standing on the bottom step, Charlie drank his brother's happiness in with a sense of utter relief. The tiny fragile-looking thing beside his tall athletic brother had stars in her eyes and a big smile on her pixie face, while his brother looked positively besotted. Nothing like the jaded rake he'd been the last time Charlie saw him.

The last time they'd met, Charlie had let his brother down. He'd supported Father against his twin, when they'd always stood shoulder to shoulder. At the time he'd thought he was doing the right thing for his brother. Robert's shock, his sense of betrayal, had shown in his eyes. That look had haunted Charlie all these long years.

Perhaps Robert still held a grudge. Perhaps he wouldn't care to see him at all. It would explain the lack of any word. He drew back, unsure.

As if sensing Charlie's presence, Robert's gaze searched the crowd. The moment their eyes met he grinned and waved.

The welcome in his smile swelled Charlie's heart to breaking. He tore up the steps and dragged his brother into an embrace.

The next few moments were chaos. Father taking him to task for being late. His mother hushing Father. An incomprehensible conversation about Zeus with the bride and not a moment for questions.

Somehow, Robert had found the path to happiness. He could see it in his brother's face, but when Charlie tried to seek answers, his brother had sloughed him off.

Apparently a ship to Italy awaited the bride and groom.

Stunned, Charlie stood with his mother, father and siblings and waved as the happy couple departed.

When the carriage disappeared around the corner, the governess gathered her charges and walked them to one of the several waiting carriages.

Father and Mother remained, receiving the well wishes of members of the *ton* who had crowded into the church. Charlie ranged alongside them, shaking hands and muttering appropriate words of thanks.

Finally it was over. Father frowned. 'Glad to see one of my sons still knows what is owing to the Mountford name,' he muttered.

The heavy weight of responsibility strangely missing these past few days descended squarely on Charlie's shoulders. The burden felt heavier than ever before.

'Stantford,' Mother said in warning accents, 'she is a lovely young woman. They will do very nicely together.'

'Who is she?' Charlie asked in awe of any woman who could capture his younger brother's wandering eye and make him look so bloody happy.

'Abernathy's by-blow,' Father said gloomily.

'Oh, really, Alfred,' Mother huffed. 'You promised you would say nothing more. She is Endersley's legitimate daughter. Lord Wynchwood's niece. And an accomplished artist.'

Father snorted.

Charlie wanted to laugh. Of course Robert wouldn't marry a suitable gel. He'd marry where he pleased. And be happy. 'Good for him,' he said, smiling at his mother.

He hadn't seen her looking this happy since Robert had disappeared. The worry had gone from her eyes. She was even standing up to Father.

'How is Lady Allison?' Father asked.

His heart grew cold.

As he'd promised, Father had taken Robert back into the family. Now he wanted his pound of flesh. A trickle of envy ran like acid in Charlie's veins. No choice for him. No odd little artist or outspoken industrialist's daughter. He had a position to uphold. He'd accepted it on his return from the war, embraced it as a way to make amends. After all, he had no right to expect happiness when he'd destroyed so many good lives. If doing his duty gave him pain, so much the better. It was well deserved. But now, right at this moment, the yoke of responsibility irked.

'I did not yet see Lady Allison,' he replied. 'I barely reached Durn when you called me home.'

Father frowned. 'Unlike you to delay.'

Charlie clenched his jaw, holding in the unreasoning surge of anger. 'You are right, Father. That is why I am returning right away.'

'In the morning?' Mother said.

Charlie glanced at his father's deeply lined face, at the weariness in his eyes and the fear his eldest son would fail. 'No, Mother. Today. Now.' He took her hand and kissed it. 'I'm sorry to rush off, but duty calls.'

She shook her head. 'Life is more than duty, Charles.'

Not for him. He'd seen the results of straying from responsibility when he joined the army against his father's wishes. He gave her a reassuring smile. 'I'll return to town as soon as I can.'

Her eyes misted. 'You brother looked so very happy.'

He had. And Charlie had to be happy he'd been able to heal the breach between his father and his brother, even if neither of them seemed to give a damn one way or the other. Charlie could take comfort in seeing his mother's smile. 'Yes. He did. I'm glad I got back in time.'

Mother's eyes misted. 'I want that for all my children.'

There was happiness, or at least satisfaction, in doing one's duty. There had to be.

His father gave an impatient sigh. 'Tonbridge,' he said, with brows drawn low. 'I'm looking forward to seeing you standing in this church very soon. Hopefully, at least one of my sons knows what is due to the name of Mountford.'

He forced a smile. 'I know where my duty lies, Your Grace.'

'Next time dress in appropriate attire.'

Charlie inclined his head. 'My apologies, Your Grace. It was either change or see Robert and his new wife.'

'Hmmph,' Father said.

'Really, Alfred,' Mother said.

Charlie bowed to his parents, the weight on his shoulders more unbearable than it had ever been, and left for Durn.

Chapter Fourteen

Charlie handed his hat to his butler and shrugged out of his coat. If anything, Logan looked more prune-faced than usual. 'Miss Draycott about, Logan?'

The butler's thin lips pursed. 'In the long gallery, my lord. With that other female and the child. If I may say, my lord, this is not what I expected when I joined the household of one of the first families in England.'

'You may not say,' Charlie said, putting all the chill of a displeased cavalry officer in his voice.

Logan shrivelled a bit, but the resentment in his eyes showed he wasn't completely cowed. Damn it, what were Merry and her ladies up to that they had upset Durn's staff? What was it about the woman that continued to turn all about her upside down?

He took the stairs to the first floor two at a time and made his way through the maze of corridors to the back of the house. The long gallery displayed the pride of generations of Mountfords. Portraits, royal warrants, the odd suit of armour.

As he drew closer squeals of delight echoed along the

hallway. The high-pitched voice of a child and women's laughter.

What was she up to?

The cheerful sound brought an unwilling smile to his lips. He approached the wide corridor running the length of the back of the house on silent feet, determined to catch her and her accomplices in the act.

Remaining in the shadows, he glanced along the gallery. Light from the bank of windows flooded the Gothic-style room, which was lined with heavy oak panels and covered in portraits and coats of arms. He'd never before seen all the shutters flung back to let in the daylight, not even the muted daylight of a grey winter afternoon. Bad for the artwork.

Two suits of armour had been moved from their corners to stand at the midway point of the room; a length of line attached one neck to the other. But that wasn't what had his gaze wide-eyed. It was Merry, her skirts looped under a ribbon at her waist, so she showed an extraordinary amount of ankle, calf and knee, with a battledore in her hand, diving for a shuttle-cock bashed with great vigour by Beth.

Somehow she managed to hit it back. Beth collapsed laughing as the feathery object fell on the floor at her feet.

'Ten times,' cried little Thomas on the sidelines. 'Now it is my turn.'

Good Lord, he'd forgotten all about those old racquets. He and Robert used to play outside in the summer. Using the long gallery on a winter's day would never have been approved.

This would be how it would be with Merry. Fun. Surprising. Spur of the moment. When she wasn't working, of course. She seemed to have achieved a balance in her life. Duty and pleasure.

Why did he find it so difficult?

Her face was flushed and alive with joy as she tossed her

hair back and handed over her bat to the small boy. She looked more beautiful than he remembered.

Frowning, he sauntered towards the players.

Beth shot to her feet with a scared look. Merry turned and her expression of dismay made him cringe inside. With fumbling fingers she untied the ribbon at her waist and, disappointingly, her skirts fell to the floor with much brushing and tweaking from their owner.

'Lord Tonbridge,' she said, sounding breathless. 'We didn't expect you back so soon.'

'Clearly.' He raised a brow and glanced at the wooden-and-vellum bat in Tommy's hand.

'Oh, er...I hope you don't mind,' she said. 'Tommy was restless. Caro has come down with the ague, but he is so much better.' She pointed at the battledore. 'I found these in the schoolroom. I made the shuttlecocks from corks and pens from the library.'

No wonder they flew so badly. Beth and Tommy were looking at him as if he was an ogre. He couldn't hold his serious face any longer.

He chuckled, then he laughed out loud. 'If you could have seen yourself just now. I thought you were going to break your neck trying for that shot.'

Merry grinned back. 'I used to be champion at this game as a girl, I'll have you know.'

'I bet you were.'

He ran a finger along the string. 'Interesting innovation.'

She chuckled. 'Tommy kept running into us. We put that there to keep him back at bit.'

'Does the shuttlecock have to go over it or under it?' he asked.

'It doesn't matter,' the boy said. 'Just so long as you stay on your side.'

'Can I have a turn?' Charlie asked.

'Of course,' Merry said.

'You can have my turn,' Beth said, bobbing an awkward curtsy. 'I really ought to see how Mrs Falkner does.' She handed her battledore to Charlie and scurried away.

Tommy pouted. 'He's too big.'

'All right,' Charlie said. 'You play with Miss Draycott, and I will keep count.' He lowered himself to the floor and rested his back against a priceless tapestry. 'Off you go.' He gave Merry a saucy look. 'Feel free to adopt your new style of clothing, Miss Draycott, if it makes it easier to play.'

'Rogue,' she said.

Sadly, she didn't. But from this angle Charlie had plenty of glimpses of her shapely ankle to keep him happy, as well as the view of her lovely bosom bouncing beneath her gown. Her ready smiles and laughter were even better.

It was like watching poetry. It brought back the flashes of happiness he'd had before Waterloo. He sat on the floor and smiled until his cheeks ached.

He counted out each hit and was delighted to see how carefully Merry knocked the flighted shuttlecock back to Tommy so he could hit it. The boy was wild in his returns, but Merry was agile and light on her feet.

Finally, after twelve hits back and forth, Tommy let the bird drop to the floor.

'Oh, well done, sir,' Merry cried. 'That is the longest number of hits we've had all afternoon.'

The little boy instantly cheered. He grinned.

Merry dabbed at her face with her handkerchief. 'My word, I am hot. I think we will call it a day.'

'What?' Charlie said, leaping to his feet. 'Just because it is my turn? You fear I will best you.'

Tommy giggled at his expression of outrage.

Merry laughed. 'You take unfair advantage, sir. I have been playing for almost an hour.'

'And I have been driving neck or nothing for several.'

She made a mock curtsy of defeat. 'Count for us, will you, Tommy?'

The boy took up Charlie's position on the floor.

Charlie released the string around the neck of one of the suits of armour. 'If I remember correctly, there is a lot of dashing about in this game. I don't want to knock these fellows over. Logan will have my hide.'

Merry covered her mouth with her hand. Her eyes twinkled above her fingers. 'I'm sorry. I should not have moved them.'

'He's cross with us,' Tommy said.

'He's always cross with me, too,' Charlie replied. 'I shall pay it no mind. Please serve, Miss Draycott.'

He loved the way her cheeks flushed red, and the frown on her brow above her sparkling blue eyes as she determinedly returned each of his shots. She was good at this game, as she was good at so many things, and she kept trying to catch him off guard, sending her shots in unexpected directions. It wasn't so much about how high the count went, but about who would miss the first shot.

Tommy's voice rose in pitch as they exceeded twelve and headed for twenty.

But Merry was tiring, he could see her energy flag and he was about to miss her next shot out of sheer kindness, if he could do it without making it obvious, when she tripped on the carpet.

She went flying at the suit of armour in front of the fireplace.

He dove to catch her, somehow managing to pull her clear of the hearth and land beneath her. A very sharp elbow jabbed him in the ribs as he hit the floor. Winded, he lay gasping beneath her. Laughing so hard, he couldn't stop.

'It's not funny, ye great lummox,' Merry said. 'You made me miss my shot.'

Tommy dashed over, his face terrified.

'I made you miss it?' Charlie said. 'I thought you had abandoned the game in favour of a waltz with Lord Stanley there.' He tickled her beneath the ribs.

'Oh, stop.' She dissolved into helpless giggles and Tommy joined the heap on the carpet, his little fingers more like claws as he tried to tickle them both.

Charlie gathered them up, one under each arm and staggered to his feet. 'That's it, you two. You are going in the duck pond for insulting the heir.' He whirled them around, aware of a twinge in his arm, but not giving a damn for the sheer joy of the moment.

Merry, the little wretch, blew in his ear, bringing him up short.

'Enough,' she commanded. 'Enough, both of you. Put me down, my lord. It is time I retired from the lists to change my gown and tidy myself.'

Charlie grinned down into her face. The pull of desire left him hard and wanting. Not at all suitable in front of a child. He put them both down.

'Run along and see your mama,' Merry said. She smiled at Charlie and there was tenderness in her gaze. 'Thank you for playing with him. He lacks for male company.'

She looked lovely. Beautiful. All flushed and happy. And beyond his reach.

He bowed. 'Thank you for the game. When you have freshened up, I would like to talk to you, if I may.'

Her face sobered. 'Did your steward find out any information? I have tried to speak to him once or twice, but he has been too busy to see me.'

'I called in on him on the way home. He found no news of the men who shot at us. Nor anything about Mrs Falkner before she arrived at the inn where you met.'

She gasped. 'I did not ask you to poke around in Caro's life.'

'She is hiding something, Merry. Who is she?'

'My true friend. And that is all you need to know.'

Until someone proved her wrong. Frustrated, but admiring of her loyalty, he bit down on the words. 'Very well. But we do need to plan our next course of action.'

'I'll change and join you in the drawing room in half an hour.'

Heavy hearted from what he knew he had to say, he watched her walk away and pulled himself back to business. He also needed to freshen up after his journey, but he'd use one of the guest rooms. Their affair had to end and he'd decided he would hire someone to guard her at Draycott House while they continued searching for the attackers.

He didn't have an alternative. Her staying at Durn made it impossible for him to follow through on his promise to Father. Her Purtefoy connection added yet another dimension to the complications. Agreeing to her plan had been a mistake of epic proportions, for them both.

Merry started down the stairs for her meeting with Charlie. She was still smiling after their game. She'd never seen him so unreservedly happy. But the joy had faded as swiftly as daylight left the evening sky. Something was troubling him.

'Psst,' a voice said, bringing her head around to the source of the noise. Beth.

She retraced her steps to where Beth hovered in the doorway to the other wing.

'Did you need me?' Merry asked.

Beth glanced at a stolid footman. 'I wants to speak to you in private. I was going to do it afore, but his lordship came along.'

Her heart gave an uncomfortable thump. 'Is Mrs Falkner worse?'

'No, miss.' She winced and again glanced at the footman who was looking down his nose.

Merry gave him a haughty glare. 'Would you mind stepping further down the hallway? Out of earshot.' She spoke with calm authority. The man's ears reddened and he strode away, all offended dignity.

'What is it, Beth?'

'I made friends with one of the kitchenmaids.' She grinned. 'Never know when an extra bit of food might come in handy. She snuck out to see her man last night. This mornin' she said there's a woman staying at the inn asking about visitors here at Durn.'

'What sort of woman?'

'I thinks it's Jane. I was wondering if she wants to come back, like. Changed her mind and followed us here. She weren't very keen on t'house when we was there, but mayhap she's thought better on't.'

'How did she know to look for us here?'

'We all saw how it was between you and his lordship. April and May, she said. Seemed a bit put out by it. But she must 'ave guessed he'd bring you here.'

Hardly April and May, but the attraction must have been more obvious than Merry thought. She frowned. How could a woman like Jane afford a room at the inn? Unless she'd returned to her old work. One of Caro's rules had been no more male customers.

Beth was watching her eagerly. 'Shall you tell them to let her in?'

'I can't override his lordship's orders,' Merry said, suddenly glad for Charlie's autocratic edict. Every instinct told her not to trust Jane, but Caro had always accused her of prejudice and Merry, unable to deny it was something about Jane's hardness that troubled her, had pushed the feelings aside. 'But I will see what can be done when I talk to his lordship in a few minutes. I will let you know what he says.'

Beth shifted her feet. 'You won't tell him about the maid?'

Heaven help her. 'No, Beth. I won't give your friend away.'

Beth bobbed a curtsy and ran back down the hallway. Merry continued down the stairs.

Charlie was waiting for her in the drawing room. Oddly, Logan followed her in, though she had not heard him behind her. He'd been following her around quite a bit. Her and Beth. Making sure they didn't run off with any valuables, no doubt.

Charlie glared at him. 'What is it, Logan?'

'My lord, I'm sorry, but a party of visitors have been admitted through the front gate. The lad ran all the way here to let us know, but they are not far behind.'

Charlie's face darkened to thunderous. 'I instructed no one was to be admitted.'

Merry froze. 'I had better return to my room.' She hurried out into the hallway and headed for the stairs. Charlie followed her out. 'Logan, hold them off until Miss Draycott is upstairs.'

Before Logan could move, the door swung open.

'Honor Draycott,' a shocked voice said. 'Is that really you?'

Merry swung around and stared at the fair-haired young man and fashionably attired lady in the opening.

The Purtefoy siblings. Digby and Allison: blond, blue-eyed, beautiful and aristocratic. They looked horrified.

They stepped into the entrance hall.

'Tonbridge,' Digby said, removing his hat. 'I knew it was you who passed us in the village. The stupid fool at the gate tried to tell us you were absent.'

'My lord,' Allison said, stepping into the vestibule and making an elegant curtsy. 'And my cousin. How delightfully unexpected.' Her smile was sweet. Her eyes glittered like glass. Lady Allison was furious.

Merry couldn't move. She couldn't speak. Her throat simply didn't have enough moisture to utter a word. She looked help-lessly at Charlie, who seemed equally shocked.

She swallowed hard. 'Good morning, Digby. Allison.'

Allison raised a brow. 'I hardly know what to say. Although, perhaps we shouldn't be surprised, should we, Digby? We do sometimes hear of your exploits.'

Merry felt herself flush at the poison-laced words. She drew herself up to her full height. 'You should not believe all you hear.'

'I should hope not,' Allison said, batting her eyelashes at Charlie. Her heart-shaped face looked particularly pretty beneath the brim of a green velvet bonnet with its dashing ostrich feather dyed to match.

'When we saw your curricle haring through the village, Tonbridge, we came to make sure you hadn't forgotten our invitation,' Digby said. He glanced at Merry and winced. 'If you are free, that is?'

In other words, Merry wasn't invited. Good thing, too.

There was no way she would ever enter her cousins' house. Not for a thousand pounds, or if she was starving in the street.

A faint look of embarrassment crossed Charlie's face and then his jaw hardened as if he'd come to an unpleasant decision. He faced his visitors and squared his shoulders.

'We weren't expecting callers this morning,' he said, rather pointedly, Merry thought with a flash of glee. 'However, since you are here, and are now practically family, you might as well be the first to hear the news.' He gestured to Merry, calling her back to his side. 'Miss Draycott has done me the great honour of accepting my offer of marriage.'

Allison gasped. Digby's jaw dropped.

As did Merry's. Her heart stumbled strangely. Her head felt oddly light. Trembles shook every bone in her body, fear and hope mingling. Hesitantly she walked back down the stairs to stand beside him. He pulled her close and gave her hand a squeeze. His smile, when he looked at her, didn't reflect in his eyes.

A blade twisted in her chest. He was keeping to his side of their bargain. Nothing more. And she should be grateful, not feeling hurt.

Lord Digby recovered first. 'Congratulations, old man. Father will be pleased. Finally, he'll be able to boast a duke in the family.'

A flush appeared on Allison's cheeks. Of course. She'd hoped to be the one to catch the ducal heir. That was why they'd hurried over here at the news of Charlie's arrival.

Merry found herself smiling. 'By gum, Purtefoys is going up in t'world.'

Allison narrowed her gaze on the hand tucked beneath Charlie's arm. No ring. Not that there need be one, but it was unusual for a family like the Mountfords not to provide the heir's future bride with a promise ring. 'A sudden decision, I assume,' she said with a sneer.

Charlie must also have seen her gaze, because he covered Merry's hand with his. 'I am the luckiest man alive.'

'When is the wedding?' Digby asked, still having trouble controlling his jaw.

'We haven't yet set a date,' Merry said, before Charlie made up another monumental lie that would have to be explained away.

'The sooner the better,' he said, giving her a wolfish grin that made her heart lurch and her insides clench. So inappropriate.

More heat scalded her face. She tried to tug her hand free, but found it held fast.

Allison's head tilted to one side. 'Did you two lovebirds travel here alone?' A wealth of suspicion tainted the sugary-sweet voice.

'Certainly not,' Charlie said. He seemed to have recovered his wits very nicely and Merry was quite happy to have him respond to her cousin's barbed words. 'Miss Draycott is accompanied by her companion, Mrs Falkner.'

'Perhaps we should introduce ourselves to the lady,' Lady Allison said with a sweet smile that dripped acid. 'Invite her to our party. You will both come, won't you? It will be a wonderful way to celebrate your approaching nuptials, which seem to have been a well-kept secret until now.'

They were done for. Allison knew they weren't betrothed. The Purtefoys, with their close connections to the duke, would have been the first to know.

Before she could refuse the invitation, Charlie smiled. 'It isn't public knowledge, I'm afraid. We haven't yet spoken to His Grace.'

The look of triumph on Allison's face was a sight to behold.

'Oh, I see.' She surreptitiously nudged Digby in the ribs. 'We really ought to make the acquaintance of your companion before we go.'

'Mrs Falkner is indisposed at the moment,' Merry said. 'The doctor fears scarlet fever.'

Charlie made a sound like choking, then coughed.

'Scarlet fever?' Allison's voice rose. 'Why did you not say so at once? It is very dangerous. Why, my aunt died of it in less than three days.' Allison's pretty face changed to sly. 'How very inconvenient of your chaperon to be ill right at this moment.'

The aunt she spoke of so cavalierly was Merry's mother. Merry wanted to bash her over the head with her green parasol.

The last time she'd done so, she'd been expelled from school. Although it was not the reason given. The hours spent with Jeremy in the garden shed had provided the excuse they needed to make her *persona non grata*, courtesy of Allison. The girl had a knack of making herself look like a saint.

'We do not yet know for sure,' Merry said.

Charlie had a strange look in his eye. 'Perhaps you would like to join us for tea,' he said. 'If Mrs Falkner has a debilitating condition, I am certain we will not be going out in company.'

Digby looked as if he might agree, but Allison grabbed his arm. 'No, no. We wouldn't dream of putting you out with illness in the house. Good day to you both.'

She turned and trotted down the steps. Her brother had little option but to follow. At the bottom, they climbed quickly aboard their brougham.

Like a long-married couple, Charlie and Merry stood on the front steps watching them depart. It seemed odd. And somehow right. And completely impossible.

'It seems we stirred the mud at the bottom of the pond,' Merry said, half-laughing.

The grim expression on Charlie's face said he couldn't agree more, but not in a good way.

She let him escort her to the drawing room without saying a word. What was he fretting about? The betrothal could be dealt with right away. The sooner they ended this terrible farce, the better. Dash it. If Caro hadn't fallen ill, they would have been on their way before the Purtefoys arrived on the doorstep.

She sank on to the sofa and looked up at his distant expression, his tight shoulders. He looked as if he carried the weight of the world. 'How did your family business fare?' she asked in what she hoped were calm accents.

A faint bitter smile curved his lips. 'Everything was fine.'

A lie.

'Right now we have a more pressing problem,' he said.

Their betrothal no doubt. Merry Draycott solved her own problems. 'Simple. One of us will cry off, now, today, and I will return home. It would have been better if you had said nothing at all about our supposed engagement to the Purtefoys just now, but the damage can be soon undone.'

He looked taken aback. 'What other explanation could I have given for your presence in my house?'

'Do you think they didn't draw their own conclusions? And besides, our agreement was for Broadoaks. For the mill owners in Skepton. People who don't move in your circles. Now the news will be all over London. You will be a laughing stock.'

He frowned. 'I hardly think so.' He sat down beside her and took her hand in his. He gazed into her eyes with a smile she could only describe as puzzled. 'The thing is, Merry, I find myself unwilling to let you go without assuring myself of your safety.'

A bubble of something light and warm filled her chest. She felt as if she might float away. And beneath it was an odd sort of longing. The bond between them seemed stronger than ever, despite his absence. No doubt about it, she'd missed him dreadfully.

He dipped his head for a kiss. She fought the insidious longing in her body. Fought the desire to melt into him, to surrender to the drug of his kiss. Fought the lonely ache in her heart. Her hand pressed against his chest to push him away; instead, it crept up around his neck and she kissed him back with the passion he aroused.

Long moments passed. His tongue swept her mouth. Her body pressed close to his hard length, loving the strength and the power against her soft pliant curves.

He broke the kiss and held her by the shoulders. His smile was just a little smug.

All she could think of was getting him in her bed.

'Why on earth did they have to show up right at this moment?' He rubbed his chin. 'It would serve them right for barging in if we did get married.'

What would it be like to be married to a man like Charlie? The heir to a dukedom. A man who moved in the first circles of society—the kind of society that looked on the Merry Draycotts of the world with scorn.

The thought chilled her to the bone.

He wasn't serious, though. He couldn't be. He was just angry at her cousins' intrusion. She struck at his shoulder with her fist. 'You gormless lump. I can't marry you.'

'There you go, hiding again.'

She pushed him away. 'You have no idea what you are talking about.' One thing she knew for certain: for him, marrying her would be a disaster.

Rueful regret filled his eyes. 'I certainly can't force you if you don't want it.'

Not want it? How could she explain what she didn't want were all the trappings that went with the dukedom. Just the thought of it made her shudder. 'All I want is to go home.'

He pressed his lips together and drew away. 'As you have said before. I wrote to a friend of mine. A soldier stationed at York. I asked him to recommend a couple of good men no longer employed by the military who will guard you until we get to the bottom of these attacks.'

She shook her head. 'I don't want to be surrounded by guards. People will think I'm afraid.'

'You should be afraid.' He held up a hand. 'Don't argue. Wait until we see who he suggests. It will make it easier for me, Merry, if you go along with me in this.'

This is what it would be like if she married him. He would control her life. But it was because he cared. She let go a breath. What harm would it do, to put up with a couple of retired soldiers underfoot for a while? They probably needed employment. At the moment, her desire to have speech with Jane was a more pressing issue, because Charlie's hints that he thought Caro responsible for the attacks still worried her.

If Charlie discovered Caro was to blame, she feared for her friend's life. Charlie would have no problem having her incarcerated, whereas Merry would prefer to give her friend enough money to send her away.

Not that she believed Caro was guilty of such a betrayal. She didn't. She just had to know for sure. If Caro was involved, then Jane must be, too, and Merry needed to talk to her—before Charlie found her himself.

She let her shoulders sag in defeat. 'Very well. I will leave

my decision until we have your friend's reply. In the meantime,
I would like to go to the village.'

He frowned.

'Caro is ill. The doctor suggested willow-bark tea, but there
is none to be had here at Durn.'

'I'll send one of the footmen.'

The blasted man had an answer for everything. She shuffled
her feet. 'She also has need of other things. Female things.
She brought very little with her, we left in such a rush, and
Beth tells me she is too proud to ask. I would like to make her
a gift.'

He started to look uncomfortable. 'Give the footman a
list.'

She gave a disappointed shrug. 'I can, I suppose. It would
not be the same, though. Such intimate apparel needs a woman's touch. I hoped you would come with me. I should not have
troubled you with such a trivial request, you must be tired after
your journey.' She rose to leave.

'Merry, no,' he said, stopping her mid-stride. 'I'm sorry for
being such a dreadful host. I will be happy to drive you to the
village.'

Now she felt terrible. But the die was cast. 'Thank you.'

In a few swift strides, he drew close and captured her face
in his hands. He gazed down into her eyes with a frown, as if
seeking assurance. Then he kissed her gently, briefly, on the
lips. 'I was rough on you earlier.'

'I was a shrew.'

They laughed at the same moment. He stroked her cheek.
'May I make it up to you properly later?' he whispered, his
dark gaze hot. Again he brushed her lips with his mouth.

She felt worse than ever. Heartsick at playing off such wiles,
when he was being so sweet, and the thought of one last night
in his arms made her weak. 'I shall look forward to it.'

He gave her a swift kiss. 'Enough of this or we will not be going anywhere.'

'Shall I ask Logan to have the carriage brought around?'

'Please. Ask for the closed carriage. For safety.'

She hurried away before guilt made her admit her request was all a plot.

The carriage ride passed delightfully, despite the sinking feeling Merry had every time Charlie smiled at her with approval. Twice she almost owned up but then bit her tongue. Fortunately, their swift arrival at Durn village, a collection of stone houses with slate roofs, occurred before she plucked up the courage.

The village boasted an inn, a mill, an apothecary and a haberdasher's, which also served as the post office. Numerous cottages wound along a fast-running beck, with the grand Norman church set at one end. They started at the haberdasher's. While Charlie enquired after the mail, Merry picked up an assortment of items. Handkerchiefs, a nightdress of serviceable cotton, stays, a matronly cap of the sort Caro favoured, some stockings. Soon her arms were full. Pretending to browse, she made her way to the back of the shop where an open door led to a storeroom.

'What are you doing?'

She spun around at the sound of his voice. 'Looking for buttons.'

Charlie raised an eyebrow at her collection of items. 'Mrs Falkner needs all of those?'

Merry couldn't help her blush. Lying to him felt horrid. 'She does,' she said firmly. She carried them to the clerk at the front of the shop and dropped the pile on the counter. She picked up the nightgown. 'It is very plain.'

'Ah...' the clerk nodded. 'Most ladies makes their own.'

He pointed to the bolts of cloth behind him. 'I have some nice white linen.'

'How much is the nightdress?'

'One and six.'

'Daylight robbery,' she exclaimed. 'I'm no bairn wet behind the ears, you know.'

He grimaced. 'All reet. A shilling.'

'Give him what he asks,' Charlie said, clearly embarrassed by her haggling.

She frowned. ''Tis my brass,' she said. 'And I'll not be gilding his lily.'

The clerk muttered something under his breath.

Charlie winced.

Merry turned to face him. 'Why don't you wait outside in the carriage? It will probably be quicker.'

Brow furrowed, he looked doubtful, though she had the feeling he was dying to leave her to her negotiations. 'Better yet, why don't you see if the apothecary has the willow-bark tea?'

His expression cleared. 'Good idea.'

No doubt he had a vision of her trying to bargain with the apothecary, too.

He strode from the shop.

Merry picked up the stays. 'I'd like to try these on. Do you have a private room?'

'In t'back.'

'I won't be a moment. If his lordship comes back, tell him I'll be quick.'

The storeroom had a screen secluding one corner from view. It also had a door into the laneway, which traversed past the Red Lion. If she hurried, she could be back before Charlie noticed her absence. Perfect.

She picked up her skirts and ran along the rutted alley and, breathing hard, entered through the side door.

'I'm looking for a Miss Jane Harper,' she said to the lad sweeping the parlour floor. 'She is expecting me.' She tossed him a sixpence.

'First room at the top of the stairs,' the boy said, pocketing the coin and returning to his sweeping.

Beth was right. Jane had followed them. Hoping there was an innocent explanation, she ran up the stairs. Pressing down on the latch, she pushed the door open into a private parlour with Jane sitting at a table in front of the window beside a swarthy young man with close-cropped hair and a brutish face.

A premonition all was not well made her heart race. 'Jane Harper, what are you doing here?'

The man rose to his feet, a nasty look on his face. 'Now here's a surprise.'

Merry narrowed her eyes on the woman. 'I heard you were here and wondered if you wanted to return with us, but now I see you have other friends.'

A rather unpleasant smile split Jane's narrow face. 'Nice of you to call, Miss Draycott.' She gestured to the man. 'Why don't we make our guest comfortable?'

He pulled out a chair.

'No, thank you, his lordship is waiting for me.'

The man lowered his beetling brow and pulled a pistol. 'Sit.'

'All right,' Merry said, sitting down opposite Jane. She eyed the woman warily. 'Are you working alone, or is someone paying you to cause me harm?'

'I'm saying nothing,' Jane said, her lips tight.

Merry's heart sank. 'Then tell me if Mrs Falkner is involved?'

Jane's eyes widened a fraction. Surprise? Because Merry had guessed wrong or because she'd guessed right? 'Tell me. I'll pay you well and tell no one how I found out.'

'There isn't enough money in the world to pay me off.'

How odd? 'It is not the marquis, is it?'

Jane openly laughed. 'Guess all you want, missy.'

Chapter Fifteen

The trip to the apothecary should not have taken Charlie more than five minutes. Unfortunately, Mr Quire, the owner, had served the needs of the Mountford family for years. Charlie could not escape without a full accounting of the health of his family and a discussion of his brother's wedding, which had appeared in *The Times*.

Twenty minutes passed before he returned to the carriage outside the haberdasher's. He glanced inside his coach.

'Not back yet, my lord,' the footman said.

'Blast women and shopping,' he muttered.

'Yes, my lord.'

She was probably still bargaining. His mother had always complained about the haberdasher's exorbitant prices, but she had always paid him without comment. He should have done the same and dragged Merry out. He squared his shoulders and entered the shop. The pile of goods lay where Merry had dropped them. The clerk was busy tidying a tray full of brightly coloured ribbons.

'Where is the lady?' Charlie asked.

The clerk gave him a disgruntled glance. 'Trying something on in t'back room.'

Charlie heaved a sigh. He leaned one hip against the counter and folded his arms across his chest. Minutes passed. The clerk went around to the other side of the counter. 'Do she want these or not?' he asked.

Oh Lord, if she was going to start haggling when she came back, they were going to be here all day. He'd decided he'd rather spend the afternoon in bed, with her, because they had very little time left.

'Tot up the bill, package them and I'll pay while I am waiting.'

The man's eyes gleamed. Clearly, he was going to pay far more than any of this stuff was worth. The man was a Captain Sharp. He would speak to Father about not renewing his lease the next time it came up.

The clerk parcelled up the goods and handed Charlie the bill. He forked over the dibs.

Still no sign of Merry. 'What was she trying on?'

The man coughed. 'Stays.'

Why on earth…? 'Where did you say she was?'

The man pointed to the door leading to the rear of the building. As Charlie made his way back there a band around his chest tightened. He had no doubt what he'd find when he entered the back room full of boxes.

'Merry?'

No answer. Of course there was no answer. The little minx. She'd given him the slip. Reckless. The woman had no care for life and limb. But where the hell had she gone? He dashed through the back door and looked up and down the lane. Nothing suggested where she could have got to. The only other building of any size nearby was the inn.

The inn had horses for hire. Could she really be that desperate to leave? It made no sense.

'Hey,' the clerk called. 'What about your parcel?'

'Have it put in the carriage,' Charlie said. Anger balling in his chest, he strode down the lane and into the inn.

A lad stood at the bar tossing a coin in the air.

'Did you see a young lady come in here in the last few minutes?'

The boy's grubby face took on a crafty expression. 'Wot if I did?'

'Sixpence if you tell me where she went.'

'It's my lucky day,' the lad said. 'First door at the top of the stairs.'

Not renting a horse then. Charlie dropped the promised coin in his hand. 'If she's not there, I'll want it back.'

'She ain't come down yet.'

What game was she playing? Who was she meeting? The hairs on the back of his neck rose. A warning. Not to be ignored.

Cautiously, he climbed the stairs. The door stood ajar a fraction. He pulled the pistol from his pocket and pushed it open.

The first face to meet his gaze was Merry's. She was seated at the table facing the door. Pleasure did not describe her expression when she saw him.

The other woman grinned. Jane. The missing lightskirt. 'What in hell's name is going on, Miss Draycott?' He stepped into the room.

Merry's gaze darted off to the right. She had an odd look on her face as if she was trying to tell him something.

The door swung closed.

He whipped his head around. Too late. The cold metal of a

pistol muzzle pressed against his neck. 'One move and you're a dead man,' a coarse voice said.

'It seems we have a stand off,' Charlie said, keeping his pistol levelled on Jane.

'Nah,' another voice said. 'See, if you don't put down your pop, I shoots Miss Draycott here.' A second man, a lanky pockmarked fellow, stepped into his line of vision from the other room, a bedchamber, with his weapon directed at Merry.

With a curse, Charlie lowered his gun. He'd walked into an ambush like some Hyde Park soldier fresh on campaign. 'What is it you want? Money?'

The first man snatched the weapon from his hand.

'They are nothing but cowards,' Merry said, her voice full of scorn. 'They won't even admit who they are working for.'

'Whoever it is, I'll offer you double to let us go,' Charlie said swiftly.

The second man laughed. 'You ain't getting off so light.'

Charlie glanced at Jane with a frown. 'Are they holding you hostage, too? Is that why you disappeared?'

Jane rose. 'Certainly not.' Her voice was cold enough to freeze a pond in mid-summer. 'These men work for me.' Her voice no longer had a nasal whine and her clothes were better quality than those she had worn at Merry's. She looked more like a housekeeper than a maid. Or a prostitute.

'What do you want?' Charlie asked.

She smiled. 'I have everything I want.'

None of this made any sense. 'And that is?'

'The end of Merry Draycott.'

Blunt and to the point. Merry's face paled and Charlie's fists bunched in futile rage. He should have brought reinforcements. He'd been so annoyed with Merry for giving him the slip, he'd not stopped to think it through. *Too bloody hot-headed.* His colonel's voice rang in his ears. It chilled his blood. He could not let the past tie him in knots.

'Don't you know who I am?' he said. 'Do you know what will happen to you, if you harm me or my betrothed?'

Jane laughed. 'Your whore, you mean.'

Merry flushed red.

'I'll have none of your lip,' Charlie said, clenching and unclenching his fists, watching for some sign of weakness, some lack of attention on the part of the men.

'Don't worry about your skin, my lord. We've no axe to grind with you. We just need you not to interfere for a day or so. Tie them up.'

Poor Merry. Her lower lip trembled, showing her fear. He gave her an encouraging smile, though what the hell he had to be encouraging about he didn't know.

The two men pushed them to the floor roughly and bound them hand and foot. The ropes were tight about his ankles and his arms. Merry winced as the other man pulled at her restraints.

'Be careful,' Charlie growled. He wanted to tear the man apart for that wince. 'My men will come looking for me,' he warned. 'My coachman is standing out in the street. He will wonder what has happened to us.'

Jane looked thoughtful. 'He's right.' She pointed to one of the men. 'Go give the coachman a message from his lordship, here. Tell him they've decided to spend the afternoon at the inn and he's to come back for them after dinner.' She fumbled in Charlie's coat and pulled forth his purse. She fished around and found a half-crown. 'Give him this. Tell him mum's the word. He'll know. The servants all know what the two of them are like.'

Merry gasped.

'Servants talk, Miss Draycott.' Jane curled her lip. 'They

say what they think when they know you're not listening. They know his lordship's had you in his bed and they won't be a bit surprised to hear he stopped off to dance a blanket hornpipe after an absence. You always were a slut.'

'You are a nasty piece of work, Jane Harper,' Merry said.

'Blindfold and gag them,' Jane said. 'Take them down through the cellar until tonight. Just make sure no one sees you. Be careful with the girl—he wants her in one piece until he deals with her himself.'

Charlie's blood ran cold. 'If you value your life, you won't do this.'

Jane grinned.

The man closest uncocked the pistol in his hand and raised it by the barrel.

Merry's eyes widened. 'No!'

The sharp blow to Charlie's head sparked stars behind his eyes. Darkness descended.

Merry screamed. One of the men heaved Charlie up on his shoulder with a grunt. 'Bloody heavy, he is,' he said, looking at Jane.

She waved him away. 'Get on.'

The other man approached Merry. 'You don't have to knock me out,' she said.

He looked at Jane.

'We don't want her hurt,' she said. 'A blindfold and a gag will do, if she doesn't struggle. Then cover her with a sheet.' The blindfold came first, followed by a rough cloth shoved in her mouth.

The man hoisted her over his shoulder like a sack of coal. His shoulder ground into her stomach, making it hard to breathe. She held still.

The journey to the cellar being carried like a bag of washing was something of a nightmare. When Merry was carried outside, she began to worry. They weren't out there long. The smell led her to think they had entered a barn. After another set of stairs, they seemed to turn in circles and the direction became muddy in her mind.

She was dumped on a cold damp floor. Her ribs felt bruised from the rough handling, but at least she could catch her breath. She inhaled the stink of stale beer, mould and rodents. They must be underground. She shivered.

The men walked away, leaving them alone in this horrid place. But why? What had she done?

Jane had let slip the word 'he', so she hadn't acted alone. Did it mean Caro was not involved? Lord, what did it matter? The situation was hopeless, whoever it was. One thing she was sure of. Charlie was not part of the plot.

And the man who was involved was coming tonight. One of the mill owners? Grandfather's friend? One of her employees? Bile rose in her throat. The gag tightened. She swallowed hard. A hollowness filled her chest. Stupid tears burned the backs of her eyes.

Dash it, she would not cry. Despair would not help them escape and she feared if she was here when the *he* arrived, things would go very badly indeed.

She couldn't see a thing through her blindfold, and her hands were going numb, but she could hear Charlie's breathing. A harsh rough sound through his nose. At least they hadn't killed him when they hit him.

She lay still in the dark, listening. He was panting as if he'd run a mile and making the same kind of noises she'd heard him make in his nightmare. Sounds of terror.

Was he conscious?

She wriggled backwards, towards the sound. 'Charlie,'

she mumbled. It sounded more like 'Uhhhn uhhhn', but his breathing slowed as if he was listening.

He groaned when her legs touched him and flinched away. She tried again, slowly running her bound feet up and down some part of his body. His legs, she thought.

He inhaled a deep noisy breath and shifted closer. Something touched her arm. He was trembling. Shaking as if he had the ague.

'Mmmmm?' she mumbled.

His breathing picked up speed again like a startled horse. The sound of panic.

How could he be so afraid? What did he know? Her heart raced. Her breathing shortened.

No. There was nothing to be afraid of. Not yet anyway. No sense in getting into a lather until they knew what they were dealing with, as Grandfather used to say. 'Stop it,' she snarled, furious he couldn't understand the stupid sounds coming from her throat.

He stopped breathing.

Damn. What was the matter with him? Was he afraid of the dark? Was that why he left the candles burning all night? A grown man fearful of his dreams? Dreams like the one he'd had the other night?

When she used to be afraid at night after her parents died, Grandfather used to sing her to sleep. It took her mind off all she'd lost. It had always felt comforting.

She started humming an old lullaby.

He drew closer, touching her down her length. She felt him relax. She hummed 'Lavender's Blue', then 'Sweet Lass of Richmond Hill'. He joined in, his deep hum echoing off the walls. They sounded more like a church choir than a couple of terrified prisoners.

After a while her dry throat gave out. 'Sorry,' she said. He rubbed his forehead against her shoulder blades in acceptance. He wasn't shaking any more and his breathing had slowed.

They lay still, bodies touching, for a long time.

Then he moved, pressing his knees into the small of her back.

'Uhhn?' she said.

'Uh,' he said. It sounded like a command.

How was she supposed to know what he wanted?

He pushed her leg with the toe of his boot.

'Uh?' she asked.

He pushed her again. Harder. Why was he kicking her? He had boots on. The same boots he'd worn when he cut her traces and when they were attacked. The boots where he hid a knife.

'Ooooh,' she said.

He made a sound like a chuckle followed by 'ugh ugh'. That had to be *good girl*. Had to be.

She wriggled until her bound hands found the tops of his boots. He pushed one at her, so she concentrated on it. Found the hilt of the knife with her fingertips. After much grunting and muffled cursing she managed to pull it clear.

'Now what?'

He seemed to understand because she felt him move away, then he was hard up against her again, his fingers feeling her sleeve. Back to back. Oh God, he was going to try to cut the ropes against the blade. His fingers passed over her hand and she felt the blade shift.

'Careful.' Oh, this stupid noise coming out of her mouth was so annoying.

'O I,' he said.

Hold still.

'Mmmm,' she agreed.

She gripped the hilt hard in her palms and prayed she

wouldn't drop it. The pressure of him sawing back and forth made it so difficult to hold the knife. She hoped he was cutting hemp and not flesh. She swallowed at the stomach-wrenching thought.

After what seemed like an age, the pressure stopped. He scuffled around beside her.

He stilled.

Footsteps. They were too late. Someone was coming. She heard him move again. His breathing becoming rapid. Oh, no, don't say he was going to start panicking again.

'Mmmm,' she said.

'Mmmm, mmmm,' he murmured softly. He didn't sound upset. Then what was he doing?

Light pierced the blindfold. She turned her head in its direction.

'Dear God,' a well-educated voice said in horrified tones. 'Do you know who you've got there?'

Merry strained to hear something familiar in the voice, but the echoing chamber distorted it. Oh, well, she would see who it was soon enough, when they set her free. And then he'd get a piece of her mind and some besides.

'Naught we could do, your lordship.' Jane. 'They came looking for me. They know who we are.'

A lord? What lord?

Some whispered mutters. Merry held her breath, waiting for Charlie's signal.

'That's no good,' Jane said, sounding furious. 'He's seen us. You have to do away with them. Today. Now.'

'You people are idiots. Kill Tonbridge and the world will be looking for you. Let them go as soon as I am clear,' the new man said in a harsh whisper. 'I'll deal with her later.'

Merry shivered. If only she could recognise his voice, but

the echoes and the whispering made it impossible. He had recogised Charlie at a glance, though.

The muttered voices drew further away. Footsteps drowning out their words. They were leaving.

And Charlie, beside her, was moving. He took hold of her wrist and began sawing at the ropes.

No, someone was coming back. A light hurried step. Had Jane returned to set them free?

'Mmmm,' Merry said. Charlie must have heard, too, because he stopped cutting at her ropes.

Liquid splashing on the floor. The smell of brandy hit the back of her throat.

'Mmmmm,' she said.

He kicked her foot. She lay still.

'Bloody coward,' Jane said. 'He'd see us all hang. But not me. 'Tis bad enough she caused the death of my brother.' The voice receded. Then the sound of a striking flint, followed by a woof of rushing air. And heat.

'Hey,' Merry yelled through her gag.

'That'll teach you,' Jane yelled and then she was gone, running after the others.

And Charlie's hands were on her ropes, cutting frantically, then pulling at her blindfold.

Merry blinked at the dazzle of flames. Jane had set a fire. It licked up the side of a barrel. They were surrounded by barrels on racks. The flames ran like rivers along the liquid Jane had poured. Fumes filled Merry's head and made her feel dizzy.

'Come on,' Charlie said, working on the ropes at her feet. 'We have to get out of here.' He freed his own ankles and pulled her up.

Pain. Hands, feet, legs—all prickled with the rush of blood. She rubbed at her wrists.

Charlie grabbed her hand and they headed for the doorway. Flames curled up around the doorposts.

They broke into a run.

With a crack and a rumble, the rack nearest the door collapsed. Barrels rolled off it to the floor. One, maybe more than one, split open. Flames roared up to the ceiling.

Heat. Merry put her arm up, to protect her face. 'We are trapped.' There was no way out.

'This way,' Charlie shouted.

He ran to the racks on the other side of the cellar. He put his shoulder to it.

She ran to help. 'What are you doing?' She pushed at the wooden structure and felt it move.

'I think there's another way out,' he said, heaving with a grin that looked demonic in the blaze of flames. With the place lit up like Guy Fawkes's night, he looked positively happy. She wanted to strangle him.

'Come on, Merry, together. Heave.'

She pushed with all her might. It shifted a little. She was sure it moved. The flames were spreading to their side of the cellar.

'Again,' he panted.

She put her shoulder beside his and grasped the wood frame.

'Heave,' he said.

The rack rolled, picked up speed, slid away from the wall.

A gaping black hole. A tunnel. A draught of sweet fresh air fanned the flames behind them. Shadows danced on the wooden ceiling.

'Come on. Before those explode.' Charlie grabbed her hand.

Explode made her legs work really well.

They ran for their lives, only stopping to catch their breath when they could no longer feel the heat of the fire, or hear its horrid roar.

She put her hands on her knees and bent over, gasping for air. 'She meant to burn us alive.' The horror of it made her want to throw up.

Charlie put an arm around her shoulders. 'It's all right. You are safe. I remembered this when we were singing; my brain started working instead of panicking. Robert and I found a smuggler's tunnel in the riverbank years ago. It led to a barn. This barn.'

'Thank God you remembered.'

Her mind froze, refusing to think about what would have happened if he had not.

He took her hand. 'The tunnel comes out below the mill. Smugglers row the contraband upstream and bring it this way to the inn. If you don't mind, I'd rather like to get out of here.'

Merry glanced back down the tunnel at the distant glow of flames. 'The innkeeper is going to be very upset about losing his wares.'

'If I find out he is part of this, he'll lose more than contraband brandy. And if he isn't, Father will be furious. He's one of his best customers.'

Merry giggled. Then started to laugh. She couldn't stop. It just sounded so ridiculously funny.

Still laughing, she let Charlie drag her along by one hand, using the other to guide himself along the wall. Walking this time, thank goodness. If she tried to run, she'd fall down.

The exit appeared as a small circle of grey and grew swiftly. A few moments later they were standing in snow in the gathering dusk. Never had Merry been so happy to see snow. Luckily the tunnel did not end in the river, but in the bank a few feet above water level.

She heaved a sigh of relief as they climbed up beside the mill.

'Nothing,' he said, striking his fist in his hand. 'All that for nothing.' There were soot streaks on his face. His face was grim, his eyes dark. 'No Jane and now this other man. This lord.'

She winced. 'I suppose you didn't recognise his voice.'

Thin-lipped, he shook his head. 'No. We go back to Durn.'

'Shouldn't we find the constable? Tell him what happened? Start a hue and cry for Jane?'

'You forget the man who set all this in train.'

'We don't know who he is. Catch Jane and we can catch him, too.'

'In the meantime, he is still at large and you are in danger. You heard him. He planned to deal with you some other way, and when Jane learns you did not die in the fire, she will come after you again. I can't take that risk.'

Across the field, a pillar of smoke was beginning to rise. 'Everyone will be too busy with the fire to look for our criminals for a while,' he said. 'And I will not be sure you are safe until we are inside Durn's walls.'

'But—'

'I mean it, Merry. I'll put you over my shoulder and carry you all the way home if you won't come willingly.'

Exhausted, she let him lead her along.

'Bully,' she muttered, but never in her life had she felt so protected as she was leaning on Charlie's steady arm.

They met the carriage returning for them just beyond the mill. To his coachman's obvious shock, Charlie refused to help the people trying to put out the fire and insisted on speeding back to Durn. His servants would think him heartless. Hopefully, he would be able to set their minds at rest at a later date. Given the amount of brandy burning there was no saving the barn, but no lives would be lost, since he and Merry had got out.

He'd almost got them both killed by charging after Merry. Always impetuous. His commanding officer had said so and his father had said so. It seemed he had learned nothing by his experience in the army.

The thought of Merry burning in the fire sent cold chills down his spine every time his mind wandered back to the scene in the bowels of the earth. Hell could not have looked worse.

The carriage halted outside the front door of Durn.

Charlie looked at the glower on his coachman's face. 'Take some men, return to the village and see if you can help,' he said. 'But say nothing about picking up Miss Draycott and me on the road, if you please. Also remind those at the gate of my orders. No one other than members of the household are to be admitted tonight without my express permission.'

The man gave him a look that said he thought Charlie touched in the head, tugged his forelock and set his team in motion.

Charlie guided Merry up the steps. She'd sat with her eyes tight shut all the way home. He'd been glad of her silence. There had been too much going on in his head for sensible conversation.

Logan opened the door. For once his expression showed shock. 'Has there been an accident?'

'Oh, no,' Merry said, before Charlie could speak. 'It was all quite deliberate. If you'll excuse me, I would like to see Mrs Falkner.'

'Perhaps you will scare her, appearing covered in soot.'

Merry narrowed her eyes. 'Perhaps she will be shocked if I appear at all.'

She headed for the stairs.

Charlie caught her halfway up the staircase. 'All this time you have defended her. What makes you suspect her now?'

She looked on the edge of breaking. Tears stood in her blue eyes. The tears of betrayal, and fear and pain. He wanted to hold her close and comfort her. When he tried to put his arms around her, she pushed him away.

'She brought Jane into my home. She insisted she stay when I said I didn't like her. And she is so damned secretive. She is the person who will benefit by my death.' Her voice broke. She covered her face with her hand. 'I can't really believe it but I just don't know any more.'

So this was why she'd been so quiet in the carriage, brooding about her friend. Damn it, he should have asked her what was wrong. She'd been so brave up to now, so courageous—he couldn't bear to see her so utterly lost.

'If you confront her and she denies it, how will you know if she is telling you the truth?'

She swallowed, blinking back the moisture before it spilled. He wanted to hold her close but feared too much sympathy and her spirit would break entirely. 'Would it help you to know I am starting to doubt her involvement?'

'You are?'

'I believe our man in the cellar is behind it all. And Jane was acting out of revenge. You heard her speak of her brother.' He frowned. 'Have there been any accidents at your mill? Lives lost?'

She gazed up at him. 'None. I swear it. Grandfather ran the safest mill in Yorkshire and I have kept to that standard.

There have been a few accidents, but nothing fatal. And all victims well compensated, I swear.'

'And I believe you.' He kissed the tip of her nose. 'You are covered in soot and dirt. You are cold, you are tired and these things are playing on your mind. Questioning Mrs Falkner can wait.'

'It can't. I have to hear it from her lips. Will you come with me?'

He sighed. He'd learned that if Merry Draycott made a decision, he might as well go along with it, because she was stubborn and determined and rarely took no for an answer. 'If that is your wish.' They walked up the stairs together. 'First, though, we wash and change. Quite honestly I can't stand the smell. I don't think I'll ever be able to drink brandy again.'

She managed a small chuckle.

When Beth met them at the door to the nursery, Merry was feeling a little less shaken.

'How is Mrs Falkner?' Merry asked. All her old fears about fevers and sickness that she'd had since her parents' deaths pressed down on her. She pushed them away. She needed to look into Caro's eyes when she asked her questions.

'Better, miss. Sitting up, giving orders.' Beth grinned.

With Charlie behind her, Merry crept into the dimly lit room. The flush of fever lay on Caro's cheeks and her eyes were unnaturally bright.

'What are you doing here?' she croaked.

'Nice welcome,' Merry said, surging forwards, forcing the dry panic in her throat down with a quick swallow. 'How are you?'

'Better.' Caro smiled. 'Poor Tommy has been worried, but Beth has been a wonderful nurse.' She glanced at the girl with a fond smile. Beth bobbed and left. 'I will be up and about in a day or so.'

'Thank goodness.'

'You look pale,' Caro said. 'You should not be here. We do not want you taking ill, too.' She gestured to Charlie, who had remained in the doorway.

'We need to talk to you. Whoever attacked us at Draycott House has followed us here to Durn,' Merry said.

Caro's blue eyes widened; she paled beneath her flush. 'What happened? Are you hurt?'

Merry took her hand, felt the dampness and the heat. 'I am fine, Caro. But I must ask you some questions, if you would agree?'

A shuttered expression passed over Caro's face. It always did whenever anyone questioned her. Merry clenched her hands, trying to believe her friend had nothing to do with what was happening.

'We wanted to ask you about Jane, Mrs Falkner.' Charlie's deep voice was gentle. 'How did she come to be in your company?'

Caro swallowed.

'Would you like water?' Merry asked.

Caro nodded and sipped from the glass Merry held to her lips.

She pulled her shawl tighter around her shoulders. 'She arrived at the house in Skepton two days before the fire. She said she had heard it was a refuge and begged admittance.'

'You had never met her before?' Charlie pressed, stepping closer to the bed.

Merry watched Caro's face, looking for anything—guilt, fear.

Caro looked Merry straight in the eyes. 'Never. Nor had the other girls.' She pressed the back of her hand to her forehead.

'Are you saying Jane has something to do with this? Wretched woman. I wish I had never set eyes on her.'

'We were captured by Jane and some men, one of whom spoke like a gentleman,' Merry said.

Caro gasped and looked horrified. 'Captured? What do you mean captured?'

A wave of relief washed over Merry. She knew people. She'd studied them. Caro was genuinely shocked and concerned. Merry turned her gaze to Charlie. His expression was unreadable, his eyes shadowed.

Caro stared at him. 'You think I—?' Her voice broke. Her eyes swam with tears. 'I had something to do with this?'

Merry picked up the water, but Caro waved it away. She struggled upright in the bed. 'If you believe such a thing, I must leave.'

'I don't believe it,' Merry said, feeling her own throat become thick and damp. She sniffed. 'Not for a minute.' Well, it was only a small white lie. She gazed up at Charlie. 'And nor does his lordship.'

'Not any longer,' he said abruptly, as if he'd finally made up his mind. 'I keep thinking I had heard the man's voice before, though. Did you recognise him at all, Merry?'

Merry thought back to the dank cellar, to the few words she'd heard, before the conversation became muffled.

She shrugged. 'He sounded like a toff. And he knew you right away.'

Caro frowned at Charlie. 'A friend of yours?' She tilted her head. 'An odd coincidence. Was it also merely chance you found her on the road, my lord?'

Charlie's lip curled. 'Nice try, Mrs Falkner.'

'Stop it, both of you,' Merry said. She stared at the counterpane, a gorgeously embroidered work of art. She ran her fingers over the threads, tracing the outline of entwined roses.

'We know Jane is involved. If we find her, we will find our answer.'

'I don't agree,' Charlie said. 'I think it is the man we need to find. He was clearly in charge.'

'But Jane will surely lead us to him. Or her accomplices will. They would probably betray their mother for a guinea or two. I know their type.'

'I don't doubt you are right on that score,' Charlie said. He looked down at Caro. 'I am sorry if I was overly harsh, Mrs Falkner. My concern is for Merry.'

Caro looked at him for a moment. One of her all-too-rare sweet smiles curved her lips. 'Mine too, your lordship. I apologise for voicing my suspicions also.'

He grinned at her. 'We will leave you to rest. Come, Merry, you are exhausted. We will decide our next step in the morning.'

There he went, ordering her about again. But it had been a gruelling day and her head felt filled with thick wool; she could do nothing more than take his arm.

Aware of Merry sleeping in her chamber upstairs, Charlie paced his study. He would not go to her. She needed her rest.

God, she'd seen him naked, his very soul exposed, and she'd been wonderful. Calm, courageous and kind. Unbelievably, the sound of her voice in that cellar had held his dark visions at bay.

He'd found a light in the darkness and now duty required he let her go.

Earlier today he'd proposed they marry, out of a sense of frustration, but then when he thought she might say yes he'd felt an unexpected flood of joy. Until she turned him down.

Why shouldn't he be happy? Like Robert. Nothing Father

could do would harm Robert any more. He had married an heiress.

What harm would it do if he also married where he willed? Where he—God was he even thinking this?—where he... loved.

Was love this strange restlessness inside him, this need to meld with Merry, to be as one? Or was this just him again trying to escape? Had he lost any sense of himself, who he was, what he owed his position, his father, the men who had died because of him? Had sleepless nights and guilt finally taken their toll?

It seemed more than likely, given that men in his position did not marry for love. They married for political reasons. For reasons of power and increased status. To acquire a suitable hostess. And to beget heirs.

They married women like Allison Purtefoy because the arbiters of his world said women like Merry weren't good enough.

They were wrong. So bloody wrong.

Merry was worth twice most of the females of his acquaintance and three times the vapid Lady Allison. He pressed his fingers to his aching temples in an attempt to ease the residual headache from the blow to his skull.

Only Merry had no interest in marrying him. She'd made that perfectly clear.

He rubbed at the pain in his chest.

She was right not to want him. He was little more than a shell since Waterloo, going through the motions, clinging to his duty to stop himself from tipping into darkness.

Which meant he had no right to hold Merry to their promised betrothal. The only thing he could do for her was rid her of whoever was trying to harm her. He'd at least have the satisfaction of knowing she was safe.

Damn it. All that torture in that bloody black cellar and he'd walked away with nothing. He put his glass down on the table.

The man who had come to their prison beneath the barn had spoken with power and authority. He was a far more dangerous opponent than Jane Harper. Merry was right, though, the woman was the key. And he needed to find her quickly.

He rang the bell.

While he waited for Logan, he went to the pigeonholes at one end of his bookshelf and pulled out a map. He spread it flat on his desk. He stared at the map of the moors and villages around Durn. 'Where are you hiding, Jane Harper?' he muttered.

'My lord?' The butler looked as if he'd dressed hurriedly.

'I'm sorry to disturb your rest,' Charlie said. 'I have need of men tonight. Grooms, footmen, anyone you think useful in a brawl.'

Horror filled the butler's eyes, though he clearly tried not to look as if he thought his master had run mad. 'Yes, my lord.'

'Have them meet me in the gunroom in half an hour.'

'Right away, my lord.'

Poor Logan, he might never be the same again.

He stared at the map. He'd start at the inn. There might be tracks in the snow. If he found nothing there, he would visit every farmhouse and hovel within ten miles. There was nowhere she could hide.

At the inn, the smell of smoke hung in the cold night air, oppressive and choking. While his men waited outside, Charlie spoke to a very disgruntled landlord. Not only had he lost his stores, his guest had disappeared, leaving behind her belongings and her unpaid shot. 'You have no idea where she went?'

The man glowered from beneath his nightcap. 'She ain't been seen since yesterday afternoon. Her and the bully boys she had with her ran off and left me trying to save my barn. Not a hair of 'em have I seen. They must have done it. I'm ruined.'

Charlie felt a twinge of guilt. He'd have to do something to help the fellow. But not now. 'I will inspect her chamber, if you please.'

'Help yourself, my lord. An' if you finds her, you leave her to me.'

'The magistrate will deal with her.' Charlie ran up the stairs to the room from which he'd been so rudely carted that afternoon. The smell of smoke seemed worse up here than it had below.

He rifled through her meagre belongings. Her valise contained a few clothes and some old yellowed letters tied in a ribbon. Love letters? It seemed odd that she'd left without such personal items. Very odd.

He lifted the mattress. Nothing. The pillows. He opened the drawer of a small roll-top desk. Among her handkerchiefs, he found a note in a bold hand. Dated two days ago, it set up a meeting at an abandoned cottage a short distance outside of the village. No signature.

The mystery man? Perhaps he'd find the pair of them at this cottage? He stuffed the correspondence in his pocket in case it gave some clues as to where she might have gone if the cottage proved a dead end and headed down to his men.

The ride took mere minutes. The cottage was dark and silent. He huffed out a breath, the fog of cold drifting away on a breeze. 'I'll take a look,' he said to the head groom, Fred, who had leaped at the idea of a nightly adventure. 'If anything happens, ride for the magistrate.' He dismounted.

The man drew a pistol from the holster in his saddle and climbed down. 'I'll come with you.'

Charlie tried the door. It swung open. Sprawled on the floor in a patch of moonlight from the window, a bullet hole in the middle of her forehead, lay Jane Harper. The stink of death hit him in the face. A too-familiar odour. His gut churned. Images rushed into his mind. Darkness edged his vision. He fought down the panic. 'Hold the torch higher,' he growled at the man at his back.

'Dear God,' his groom said, looking over his shoulder. 'What sort of fiend would dispose of a woman in cold blood that way?'

It had been a long time since Charlie had seen a dead body, but he had no trouble recognising its lack of life. Bile rose in his throat. He swallowed. 'Someone who feared discovery. Someone she trusted.'

He was no closer to discovering who that someone was than he had been yesterday. In fact, now Jane was dead, perhaps further away.

After a cursory glance around the cottage, he and Fred returned to the waiting men.

'Fetch the constable and the magistrate,' he said to Fred. 'Take a couple of men with you. I'll search around here to see if we can find anything to tell us who might have done this.'

Fred grabbed his horse, picked two of the four men they'd brought and set off for the village.

'You two can help me search for tracks,' Charlie said to the others. 'You in that direction, you over there. I'll take the centre. If you see anything, call out and lift your torch high so we can find you.'

The men nodded their understanding and fanned out.

Charlie swung his torch in an arc around him after each step. He'd gone about five yards when one of the other men sang out, 'Found something.'

Charlie retraced his own footprints back to the cottage, then followed the footprints of the man signalling. The other man followed suit.

'What have you got?' Charlie asked. The man, another groom, pointed. 'Someone tied a horse here earlier this evening.'

Hoof-flattened snow and a pile of dung. Whoever had tied his horse here had not stayed long. The man pointed to boot prints leading away from the horse. 'He must have circled around and taken her by surprise.' The boot prints could have been anyone's. The horse was large. That was all Charlie could tell.

'Damn it,' he said. 'Not a thing to say who the murderer might be.' And Charlie would have to explain to the magistrate exactly why he was prowling around in the middle of the night and had just happened on the grisly scene.

He also had to decide what to tell Merry.

It was ten in the morning when he handed a distinctly disgruntled Logan his greatcoat. 'Miss Draycott is in the breakfast room,' the butler said with a slight curl to his lip.

Charlie ignored the butler's tantrum. He'd get over it. 'Wondering where I am, no doubt.'

Logan bowed. 'I wouldn't know, my lord.'

He was starving. He flung open the door and caught Merry tucking into ham and eggs.

The smile on her lips drove all thought from his mind. He wanted to hold her close, kiss her lovely lips, nuzzle against the column of her throat.

'You were up early?' she said.

He picked up a plate and helped himself to some ham and a couple of coddled eggs. He sat down beside her. 'I couldn't sleep.'

A soft smile curved her lips. Sympathy. No doubt she thought him in need of comfort. A weak puling creature. A chilling thought. 'I had to find Jane.'

She frowned. 'Are you saying—'

'I went looking for her.'

'Alone? Are you mad? Why didn't you wake me?'

'Not alone. I took some of my men. We found her.'

'You did?' Her voice rose in excitement. 'What did she say?'

'She's dead.'

The pallor in her face grew worse. 'No,' she whispered. 'You can't—'

'Blast it, Merry. What do you think I am? I didn't kill her. She was dead when we found her.' He spoke more harshly than he intended.

'I...I'm sorry.' She bit her lip. 'So we have no way of knowing who employed her?'

'None at all. The men with her have disappeared. Likely left the county if they've any sense.' He pulled the letters from his pocket. 'We found these at the inn. Letters from a brother, forced to leave England from the sound of it, and instructions for a meeting, presumably from our mysterious man. But no clue as to his identity. I went back to her room at the inn to make sure.'

She picked up one of the letters. 'It seems rude to pry, but perhaps there is some clue as to her identity. Perhaps a family who should be informed.' She winced.

'There is an address in Cumberland.'

Merry's hand stilled. 'Cumberland?'

He nodded.

'It can't be.' Her hand shook as she unfolded the letter.

'What can't be?'

She scanned the note, stopping when her gaze reached the signature. She picked up the next one and the next and with each reading her face held more and more pain.

She let the last one fall to the table. Charlie covered her limp hand with his. It felt cold. Freezing. He picked it up and held it within his palms. 'What is it, Merry? Do you know something of this woman?'

She turned her gaze to meet his and he had never seen her look so devastated, not even the first time she'd realised someone wanted her death.

'She was Jeremy's sister.'

'Jeremy?' A cold fist clenched in his chest.

'A gardener's boy from school.' Her voice choked with tears.

'Merry.' He put an arm around her shoulders, but she shrugged him off. Rose to her feet and strode to the window.

He wanted to go to her. He wanted to hold her close, but something held him back, as if a shadow stood between them. The shadow of this man Jeremy.

He hadn't read the letters, just the address. He'd been focused on the note from the man to whom Jane had reported.

'I never meant him any harm,' she whispered to the glass.

'What are you talking about?'

She turned and gestured to the letters. 'We were close. At school. There was a scandal.'

Charlie winced, his imagination running riot and a sudden surge of anger making him hot. Jealousy. How could he be jealous of something that happened so long ago?

'It seems Grandfather had him shipped off to the West

Indies.' She covered her mouth with her palm, her eyes wide and moist. She blinked a couple of times and, removing her hand, took a shaky breath.

'He hated it, according to those letters, but he repeats over and over to Jane not to hold a grudge against the Draycotts. He meant me. Jane must have railed about me in her replies.'

She wrapped her arms around her waist. 'The last one is started by him and finished in another hand. He died from a fever. By the date, he can have been no more than twenty.' She lifted her sorrowful face, her eyes focused in the past. 'So far from his home and his family,' she whispered. 'No wonder Jane wanted me dead.' She bowed her head and covered her face with her hands. 'I didn't know.' Her muffled voice was full of tears. 'Grandfather never told me. I kept wondering why Jeremy never wrote to me. I even wrote to the school once asking for news. They never answered.'

He felt sick, not for himself, but for her, for the sorrow he saw on her face. Was this why she'd never married? She'd been waiting for this man to return? 'You loved him.' The thought was a blow to his kidneys.

She uncovered her face and there were tears on her cheeks. He'd never seen her cry. 'Passionately.' She choked down a sob. 'As young people do. I wondered over and over why he never tried to contact me. And now there is nothing I can do.'

Her shoulders sagged. She stared at the letters as if seeing the boy she'd loved.

Charlie strode to her side and put his arm around her shoulders. He inhaled the lavender fragrance in her hair and ignored the anger at her grandfather for keeping her in the dark and Jane for wanting revenge. 'We can find out who killed his sister. Who used her against you. We can do that much.'

She leaned into him, and he held her gently against his chest, lightly in case she would break. Slowly the tension eased from her body. Her warmth felt good in his arms. He wanted to keep her there forever.

She raised her face. 'Thank you.'

He bent to kiss her lips. Something wrenched in his chest. Loss. But you couldn't lose what you never had. 'Come sit down. You look exhausted. Worn to the bone.'

She managed a shaky laugh. 'Thank you for the compliment.'

'Eee, lass,' he said softly. 'Would you have me lie to your face?'

Her eyes shone with tears, but her smile was sweet. 'No. That I would not.'

'Come then, drink some tea. We will find this man, I promise.'

Logan entered with a silver tray.

Charlie frowned at him.

'I'm sorry to disturb you, my lord, but a reply by return is requested.'

Charlie took the note. 'From Purtefoy,' he said glancing at Merry.

Her mouth tightened.

He broke the seal. 'He's apologising for his sister's lack of courtesy and requesting that the family be permitted to show their pleasure at our betrothal at the ball. He begs our attendance.'

'Really? When they know my chaperon is laid low? It will be yet another opportunity to prove my lack of breeding.'

'Show them they are wrong.'

'By playing off our sham on members of society? We must not continue this pretence.'

His gut rolled. Unfortunately, she made perfect sense, but... He glanced down at the note. 'Everyone in the county will be present.'

'Precisely.'

'Including perhaps the blackguard from the cellar.'

Her eyes widened. 'Of course. Why didn't I think of it?'

'I might recognise his voice.'

'All right, we will go.'

The sudden about-face made the hairs on his nape tickle. 'I can manage alone.'

'What, and speak to every male guest? Also you might need my confirmation, once you think you have found him.'

There was excitement behind her reasoned words. He raised a brow. 'He...he may try again. Give himself away,' Merry continued.

'Are you suggesting I use you as bait?' His back stiffened. Outrage. He would never knowingly endanger a woman. He'd led enough people to their deaths. 'Certainly not. The man is dangerous.'

'And he will continue to be dangerous until he is caught. This time, we will be the hunters.'

A cold chill ran across his shoulders. 'As well as the hunted. No, Merry. I will not allow it.'

She rose to her feet and he followed suit. 'What can he do in a ballroom full of people? As long as we stay together, a loving couple besotted with each other, nothing can happen.'

'I will not put your life in danger again.'

'Then I will go alone.'

'You forget, your chaperon is indisposed.'

A gleam of triumph lit her eyes. 'I do not need a chaperon to visit family.'

He tipped her chin and gazed down into her defiant eyes. 'Miss Draycott, you truly are the most infuriating female it has ever been my misfortune to meet.'

'Because you know I am right.'

'I really think it is better if I go alone,' he said into her hair, knowing full well her answer.

'I'm going with you.'

'Then we must take great care. I'll send a note to my soldier friend.'

'And I will enlist Caro's help with my gown. I think it a little *risqué*.'

'Never.'

She grinned, but there was a touch of sadness in her eyes. 'Still, I would not wish to disgrace you.' She got up and strode to the door. She turned back. 'For what time are we invited?'

'Eight of the clock. It will take at least an hour to get there.'

She nodded. 'I will be ready.'

So would he. Forewarned was forearmed in more ways than one.

As the carriage drove up the drive to the Chepstow country seat, Caro's admonition rang in Merry's ears. *Trust no one.* She trusted Charlie. With her life. She leaned against his broad shoulder in the dark of the carriage and he pulled her comfortingly close. Her heart, that stupid organ, squeezed painfully. Because this was a bit like Cinderella's ball, but this time there would be no happy ending. No prince on her doorstep. He would go back to his life and she to hers.

It was the only possible outcome. Neither would be happy in the other's world.

The carriage halted and a footman opened the door. Once again snow threatened. She could smell it in the air. Any sensible Yorkshire person would remain home on a night like tonight. It seemed being sensible was incompatible with being a member of the nobility. They only cared about entertainment.

She pulled her fur-lined cloak around her, stepped out of the carriage and looked up at the sprawling red-brick Tudor mansion.

'Looks like quite a party,' Charlie said, taking her arm. Every window blazed into the night and carriages lined the driveway.

'It does.'

An elderly butler opened the door and took their outer raiment.

'Welcome.' In the entrance hall, all black-and-white tile and medieval beams, Digby looked very much the viscount. He smiled in lordly greeting. 'Merry, you look lovely. Good to see you, Tonbridge.'

The bonhomie felt forced, but at least the man was making an effort. Her cousin Allison likely would turn up her nose.

'Through there to the ballroom,' Digby said. 'You'll find Allison in there somewhere. You've never been here before, have you, cousin?'

Merry shook her head. 'No, indeed. Are your mother and father here?'

'No, Father stayed in town for the holidays and Mother is visiting relatives.'

'While the cat's away, mmm?' Charlie said cheerfully, peering into a ballroom filled to capacity with every conceivable member of Yorkshire aristocracy. Feathers bobbed, diamonds winked and perfume thickened the air.

Her cousin laughed. A little too heartily, Merry thought. 'No, no. We always host a ball at this time every year.'

'And Merry was never invited?' Charlie's tone sounded just a little dangerous.

'Glad not to be,' Merry said quickly. 'All these nobs. I've nowt to say.'

Digby winced. Charlie touched her ankle with his toe. A

be-good admonition. She remembered her promise not to put him to shame with a flicker of resentment, but she didn't really blame him for wanting her to behave like a lady, not when she was supposed to be his betrothed.

'Shall I take you around?' Digby said. 'Introduce you?'

'I pretty well know everyone,' Charlie said. 'Don't worry about us. We will be fine.'

'All right. It will soon be time to start the dancing, and I still have guests to greet.' He hurried off.

Charlie placed her hand on his arm and walked over to the nearest group. 'Lord Tonbridge,' a pretty blonde lady in a gown of pink crepe, hemmed with enormous twining roses, cried. 'I heard you might attend.'

'Allow me to introduce my fiancée, Miss Merry Draycott,' he said, pulling her forwards. 'Merry, this is Lady Argyle.'

Merry curtsied.

Lady Argyle ran her gaze from Merry's head to her heels and, seeming to approve, introduced her to the rest of the party. It seemed that Tonbridge gave her an entry where none would have been possible before.

Wouldn't they be surprised when they learned the engagement was off? Perhaps even insulted. Her heart sank a little.

Soon they were moving from one group to another, Merry being introduced and conversations rippling around them. She did not feel quite as out of place as she expected. Many of these people were pleasant, and were anxious to talk about the manufacture of cloth. Many of them depended on it for their livelihoods. While she and Charlie conversed, she strained her ears to hear that one voice.

When the dancing began, not only did they have to listen to male voices through the general chatter, they now had to contend with the music. Not once did she hear a man she recogised as being the one in the cellar; judging from Charlie's air of frustration, nor had he.

'Perhaps he wasn't invited,' she murmured as they strolled around the dance floor, looking for people they'd not yet spoken with.

His lips thinned. 'Perhaps he disguised his voice.'

'Then him taking the bait might be our best chance after all.'

He didn't look any happier.

The orchestra announced a waltz. 'Dance with me,' Charlie said.

'How do you know I can dance?' she said, smiling up at him.

His eyes crinkled at the corners and gleamed wickedly. 'A man canny enough to send you to the most exclusive girls' academy in England is hardly likely to neglect the rest of your education.'

'*Touché.*'

He swept her into his arms and they circled the floor in fine style. He was the best dancer she'd ever encountered, including her teacher.

'I see you had lessons too,' she said.

'Required curriculum for ducal heirs.'

'And also for rakes.'

'Who are you calling a rake?'

She smiled. He looked charmingly boyish. You would never know he was trying to catch a murderer.

Beneath the air of sophistication, beneath his cool reserve, resided a man with a very good heart. If only she had been of his world, things might have been different, but she wasn't. The ache in her chest for what could not be made no sense, so she smiled as he whirled her around.

She relaxed in his arms, living the dream of being his fiancée for one more night.

And when he smiled down at her, the gold burst around his pupils as bright as a guinea, she could almost believe it would last forever.

But it didn't.

The orchestra played the final notes and, looking down into her face, Charlie slowly released her. Was it regret she saw in his gaze, sorrow in the slight tightening around his lips, or was it all wishful thinking?

She gave him a bright smile. 'That was grand.'

He smiled. 'Thank you. You dance like an angel.'

'More like a baby elephant.' They laughed and linked arms.

Many eyes followed their progress off the floor. Men and women. Wondering eyes.

Did one pair belong to the man in the cellar? Would he strike? The joyful mood from their dance dissipated as if a cold wind had blown through the room.

Charlie guided Merry to the refreshment table.

'Mountford,' a male voice said behind them. 'I got your letter.'

Charlie swung around. The man before him held out his hand.

'Blade,' Charlie said. 'I'm Tonbridge, remember?'

'Sorry, I forgot.' Blade grinned beneath his magnificent brown moustache.

'Merry, this is Captain Bladen Read. Read, this is my fiancée, Miss Draycott.'

'Delighted to meet you.' The captain bowed.

'So, Blade, how are you finding Yorkshire?'

He grimaced. 'Cold on more than one front. Several of us from the York camp are here tonight. Out of uniform. The army is not popular at the moment.' He spoke carefully, like a man well on the way to half-seas over and his twinkling hazel eyes looked a little bleary.

Everyone dealt with the aftermath of Waterloo in their own way. Charlie could only wish brandy worked for him.

Blade turned his charming smile on Merry. '*The* Miss Draycott?'

Merry's eyes widened. 'I don't know of any others.'

'Don't tease her.' Charlie knew Blade of old. The man was an incorrigible flirt. And a confirmed bachelor.

Digby sauntered up. 'May I have this waltz, coz? Show family solidarity and all that?'

Merry glanced at Charlie. He nodded. A private word with Blade was just what he needed.

They watched Merry dance with her cousin. 'She's a lovely woman,' Blade said. 'An heiress and not a wart or bristle on her chin. Can't think why she's not been snapped up before.'

Charlie's nape hair rose. 'Well she's snapped up now.'

'No need to poker up, old fellow. I'm not in the market for a bride. Although with a fortune like hers, I'd be tempted. Not that you are in need of money,' he added swiftly at Charlie's glare and rigid shoulders. 'She's a very attractive woman in her own right.'

They moved a little apart from the dance floor, seeking a quieter place for conversation.

Charlie flexed his fingers. 'How have you been?'

'Well enough. Regiment's gone downhill. We lost too many of the good ones.'

Cold steel twisted in Charlie's gut. He glanced down at his friend's left hand.

Blade grinned when he saw the direction of Charlie's gaze. He raised his arm and the sleeve fell back, revealing a wickedly sharp hook. 'Makes a great weapon. And holds the reins just fine.'

The recollection of Blade's screams when the women took his finger sent a shudder of revulsion across Charlie's shoulders. He hoped Blade didn't see it. But of course he did, because his grin widened. 'I was one of the lucky ones. If you hadn't stabbed that old crone, who knows what she would have cut off next?'

'If I hadn't led that bloody charge, you wouldn't have ended up off your horse.'

'It was glorious, though, wasn't it?'

Glorious and foolhardy. Utterly mad. Their commanding officer had been beside himself with anger, when he'd finally found Charlie in hospital.

So many good men lost, because Charlie lost his head.

Bitterness rose in his throat like bile. He swallowed it down. He lived with the guilt as best he could. 'As I wrote, I need your help.'

'Name it.'

'Someone is trying to do my heiress harm.'

Blade's eyes sharpened. 'Gad, an adventure. Who?'

'I don't know. But he may well be here tonight. I might need you to watch my back.'

'Like old times.'

'You will need your wits about you.' He looked pointedly at the glass tucked inside Blade's left elbow.

Blade shrugged and set the glass on the windowsill. 'I'm better than I was.'

'Glad to hear it.' He scanned the dance floor. He couldn't see Merry. She had been there moments ago, waltzing with her cousin in prime style. She'd drawn many envious glances from the other women. But now she was gone.

He cursed under his breath.

'What is it?' Blade asked.

'Where is Merry?'

He frowned. 'I didn't see her leave.'

'Look around, will you? I don't see her damned cousin either.' They circled the ballroom in opposite directions.

Anxiety closed his throat. How the hell could he have let this happen?

'There you are,' Lady Allison said, appearing at his elbow. 'There are young ladies dying to meet you.'

'In a moment,' he said. 'Have you seen Miss Draycott?'

She smiled brightly. 'Ladies' withdrawing room. Digby stepped on her train. She went off to pin her lace.'

He let go a sigh of relief and let Lady Allison introduce him to a group of debutantes—vestal virgins he always called them because he never could remember their names. They all giggled and blushed and peeped sideways over their fans. Unlike Merry, who looked him straight in the eye.

He shot a not-to-worry grin at Blade across the room.

His friend nodded.

Several minutes passed and still Merry didn't return.

Worry returned, more intense than before. 'Excuse me, ladies. I see an old acquaintance.' They chorused their dismay as he strode from the ballroom.

'Ladies' withdrawing room?' he said to the footman at the door.

'Down the hallway to the right.'

Blade caught him up. 'Still no sign of her?'

'Or her cousin. Lady Allison said she'd gone to the withdrawing room.'

'With her cousin?' Blade said, meaningfully.

Charlie stopped. 'They are family.'

'Family members don't always like each other. More betrayal in families than anywhere else.' He sounded bitter.

Charlie's heart stopped. The educated voice in the cellar could easily have belonged to Purtefoy. The undercurrents of dislike had been palpable when he and Allison visited Durn. But what would he gain by her death? Even if the family thought her a dirty dish in their cupboard, it hardly counted. Everyone had one or two of those.

His heart drummed louder. His chest tightened. 'We'll check the withdrawing room first. No sense in yelling "fire" before it happens.'

They sped down the hallway. A woman emerged into the corridor. She smiled at them vaguely.

'Is Miss Draycott in there?' Charlie asked.

The woman looked startled. 'No one is in there.'

Charlie closed his eyes. Damn. His stomach churned. Merry had gone off with her cousin. She could be anywhere. How like Merry not to let him know.

'Where next, old fellow?' Blade said.

Charlie narrowed his eyes. 'Lady Allison.'

They hurtled back to the ballroom, but she also was nowhere to be found.

'If they meant to do Merry harm, where would they take her?' Charlie asked, looking around as if the walls might give him a clue.

'Somewhere away from the guests, where she wouldn't be heard. Lots of people staying tonight, because of the snow.'

'The stables?'

'The attic.'

'Bloody hell.'

Blade grinned. 'I have an idea.'

He went back to the footman at the door and leaned heavily on the wall beside the man. 'Whersh your mashter?'

'I don't know, sir.'

'Got to know. Servants always know. Thing ish, see, I'm a

war hero.' He held up his hook. 'Losht this at Waterloo. Want him to help me find it.'

He put an arm around the man's shoulders and leaned hard. He stroked his cheek with the pointed metal. 'Where ish he, old chap? Don't want to damage anything, but I need hish help.'

The man turned bright red. 'He is otherwise engaged, sir.'

'Where?' He placed the hook against the man's throat.

'In the library. But he won't appreciate being disturbed.'

'Too bad.' He clumped the man over the head with the base of the hook hidden beneath his coat sleeve and the man slumped to the ground. Blade showed his teeth. 'Great weapon in a brawl that hook. Give me some help here.' They dragged the unconscious footman along the hallway and pushed him into a niche.

Blade always was a ruffian at heart. 'Did you have to hit him?' Charlie asked.

'You are getting soft, Major. Don't want him raising the alarm, do we?'

Charlie shook his head. 'Right.'

They hurried down the corridor to a set of double doors. Charlie placed his ear against the door and heard voices. He pulled his pistol from his pocket.

Blade grinned and produced his pistol. 'In case of insurrection, don't you know.'

They tried the doors handle very carefully and quietly. Locked.

A scuffling sound could be heard on the other side of the door. Charlie's blood congealed.

'We have to get in there.'

'Take more than a boot to smash that lock,' Blade said.

He fired his weapon and they went in through the puff of smoke.

'Good God.' Purtefoy, bending over the fireplace, whirled around to face them. 'Oh, it's you, Tonbridge. And Captain Read.' His gaze shifted from one to the other. He smiled awkwardly. Guilt flashed in his eyes as he sank into the nearest chair. 'Can't a fellow blow a cloud in peace?' He waved the cigar he'd been lighting from the coals in the fire.

'Where is Merry?' Charlie said.

'Cousin Honor, you mean? I left her in the ballroom moaning about her gown.' He shook his head. 'I can imagine why you might fancy a roll in the hay with her, but engaged? You really can't, not unless the Mountford fortunes have plummeted.'

The insult drove a spike of heat to Charlie's brain. Somehow he kept a grip on his temper and prowled closer, his pistol cocked. 'Mountford fortunes are as they ever were, Digby. What have you done with her?'

The other man waved a languid hand. 'She's probably tupping a footman, or one of the stable boys. You do know that's why she was expelled from school.'

Charlie recoiled.

'Didn't you know?' Digby sneered. 'You do now. Everyone else will, too, if you continue with this engagement. You were supposed to be courting my sister.'

'Shut your filthy mouth and tell me where she is.'

'She's nothing but a thorn in my family's side, but as for her whereabouts, you are welcome to search for her.'

The man was just too confident. Charlie's gut dipped. Wherever Merry was, she would not be easily found. In an old house like this there could be any number of secret staircases and priest holes. If she was still alive. His stomach did a sickening roll.

No. He wouldn't believe it. The man hadn't had time. Had he?

He looked around. 'I heard voices. She has to be here.'

'Check behind the curtains, why don't you, or under my chair,' Digby mocked.

Blade was looking distinctly annoyed, his smile all teeth and cold eyes. 'So you don't have a clue where she went, old fellow?'

Digby shook his head. 'As I say, ask the stable boys.'

'I'd sooner have a drink.' The soldier pointed to the decanter at Digby's elbow. 'D'you mind?'

'You've had enough,' Charlie said, wondering what his friend was up to.

'None of your business,' Blade said and closed in on the decanter with a slight stagger that hadn't been there a moment ago.

Charlie tensed.

Blade poured a glass and turned to look at Charlie. 'Looks like you've tangled yourself with an unsavoury young woman, my friend. If you want my advice, you'll forget all about her. Cry off.'

Charlie clenched the grip of the pistol. Digby didn't know just how much danger he was in.

Digby nodded agreement. 'Leave her to us,' he said. 'I'll sort her out. As head of the family, it is my responsibility.'

Blade took a long swallow from his glass and leaned on the high back of Digby's chair. 'Good advice,' he said, patting Digby's shoulder with his hook.

Digby glanced down at the sharpened metal and swallowed. He started to rise. 'Well, if that is all, gentlemen—'

'Not so fast,' Blade said. He patted Digby's cheek. The man paled.

Blade chuckled. 'What are you afraid of, man? This old

missing hand of mine?' He ran the tip down Digby's cheek, leaving a red line on the pale flesh. 'It's taken out an eye or two and leaves a nasty scar.' He traced a path from the corner of Digby's mouth to his ear. 'Accidentally, of course.'

Charlie curled his lip. 'And who wouldn't believe two heroes of Waterloo that it wasn't an accident?'

Digby sat still. Utterly frozen, his eyes wide and terrified.

Blade moved the hook to hover over Digby's eye. 'One eye, I think. A drunken stagger, an arm outstretched for balance, drags right across his face. Nothing left to sew together. I've seen it many times.' The words were as chilling as his face.

The coward shuddered. 'No! She's in there.' He pointed at the fireplace. 'A priest hole. Twist the cherub to the right.'

'You bastard,' Charlie said. He tossed his pistol to Blade. 'Keep him covered. He's going to pay for this. And for Jane's murder.' He released the catch and a portion of the wall swung clear of the chimney breast. Gagged and bound, Merry dropped to her knees.

Charlie pulled his knife from his pocket and cut her free.

'Charlie, thank God.' Her face was ashen.

'You have nothing to tie me to any murder,' Digby cried out. 'No evidence at all.'

Charlie picked a dazed-looking Merry up and put her in a chair. He chafed her hands. 'Don't be so sure. The simple fact of your treatment of Miss Draycott is evidence of wrong doing.'

'The bitch brought it on herself. She as good as killed Jane Harper's brother. Then she changed her will in favour of some destitute whore. Our family was supposed to inherit Draycott's. The old man's will left it to us on her death.' His face twisted in disgust. 'Now Father insists I marry the slut.'

'What?' Merry gasped. 'I wouldn't marry you if you locked me in that place for a hundred years.'

Charlie looked at the dark and narrow place beside the hearth and bit back a curse. He wouldn't want to be in there for a hundred seconds.

Digby's lip curled. 'Forget marriage. All I wanted you to do was change your will in my favour.'

'And if she refused?' Charlie asked.

He shrugged, the sneer on his face more pronounced. 'She's a woman. Any judge learning of the reckless way she's behaved, setting up a house for whores, trying to run a business by herself and losing money hand over fist, would put her finances in the charge of her male relatives. To protect her interests. It stands to reason. She'd be thanking me for stopping them from incarcerating her for operating a damned bawdy house.'

'It was not a bawdy house.'

He looked morose. 'Jane would have testified otherwise.'

'You beast!' she yelled.

Sickened by the man's machinations, Charlie put up a hand. 'It looks as if you are the one going to prison. For murder.'

Digby pressed his lips together briefly. His blue eyes flashed. 'Prove it.'

'I don't think I'll have much trouble convincing a jury,' Charlie said. 'A duke's heir trumps an earl's, you'll find.'

Digby paled. 'You are a disgrace to the title. You should be supporting me, not her. I will be a peer. Your equal. Hell, you were going to marry my sister, for God's sake. What an insult, turning up here with that.' His scornful gaze turned on Merry.

She wilted under his gaze.

Charlie clenched his fists. Hitting Digby wouldn't help their case against him.

Blade waggled his pistol. 'I suppose we'll have to see what the magistrate says.'

The viscount pushed to his feet. He pulled a pistol from his pocket and pointed it at Merry.

Charlie's heart lurched. He stepped in front of her. 'You will have to kill me first.'

The man's chin bobbled. 'You self-righteous bloody bastard.'

Charlie glared at him.

Digby's face crumpled. Resignation filled his eyes. 'Allison knew nothing of this.'

His gaze begged for belief. Charlie nodded, his gut rebelling as he saw in those eyes what came next and would do nothing to stop it.

Digby turned the pistol to his temple and fired. He fell to the floor with a hollow thump.

Merry screamed.

'Don't look,' Blade said, kneeling beside the body. 'He's gone.' He picked up the edge of the carpet and tossed it over the fallen man. 'We'll leave him for the magistrate, who luckily is here at the ball.'

'His father wanted him to marry me,' Merry whispered. She gave an odd little laugh and covered her mouth with her hands, her gaze tangling with Charlie's. 'And he killed himself.'

'It's over, Merry. He was mad,' Charlie said.

'As queer as Dick's hatband,' Blade agreed. 'Come on, Miss Draycott. I think you should go home.'

'My house,' Charlie said.

Durn's front door swung open. The stiffness in Merry's shoulders eased. A sigh escaped her lips. She wanted to crawl into bed and stay within the circle of Charlie's arms. Arms that had held her all the way home. Strong protective arms.

Only there would she be able to forget the happenings of this night.

She smiled up at him. 'Home at last.'

He smiled. The warm light in his gaze said he would be very happy to have her in his bed one last time.

Logan took her cloak. He gave Charlie a worried look. 'The duke and duchess are waiting for you in the drawing room.'

Charlie stiffened.

The bubble of comfort surrounding Merry burst. She swallowed. 'I will retire.'

'They asked to see you too,' Logan said with a flicker of emotion on his face. Triumph, Merry thought.

'Very well.' Charlie straightened his shoulders, a small movement, but Merry felt his discomfort, his expectation of trouble. He took her arm with a hard set to his jaw and a martial light in his eye.

Cold gripped Merry's stomach. The duke must have heard rumours of the betrothal and come to stop it. It would not take long to set their minds at rest. She stiffened her backbone.

A footman Merry didn't recognise threw open the drawing-room door. Merry stepped inside.

She stopped and stared.

Behind her, Charlie cursed softly.

Caro and Beth were perched on the edge of a sofa, their gazes pleading for rescue.

A tall grey-haired gentleman stood by the hearth, his face lined and grim.

A small but vital lady sat opposite the girls with a cup of tea in her hand. She smiled at Charlie. 'How was the ball?'

'Mother.' He bowed stiffly. Merry's heart twisted at his obvious chagrin. 'Your Grace,' he said to his father with a deeper bow. 'What brings you to Yorkshire? May I introduce my friend Miss Draycott. I see you have already met Mrs Falkner and her child's nurse, Beth.'

The grey eyes of His Grace bored into Merry. His lip curled with distaste. 'I knew your grandfather.'

'Come, child,' Her Grace said. 'Sit down. May I offer you tea?'

Merry would have preferred a hole to open up in the floor. She glanced at Charlie. His face was expressionless, his eyes dark and unfathomable.

She took the chair indicated. 'No tea, thank you.'

Charlie stood, feet apart, his hands clasped at his back. Rigid. Formal. 'As I am sure you know, Miss Draycott has kindly agreed to accept my proposal of marriage.' The harshness in his voice, as if the words had been forced from his throat, caused Merry to cringe inside.

The duke glared at her. She lifted her chin. He turned his cold gaze on his son.

'So, the rumours are true,' the duke said.

'They are not rumours,' Charlie said. 'We were waiting to inform you before making an announcement. You have saved us the trouble of returning to London.'

'Lord Tonbridge,' Merry said, 'I—'

Charlie crossed to her side and picked up her hand. He kissed it, deliberately displaying the ring on her gloved finger, one he'd given her that afternoon. He was making it worse. Why did he not just admit the truth?

'I beg you to excuse me,' Caro said, rising, then making a deep and elegant curtsy. 'My son is alone upstairs. I would prefer to go to him than take tea.'

Her Grace turned her gaze on Beth squirming on the couch. 'I found this young lady in the servants' hall kicking up larks. I understand she is one of your servants, Miss Draycott?'

Caro turned a reproachful gaze on Beth.

'I weren't there for more'n a minute or two,' Beth said. 'I've been locked up in the nursery for days.'

Caro smiled gently. 'You have been a great help. And you deserve a little fun. I beg your pardon, Your Grace. It was quite my fault.'

'Bad influence, she is,' His Grace said. 'Found her sitting in a footman's lap.'

Beth flushed scarlet. 'Sorry, Mrs Falkner.'

'What kind of woman employs—?' His Grace began.

'Father,' Charlie said.

'Please do go to your son, Mrs Falkner,' Her Grace said mildly, but with the authority of a woman who is sure of her place in the world. 'I know what it is to worry about children. I suggest you take your nurse with you.'

Head down, Beth scurried to the door with Caro close behind. Cowards. And Merry didn't blame them one little bit. She felt quite cowardly herself and rose to follow them.

'I wonder if I might have a moment more of your time, Miss Draycott,' the duchess said.

The command hung in the air. No way to refuse, it was uttered too softly. Merry sank back into her chair. She swallowed against the rawness in her throat.

The door closed behind Caro. Lucky Caro.

'Hmmph.' The duke cleared his throat. He looked at Merry, then at his son. 'Why did you bring these females into my house, Tonbridge?'

Charlie stiffened, muscles flickering in his jaw, his hands opening and closing. 'You will not speak in that tone of voice about my fiancée's friends.'

There was something in his eyes. Embarrassment, perhaps? Regret? Whatever it was, it was Merry's fault for letting his chivalry overcome her objections. She didn't belong in his world. She never had. And never would.

The dryness in her throat made it hard to speak. Her voice sounded rusty. 'Your Grace, Lord Tonbridge gave us needed sanctuary. Please be assured we will be leaving first thing in the morning.'

She removed the ring from her finger and placed it on the tea tray. 'I hereby relinquish any claim to your son's hand. We find we do not suit.'

'I'm witness to your statement, miss,' the duke said.

'Oh, my dear,' Her Grace said. She glanced up at Charlie. 'Have you argued?'

He stared at Merry, his face grim. 'No. The engagement stands,' Charlie said.

'What?' His Grace roared, his face flushing with an unhealthy colour of puce.

The room blurred. Charlie's face wavered in and out of focus. She could not quite make out his expression, but she knew what was there. Determination. Perhaps even a desire to protect her feelings. Chivalrous kindness. She could not let him do it. She swallowed the hard lump in her throat. Forced the shake out of her chest with a deep breath.

She rose to her feet and brushed the wrinkles from her skirt. 'Tha's been reet kind, Charlie. Helpin' out with the Purtefoys an' all.' She cast him a saucy smile as she headed for the door. 'If you ever need a favour, or a tumble, Merry Draycott's your lass. But I'll not hand over my brass to any man.'

'Damn it, Merry,' he said.

She turned at the door and swept a magnificent curtsy. 'It was a pleasure to meet you both.' Dignified and straight-backed, she walked out.

The footman quietly closed the door.

Heart in her throat, so large and painful, Merry hesitated, listening, praying everything would be all right between Charlie and his father.

'How dare you bring a common trollop into *my* house?' The duke. It seemed her little act had worked.

'You are wrong about Miss Draycott,' Charles said, his voice low. 'She deserves nothing but respect.'

'What about you, Charles?' The duke's voice, harsh, angry. 'How can I respect a man who forgets his promises so quickly? Did I not keep my part of the bargain? Have I not paid out a fortune to widows and orphans from the last time you ran from your obligations? At your request? Based on your promises to do your duty?'

What on earth could he be talking about?

The footman shook his head, his face disapproving. Merry glared at him.

Charlie cursed. 'This is different.'

'Charles,' his mother said sharply.

'Is it?' his father said, overriding his apology.

'Please, both of you,' Her Grace said. 'Can we not discuss this sensibly?'

'Sensibly?' the duke roared. 'He doesn't understand sensible. Or honour. He destroyed a regiment and with it our good name with his foolhardiness. I'll be damned if I let him destroy anything else with this latest peccadillo.'

Merry covered her mouth with her hand, shock catching her by the throat in a vice. The footman inched closer, his face red beneath his peruke. She held her ground.

'Damn you, Father,' Charles said. 'Miss Draycott is worth a dozen Lady Allison Purtefoys as you will soon discover.'

'Oh, I know you burnt your bridges there, Tonbridge. Ruined my hopes. But I'll not let you marry that woman. I'll cut you off without a penny. You'll get nothing that isn't entailed, d'you hear me? Not a thing.'

Merry whirled away. She'd heard enough to know exactly what she had to do.

* * *

Charlie wanted to plant his father a facer. And he might have if the old fellow had not looked as sick as a horse. He crossed the room and glared down at him. 'Do it. Cut me off. See if I give a damn.'

Father glared back. 'You are a Mountford. Act like one.'

'I am also a man.' He looked at his mother. 'There is more to life than duty.'

'What about Robert?' Father said. 'Don't you care about your brother now? Are you so blinded by lust you'd abandon him?'

The realisation hit Charlie like a blow to the solar plexus. 'He doesn't need you or your title or your money. Any more than I do.'

Father's jaw dropped. He narrowed his eyes. 'Don't test me, my boy.'

'I'm no boy, Father, to be bullied by you or anyone else. If you'll forgive me, I have your apologies to make to Miss Draycott.'

'Damnation, Charles. You will not leave this room.'

Oh, but he would. It was time he and Merry sorted out just where they stood.

He walked out of the door and ran up the stairs.

He found Merry in her chamber, folding a gown into her valise. She did not look up.

'What are you doing?'

Merry turned to face him. 'Preparing for our departure.'

He felt something tear in his chest. 'Marry me, Merry.'

Open-mouthed, she stared at him and he swore he saw a yes in her gaze, and yet there was a brittleness about her smile he couldn't quite understand. 'A tempting offer, my lord, but, no, thank you. I am more grateful for your help than I can say, but it is time to return to reality.'

Refused. Again.

Damn it all. 'Why not?'

She looked over at the valise and then back to him. 'I'm not the marrying kind. I have a business to run. I have been away too long.'

Unable to look at the regret in her eyes, Charlie turned away. He crossed to the window and looked out. Ice frosted the panes. Merry wouldn't be speaking of her business if she felt as he did. Perhaps this was his punishment for all those lives lost. He was to be deprived of the one thing he really wanted. No doubt he deserved it. 'I will come with you,' he said. 'See you safe home. Stay a while.'

Try to get her out of his blood. Except he had the feeling it would never happen.

'Running the mill keeps me far too busy for such distractions.'

'Damn it.' He crossed to her, pulled her into his embrace and looked down into her lovely face. 'You know I will miss you.'

She stroked his cheek. 'I'll miss thee, too. But duty is duty. You have yours and I have mine. The reason for our bargain is over. I thank you for standing up for me to your father, but I have cried off and there is no sense in drawing this out.'

Regret shadowed her eyes, as if she was holding something back. Something she didn't want him to know.

Of course. It hit him like a blow between the eyes. She'd seen him cowering in the dark, seen his weakness and wanted no more to do with him. It had to be something, because if Merry wanted to stay with him, nothing would stop her.

'Then there is no more to be said.' His voice was hoarse, his throat tight.

She nodded and raised her brows. 'We do have one last

night, before we set our feet back on the path of duty. Should we waste it talking?'

His blood heated. His body hardened. How could she still have this effect after all she had said? He should walk away. At least he'd retain a shard of pride.

She must have seen the thought in his face, because she gave a wry smile. 'Happen you are right. I'll move into Caro's apartments in the other wing.' A small sniff undid him.

Tipped her chin and brushed a tear away with the ball of his thumb. 'Oh, Merry, why are you crying?'

She cupped her hands around his face. 'I need you tonight, Charlie,' she whispered. 'I need you to hold me and make me forget.' Inevitability shone in her eyes. This or nothing.

He looked down at her, and his heart felt full and empty at the same time. He felt as if a step in any direction was the wrong one, but he did know he wanted Merry. And probably always would. He pushed aside thoughts of the empty future, because tonight he would hold her, bring her bliss and pretend she was his. Something in his chest stretched tight like a bowstring. No matter what happened, it would break. 'So be it. We will not waste these last few hours. Instead we will make memories neither of us will forget.'

He let her see the heat of his desire.

Merry tipped her face for his kiss. Her heart ached. The pummelling it had received from her betraying family seemed insignificant to the tearing in two she felt now. He'd stood against his father and defended her honour, but the sacrifice he faced was too great. The scorn in his father's voice, the threat of banishment, were too much for her shoulders to bear. She'd already separated one man from his family—she could not do the same thing to Charlie. She loved him too much.

Love? How had love happened? Wasn't it gratitude? Friendship? The pain in her chest increased. If she truly loved him, she had to let him go. For his sake.

He plied her lips with his until she opened to admit him. The kiss was delicious, expert, teasing and demanding. She let her senses drift on sensual delight, until they were both breathless.

'Let me help you out of that gown,' he whispered in her ear. Delicious shivers ran down her spine. Sensations she would never feel again. Regret flowed through her veins, an aching sadness. The urge to weep caught at her throat. Burned in her eyes. Pain she must not let him see.

'Tha's a bad lad,' she said with a smile that felt forced. To hide it she turned her back to grant him access to her ties.

He made short work of the hooks and the laces. 'Oh, Merry,' he whispered, 'I am going to miss you.'

She would miss him too.

He slipped the sleeves of the gown down her arms and held it there. 'Now I have you,' he whispered wickedly. 'You cannot get away.'

She chuckled low in her throat.

A shudder of pleasure ripped through her body. Helpless, she waited for the onslaught of his lips.

Slowly, he pulled the pins from her hair. Heavy black tresses fell down around her shoulders. From behind, he cupped her breasts covered by her chemise, rubbing her nipples with his thumbs while he buried his face in her hair, nuzzling until he found her nape. He licked and nibbled at her neck and shoulders until the sensations had her writhing with pleasure.

He breathed a soft laugh against the tender place beneath her ear. 'Patience, my lovely.'

'You will suffer for this,' she gasped as his tongue explored her ear and shivers ran across her spine.

'I'll look forward to it, sweet darling.'

His endearments tugged at her heart. Unbearably sweet as well as sensual. Wanting to see his face, hold him in her arms, Merry twisted around. He'd trapped her arms at her sides within the gown. Left no option, she attacked his mouth with her lips and pressed her body to his hard length.

With a grin, he relaxed his hold, allowing her to ease her arms free. She flung them around his neck and showered his face with kisses as light as butterfly wings.

While she kissed him on his lips and cheeks and jaw and chin, he pushed the dress down over her hips. It slid to the floor. Taking her shoulders in his hands, he pushed her a little away. 'You are beautiful,' he said. 'Do you know what word came to my mind when I saw you out on the moors?'

She shook her head.

'Perfect,' he breathed. He shook his head. 'Nothing else. Simply perfect.'

Thrilled and honoured, she wanted to melt. She forced herself to grin. 'Now you know better.'

He laughed. 'Yes. I do. You are sublime.'

The reverence in his voice smashed through her defences tearing down walls, crumbling armour to dust, yet she could not let him see. She forced a smile and hoped he would not hear how close she was to breaking. 'Thank you,' she murmured. *I love you*, she whispered in her heart.

Brightening her smile, she cocked her head on one side. 'You are behind in the undressing department.' With trembling fingers, nerves and excitement tangling together to render her awkward, she attacked the knot at his throat while he shrugged out of his coats.

The strip of muslin followed them to the floor. Obliging her, he pulled his shirt off over his head. She looked her fill at his chest, so broad and manly, at the scar gleaming silver in the candlelight, and branded it all on her mind and in her soul.

A corner of his mouth lifted. A purely male arrogant smile. It hit her low in her belly and her blood raced through her veins, hot with desire.

It hurt to know she would never see him like this again. She wanted to see all of him.

Her fingers went to his waistband, hesitated. Would he think her too bold. 'May I do the honours?'

'Please.' His voice sounded strained as if he, too, battled with words he could not say.

The buttons came undone with a little tugging. Free of the confines of tight fabric, his shaft rose proudly between them. She took it in her hand, curled her fingers around his width and stroked hard and firm. A hiss of indrawn breath tightened her insides with a steady pulse beat of blood. She slipped her hand beneath the base of him, and rolled his testicles, heavy and hot, in her palm. Exquisite velvety heat. He groaned his pleasure and sent hers rocketing out of control.

She leaned close to his lovely sculpted chest and grazed his nipple with her teeth.

'Careful, sweet,' he said on a sharp exhale of breath. 'You will undo me too quickly.' He picked her up and laid her on the bed, before slipping off his shoes and peeling off his evening breeches and stockings.

Magnificent man lit by candlelight. Sculpted warm skin and muscle. A god of love bearing the scars of a warrior. She would always remember him like this.

His expression softened as he gazed on her. Regret filled his eyes. It echoed in her heart and her soul.

Then he covered her with his body.

Her core ached for his entry, but her mind yearned for more. This would be the last time they would lie together and she longed to bring him more pleasure that he had ever known. A gift he would never forget.

He didn't resist when she pushed at his shoulder. He rolled on his back, the candlelight and the wicked smile curving his lips making him less angel and more devil. She straddled his hips.

He grinned up at her. 'Feel like going for a ride?' He reached down to lift her up.

'Lie still,' she ordered. 'If I am the rider, you must obey my commands.'

His jaw clenched. For a moment she thought he would refuse, but he let his hands fall to his sides. 'Tally ho.'

She dipped her head and kissed his lovely mouth, nibbling his lips, tasting with her tongue the fruit of wine and his own special flavour. When he responded with his own darting taste, she sucked hard, holding him fast, punishing him for his boldness. Immediately he held still, clearly understanding.

Her insides tightened deliciously. This would be a night to remember for them both. She faltered at the thought of never seeing him again. Never knowing his touch again. Or the feel of his mouth on her body. Agony speared between her ribs. She fought a cry of anguish.

Now was not the time for sorrow. There would be years and years to feel sad. Now was the time for taking pleasure and giving pleasure and sharing pleasure.

She broke free of his mouth, pressed her breasts to his hard wall of chest, moving her lips over his cheekbone, his stubble-hazed cheek and jaw, feeling the roughness of beard and the strength of bone beneath. She licked the rise of his Adam's apple and the hollow beneath and inhaled the faint scent of bay and musky sweat.

She learned every dip and contour, every bone and pulse

point, where he had hair and where his skin was silken smooth and warm beneath her hand.

She tweaked first one nipple, then the other, feeling his groan of pleasure laced with pain deep in her core.

Reaching down between them, she found his shaft hard and eager. Felt his need to drive home in the tension of muscle and sinew as he drew in a swift gasping breath.

'There is something I have always wanted to try,' she whispered.

He looked down at her, one of those male considering glances that is full of amusement laced with a healthy dose of wariness.

'You'll think me very strange. You might not like it. Perhaps it is better left unasked.'

His expression changed, became more heated. Feral. 'Try me.'

Dare she? She took a breath. 'I've had the dream of a man who obeys my every command.'

His eyelids lowered a fraction and she looked away, suddenly embarrassed, wishing she hadn't spoken.

A warm hand gently drew her face around. 'I'm hard just thinking about it. If it is your wish, it will be my very real pleasure.'

Excitement clogged her throat. 'Put your hands above your head,' she ordered in a husky voice.

She sensed a slight hesitation, but he did as requested.

'Open your legs.'

'Merry—'

'No talking.'

He pressed his lips together and widened his thighs.

A generous relinquishing of control for a man who liked to be in command. The heat of shared passion in his eyes drove her to heights of arousal such as she'd never encountered before. She could scarcely breathe for the thrill of it.

One hand on his shaft, she brought him to her entrance, the other she used to torment his erect nipple. His chest rose and fell on ragged breaths as he fought to hold still beneath her hands. His eyes squeezed shut. His lips drew back in a grimace, revealing white even teeth. She traced the outline of muscle on his chest with the tip of her forefinger. She stroked him against her folds. 'Do you want to be inside me?'

'Yes,' he said, hoarse and low.

'I don't think you are ready.'

He opened his mouth to protest and then must have thought better of it, because he simply gazed at her from eyes hazy with pleasure and sadness.

'Raise your knees.'

He followed her order. Straddling his groin, she rested her back against his thighs. His shaft jutted straight up between them. She circled the tip with her finger. So silky soft. She bent forwards and flicked it with her tongue. He pressed upwards, seeking more prolonged contact.

She straightened and looked down at his face. 'Bad boy,' she said. 'Is that what you are? A wicked boy? You can answer.'

'Yes.' He grinned wickedly. 'I'm evil.'

'I like bad boys.' She leaned forwards and took him in her mouth. She licked and sucked and tormented his shaft until his body shuddered beneath her. He was hanging on by barely a thread and not once had he tried to wrest back control. The man was a god. She would adore him forever.

She released him. 'Please, Charlie, join with me.'

Pride filled his face and he helped her rise up. She guided him to her entrance. Slowly, delicately, she slid down his shaft, a gentle glide when he wanted hard pounding force. Each time his hips shifted, she pulled away. He groaned his frustration, the sound zinging through her blood to heighten her tension.

When finally he was seated deep within her, she held perfectly still, squeezing him with her inner muscles, each new pull a little harder than the one before.

He panted with the effort of remaining immobile beneath her, his shaft twitching and throbbing until she thought she might go mad with the tiny sensations tormenting her insides.

Nothing remained of her mind, every fibre of her being focused on their joining.

In a steady rhythm she began to ride. Lifting and lowering herself with smooth long strokes, leaning back to increase the pressure where it felt unbelievably good, watching the pleasure in his eyes and expression as he submitted to her enjoyment of his body.

He lifted his lashes and gazed into her face with smoky eyes, his lips curved in a sensual smile, and all control left her as she rode him hard and wild, driving to completion. The tightness within stretched to breaking point.

She shattered.

He followed her over the edge with a moan deep in his throat, a sound of joy and despair.

She caught the cry in her mouth and collapsed against his chest as his hips pumped his hot seed into her body.

Shivering and shuddering, they lay together in heat and bliss. The shadow of their parting returned, like a presence in the room. Merry tried to pretend it wasn't there.

Charlie lay beneath her, his gaze following the shadows and patches of light cast by the candles. Never in his life had he felt so drained and replete. Or so alive. His skin prickled with excitement, while his limbs remained languid and heavy beneath her sleeping form. Tonight they'd become one. Losing her was like losing part of himself.

Regret left an empty space beneath his ribs. A hollow in his stomach. This was goodbye. Sorrow filled him. A black emptiness. A knowledge that he would never find another woman like his Merry. Except she wasn't his to have and to hold. She was quicksilver. Beautiful to look at. Impossible to grasp.

But he didn't know why.

She stirred. Her hand tracing circles on his chest. 'What happened at Waterloo?'

The urge to deny tightened his throat. The thought of putting his guilt into words made his spirit shrink. She'd despise him. As she should. Hell, he despised himself for the suffering he'd caused because he'd rebelled against his lot in life. He'd done so much damage.

She more than anyone ought to know.

He drew in a breath. 'Against my father's wishes I joined the cavalry. I commanded a troop of horse at Waterloo. My orders were to take a French cannon. We charged. The French saw what we were about and sent a troop to meet us. We clashed right in front of the cannon's mouths. The French broke really fast. In hindsight, some of us think it was a trap.'

'Who thinks?'

'Read, for one. A good friend. And a good soldier.'

The caresses ceased. 'I didn't think heirs of dukedoms went to war any more. I thought they left it to their younger brothers.'

'I switched places with my twin, Robert. He took my place here. I went to war as him. Looking for excitement.'

'Didn't you get found out?'

A smile pulled at his lips. 'We are like peas in a pod. We

changed places so often as lads, it was like second nature. Father always hated it when we were young.'

'What happened next?'

'When the French turned and ran, we followed. Half of my men took the cannon. The rest of us, on my orders, followed the French over the hill straight through a company of their infantry waiting to cut us to pieces. A more experienced officer would never have continued the charge. I led them to their deaths.'

'No wonder you have nightmares.'

'The worst came later.' He swallowed the dryness in his mouth. 'I was cut down by a French officer's sabre. My horse fell on top of me and I lost consciousness. When I came to my senses, I was still beneath my horse, crushed, having difficulty breathing. It was dark and it was raining. All around me men were screaming, begging for water, unless they were dead. The appalling stink, the horror. The fear. It's all there waiting every time I close my eyes. I called out. Read answered from a few feet away. We talked to keep our spirits up. Then the women came. The camp followers.'

'They helped you?'

'Hell, no, Merry. If they find you alive, they kill you for whatever they can find on your body.'

'How could they?'

'Mostly because they are starving. In daylight I don't blame them. In the dark, they are unholy horrors. Blade and I lay very still, pretending to be dead whenever a party of them came by. Hours passed. Every now and then you'd hear a man cry out and know they'd finished him off. I let them finish off what was left of my men and did nothing to stop it, terrified I was next. I even played dead while one of them dragged me out from under the horse and stole every stitch of my clothes.'

She gasped. 'No wonder you have bad dreams. You could have been murdered.'

He should have been. 'She started hacking at Blade's finger for his ring. He screamed. She lifted her knife to cut his throat.' He shuddered, then chuckled grimly. 'I stabbed her with my knife. I'd been using it to try to keep the rats away. I tied up his hand as best I could, but I was so damned scared they'd hear him and come back and finish us off I stuffed his mouth with a rag to keep him quiet. He almost suffocated.'

'But you saved his life.'

'Hardly. He would not have been there but for me. My men trusted me to see them safe and I led them to their deaths.' Guilt roiled through him, bitter and black, writhing in his gut as the visions filled his mind. An older wiser officer would have seen the danger.

'What happened then?'

He shrugged. 'They found us at first light. Me and Blade and a couple of the others.' Then, only then, in the grey dawn, had he realised the full extent of his mistake. 'Twenty good men died or were badly injured because I didn't follow orders.'

'But you captured the cannon.'

'We captured the cannon, but my commanding officer was furious. Even more so, when he realised I wasn't Robert. He half-expected Father to have him put in the Tower.'

'I think you have to stop blaming yourself. You did your best. War is terrible, but it is over now and because of men like you the world has peace.'

He kissed the top of her head and inhaled the scent of her hair. He felt easier within himself than he had for years. Never had he talked about the horror of that night, the fear, not even with Blade who had been there, and while the guilt would never leave him, some of the darkness in his soul had faded.

Because of Merry. It was as if by listening she had taken some of the worst of it into herself. Relieved him of the worst of the burden.

He rolled on to his side and took her face in his hands. He thought he saw the sheen of tears in her eyes. He kissed her mouth, her cheek, her eyelids and tasted salt. 'Don't leave, Merry.'

Her answering half-laugh, half-regretful sob wrenched at his heart. 'I can't stay. You know I can't.'

He didn't, but the finality in her voice blocked his objections. She didn't want to stay.

For the last time, he enfolded her in his arms.

A fortnight had passed since Merry's departure when Charlie joined his mother for afternoon tea in the drawing room. She always looked lovely, but in the sunlight from the window, and wearing her favourite pale lilac, she positively glowed. Robert's news, no doubt. They'd had a letter from Italy announcing a grandchild in the autumn.

He hoped his decision would not dim her sparkle.

'Did you enjoy your ride, dear?' Mother asked as he sat beside her on the sofa.

'I did.' He stirred the tea. Then put the cup down. There was no sense in procrastinating. 'I went to visit Lady Allison.'

'That was kind of you. I really must call in again myself before we leave for London.'

'You are going soon?'

'In two days' time. Your father is needed in town.' She sighed. 'Politics. How is poor dear Lady Allison?'

Charlie gritted his teeth. Poor dear Lady Allison had been horrendously unkind to Merry, even if she didn't know of her brother's plans. 'Her brother's death hit the family hard. While she has my sympathy, she knows any chance of a betrothal is out of the question.'

Mother frowned. 'Is this your father's decision?'

'No. It is mine.'

Mother sipped her tea, then, head tilted on one side, looked at him. Her grey eyes twinkled. 'Do you have some other gel in mind?'

He grimaced. 'You know I do. But she won't have me.'

Mother made a scoffing noise. 'What girl wouldn't have you?'

Mother never could see anything wrong with any of her children.

'I'm going to try once more to change her mind.'

She put down her cup and put her hand over his on his thigh. Her hands were small and the skin fragile. She gave his hand a pat. 'Why, Charle? Why this girl?'

It was a question he'd been torturing himself with for days. Why couldn't he just get on and do his duty as he'd promised his father when he came back from Waterloo? It wasn't a matter of honour. She'd refused him twice. The answer had come to him in the middle of the night.

'She makes me laugh. She makes me remember there is more to life than abiding by the rules.' He turned to face his mother full on. 'With her I believe in myself.' He thought about speaking of love, but decided that could only be spoken of in one person's hearing.

'I wish you good fortune, my son.'

For a moment, Charlie stared at her serious face in bemusement. She raised her brows above twinkling eyes. 'I hadn't seen you look happier for years, than I did the night before she left. Until your father got in his high stirrups.'

He took her hand and kissed it. 'Captain Read is travelling to Skepton, I am going with him, then on to Draycott House to seek out Merry.' He let go a sigh. 'I'm sorry if this upsets Father. I just hope he doesn't take his spleen out on Robert as well as me.'

The thought of being cast adrift the way Robert had left a bitter taste in his mouth, but Robert had survived and so would he.

Mother picked up her teacup. It hovered at her lips for a moment, then she looked at him with a frown. 'Your father gets a bee in his bonnet sometimes, you know. Why he thought I would permit him to cut Robert out of the family, I cannot imagine.' She sipped.

'Permit?' Charlie said cautiously.

Mother looked at him with surprise. 'Power has a way of corrupting a man, Charles. Makes him think he can never make a mistake. Don't let it happen to you. Though I doubt a woman as strong as Miss Draycott will allow it.'

'I'm not sure I understand what you mean.'

Mother put down the cup and picked up her embroidery. 'Alfred can pass laws and write bills—' she smiled a small smile '—but our family is my concern.' Mother cut a skein of blue silk with a decided snip. 'You leave your father to me.'

An odd feeling, something like horrified laughter, rose in Charlie's throat. He managed to keep it behind his teeth. When he finally managed to breathe, he was able to ask his question. 'Are you saying you have Father under your thumb?'

'Not when it comes to important matters of State. But here in this family, your father is not the one in charge. Believe me, none of my sons will ever be cast out again. Not if your father plans to live to a peaceful and ripe old age.'

Side by side with the laughter in his chest, hope blossomed that no ill would come to his twin as a result of what he was about to do. Not that he was sure his efforts would be rewarded.

Merry was a conundrum he hadn't yet solved.

Mother set a stitch, peering at it closely, then her grey eyes flashed up to meet his. She touched his hand. 'Be gentle, son. She's been hurt, I think.'

Merry? Strong outspoken Merry? Was that what she hid behind her blunt exterior? She had a kind heart. And a courageous soul. The thought she might be in pain tied his gut in knots. That he might have added to it…

Mother flapped her embroidery in front of his face. 'Stop blaming yourself and go and make amends, Charles.'

He grinned. His mother might be small, but she was exceedingly formidable and clearly very wise. 'There is one thing I would like to say, Mother, if I may.'

An eyebrow shot up. 'Indeed?'

'Heaven help anyone who crosses you.'

Laughing, Charlie went off to set his affairs in order, because who knew how long it would take Merry to change her mind.

If she would.

He pushed that cold thought aside.

Chapter Sixteen

'Let me show you the refectory,' Caro said, leading the way to the back of the new house Merry had acquired in Skepton. 'The workmen finished yesterday. It is perfect.'

Perfect. The word struck a painful chord. Somehow Merry managed to smile. 'Then lead the way, my dear.'

In the two weeks since she'd returned to Draycott House, Merry's life had settled back into its old rhythm. At least, outwardly the rhythm remained the same. Inside, she felt like a clock with a broken spring, with little rushes of time full of busy work and long empty gaps in which the seconds ticked by like hours.

Even here, visiting Caro's new refuge for needy women, she couldn't feel any excitement. It was as if a piece of her was missing.

Charlie. Each day she scanned *The Times*, looking for word of him, dreading to see the announcement of his forthcoming wedding and steeling herself to read it and smile.

Caro flung open the door to a long room, with a bank of windows down one wall, a polished plank wood floor and furnished with a rectangular table surrounded by chairs. A door led off it to the kitchen. 'We can feed at least six ladies in here,' she said with obvious satisfaction. 'Once they have real work and can afford to rent accommodation, we can take another batch.'

'The workmen did a good job. It looks very welcoming.' Prior to the renovations, there had been three small rooms at the back of the house.

'They will start the dormitory next week.'

'Mummy, Mummy.' Tommy rushed into the room, his face flushed with excitement. 'There's a soldier at the door.' He shot off again. Tommy loved all things military and was no doubt intending to ogle their guest. If he was a guest.

Caro looked at Merry with consternation in her eyes. 'Not more trouble.'

'I haven't heard any grumblings. Mr Broadoaks tackled the other mill owners and their wives. He promised money, too.'

Beth appeared at the door. Her face held suppressed excitement, but no concern. 'Two gentlemen to see you, Miss Draycott.'

'Me?' Merry said. 'Who on earth knows I am here?' Instead of working in her office as usual, she'd used the finished refectory as an excuse to leave her empty house. Not that she was getting much work done even when she was there. Her mind wouldn't focus. It kept wandering off to think about Charlie and the events of the past few weeks.

Beth had a secretive smile on her round face. 'I've put them in the front parlour, miss.'

'Did the gentlemen not give you their cards?' Merry asked. She really didn't want to see anyone. Making small talk took too much energy.

'They did, mum, but I couldn't read them too good.' She sauntered off with a swing of her hips.

Merry glanced at Caro and laughed. Beth's role as house-keeper had it drawbacks, but she was learning.

'We should see who it is, I suppose,' Caro said.

'Yes, we should.' Merry tucked her arm through Caro's and they strolled back to the front of the house.

Merry gestured for Caro to go ahead. It was, after all, her house. Merry had put it in her name.

Caro came to a sudden halt with a gasp of shock. Merry almost bumped into her. She stepped around her friend.

Two gentlemen rose to their feet. Tommy hung on the arm of the chair from which Captain Read had risen, hero worship on his angelic face.

And looking haughty and reserved across the room was... Charlie.

Merry's stomach pitched. Her heart stuttered to a halt, then broke into a gallop. She grabbed the doorpost for support. 'Lord Tonbridge?' Her voice sounded reedy. She swallowed and realised the captain was staring at Caro open-mouthed.

Charlie bowed. 'You remember Captain Read, don't you, Miss Draycott? Mrs Falkner, Captain Read is a friend of mine, here in Skepton looking into rumours of unrest at the mills.'

The captain glanced down at the boy and back at Caro. 'Mrs Falkner?' He looked stunned.

As did Caro, who backed towards the door, her hands fluttering at the ribbons of her cap. 'If you gentlemen will excuse me, I have remembered an urgent appointment. Thomas. Come along.' She made a stiff curtsy and left the captain frowning after her.

Tommy dragged his feet in her wake.

'If you do not mind, Miss Draycott,' the soldier said. 'I would like a word with Mrs Falkner.'

Whatever the captain wanted to say to Caro, the desire for speech was clearly not mutual. Merry put out a staying hand.

'Please, Captain, may I not take the opportunity to express my deep thanks for your help the other evening?'

Reed glanced down at his coat sleeve tucked inside his jacket. His mouth curled in a wry smile. 'I wouldn't have missed it for the world, my dear Miss Draycott. Quite like old times, eh, Tonbridge?'

'Quite,' Charlie said drily.

The captain bowed. 'If you will excuse me.' He marched off.

'Oh, dear,' Merry said. 'I think he knows Caro.'

'I shouldn't be surprised. Blade is a bit of a rake. And the hand doesn't seem to hold him back.'

'Perhaps I should go and make sure she is all right.'

He blocked her from leaving. 'She won't come to any harm. He's an officer and a gentleman.'

'Why are you here?' Merry asked, struggling to ignore her quickened heartbeat. 'Are you visiting in the neighbourhood or passing through on your way to town, perhaps? It is very kind of you to call and see how we do.'

'Merry,' he said sternly, 'I came specifically to see you.'

A lump rose in her throat. She swallowed. 'We have nothing left to discuss.'

He looked down at his hat, turned it in his hands and set it on the table. 'I think we do. Or at least I have things I need to say.'

She really didn't want to do this again. Her heart was aching quite enough at the sight of him without adding further pain. Nothing had changed. He was still heir to a dukedom. She was still common-as-muck Merry Draycott, a mill owner's daughter. She had done the right thing for him. Left him with his own class of people. Why could he not let it lie?

'Please, Charles, can we not do this?' She went to the window and looked out. Dark grey clouds hung over the moors beyond the edge of town. 'My business in Skepton is concluded. I called in on Caro on my way home, but I really must be going. It looks like snow.'

'It doesn't smell like snow,' he said.

She spun around and just caught the flicker of a smile on his lips. Teasing her? The wretch. Didn't he know how painful it was for her to see him again? Probably not. He was likely doing what he considered his duty. A courtesy call.

She managed to draw a shaky breath, something to sustain her next words around the pain. 'If the captain needs information from me, he may call on me at Draycott House.'

'But I may not,' he said, his voice low.

'No. You may not.' It hurt, but still she smiled. 'I am not looking for an affaire at the moment.'

He smiled. 'Are you sure?'

His voice was low and husky. Sensual. His eyes hot. Heat fired beneath her skin, her body tingled where it should be quiet and still. 'Perfectly sure,' she said coolly. She couldn't bear the thought of it, knowing eventually he would leave her.

In three steps he was at her side, his hand holding hers to his lips. His brown eyes regarded her steadily, intently, as if he would look into her soul. 'I miss you, love.'

The words melted her insides. Her arms yearned to hold him. What good would it do? There would be more pain, more longing when he left. Nothing good could come of it, but a few fleeting hours of passion.

Surely he understood. 'We are not children, Lord Tonbridge. We are adults. We know that it is not the end of the world if we are denied the thing we most want at any particular moment. Find somewhere else to cast your eye. Lady Allison, perhaps.' Oh, dash it, that sounded terribly bitter.

The twinkle did not leave his gaze. 'Lady Allison is in mourning.'

Merry recoiled, forced herself to remain calm. 'There are many others, I am sure.'

'Yes,' he agreed, smiling, his face devilish. 'There are.'

'Well, then.' She tried to recover her hand, but he held it fast.

His gaze searched her face. 'Unfortunately, there is only one Merry Draycott.'

Captain Read charged into the room. He winced when speared by Charlie's glare. 'Mrs Falkner has disappeared.'

'And you are telling us this because...?' Charlie said coldly.

'I thought Miss Draycott might know where I should look.'

'If Mrs Falkner does not wish to be found, Captain Read,' Merry said, 'don't you think you should leave her unfound?'

He swallowed and turned red. 'I...I... Yes. I beg your pardon.' He bowed and left.

'Idiot,' Charlie said.

The interruption had allowed Merry a chance to gather her scattered wits. She pulled her hand free, put a few feet between them, where she found air enough to draw breath, and escaped his sensual pull. 'It's reet kindly of you, my lord. Flattering. If you are concerned for my reputation, you needn't be. It is as ever it was.'

'Merry, dearest Merry. It is no good hiding behind that accent. It is music to my ears, love. I have done a great deal of thinking these past two weeks about what is right and what makes sense.'

He'd been thinking? She'd been going round in ever-decreasing circles. 'Nothing between us makes sense.'

'I know I am not happy while we are apart. And I know I was never happier than when we were together.'

A rush of tears filled her eyes. She turned her face away. 'Please, I am begging you, do not ask this of me.'

'What am I asking, Merry? You have to tell me, so I understand.'

'How can you understand? You are the son of a duke.'

'Try me. Give me a chance. Please, Merry.'

Oh, he knew her too well. If he had commanded her, she could have called on anger and resisted, but this gentle question was so much harder to fight.

She took a deep breath, panicked and grabbed the first thought in her mind. 'I won't be the reason for estranging you from your family.'

'Heard that, did you?' he said grimly. 'I should have guessed. This has nothing to do with my father. I am talking about *our* future, *our* happiness. Doing my duty, as Father calls it, won't make up for past mistakes. I know that now. Nothing can. I can only trust I have learned enough to do better in the future. Merry, I want that future to include you. I need you there with me.'

Oh, it wasn't fair, that he should be so wonderful, so sweet, so terribly tempting. She sniffed and he handed her his handkerchief. She dabbed at her eyes. 'But I don't fit in your world.'

'How can you know if you don't try? With me beside you—'

'I did try.' The old hurt rose up like a poisonous mist, clouding her mind with the anger, the hurt. 'At school. When I first arrived, they laughed at my speech. I'd been copying Grandfather, you see. I learned quickly. I said nothing out of turn. I was a model pupil. I even bought things for the other girls. Grandfather sent me whatever I asked for, money, hair ribbons. A puppy.' A hard laugh escaped her at the memory. 'Can you imagine the stir? I was the centre of attention.'

She tugged her hand free and paced to the other side of the room. She forced a smile to her lips and turned to face him. He was watching her gravely, trying to understand. How could he understand? He had never known what it was like to feel rejected, unworthy. 'I loved how they gathered around me.' A hot lump formed in her throat. She breathed around it, her chest rising and falling painfully. The schoolgirl of those long-ago years, curled up in a ball. Curled around the hurt, protected it from view.

'All the while I was trying to fit in, those girls were laughing behind my back.'

'You don't know that for sure.'

'I do know it. Lady Allison kindly told me. Why do you think I sought comfort from Jeremy?'

'No one will laugh at the Marchioness of Tonbridge.'

'You don't understand, Charlie. They expelled me from school because I wasn't the right class of person. Not because of what I did in the potting shed. I wasn't good enough. Nothing has changed.'

He shoved a hand through his hair. He looked tired and frustrated. 'All right, we will live in seclusion. We don't need to mingle with the *ton*. It will be just us. You and I and our children, if we are blessed.'

She grabbed on to his words like a life line. 'You'd hide me away, you mean. You see. You know I'm right. You'd be ashamed of me.'

'You are twisting my words.'

'And what of the children? Will they be laughed at, too, when they go to school?'

'Of course not.'

'You don't know that. You can't know that.'

'I'm sorry you had such a bad time of it. Children are cruel. And, yes, the *beau monde* is rabid about guarding their privileges. Show weakness and they will tear you to pieces. But you aren't weak. And nor will our children be weak.'

'I can't do it.'

His jaw hardened. His eyes grew bleak. His expression turned to granite. 'Merry, these excuses of yours encourage me to think I can find a solution, but if the real truth is you don't want me, then say so. Put me out of my misery.'

She wanted to weep. To see him looking so hurt, so confused, and to let him suffer. She wrung her hands. 'You don't understand.'

Sadly he gazed at her. 'No. I don't. I have tried. But I really do not understand why you would care more about the views of a pack of jackals than about us.'

Layer by layer he peeled away the fabric she'd woven to protect her innermost secrets until she could no long hide the raw and bleeding bitter truth.

'Do you know what I did?'

Silent, watchful, he waited for her to tell him.

'At the end of term, I asked Grandfather not to come to the school to collect me. I told him to meet me around the corner, so no one would see him. I was ashamed of him. The man who gave me everything. I didn't want them to meet him.'

'Oh, Merry, a child's mistake.'

'I was old enough to see the hurt in his face when he realised what I had done. The kindest, most generous man in the world and he knew I was ashamed. And yet I did nothing, said nothing.'

He took a half-step forwards as if to offer comfort. She held up a hand to ward him off.

'I knew it would hurt him. I knew. And still I did it.'

'But he forgave you?'

'We never spoke of it. He was kind and cheerful as always. But he knew what I had done.'

'Then he forgave you. And you must forgive yourself. He would not want you to dwell on such a small thing.'

She curled her lip. 'It sounds simple when you say it, but what about you? You haven't forgiven yourself for what happened at Waterloo and you came home a hero.'

'That is different. Men died because of my stupidity. And to tell you the truth, since we talked, I seem to have come to terms with it.'

'I'm glad.' She was glad. Thrilled that she might have been of help. She smiled brightly. 'At least something good came of our time together.'

'Merry, I love you. I want to marry you. Don't push me away.'

Love? She stared at him open-mouthed. She thought he'd come for honour and duty's sake. Because he'd taken her to his bed. He loved her?

'Oh,' she said. Her legs felt weak. She sank on to the sofa.

'I should have told you before. It took me a while to work it out. It took your leaving for me to understand my own heart.'

'You honour me,' she said.

'But?'

'It can't work.'

He took her hand and kissed her gloved knuckles. 'It can if you want it, too. If you love me.'

Everything she'd ever wanted shone from his eyes. Love. Affection. Honesty. She shook her head.

'Why, Merry. Give me a reason I can understand. Tell me you don't love me in return and I will never bother you again.'

She loved him with all her heart.

The tears, pushing up in hot waves in her throat, spilled over. 'Charlie, what if our children are ashamed of me? I don't want that for them. The shame and later the guilt.'

He put an arm around her shoulders and drew her against his wide chest. 'I won't allow it, love. They will love, honour and respect their courageous, beautiful mother or I will cast them off without a penny.'

A shaky laugh pushed its way through the tears. 'You sound like your father.'

'Don't I just.' He gave her a squeeze. 'It won't happen. If your parents had lived, do you think your mother would have been ashamed of your father?'

'Oh, no. Grandfather said it was love at first sight.'

'And do you think either one of them would have left you to the mercies of callous schoolgirls like Lady Allison? No. Your mother would have given you the tools you needed to deal with their ilk. Instead of that you had to work it out for yourself. Our children will not be ashamed of their mother because not only will they love her, but their father will make sure they respect her. They will know how brilliant you are and how beloved.'

It sounded plausible when he said it with such conviction. 'Your father won't like it.'

'Father will come around.' He shrugged. 'And if he doesn't, then I'll find some gainful employment. After Waterloo, I swore I would follow the rules and never risk harming anyone else. God, I even tried to make my brother fit the same mould. He tried to tell me a life of only duty is no life at all. I wouldn't listen. You taught me to listen, Merry, and gave me joy. Something I thought I didn't deserve. Don't send me back to an empty life. I need you. Together we can face the world. I would be proud to call you my wife.'

Proud? Of her? 'How can you be?'

He kissed the tip of her nose. 'Because you are clever and kind. You stand up for what you believe in no matter what others say. And because I love you.'

'I love you, too.' The words held so close to her heart she hadn't known they were there spilled forth like heady wine. 'I love you, Charlie.'

He let go a sigh of relief. 'Thank you.' He slid off the sofa and on to one knee. He withdrew a ring from his pocket. The one she'd left on the tray at Durn. 'Merry Draycott, will you do me the honour of becoming my wife?' He slipped the ring on her finger.

She stared down at it. Everything clicked into place, her heart, her mind, her soul, joining together with his, like some well-oiled lock. The little schoolgirl who everybody had scorned danced in circles of happiness. What had he said earlier? They would face the future together. With Charlie at her side, no one could cause her hurt. Because no one else counted. Only Charlie.

She lifted her gaze to his eyes, saw the question and the hope and the love. 'Yes,' she said. 'Yes, please.' She flung her arms around his neck.

He found her lips with his and she lost herself in his kiss.

After a while he broke away and tucked her against his chest, his arm around her shoulder. 'Miss Draycott, you certainly know how to lead a man a merry dance.'

'Mmmm,' she said. 'And I am looking forward to many more dances with you.'

He grinned. 'Other things too,' he said. 'After our wedding.'

'About the wedding. Do we have to have a grand affair in London?'

'I want everyone to see you. To know you are the woman

I have chosen as my wife. To see my pride and my happiness and gnash their teeth.'

A laugh escaped her. 'Oh, Charlie. You couldn't have said anything better.'

He grinned. 'Let us be off, sweet. We can reach Durn tonight and break the news to my parents before they leave for London.'

She winced.

He rose, pulled her to her feet, and kissed her forehead. 'Courage, love. That is what I admired about you from the first, your courage as well as your beauty.'

She raised a brow. 'You thought I was a lightskirt.'

'Instead you are the light of my life.'

He drew her into his arms and kissed her lips. Happiness was a bright golden thing in her heart. It filled her with warmth. True love didn't care who your parents were, or what had happened before, she realised. True love was a beginning.

'Has he gone?' Caro asked, peeping around the door.

They separated like naughty children.

Caro flushed scarlet. 'Oh, I am sorry. I didn't mean to interrupt.'

Merry held out the hand with the ring. 'You are here just in time to hear my news. I am to be married.'

Caro's eyes widened. 'Really married?'

Charlie grinned. 'Leg shackled. Permanently.'

'Oh, Merry, I am so happy for you.' Caro rushed forwards and hugged her. 'So very happy.' She stepped back and there were tears of joy in her eyes.

'Why did you run from Captain Read?' Merry asked.

Caro paled. 'He is someone I knew a long time ago.'

Merry glanced at Charlie. 'Perhaps I should stay and—'

'No,' Caro said, her voice firm. 'I should not have run. He never did me any harm. It was just the shock of seeing him again.' She smiled. 'I have made a new life for myself and it is past time I stopped hiding.'

Merry sensed an underlying disquiet beneath the calm face. 'If you are sure?'

'Merry,' Charlie said, capturing her hand, his face serious. 'If Mrs Falkner finds herself in any difficulty she must send word to me. I will do all in my power to help her. But now we must speak with my parents.'

'Go,' Caro said, laughing. 'Invite me to your wedding and I promise I will come.'

The fear for her friend lightened. She kissed her cheek.

'Come,' Charlie said, urging her out of the door. 'The sooner we get this over, the sooner we can be wed.'

Wed. Common-as-muck Merry Draycott, wed to the heir to a dukedom. It hardly seemed possible, but when she gazed up into Charlie's face, she knew it had nothing to do with who he was and everything to do with the love shining in his eyes.

She reached up and kissed his cheek. 'No need to fuss, love,' she whispered. 'We have the rest of our lives.'

'We do.' He swept her up in his arms and carried her out of the house. 'And the sooner we get started, the better.'

He'd brought the closed carriage she noticed with a sigh of anticipation and a flood of heat. The ride back to Durn couldn't start soon enough.

She twined her arms around his neck and smiled.

* * * * *

The Rake's Inherited Courtesan

ANN LETHBRIDGE

Chapter One

Dover, Kent—1816

Safe behind her black veil, Sylvia Boisette steeled herself to confront those who, because of her birth, were a part of her world, but who would never accept her as part of theirs.

Dusty fingers of gold streamed through the bank of windows along the library's west wall, highlighting the room's comfortable shabbiness. On the threshold behind her, the eager servants murmured in anticipation of the reading of the will.

'I believe Mr Tripp wishes you to sit there, *mademoiselle*,' the butler muttered over her shoulder. He gestured to the far end of the room.

In front of the bewigged, craggy-faced lawyer, ranged the backs of three seated figures, a black-clad bastion of stiff respectability, and beside them, one empty chair.

'Who are they?' Sylvia whispered to the butler. Isolated in painful solitude at the funeral, she could only guess the identity of the strangers in attendance and the servants always knew everything.

'Imogene Molesby, the master's sister, to the right,' Burbridge murmured. A large-boned woman, she wore an outdated black bonnet and sat closest to the windows. 'Her husband, George.' Molesby's bulk seemed to overflow his straight-backed chair.

Beside him sat the handsome young man whose height and breadth had overshadowed the pitifully small group of mourners at the graveside, his aloof, patrician countenance full of disapproval. She nodded towards him. 'And the other?'

'Mr Christopher Evernden, Lord Stanford's younger brother.'

A buzz of anger in her veins chased off the numbness that had held her in thrall all morning. Lord Stanford, the head of the Evernden family, hadn't even bothered to come to his uncle's funeral. And Monsieur Jean had always spoken so well of his nephew.

Pauvre Monsieur Jean. How she would miss reading to him in this very room, his smiling face lit by the glow of a fire-place now as cold and empty as her heart. Sometimes, moisture glinting in his tired eyes, he had told her how much she resembled her beloved mother. Icy fingers clenched in her stomach. She might carry the burden of her mother's beauty, but she would not follow her path to ruin.

A deep breath steadied the beat of her heart. With a solemn swish of black silk skirts, she trod the bars of light and shade on the faded Axminster rug as if they formed the rungs of a ladder to her future, or an escape from her past.

Mr Tripp acknowledged her presence with a nod.

Fighting the sudden trembling in her knees, she sank on to the empty chair beside Mr Evernden. His sharp, sideways glance projected his distaste with the sureness of an arrow, while a chill disapproval emanated from his companions. She forced her spine straight. From this moment on, she would forge her own destiny.

Behind the ancient walnut desk, the lawyer glanced down at his papers. 'That is everyone, I presume?'

The straight-backed chair beside her issued an impatient creak and, from behind her veil, she risked a glance at its occupant. Polished Hessian boots planted flat on the floor, his muscular thighs extended well beyond the chair seat. Gold glinted in his dark-honey, wind-tousled hair. Fair skinned, with a chiseled jaw and high forehead, he bore the stamp of English nobility. His expressive mouth, set in a straight line, spoke of firmness of purpose.

Her stomach tumbled over in a strangely pleasurable dance.

Caught midbreath, she froze. She never allowed herself to notice men. One glance and the lascivious greed in their eyes sent her diving for the cover of cold disdain. She tried not to see them at all. Her interest stemmed from curiosity, nothing else. She focused her gaze on the lawyer.

Mr Tripp began to read. 'Being of sound mind…'

Beyond the window, fleecy clouds scudded across a robin's-egg-blue sky, their shadows gambolling like lambs across the familiar green, rolling hills. She would miss walking those headlands between here and Folkestone.

Tripp droned on and she forced herself to listen. Monsieur Jean left small sums of money to his butler and the housekeeper. He left a guinea to each of the other servants. How like the gentle man to remember them. His prized books, already boxed and waiting for transportation, went to an old friend too ill to travel to the funeral.

'To my sister, Imogene, I leave the ormolu clock which belonged to our mother,' Tripp intoned.

The clock Mrs Molesby and monsieur had fought over for years. How he had chuckled over that tale. She repressed a smile.

'Cliff House will be sold to pay my debts,' Mr Tripp read.

Monsieur Jean had promised her something for her future. She needed very little. Sylvia held her breath.

Pausing, Mr Tripp looked over his pince-nez at the assembled company. He cleared his throat. 'I leave my ward, Miss Sylvia Boisette, in the charge of my nephew, Mr Christopher Evernden.'

Sylvia gasped at the same moment Christopher Evernden smothered a startled oath with a cough.

The lines etched in Tripp's face deepened. 'He will receive whatever funds remain from the sale of Cliff House for her future care. The balance, when she marries, is to be used for her dowry.'

The room rocked around Sylvia as if Cliff House had toppled from its chalky perch and now floated on the wave-tossed English Channel. Sylvia closed her eyes against a surge of nausea, holding her body rigid until her head ceased to spin. She would not let them see her distress.

What had Monsieur Jean done? The dagger of realisation stabbed through her whirling thoughts. By trying to protect her from beyond the grave, he had ruined her plans.

'Disgusting,' Imogene Molesby exploded. 'How dare he foist his ladybird on to a respectable member of this family? It's disgraceful. There ought to be a law against it.'

Heat scorched her face at the damning tone. She clamped her mouth shut against the desire to cry out against the woman's injustice. Not for her own sake, but for sullying her beloved Monsieur Jean's memory.

At the back of the room, the servants moved restlessly and low mutters broke out. She turned and shook her head to stem their loyal defence. She wanted no public outcry marring this day.

Mr Tripp mopped his brow with a large white handker-chief. 'That concludes the reading of the last will and testa-ment of Mr John Christopher Evernden. A cold collation is offered to the family and mourners in the blue drawing room.'

The ormolu clock on the mantel ticked into the silence.

Hopelessly kind and a dreamer to his dying day, Monsieur Jean had buried her dream of starting a new, respectable life.

The chair arms solid beneath her shaking hands, Sylvia pushed to her feet.

Mr Evernden, shock and horror reflected in his hazel eyes, rose with her and executed a stiff bow. He wanted this as little as she. What English gentleman wouldn't be horrified at such a dreadful imposition? To be required to care for a woman of ill repute went beyond the pale of family duty.

Tears scalded the backs of her eyes and her mind unravelled at the speed of a spool of wool batted by a cat. She hadn't felt this lost since, at the age of eleven, she learned she would never see her mother again.

The tattered remnants of her composure her only shield against their censorious faces, she sketched a curtsy to Mr Evernden and the irate Molesbys. She nodded to Mr Tripp and, head held high, strode for the drawing room. The servants parted to allow her through the doorway. She acknowledged their murmured words of support as she passed.

She would not allow this to happen. There must be some way to be rid of this grim young Englishman.

Christopher, appalled and astonished, stalked towards the lawyer. He needed this error corrected immediately.

A hand clutched at his arm. 'I say, Evernden, we didn't expect to see you here today.'

Damn. The presence of the Molesbys added another layer of complication to the situation. He reined in his impatience. 'Mother insisted one of us had to attend. Unfortunately, Garth had another engagement.'

His chubby face shining and his gaze greedy with anticipation, Uncle George slid him a grin. 'That really is doing it rather too brown, don't you know. Leaving you saddled with his...' He coughed delicately into his hand and glanced at the affronted expression on his wife's horsy face. 'Well, I mean to say, his ward.' He winked. 'I hear she's ravishing.'

Christopher's heart sank. Garth's exploits, along with those of his infamous uncle John, were bad enough. When this news hit the clubs, Christopher's name would also be dragged through the Evernden mire. No doubt Uncle George would dine out on the story for weeks.

'Don't beat about the bush, George,' Aunt Imogene said with her habitual snort. 'We all know what sort of female she is.'

Knowing Aunt Imogene and her tendency to take the bit between her teeth, Christopher held his tongue. George stared at his boots, a penitent in purgatory.

In a travesty of a grimace, Imogene bared her protruding yellow teeth. 'And that is why your father banished him from the family. A young fool, he turned into an old fool. Can you imagine? He left all his money to her. All I got was the ormolu clock.' Her indignant voice rattled the ill-fitting windows.

Christopher kept his expression bland and his growing ire under firm control. No one could require him to inherit his uncle's mistress.

'Excuse me, Aunt Imogene, Uncle George. I need to speak to Tripp.' He bowed to the old couple and followed the lawyer into the drawing room.

While its cream walls and furnishings gave no indication of its designation as blue, at least this room looked more like a gentleman's home than the drab library.

At the window, stiff and forbidding in her deep mourning, Mademoiselle Boisette stared out across the English Channel. Outlined against the light, her high-collared black gown revealed shapely curves and a narrow waist. A deliberate ploy to display her charms to advantage, no doubt.

He wasn't interested.

Tripp hovered beside the sturdy Queen Anne sideboard piled high with pastries and platters of sliced roast beef, fruits and cheeses. Red tulips and sunny daffodils in a crystal centrepiece splashed colour into the muted room.

A glass of red wine in one hand and a fat meat pasty in the other, Tripp had the expression of a well-fed bloodhound. Apparently, reading wills sharpened the appetite.

'Help yourself,' Tripp said, spraying Christopher with crumbs. 'Oh, dear me. Excuse me, sir.' He dabbed at Christopher's coat front with his napkin.

Aware of the Molesbys' entrance into the room and their curious stares as they joined the vicar near the hearth, Christopher smiled and waved Tripp off. 'No, really. Don't be concerned.'

Tripp stopped flapping and gestured to the butler. 'Drink?'

For once, a drink sounded like a good idea. Perhaps several, after this got sorted out. Christopher selected a glass of burgundy from the butler's silver tray. He sent a swift glance towards Mademoiselle Boisette and turned his shoulder to the room at large. 'Now about this will,' he murmured. 'There's been a mistake.'

'I don't think so, sir,' Tripp replied. 'I helped Mr Evernden draw it up myself last month.'

'Last month?' Christopher reeled at the implication. Twelve years ago, Christopher's father had given his younger brother the cut direct and deemed him *persona non grata*. Christopher never saw him again.

Until six weeks ago.

He'd run into Uncle John in London and while he'd barely recognised the gaunt, old fellow, he didn't have the heart to cut a man whom he remembered for his generosity to him and Garth in their childhood.

Tripp took another bite of his pasty, chewed and swallowed. 'That's right. The moment he returned from London, he insisted I come right around to change his will.'

Dismay plunged Christopher's stomach to the floor. He recalled Uncle John leaning on his silver-headed walking stick on St. James's Street, his eyes twinkling as he asked after Garth and his mother. They'd chatted in a desultory way about Princess Charlotte's forthcoming wedding. The old man bemoaned the slump in trade since Waterloo and Christopher expressed concern about the Bridgeport riots. And that was it. Not a word of a personal nature crossed their lips and they had shaken hands and parted company. Apparently, simple common courtesy had landed him in a dreadful coil.

Christopher groaned inwardly. He suddenly wished he had cut off his right hand before allowing the old man to shake it. 'There must be some way to change it. Pay her off.'

'Mademoiselle Boisette, you mean?'

Who else would he mean? 'Yes.'

After a wishful glance at the sideboard, Tripp said, 'Perhaps we should discuss this in the study?'

Christopher glanced around the room where the smattering of local gentry paid their respects by eating everything in sight. In the far corner, Aunt Imogene held court, complaining loudly about the poor state of the ormolu clock to the vicar's plump wife and casting dark glances at Mademoiselle Boisette's rigid back. He nodded. 'Lead the way.'

Full of old, broken-down furniture and other rubbish, the crowded oak-panelled study smelled of camphor and dust. Moth-eaten feathered and furred trophies leaned against every available upright surface in the gloomy room. Boxes and papers spilled off the shabby desk and cluttered the chairs, leaving nowhere to sit.

'He used to hunt,' Tripp observed.

Ignoring the lawyer's attempt at delay, Christopher frowned. 'What can I do about this will?'

'Nothing.'

'Bloody hell. What do you mean, nothing?'

Tripp pursed his lips and lowered his brows.

'I'm sorry,' Christopher said. 'This all comes as rather a shock.' He took a swig of his burgundy. At least Uncle John had kept an excellent cellar.

'I imagine Mademoiselle Boisette is also surprised,' Tripp said, his jowls drooping to his cravat. 'A pleasant young woman. Always a very gracious hostess.'

The revelation of unsavoury secrets held no appeal and Christopher pressed on. 'Can I just sell the house and give her the money?'

Tripp appeared to consider the question carefully. 'Your uncle thought her too young. She needs a guardian.'

'Too young?' The words exploded from Christopher's mouth. His uncle must have been nigh on sixty. He wanted to throttle Tripp. 'How old is she?'

Tripp stiffened. 'Twenty-three. Your position of guardian is to continue until she's twenty-five.'

Dear God! Twenty-three and she had lived with his uncle for twelve years? No wonder the old man had locked himself away from society all these years. His stomach churned. The normally solid ground beneath him seemed to turn into a quagmire.

'I must decline,' Christopher said.

Tripp sighed. 'I feared as much. I told Mr Evernden the family wouldn't like it. He set great store by you, Mr Christopher. He would have been sorry to learn of his mistake.'

'At the risk of being rude, Mr Tripp, I must be brutally frank. I don't care what you think or what my uncle thought. I refuse to be imposed upon. I want it sorted out. Now.'

Tripp looked as affronted as Aunt Imogene. Christopher didn't care.

'The terms of the will are quite explicit, sir,' Tripp said.

'What about her mother's family, or her father?'

'She has no family of which I am aware. Her mother died in France. Mr Evernden did not reveal the name of her father. Anyway, since I gather her father refuses her recognition, it is of no consequence.'

The thin straw of rescue drifted out of Christopher's grasp. 'Then there must be something I can do with her. Some institution where she can learn a skill, somewhere a woman like—'

Tripp harrumphed. His eyebrows jumped on his crumpled forehead like rabbits on a ploughed field.

'Somewhere for a woman like me, Mr Evernden?' The cool tone from behind him held the slightest trace of a French accent.

Hell. Apparently, the impertinent Mademoiselle Boisette had no qualms about eavesdropping. So be it. Beating around the bush only led to disappointed expectations, as he well knew from his business dealings. Christopher swung around to face her.

Mr Tripp rushed between them. 'Allow me to introduce Mademoiselle Boisette, Mr Evernden.'

Still veiled, Mademoiselle Boisette held out a small, black-gloved hand. She curtsied as he took it, a fluid movement with all the easy grace of a self-assured woman.

She turned to the lawyer. 'Would you be good enough to leave us to speak alone, Mr Tripp? We have some issues of mutual concern to address.'

To his relief, her tone sounded clipped and businesslike. No tears. At least, not yet.

Tripp rubbed his hands together. 'Certainly.'

He had food on his mind, Christopher could tell.

Tripp pulled out his calling card and handed it to Christopher with a flourish. 'Mr Evernden, if it would not be too much trouble, I would appreciate it if you would call at my office later today. I have some documents requiring your signature.'

Damned country solicitors. Why the hell hadn't he brought the documents with him? Christopher tamped down his irritation. First, he had to depress any hopes Mademoiselle Boisette might have about continuing the connection with his family.

The murmur of distant conversation and the clink of glasses briefly wafted through the open door as Tripp left and closed it behind him.

Mademoiselle Boisette glided to the desk. Her graceful movements, her calmness, reminded Christopher of a slow and gentle river. Her impenetrable veil skimmed delicate sloping shoulders and he ran his gaze over her straight back and trim waist. An altogether pleasing picture.

The wayward thought stilled him. He leaned his hip against a rickety table and sipped his wine. Nothing she could say would make him change his mind.

With her back to him, Mademoiselle Boisette set her wine-glass amid the clutter of papers. A lioness's head leaned against one corner of the desk and her hand brushed reverently over its tufted ears.

She spoke over her shoulder. 'I feared these creatures so much when I first came to live here, I asked Monsieur Jean to remove them from the walls.' A breathy sigh, as light as a summer wind, shimmered the secretive veil. 'We both know there are far more dangerous creatures than these in the world, don't we?'

Reaching up, she pulled the pearl-headed pin from her bonnet. Her slender back stretched as she removed the hat in a fluid motion. She placed it on the desk.

A crown of braided gold encircled her head. Curling tendrils at the nape of her long neck brushed her collar.

As regal as a queen, she revolved to face him, her hands clasped in front of her. 'And that is why we need to talk.'

Christopher's breath hooked in his throat. She had the face of an angel.

Fringed by golden lashes, forget-me-not blue eyes gazed out of a heart-shaped face. Not a single blemish marred the perfection of her creamy complexion or peach-blushed cheeks. His mouth longed to taste the lushness of full ripe lips. A banquet offered to a starving man.

Like a callow youth faced with his first view of a woman's bare breast, his palms dampened. He resisted the temptation to wipe them on his pantaloons. By God, he'd seen many lovely women in the salons of London, but beautiful did not begin to describe this vision.

Since when did his appetites control his reactions?

As if reading his thoughts, her mouth curved in a smile, the small space in the centre of her pearl-white top teeth an enchanting fault amid celestial perfection.

She was no seraph. Pure devilment gleamed in the cerulean gaze locked with his.

Placing her gloved fingertip between her teeth, she glanced at him. Her lashes lowered and then swept up again. A lingering question lurked in her eyes.

Eve biting the apple.

He swallowed.

She tugged the tip of her glove free and then released it.

An indrawn breath lifted the swell of her bosom beneath her close-fitting gown. He imagined rose-tipped globes peaking to his touch.

His collar tightened. Sweat trickled down his spine.

Transfixed, he stared as she repeated the manoeuvre with each remaining slender finger. In all his years on the town, he'd never seen such wanton sensuality. Blood stirred and pulsed in his loins. He shifted, spreading his thighs to ease the burgeoning pressure.

Head tipped to one side, she focused her gaze on his mouth and licked her bottom lip with a moist, pink tongue.

An unendurable desire to echo that touch on his mouth, to trace the path of her glance, tingled his tongue.

As graceful as a ballet dancer and with agonising slowness, she drew off the glove, baring the white skin of her wrist, her knuckles, her slender fine-boned fingers.

Visions of white, naked flesh writhing beneath him shortened his breath. Sensations of silky skin, slick and wet and hot for him, closing around him as he drove them both to mindless bliss, tightened his groin. He fought the deep shimmer of pleasure.

She laid the wisp of black silk across the big cat's tawny muzzle.

He curled his lip. A brazen wanton indeed.

He enjoyed the warmth of a willing woman, but had no need of a professional courtesan. And no matter how beautiful or sensual, he had no interest in a woman who had brought scandal to the name of Evernden.

A dimple appeared at the corner of her curving mouth.

Taste her. Caress her full lips with his mouth, duel with her moist, soft tongue and press her slender form hard against him. Take what she offered with brazen abandon. Here. Now. The words matched the rhythm of his pulsing blood.

Damn. This little witch wouldn't play him for a fool as she had his dotard uncle. Lust never controlled him.

He slammed his glass amid the documents on the table, ignored the red stain spreading over the jumbled papers and folded his arms across his chest.

Seconds felt like minutes as, one finger at a time, she freed the other glove and slid it off. She ran the garment through her fingers, a torturous stroking of silk against bare skin. She dropped it beside its partner.

He remembered to breathe.

'Mr Evernden.' Her husky, accented voice caressed his skin the way a lioness rubbed in adoration against her mate. 'I have a proposition for you.'

Yes, his body roared in feral triumph.

Chapter Two

Disgust roiled in his gut, both at his unprecedented lack of control and the thought of his ancient uncle with his hands on this delicate creature. 'There is no proposal you could offer that would interest me, madam.'

Raising an eyebrow, she perused his person from heel to head, her gaze lingering on his chest before sliding up to meet his eyes. She smiled approval.

Molten lava coursed through his veins at the studied invitation.

Damn her impudence. Even the most audacious of the *demi-monde* made their desires known with more discretion. He didn't deal in money for flesh. The few women with whom he'd established mutually enjoyable relationships preferred gifts of jewellery, subtle tokens of appreciation and respect.

A seductive sway to her hips, she drifted to the centre of the room, her modestly cut gown intriguingly at odds with her aura of raw sensuality.

Once more, her gaze rested on his mouth and she moistened her lush lips. 'You sound quite sure of yourself.'

The only thing he knew for certain was his body's demands in response to her blatant allure. He forced his expression to remain impassive. 'We are discussing you, not me.'

She inclined her head to one side. 'Really? What is it to be then, Mr Evernden? Not an orphanage, for I am too old. A parish workhouse, perhaps?'

Her husky, French-laced voice called to him like a siren's song. He clenched his jaw.

Tapping one slender, oval-nailed finger against her rather determined chin, she nodded slowly. 'You will take your uncle's money and leave me to the tender mercies of the town.'

Bloody hell. She made him sound like a thief. Only he had no need of his uncle's pitiful estate and no reason for guilt. He knew where his duty lay. It did not include taking his uncle's bit of muslin home. 'Nothing of the sort. You have to live somewhere suitable.'

Something hard and bright flashed in her eyes. Swept away by fair lashes, it was replaced by a mischievous gleam. 'Anywhere except your home, of course.'

The deuce. Could she read minds? 'Exactly.'

She dropped her bold stare to the floor and her imperfect top teeth nibbled her lower lip. 'Excuse me, Mr Evernden. I do not wish to be at odds with you, but I do request a fair hearing before you reach a final decision.'

'There is nothing to discuss.'

Her eyes flashed. 'There is your family name.'

A lump of lead settled on Christopher's chest. More scandal. His mother had enough misery to contend with as Garth debauched his way through life, without this female causing her anguish. 'My family is nothing to do with you.'

She turned and picked up her gloves and hat. 'Perhaps this is not the best place to discuss such a delicate matter.'

He followed the direction of her gaze around the cluttered, dirty room and shrugged.

'We would occasion far less remark in my private apartments, once the other guests have departed,' she urged.

Blast. He'd forgotten the reception. And Aunt Imogene.

She would chew his ear off if she learned he'd been alone with this female. Not to mention what she would report to his poor, benighted mother. 'Very well.'

'I will ask the butler to bring you to my drawing room at the first possible opportunity.'

Christopher nodded.

Her hat clutched against her bosom, she peered out of the door, then slipped out.

Christopher raised his eyes to the smoke-grimed ceiling. He'd fallen into a madhouse.

He followed her into the hallway in time to see a swirl of black skirt disappear up the servants' narrow staircase at the other end of the passage. At least she showed a modicum of decorum.

Christopher straightened his shoulders and sauntered back to the reception. The company had thinned in his absence and Tripp was nowhere to be seen. Nursing his wine, Christopher wandered over to the window and glanced out. A privet hedge bordered the lane leading to the wrought-iron gates at the end of the sweeping drive where a knot of coachmen smoked pipes and chatted at the head of the four waiting carriages. Beyond them, a down-at-heel fellow in a battered black hat perused the front of the house. A prospective buyer?

The ramshackle condition of the property would not attract a wealthy purchaser despite the magnificent view of alabaster cliffs, the English Channel and, on a rare fine day like today, the faint smudge of the French coast on the horizon. Small vessels, their white sails billowing, scurried towards Dover harbour behind the headland. Mid-channel, larger ships plied their trade on white-tipped waves. No wonder his uncle had hermited himself away here with his *fille de joie*.

A picture of her face danced in his mind. He shook his head. No one could be that beautiful. The dim light had fooled him.

'Christopher?'

Damn it. What now? He swung around. 'Yes, Aunt?'

Excitement gleamed in his aunt's protuberant eyes. 'I am so glad George brought me today. Lord and Lady Caldwell were my brother's closest acquaintances.'

She motioned in the direction of the well-dressed couple engaged in conversation with chubby Uncle George. 'They have invited us to stay with them for a day or two.'

'How delightful for you both.'

Aunt Molesby dropped her penetrating voice to a whisper. 'Caldwell says that John actually used that woman as his hostess. Can you credit it?'

A veritable charger in the lists, nothing would stop his aunt at full tilt. Fortunately, she did not seem to expect an answer.

'Yes, indeed,' she continued. 'The shame of it. Lady Caldwell never attended, of course. Only men friends were invited for the gambling parties.' Her expression changed to disgruntlement. 'That woman didn't attend the gentlemen in any of their gambling pursuits. She always disappeared after dinner.'

Thank heaven for small mercies.

'You really should greet the Caldwells, you know,' she said, urging him in their direction. 'They were acquainted with your father.'

By the time Christopher had accepted the Caldwells' words of sympathy, said farewell to the Molesbys and spoken to the vicar, most of the food was gone and the guests had departed.

The butler approached with a low bow. 'If you'll follow me, sir, Mademoiselle Boisette will see you now.'

Quelling his irritation at the pompous tone, Christopher followed the butler up the curved staircase to the second floor. Ushered into what was obviously an antechamber, he surveyed the delicate furnishings and the walls decorated with *trompe-l'oeil* scenes of what he assumed to be the idyllic French countryside.

Rather than risk the single fragile, gilt chair collapsing under him, Christopher declined the butler's offer of a seat.

'If you would wait here a moment, sir, I will inform Mademoiselle Boisette you are here.'

Hell. Did she think he was here for an interview? He would make his position clear from the outset.

The butler knocked on the white door beneath a pediment carved with cherubs. It opened just enough for him to enter.

More moments passed and Christopher paced around the room. This situation became more tiresome by the minute. Finally, the butler returned and gestured for him to enter. 'This way, sir, if you please.'

A gaunt, middle-aged woman, her well-cut, severe gown proclaiming her to be some sort of companion, bobbed a curtsy as he passed and Christopher stepped into the lady's bower, a room of light, with high ceilings and pale rose walls. A white rug adorned the centre of the highly polished light-oak planks. Mademoiselle Boisette, seated on the sofa in front of an oval rosewood table, glanced up from pouring tea from a silver teapot.

Stunned by the full effect of her glorious countenance, Christopher blinked. His mind had not played tricks downstairs. With hair of spun gold and small, perfectly formed features, she seemed even more beautiful than he remembered. Unfortunately, she had spoiled the effect by applying rouge to her cheeks and lips since their first meeting.

He took the hand she held out.

She smiled with practised brilliance. 'Mr Evernden, thank you for agreeing to talk to me. Denise, you may leave us. Mr Evernden and I have business to discuss.'

The woman twisted her hands together. 'I will be in the next room should you need me, *mademoiselle*.'

Mademoiselle Boisette inclined her head. '*Merci*, Denise.'

She indicated the striped rose-and-grey upholstered chair opposite her. 'Please, do be seated.'

Like the pieces in the antechamber, the delicate furniture seemed unsuited to the male frame. Careful to avoid knocking the table with his knees, he lowered himself onto the seat.

Despite the damned awkwardness of the situation, Mademoiselle Boisette seemed perfectly at ease. She might not have attended his uncle's card parties, but this young woman managed to hide her thoughts exceedingly well. Determined to remain impartial, he eyed her keenly. He would hear her out.

Pouring tea into a white, bone-china cup, she moved with innate grace. Her fine-boned fingers were as white and delicate as the saucer in her hand.

He didn't like tea. He never drank it, not even for his mother. He took the cup she held out. 'Thank you.'

She peeped at him through her lashes. 'What an amusing situation to find ourselves in, Mr Evernden.' Her husky laugh curled around him with delicious warmth.

He steeled himself against her blandishments. 'I would hardly call it amusing, *mademoiselle.*'

After slowly stirring her tea, she replaced the spoon in the saucer without the slightest chink. She arched a brow. '*Mais non?* You do not find it entertaining? A farce. The son of a noble English milor' and a courtesan's daughter, trapped together by a dead man's will? My mother was *une salope*. A prostitute, I think you say in English?'

Startled, Christopher swallowed a mouthful of hot tea. Damn. It burned the back of his throat on the way down.

He struggled not to cough for several seconds. By God, he hadn't come here to listen to this. She might look like an angel, but she used the language of the Paris gutters. 'Your frankness, madam, is astonishing.'

To his satisfaction, she looked slightly nonplussed.

She tilted her head in enchanting puzzlement. 'I thought it would be better if we did not, how do you say it…mince our words?'

Did she think he would be taken in by such contrived gestures? Christopher glared at her. 'Very well, *mademoiselle*. If it is plain speaking you want, you shall have it. My uncle's will leaves me in a damnable position. I have no alternative but to place you somewhere you can do no further harm to my family's good name.'

'Do you have any idea what will happen to me in a workhouse or some other charitable institution?' Despite her smiling expression, desperation edged her voice. 'Oh, no, Mr Evernden. I will not allow it.'

Christopher glanced around the elegant drawing room. She was right. Wherever she ended up, it would not be like this. Her beauty would leave her vulnerable to all kinds of abuse. The thought sickened him.

Damn it. She'd been his uncle's mistress for years. What difference could it possibly make to a woman of her stamp? 'You have no choice. Cliff House must be sold to pay my uncle's debts. You must go somewhere you can learn a *respectable* occupation.'

A shadow darkened her eyes to fathomless blue. Fear? Anger? Golden lashes swept the expression away, leaving her gaze clear and untroubled. He was mistaken. Women like her did not know fear.

Except that looking at her, he couldn't quite give credence to the gossip. Or did he simply not want to believe something this beautiful could be so depraved?

She surged to her feet in a rustle of stiff silk and skirted the table between them. The heavy scent of roses wafted over him. He didn't recall her wearing so much perfume in the study.

As light as a butterfly, her hand rested on his upper arm. She slanted him a teasing glance. 'The key is respectable, *non*?'

Heat prickled up his arm. How would that hand feel in his? Soft? Warm? Before he could discover for himself, she floated to the window. A vague sense of loss swept him.

Her hair molten gold and the profile of her perfect face and figure haloed by the glow of the afternoon sun, she paused, looking out.

Another pose designed to drive a man to lustful madness. He tightened the rein on his self-control and waited in silence.

She pressed a hand to her throat, fingering the trinket suspended at her beautiful throat, then turned to face him full on.

He squinted against the light, straining to see her expression.

'Your uncle made no complaints,' she murmured. 'Are you sure you do not wish to take his place?'

Once more, unruly blood stirred at the suggestion in her husky voice. For a moment, he considered her blatant offer. Blast her. He was no cup-shot, idle rake like his brother. 'Quite sure.'

She remained silent for a moment, thoughtful, then smiled and raised one hand, palm up. 'Then give me two hundred pounds from the sale of Cliff House and I swear the Evernden family will never hear from me again. Nor will I ever mention my connection with your uncle.'

Blackmail. A brief pang of disappointment twisted in his chest, instantly obliterated by a flood of relief. Two hundred pounds was a pittance to rid his family of this blot on their good name. If he could only trust her word. 'Where will you go?'

The sultry coquette evaporated, leaving a haughty young woman staring down her nose. 'That, sir, is none of your concern.'

If she thought to bleed him dry a few hundred pounds at a time, she'd come to the wrong door. 'If you want money from me, I will make it my concern.'

She hesitated, then dropped her gaze. 'I am going to Tunbridge Wells.'

'Tunbridge Wells?' The nearest town of any significance to the Darbys' estate where he planned to spend the next fortnight. He'd arranged to pick up his curricle at the Sussex

Hotel and send the town carriage back to London. 'And how do you intend to support yourself?'

While her face remained a blank page, storms swirled in the depths of her eyes. 'A friend owns a small, but exclusive, ladies' dress shop in the town. I plan to invest in her business.'

With short sharp steps, she returned to her seat. The heavy scent of roses thickened the air. 'Would you care for some more tea?' She picked up the teapot. 'I have grown fond of the English *thé*.'

Christopher placed his cup on the tray. 'No. Thank you.'

She began to fill her cup.

A conniving woman of her sort needed careful handling. They lived by their wits and their bodies. Their stock in trade relied on a man's brain residing in his breeches. 'I will drive you to Tunbridge Wells.'

Tea splashed into the saucer and rattled the spoon. 'What?'

Not quite so self-assured, then.

'I want to see you safely delivered to your destination.'

She glared at him, then her lips curved in her sensuous smile.

God, his lungs ceased to work every time she did that.

'You wish to make sure I speak the truth?' she asked.

He inclined his head. 'As you say.'

She returned the teapot to the tray. Her low husky chuckle filled the silence and she cast him a sly glance. 'Are you sure that is your only reason for wishing to remain in my company?'

Smouldering annoyance flared to anger. The little hussy delighted in tormenting him. 'Mademoiselle Boisette, the sooner I wash my hands of you, the better I will like it.'

Her gaze dropped from his, her hand creeping to touch her gold locket. When she replied, her smile seemed forced. 'The feeling is mutual, Mr Evernden.'

She rose and he followed suit. The top of her golden head barely reached his shoulder.

'I assume we have nothing left to say to each other,' she said. 'I would like to leave for Tunbridge Wells in the morning.'

'I will let you know my decision after I have spoken to Mr Tripp.'

She hesitated, then narrowed her eyes. 'I am going to join my friend tomorrow, Mr Evernden, with or without your escort. I expect two hundred pounds to be delivered to me before I leave. If not, I will apply to Lord Stanford or perhaps your mother, Lady Stanford. Your uncle promised me that money.'

Next she'd be claiming a child by the poor old man. Well, Christopher would damned well make sure she never troubled any member of his family again. She might not yet realise it, but she had met her match.

Tripp had one more task this afternoon, drawing up a settlement. 'You will have my answer after dinner, *mademoiselle*. I wish you good day.'

He executed a courteous, shallow bow and headed for the door. An urgent craving to rid the cloying scent of roses from his lungs lengthened his stride.

From the arched window on the landing, Sylvia stared down at the athletic figure in the swirling greatcoat as he climbed into a shiny black coach emblazoned with the Evernden coat of arms.

The sharp point of her locket dug into her palm. Relaxing her fingers, she tried to still her trembles and leaned her forehead against the cool glass. Had he believed her? Why would he not? The thought curdled in her stomach.

He seemed to be the solemn, honourable Englishman described by Monsieur Jean on his return from London. The disgust curling his mobile mouth had poured venom through her veins. And yet, she'd seen the heat beneath his chill exterior, the stirring of interest reflected in glittering green shards deep in his forest-coloured eyes. If lust won out, she'd wrought her own disaster.

Since she had come to his house, Monsieur Jean had protected her from the outside world of brutal men, groping sweaty hands, hot fetid breath and stinking bodies. She closed her eyes and shuddered at the recollection.

She drew in a deep calming breath and watched the coachman flick his leaders with his long whip before he steadied his horses to pass through the wrought-iron gates. The coach turned towards the winding, cliff-top road to Dover.

A wry smile tugged at her lips. The young man's contempt hadn't left her trembling and as nauseous as the day she'd crossed the English Channel. It was the ease with which she'd played the strumpet that left her weak and sick. Like a well-worn mantle, she'd donned the cloak she thought she'd left in her past.

Non. The man might be one of the handsomest she'd ever met, but only necessity forced her to speak the words of a painted Jezebel and further destroy Monsieur Jean's reputation with her lies.

She had no choice. Beneath Christopher Evernden's reserved exterior, she sensed steel and a brain. A dangerous combination in a man. All she could do was wait and see if he would take the bait.

'Mademoiselle?' Denise's hand touched her shoulder.

With an effort, she pasted a smile on her lips and turned to face her old friend, the woman Monsieur Jean had brought from France to make her feel more at home in a strange country all those years ago.

'Come to France with me in the morning,' Denise said. 'My family will welcome you.'

An icy chill ran over her skin at the thought of returning to Paris. Memories of her childhood flashed raw and ugly into her mind. 'No, Denise,' she murmured, her heart eased by the tender look on the older woman's face. She smiled. 'You will see. With Mary's dressmaking skills and my designs, I will become a famous modiste, then I will call for you to come back to me.'

Tears welling in her brown eyes, Denise nodded. 'I will look forward to it, little one.'

A gut-wrenching smell assaulted Christopher's senses when he reached the quay a short distance from Tripp's office. Behind him, the town of Dover wound away from the docks. High on the cliffs, the ancient castle loomed over the harbour.

On the wharf, he skirted heaps of cargo, coils of old rope and clusters of merchants arguing in noisy groups. A group of seamen pushed past him with rolling gait, each brawny shoulder loaded with a barrel. Their curses rang in his ears. Nothing cleared the head like sea air, unless, like here, it was befouled with the smell of rotting fish and heated pitch. He grimaced. It really was a noisome, filthy place.

His long stride carried him swiftly past the waterfront where bare-masted ships speared the cloudy sky. The events of the day pounded at his mind in tune with the sea dashing itself against the cliffs.

Clear of the busy docks, Christopher strolled along the front, savouring the sharp breeze on his skin and the tang of salt on his tongue. Exposed by low tide, the yellow pebble beach sported seaweed and blackened spars. Nothing about Dover appealed to him.

Damn it all. It had been a simple task. Stay one night at the Bull, attend the funeral and the reading of the will, then be on his way to the Darbys' in Sussex by nightfall. Only now, he had to deal with the problem of Mademoiselle Boisette.

Why not give her the money and let her go her own way? Because he hated to leave anything dangling.

He frowned. The interview with Tripp had confirmed his fears that there was little to be had from the sale of Cliff House. A half-pay naval officer had offered to purchase it for a pittance and Uncle John's creditors wanted a quick sale. Tripp thought there might be a few pounds left, perhaps between ten and fifty, after the creditors received their share. Mademoiselle Boisette would be hard put to manage on so small a sum.

To top it all, Uncle John had reached out from the grave and planted Christopher a facer. A letter, to be delivered if he refused to take Mademoiselle Boisette under his wing.

Curse it. New rage flared up to heat his blood. He dropped on to a wooden bench looking out over the harbour. Sullen, foam-crested waves tumbled up the beach and rattled the stones. On the horizon black clouds heralding yet more rain. A dousing would make a perfect end to the day.

He pulled the letter from his pocket and broke open the red wax seal. Ripe with the smell of seaweed, the stiff breeze fluttered the paper as he peered at the spidery handwriting.

Dear Nephew,

I write in haste, for I have little time left to me. If you are reading this letter, you have rejected my request to care for my little Sylvia.

Request? More like a bludgeoning over the head with a gravestone. Christopher fought the urge to ball the paper in his fist and toss it into the surf rolling around the rotting timber breakwater.

She has been a daughter to me all these years.

Then why hide her away?

Her mother was my first and only love. She chose another, but my feelings remained constant. Now, all I can do for my beloved Marguerite is take care of her little girl, Sylvia. My poor Marguerite, so tender in her emotions, dragged down into the pit of hell by viciousness and vice.

These were words a Gothic novelist like Mrs Radcliffe would have been proud to write. Gritting his teeth, he forced himself to read on.

Understand, my dear Christopher, her father deserted his child and continues to deny her. I have spent my life and most of my money trying to prove her claim.

You must succeed where I have failed. The duke must pay for his crime.

Please, do not let me down. You are Sylvia's only hope.
John Christopher Evernden.

The word *hope* had been underlined several times.

He was supposed to guess the name of this duke? He turned the paper over to see if it contained the answer on the back. Nothing. Was he supposed to walk up to each of them in turn and accuse them of siring a French bastard?

Damn. His uncle must think him some sort of knight on a white charger, riding around the countryside rescuing damsels in distress. Questionable damsels at that.

It was the sort of thing Garth would have jumped at when they were boys. And Christopher would have followed behind, cleaning up the mess. A fool's errand. The old man had to be addled in his pate. Sylvia Boisette had been brutally clear about her mother's occupation.

But not the daughter? For some obscure reason, he wanted to believe Uncle John's assertion she was his ward and nothing more. In the face of a statement made by a man facing death, Christopher ought to believe in her innocence as a matter of family honour, despite her wanton behaviour earlier today.

A sudden image of her siren smile, the languorous removal of her gloves, fired his blood. Hell, did he have no self-control where this woman was concerned? Was desire mingled with disgust colouring his judgement?

Whatever the case, the almost nonexistent funds for her support left the workhouse as the only solution unless he succumbed to her blackmail.

He stared blindly at the tumbling surf and grating pebbles. She needn't know how much would be left after the sale of the house. He could add to the balance, just be rid of her. He certainly had enough blunt left from the tidy profit he'd made on the last cargo of silks from the Orient. Even after purchasing a half-share in a ship bound for America, there was more than enough left to see Mademoiselle Boisette comfortably settled.

It would solve the problem. *If* he could be sure she would leave his family in peace.

He stuck the note in his pocket alongside the agreement drawn up by Tripp, pushed to his feet and headed towards town and the comfort of his inn. He'd think about it some more over dinner.

Taking hasty decisions on an empty stomach only resulted in trouble.

Chapter Three

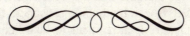

At the crunch of wheels on gravel, Sylvia turned her gaze from her beloved cliffs to the Evernden carriage rolling through the gate.

Thirsty for one last memory, she wheeled in a slow circle, the coarse fabric of her plain, grey wool travelling cloak twisting about her legs. Above her, white against grey, crying seagulls hovered on a breeze alive with the boom of crashing surf and a smattering of rain. Weighed down by the lessons she'd learned as a child, she drank in her last view of the rambling mansion's warm red brick framed by windswept larches. One could never go back.

The matching chestnuts slowed to a halt at the front door. All loose-limbed athletic grace and conservative in a black coat, Mr Evernden leaped down. The wind ruffled the crisp waves of his light brown hair. His handsome face brightened when he caught sight of her.

Warmth trickled into her stomach. Her mind screamed danger.

He waited as she strolled across the drive to his side, then glanced at her green brassbound trunk beside her valise on the steps. 'Is this everything?'

She had packed only the most practical of her clothing. She nodded. 'All I need.'

The coachman tied her luggage on the rack at the back and Mr Evernden swept open the carriage door. 'Are you ready, Mademoiselle Boisette?'

He held out his hand to assist her in. A small, polite smile curved his firm mouth and green sparks danced in his eyes.

Awareness of his size and strength skittered across her skin. She stilled, frozen by the odd sensation. Last night, his note had indicated his agreement to take her to Tunbridge Wells. After performing the harlot yesterday, dare she trust him? Prickles of foreboding crawled down her back.

She ignored his proffered aid. 'Quite ready, Mr Evernden.' Maintaining a cool expression, she stepped into the well-appointed carriage and settled on the comfortable black-tufted seats.

He followed her in, his musky sandalwood cologne heady in the confined space. Lean long legs filled the gap between the seats as he lounged into the squabs in the opposite corner. He gave her a sharp glance, then rapped on the roof and the carriage moved off with a gentle sway.

The window afforded glimpses of white sails skimming the spume-capped grey waves of the English Channel, an impenetrable moat around the castle of her past.

'Another wet day,' he said.

She kept her gaze fixed outside. 'Indeed.'

'Having caused us to freeze all winter I understand there are predictions that the Tomboro volcano will also ruin our spring.'

The masculine timbre of his voice resonated a chord deep inside her. For no apparent reason, her breath shortened as if his size and strength and even his cologne pressed against her chest. She clenched the strings of her reticule in her lap. 'So I have heard.'

An awkward silence hung in the air.

He cleared his throat. 'We will stop at Ashford for lunch and arrive in Tunbridge Wells before the supper hour.'

'Thank you.'

Tunbridge Wells and Mary Jensen and her future. Her heart swelled with optimism and she touched the locket at her throat. Everything would be all right.

An impatient sigh gusted from his corner. He shifted, stretching out his long legs until his shining black boots landed inches from the edge of her skirts.

For all his outward appearance of ease, tension crackled across the space between them. Determined to ignore it and him, she focused her gaze out of the window.

He eased his shoulders deeper into the corner. She glanced at him from beneath her bonnet's brim and cast a professional eye over his attire. After all, a successful modiste kept *au courant* with the latest styles, male and female, and she had met few members of the *ton* hidden away in Dover.

His buff unmentionables clung to his well-muscled legs, a smooth second skin over lean, strong thighs. Her pulse quickened.

Unable to resist the tempting sight, she let her gaze drift upwards past narrow hips to his broad chest, the close cut of his black coat, unmistakably Weston. Above an intricate, snowy cravat, she followed the column of his strong neck to his patrician profile, then to his hair arranged *à la Brutus*. A stray lock fell in a wave on his broad forehead. No dandy, just the quiet elegance of a man comfortable with himself.

As if he sensed her perusal, he turned his head and glanced at her from beneath half-lowered lids.

Cheeks burning, she flicked her gaze to the view.

Not another glance would she spare for her escort. Mary and her shop must be the focus of all her attention. *Their shop.* She hugged the thought to herself, a glimmer of warmth in a chilly world. Although small, according to Mary it was situated one street from the centre of the spa. No longer as popular as Bath, the Wells continued to attract older members of the *ton* because of its proximity to London. But Mary's last letter had arrived six months ago. Her business must be thriving if she could not find the time to write.

'*Mademoiselle?*'

Her stomach lurched.

Merde. She had all but forgotten him. Taking a deep breath, she willed her heart to stop its wild fluttering and forced frost into her tone. 'Miss Boisette, Mr Evernden, since I plan to make my home here in England.'

He raised a brow. 'Boisette is hardly an English name?'

He was right. It was the name her English mother had used in her new life in Paris, a life where she preferred not to shame her family name. Sylvia had simply adopted it. 'It is how I wish to be addressed.'

A furrow formed above his patrician nose, but he inclined his head. 'As you wish.'

'I prefer to be addressed as Miss. Both of my parents were English. Also, there is no need for polite conversation, since after today we will never meet again.'

His firm mouth tightened and his nostrils flared as if he held back angry words. 'As you wish, *Miss* Boisette.'

The carriage turned north away from the coast and he gazed out the rain-spattered window at the passing hilly countryside.

She let go of her breath. She infinitely preferred the heat of his anger to the other warmth she'd sensed deep in his eyes. Yesterday, he had been furious as she removed her gloves. Furious and fascinated.

Therein lay the danger. While he might have convinced the softhearted Monsieur Jean as to his honourable nature, she knew better than to trust any man.

Painful pinpricks ran over her shoulders. At any moment he might press her to make good her offer from the previous day. The dangerous game she played might yet be lost. She squeezed tighter into her corner of the carriage.

They reached Ashford around mid-day and lunched at the King's Head. There, in clipped sentences he explained the document setting out the terms under which he agreed to provide her with the promised funds. Sylvia signed it and he produced a velvet purse containing twenty-five guineas, the rest to be forwarded from his bank within two weeks. With new horses put to, the carriage jolted its way across country to their final destination and at long last, the coach bowled into Tunbridge Wells. Sylvia leaned forward for a better view of the High Street and the famous spa at the bottom of the hill. The town was smaller than she expected. It didn't matter. The infusion of funds from her uncle and the two of them sharing the work—and she would work night and day—it could not help but be a success.

The coach eased into a narrow lane and pulled up outside a timbered, bow-fronted shop with swathes of cloth draped in the window. Mr Evernden reached for the door handle.

Her heart beat a rapid tattoo. She did not want him to realise the unexpected nature of her arrival. She placed a hand on his sleeve.

The hiss of his indrawn breath shivered to the pit of her stomach.

She drew back, startled. Shaken by her response to that faint breath, she tried to keep her voice steady. 'If you would request your coachman to put my luggage on the road, I will not put you to any further inconvenience, Mr Evernden.'

He turned the door handle. 'It is no trouble at all, Miss Boisette.'

Stubborn man. She raised a brow. 'I prefer not to arrive here blatantly accompanied by a young gentleman of the *ton*.'

His expression turned grim and he dropped his hand. 'It is

impolite to leave you in the street, but it shall be as you desire.' He sat back. 'I wish you all the best in your new life, Miss Boisette, and bid you good day.'

His stern remoteness appealed to her far more than effusive politeness. He'd acted the perfect gentleman in all their dealings, while she had treated him to an outrageous display of hot and cold. No doubt he thought the worst of her. A pang of regret held her rigid for the space of a heartbeat. She must not care about his opinion. She reached for the door. 'Thank you.'

She stepped out on to the slick cobbles.

At Mr Evernden's order, the coachman heaved her belongings down beside her and climbed back on to his perch.

Shocked to discover her hand shaking in trepidation, she knocked on the door, all the while aware of Mr Evernden's intense gaze on her back. She turned, raised her hand in farewell, and the carriage moved off, affording one last glance of Mr Evernden's stern profile in the window.

The door opened to reveal a freckle-faced girl of about ten. Behind her, a passage led into the depths of the first floor and a narrow set of stairs wound upwards. Mary had never mentioned a child. She must be the maid.

'Can I help you, miss?' the girl asked.

Sylvia took a deep breath and smiled. 'Is Miss Jensen home?'

'There ain't no Miss Jensen at this address.'

Sylvia frowned. 'Are you sure?'

'Of course I am. I live here, don't I?'

'Who is it, Maisie?' a voice called from upstairs.

'A lady looking for a Miss Jensen, Ma,' Maisie yelled back.

A plump, dark-haired matron in a chintz gown, a chubby baby on her hip and a question on her face, clattered down the stairs.

Foreboding quaked in Sylvia's chest. She took a shaky breath. 'My name is Sylvia Boisette. I'm here to see Mary Jensen.'

The woman shook her head. 'She's gone, miss. The

landlady said she fell ill and her brother fetched her back to London more than five months ago.'

The entrance to the Sussex Hotel at the back of the promenade hummed with activity. Coaches rumbled in and out, grooms struggled with frisky teams, ostlers ran to and fro and passengers, rich and poor, milled around in controlled confusion in a yard rich with the smell of horse manure and stale ale.

Sylvia tried to make sense of the bustling chaos. She dug into her meagre store of small coins and gave a ha'penny to the boy who had carried her trunk from Frog Lane.

He touched his cap and dashed off, whistling a merry tune.

Oh, to be so youthful and carefree. Sylvia couldn't remember a time in her life when she hadn't been anxious about something. She clutched her reticule to her, where the slip of paper with Mary's new address, which the plump matron had given her, resided. And right now she was about to embark on an exceedingly risky course. Respectable females rarely travelled by common stage. But then she had never been considered respectable.

She had no option. She would not waste her small store of guineas on expensive modes of travel. Nor could she afford to lose them to footpads or pickpockets. Since no one in the yard appeared to notice her, she unlocked the trunk and hid the purse of guineas in its battered depths. Rising, she caught the eye of a passing lackey in brown livery.

'Can I help you, miss?'

'Please take my trunk inside.'

He moved aside to allow a gentleman and his lady to pass through the entrance into the lobby. 'Have you a room bespoke, miss?'

'I just need one small chamber.'

'I dunno. You best check with the master. Your luggage will

be safe enough with the porter while you go and see what Mr Garge has to say.'

He hefted her trunk on his shoulder and staggered to the stable entrance with Sylvia marching behind. He dropped it beside an elderly porter seated on a wooden box outside the mail-coach ticket office and storeroom. Another carriage rattled into the yard and the lackey raced off to meet it.

Sylvia smiled at the porter. 'I plan to catch the first coach to London tomorrow morning. If you would be so good as to see my trunk is placed on it, I would be most grateful.'

A pair of twinkling brown eyes looked at her from beneath straggly grey brows and the weathered face creased into a smile. 'I'll be more than pleased to oblige, miss,' he said. 'You gets your ticket in there.' He jerked his head towards the office.

'Thank you.' She gave him a penny and went inside to pay for her ticket. By the time she had completed her purchase and come outside, the porter had dispensed with her trunk. The door to the storeroom seemed sturdy and there were bars at the window. Hopefully, her money and her small cache of jewellery would be safe enough. Valise and hatbox in hand, she entered the inn.

One side of the wide entrance hall housed a counter. Across the way, a confusing array of doorways and passages led off in various directions. A bell sat next to the guest book on the counter. She rang it.

Moments later, a short, fat, florid-faced landlord in a black coat and striped waistcoat bustled out of the dining room door. 'Good evening, miss. Can I be of assistance?'

'Good evening. I will be catching the six o'clock stage tomorrow morning and require a single room for the night.'

'The name, miss?' he asked, running a stubby finger down the list in his book.

'I do not have a reservation.'

He looked behind her as if he expected someone else.

'How many in your party, miss? We are very busy today. I am not sure I can accommodate you.'

'There's no one else in my party.'

He frowned. 'Didn't you just arrive with this gentleman?'

Sylvia glanced over her shoulder. A young sprig of fashion in a many-caped driving coat and stiff shirt points swept through door.

'I am travelling alone. I… My maid took ill at the last moment.'

The landlord lowered his beetle brows. 'This inn's for Quality and their womenfolk don't travel alone. You'd best take yourself off to the Two Aitches.'

She blinked. She must have misheard. 'Where?'

'The Hare and Hounds, on the London Road. It has rooms for the likes of you. Now be off.'

The likes of her? Was her past somehow written on her forehead or branded on her cheek? Heat scorched through her veins. He had no right to treat her like some low-class female because she travelled alone and the last thing she wanted to do was wander the town looking for a room. 'My good man—'

She drew herself up to her full height and pierced him with a cool stare. 'You must have something. A small chamber will suffice.'

The landlord tapped a sausage of a finger on his reservation book. 'Well, I might have something,' he allowed. 'Not a very big room and no private parlour. I'll have to check with the missus.'

The gentleman behind her coughed and the harried landlord looked past her. 'If you'll just stand aside, miss, I'll look after this here gentleman and then I'll see what can be done.'

A hot admonition jumped to her tongue, instantly quelled. Forced to be patient or lose her only chance of a room, she drew back into the corner and watched as the innkeeper folded his stout body in half. 'Lord Albert, how good to see you again. What will it be today, a private parlour? We've got a nice bit of roast beef on the spit that might take your fancy for dinner.'

The fashionably attired young dandy with an elaborately tied cravat and rouged cheeks caught Sylvia's scornful glance over the landlord's bowed head. He winked.

Her stomach dropped. Foolhardy indeed, if she attracted the attention of this young fop. She schooled her face into chilly disdain and stared at the opposite wall.

Undeterred, the dandy gestured in her direction. 'Why, Garge, I believe this young, er…lady was here before me.' He spoke with a pronounced lisp.

Garge's face darkened. 'I'm looking after her, sir. She has to wait until I have some time.'

From the corner of her eye, she watched Lord Albert's gaze rake her from head to toe. Damn him for his impudence. Tapping her foot, she favoured him with her iciest stare.

His smile broadened. 'Perhaps I can be of some assistance, miss? I'd be delighted to be of service.' He giggled.

He actually giggled. Sylvia opened her mouth to give him a set-down, but the landlord's scowl did not bode well and she pressed her lips together.

The landlord's colour heightened. 'I'll have none of them goings-on under my roof, Lord Albert. I run a respectable house, I do.'

'I was only offering to share my room, Garge.' The dandy smirked.

Mortified, she stiffened her spine and raised her chin. 'I have a room.'

The landlord glowered. 'Not here you don't.'

Oh, no. He couldn't have changed his mind, not now. 'You said—'

'I made a mistake. We're full up.'

'As I said,' Lord Albert interjected, with a flourish of his silver-headed cane and a sly smile on his thin lips, 'I would be more than willing to accommodate you.'

Couldn't the mincing puppy see the trouble he was causing? Sylvia wanted to shake him. 'Sir, I would be obliged if you would mind your own business.'

The landlord turned his broad back on her as if she no longer existed.

For goodness' sake. She wasn't asking for the moon. All she wanted was a room for the night. She picked up her valise and sidled around him, preparing to argue.

A hand touched her sleeve. 'If you wish,' a faintly lyrical voice murmured in her ear, 'I could guide you to the Hare and Hounds Tavern. It's not such a bad place. I am sure they have a decent room.'

She swung around and found herself hemmed in by a man of medium height and a wiry frame, who must have entered the entrance hall from one of the passages. His dark green coat had seen better days and the brim of his black hat shadowed all but his lean jaw and a flash of crooked teeth.

She shook his hand off her arm. Another gallant gentleman with less than honourable intentions, no doubt. 'No, thank you, sir.'

He touched her shoulder. 'You won't get any change out of Garge, here. You will no doubt fare better at the Hare.'

In a flurry of capes, Lord Albert strode over and pointed his cane at the newcomer's chest. 'Stand aside, sir,' he lisped. 'Garge, this young lady is under my protection. I insist you provide us with a room immediately. Isn't that right, my dear?'

He caught her fingers and pressed them to his moist lips. Sylvia pulled away, but for all his fragile posturing, his grip held firm. He drew her closer.

Nausea rose in her throat and her skin crawled at the touch of his hot, damp fingers. A violent urge to flee, a fear she hadn't known in years, quickened her pulse. But she needed this room.

'Unhand me, sir.' With a jerk, she freed herself. Disguising her panic with a chilly glare, she took a deep breath.

'The young lady is with me.' A quiet, but firm voice came from behind her.

Sylvia whirled around. One hand resting on the doorframe, his shoulders filling the entrance to the dining room, Christopher Evernden glowered at Lord Albert.

A warm glow rose up her neck and warmed her cheeks. The shabby man uttered a muffled oath and seemed to fade into the shadows as quickly as he had appeared.

The landlord thrust his jaw and pendulous chins in Mr Evernden's direction. 'Now don't you start, sir. This young person ain't spending the night at this inn with any of you randy gentlemen.'

Heat raced from the tips of her ears to her toes. An irresistible urge to slap the landlord's fat face clenched her fist.

Mr Evernden shot out a large hand, grasped her wrist and dragged her out of Lord Albert's reach.

She gasped and pried at his fingers. She wasn't a bone to be fought over by men acting like curs. 'Let me go.'

'I say, old chap,' the dandy drawled. 'I saw her first. Find your own ladybird. Or get to the back of the queue.'

His high-pitched giggle scraped her nerves raw. She prayed for the floor to open up and swallow her whole. Or, better yet, for lightning to strike the simpering popinjay.

Merde. How had things come to this pass?

'The lady is with me.' Suppressed violence filled Mr Evernden's tone. All semblance of reserve gone, he radiated anger. Eyes the colour of evergreens in winter, he took a menacing step towards the mincing dandy.

Things were definitely growing worse. How typically, brutally male. She pressed back against the wall.

Cursing, Garge inserted his bulk between the two men eyeing each other like fighting cocks. He placed a heavy hand on each man's shoulder. 'I'll have no brawling in my house, gentlemen.'

Lord Albert recoiled, dusting off his coat as if Garge's touch had soiled it. 'I'm sure I don't care that much for the gel.' He snapped his fingers. 'You shouldn't leave her loitering about in public houses, if you don't want her accosted.'

'Exactly,' Mr Evernden replied with an exasperated glance at Sylvia.

Did he think to blame her because Lord Albert was a despicable rake? She returned stare for stare.

Lord Albert drummed his fingers on the counter's polished wood.

Mr Evernden glared at his back, then turned to the bristling innkeeper. 'Now, landlord, a room for Mademoiselle Boisette, if you please.'

Garge grunted. 'You ain't welcome here, sir, not you or your bit o' muslin, not nohow. I'll have your carriage brought around and your bags brought down.' He shook his head and muttered, '*Mademoiselle* indeed. Whatever next? This is a respectable house, this is, and Frenchies ain't welcome, nor their fancy men, neither.'

He turned to Lord Albert and bowed. 'I apologise for that, my lord. We don't usually get riff-raff in here. Now we've got that bit of unpleasantness out of the way, Lord Albert, I assume it's your usual room?'

A dull red suffused Mr Evernden's lean cheeks. He didn't speak. He grabbed the valise and hatbox from Sylvia's hand and strode outside.

Head held high, Sylvia trotted after him. No matter what he thought, she had done nothing wrong. If he dared say one word of criticism, she would provide her opinion of the whole male population.

'Wait here,' he said.

Long strides carried him across the cobbled yard. Neatly

dodging a liveried lackey running at full tilt with a tray of tankards to a waiting tilbury, he disappeared into the stables.

Nonplussed by yet another startling change in her circumstances, Sylvia waited as instructed. Gradually, her thoughts took some order. It seemed she would have to try this Hare and Hounds after all.

Nearby, a gentleman assisted a woman in a red-plumed bonnet into a shiny black barouche. A terrier, chased by two scruffy urchins, barked at the wheels of a departing coach. As it rattled beneath the archway into the street, she thought she glimpsed a figure flat against the wall. She peered into the gloom, but saw nothing but shadows.

More to the point, she needed a plan. She darted a swift glance around the courtyard, seeking inspiration. With nowhere to stay and Mr Evernden once more in command, she seemed to have come full circle.

'Miss Boisette.'

She stared in astonishment. The voice came from Christopher Evernden, but instead of his comfortable town coach, he perched high on a maroon-bodied curricle pulled by two ebony horses. An ostler dashed up to hold the nervous team and Mr Evernden leaped down.

She backed away. 'Where's your carriage?'

'I sent it back to London with my servant.'

Gallivanting around the countryside in an open carriage with a strange man reeked of danger. 'I'm not riding in that.'

He stalked to her side. 'Either you get in or I'll pick you up and put you in. Your choice, but make it quick.'

The set of his jaw and the angry glitter in his eyes said he would have no compunction about throwing her into the horrible thing. And yet, for all that he towered over her, she felt not the slightest bit afraid.

'Very well. I will ride with you as far as the Hare and Hounds.' At least the rain had ceased.

He handed her up. The fragile equipage rocked precariously on its long springs. While she settled herself with care on the seat, she admired the high-priced cattle in the traces. Mr Evernden obviously knew horses.

The team tossed their heads and stamped their feet. The rackety thing lurched. She grabbed for the side. It was worse than any ship.

The moment Mr Evernden climbed into his seat and took up the reins, the groom released the bridles. Solely in charge of the spirited pair, Mr Evernden glanced around him. With a dexterous twist of his strong wrist, he flicked his whip and set his horses in motion.

She'd heard a great many tales about young blades who drove like the wind in their sporting carriages. More often than not, they broke their necks. She curbed the desire to hang on to his solid-looking forearm.

In moments, the carriage eased its way through the archway. No sign of the man she thought she'd seen loitering in the shadows and yet the hairs on her neck prickled as if someone was watching. Oh, for goodness' sake. Now she was imagining monsters on every corner. The events of the afternoon must have rattled her nerves. Her biggest problem sat at her side.

They turned out on to the road.

'I assume you know where to find this Hare and Hounds?' she asked, pulling her cloak tight against the chilly air.

'I didn't say I was going to the Hare and Hounds.'

She stared at the hard line of his profile. He kept his gaze fixed on the road ahead, but the flickering muscle in his strong jaw boded ill.

'Then where are we going?'

'You'll see.'

Once more, something uncomfortable writhed in her stomach. Alone with this man, she had nothing but her wits to defend her and half the time they seemed to go begging where he was concerned. 'I expect I shall see, but I would prefer to know.'

He gave a short humourless laugh. 'What difference does it make? You're going, whether you wish it or not.'

Chapter Four

'If you are wise, you won't cause any more trouble,' he said and pulled out to pass a slowly moving town coach.

Sylvia gripped the side of the curricle and shot him a glare designed to freeze 'Without your interference, there would have been no trouble.'

'I suppose you didn't almost cause a mill back there, cosying up to some namby-pamby, titled puppy with more hair than wit.' He fired her a hard glance. 'And just what were you doing there, anyway?'

The mill, as he called the altercation, was entirely his own doing. 'My affairs are not your concern.'

A muscle jerked in his jaw and his anger sparked across the space between them. 'Really? We'll see about that.'

Prickles raced down her back. Until his resentment subsided, she risked more than sharp words from the bristling male at her side. And if he overturned this ridiculous vehicle, it would be the perfect ending to a perfectly awful day. She sat back, determined not to say another word.

The carriage bowled along at a smart clip, his strong hands grasping the ribbons with practised assurance. The spirited team ate up the road, passing everything in its path.

The traffic thinned. Signs of habitation dwindled to the oc-

casional farm along the road. The clouds rolled away and the
horizon disappeared into hazy dusk, while sunset gilded the
tops of distant trees. She nibbled her bottom lip. Just how far
did he intend to travel? If they went too far, she would not get
back to Tunbridge Wells in time to catch the morning coach.

Her trunk. How could she have been so stupid? She
clutched at Mr Evernden's sleeve.

A stony expression met her gaze. 'What?'

'I left my luggage behind.'

'You can collect it in the morning.'

The savage edge to his tone and the vicious flick of his
whip above his horses' heads gave her but a moment's pause.
'We must go back. What if it is stolen?'

'Miss Boisette, if you think I would set foot in that place
again… I have never in my life been ejected from anywhere,
let alone a common inn.' Anger vibrated from him in waves.

She quelled a sudden urge to laugh at his injured expression. 'Then you have me to thank for a novel experience.'

He scowled.

She'd gone too far. She edged away a fraction.

'It's an experience I could have done without,' he said.
'And I'd liefer not go through it again. If it is not too much
trouble, I would appreciate your behaving with suitable
decorum at this next inn.' Despite his repressive tone, he no
longer sounded furious.

A sideways glance revealed his lips in a slight curve. 'Gad,'
he muttered, staring straight ahead. 'A novel experience.'

Her lips twitched. She pressed them together, but not
before she knew he'd caught the beginning of her smile.

'Don't worry about your trunk,' he said after a brief silence.
'It will be safe at the Sussex Hotel. The landlord appears to
run a tight ship.'

'As we found to our cost.'

He smiled. 'Indeed.'

Her breath caught somewhere between her throat and her heart. The grin made him younger, almost boyish. His eyes crinkled at the corners and danced with green pinpricks of light. Unable to resist, she smiled back.

The travelling must have sent her wits to sleep. Signs of friendliness posed risks she dare not entertain. Men were dangerous enough without encouragement. She straightened in her seat and braced herself for what might lie ahead.

At a crossroads, he slowed the horses and turned them off the London Road. Sylvia tried to read the signpost, but the faded letters flashed by too fast. High hedges and overhanging trees cast deep shadows in the rutted, twisting lane. A flutter of disquiet attacked her stomach. 'Where *are* we going?'

'Somewhere we will be welcome, of that I can assure you. It is not far now.'

Did he have to be so mysterious? This stiff young man at her side thought her a wanton. So he should. She'd behaved like a strumpet, gambling everything on his desire to be rid of her. What if he changed his mind? Alone with a young and virile man, who-knew-where, tasted of risk.

Better him, than one of those other men at the Sussex Hotel. Better? A sudden tremble shook her limbs. She clenched her fingers around her locket, a familiar anchor to her past in the storm-tossed ocean of an uncertain future. If it came to a confrontation, somehow she had to make him understand she was not like her mother.

The Bird in Hand's mullioned windows flickered with warm light, a lighthouse in the deepening dusk. Wood smoke scented the cool air and the front door stood open in welcome.

Christopher hadn't been here since his grandmother had died, but it looked the same as always. The blackened Tudor timbers breathed permanence, despite the green of new thatch and a recent extension to the adjoining stables. A plaque over the weathered oak door boasted of hosting Good Queen Bess in the year fifteen hundred and fifty-six—along with half of England's other inns. He brought the horses to a stand.

A balding groom ran out from the stables and grasped the team's bridles.

A wonderful aroma of roasted meat filled Christopher's nostrils and set his mouth watering. If he could count on one thing, it was Mrs Dorkin's cooking.

'How pretty,' Miss Boisette said.

'Yes.' Christopher rolled his stiff shoulders. 'And I can guarantee we won't be turned away.'

'I am pleased to hear it.' Strain edged her voice.

The paleness of her countenance startled him. *Now* she felt nervous? She should have been a little more concerned back at the Sussex, a great deal more worried, based on his judgement of Lord Albert's intentions. The prancing ninny had his hands all over her. His gut churned.

But she had stood up to him, held her ground. He couldn't but help admire her courage, when it would have been so easy to flee, or to give in to the lordling's blandishments. And beneath the courage, he'd sensed a very real fear.

Thrusting the recollection aside, Christopher climbed down and reached up to help her alight. He caught her by the waist. Slender and lithe beneath his fingers, the heavy wool of her drab gown and grey cloak did little to disguise her womanly curves. The urge to bring her close and let her slide down his body shortened his breath.

Hell. He was no better than the popinjay at the inn.

Arms rigid, he placed her on the ground away from him, once more surprised by her small stature. For some reason, he imagined her taller. Something about her innate dignity and solemn demeanour added to her height. She had more pride than a duchess when she wasn't playing the wanton.

'Mr Christopher.' Gladness rang in the voice calling out through the door and Christopher turned to greet the generously proportioned matron who burst into the courtyard. She wiped her hands on her snowy apron and held them out in welcome.

He winced. Heaven knew what she'd say about him turning up with an unchaperoned female. He smiled. 'Mrs Dorkin. How are you?'

'Why on earth didn't you write and tell us you were coming?' she said in mock-scolding tones and her forefinger wagging. 'I would have aired the sheets special, just like your mother always ordered at the big house.'

Bloody hell. As if he needed more tender care than he'd suffered already. 'Mrs Dorkin, this is a friend of the family, Miss Sylvia Boisette.' He turned to Sylvia. 'Mrs Dorkin cooked for my grandparents at their estate near here.'

'I'm pleased to meet you,' Sylvia murmured with a smile.

Relief washed through Christopher. At least she wasn't giving dear old Mrs Dorkin her frosty face. In the old days, the cook had been his only ally against the army of doctors who insisted he eat nothing but gruel. Fortunately, she believed a lad needed his nourishment.

'We were supposed to lodge at the Sussex Hotel tonight,' he said, opening his arms in a gesture of regret. 'But somehow they let our rooms go. I do hope you can accommodate us?'

Mrs Dorkin placed her hands on her ample hips. 'The Sussex Hotel, is it? And you no more than a stone's throw from the Bird? I'm surprised at you, Mr Christopher. Come in, do. It's late and you must be tired.'

She waved a hand in the direction of the front door. 'I've a nice bit of roast pork on the spit and there's some cottage pie and I think a capon or two—cold, mind—left over from Sunday. Now then, Mr Christopher, I know that finicky appetite of yours, I'll expect you to let me know if none of it takes your fancy.' She shook her head. 'Mercy me, I am sure to find some cheese somewhere and I baked bread this afternoon.'

The warm chatter eased his tension, the way it had calmed

him as a boy racked by fever. He gestured for Miss Boisette to step inside. Shadows like bruises lay beneath her huge cornflower eyes. She looked exhausted and scared.

Damn it. The wench had been bold enough an hour ago in the face of the innkeeper's rudeness and Lord Albert's obviously dishonourable intentions.

Christopher clenched his jaw. He couldn't entirely blame the young rakehell. He'd acted like any other hot-blooded male faced with an irresistible opportunity. And Miss Boisette certainly was all of that. Why the hell had she not stayed with her friend? Suspicion reared an ugly head. Perhaps she had followed him, thinking him an easy mark after his generosity.

Mrs Dorkin pitched her voice into the back of the house. 'Pansy! Dratted girl, never around when you need her.'

A scrawny wench came at a run, her cheeks as red as if she'd been roasting her face instead of the pork.

'Show the young lady up to the second-floor bedroom.' Mrs Dorkin smiled at Sylvia. 'You'll find that's the best room, miss. Quiet.'

'Thank you,' she murmured.

Christopher grinned at the plump matron, much as he had when he had lived at his grandmother's house. 'Mrs Dorkin, we are starving. Anything you could do to hurry dinner along will be much appreciated.'

'Dinner in half an hour, don't be late.' Mrs Dorkin's voice faded away as she travelled into the depths of the old inn. 'Maybe I have some of the nice fruitcake I baked for the vicar last Sunday. You always liked fruitcake…'

Shoulders slumped, Sylvia started after the maid.

Christopher put a hand on her arm. 'I should have warned you. She's a dear, but she loves to talk.'

'She seems very kind. I hadn't realised just how famished I am. All that talk of food…'

The faintness of her voice, weary posture and attempted

smile caused him a pang of guilt. Curse it. No wonder she looked ready to wilt, she'd eaten almost nothing at lunch.

Unwelcome sympathy stirred in his chest. This was the first time today he'd seen her control slip. His questions would wait until after dinner.

He caught a glimpse of a well-turned ankle as she followed the maid up the stairs. Even worn to the bone, she radiated female sensuality. No wonder men rushed to her aid, lust burning in their eyes.

The low-beamed room with overstuffed chairs and easy country atmosphere comforted Christopher like hot punch on a cold night. Half-empty serving dishes cluttered the sideboard against the wall.

Pleasantly full, he set down his knife and fork and stared at the woman across from him. The warmth of the fire and her few sips of red wine had dispelled her earlier pallor. The faint glow in her cheeks and the sparkle in her eyes rendered her utterly lovely.

Mrs Dorkin hadn't asked him any pointed questions about Miss Boisette's presence under his protection. No doubt she'd seen and heard enough about the Evernden men and their dissolute ways not to be surprised at Christopher's arrival with one of the world's most beautiful women on his arm.

Despite her assertions, Miss Boisette needed proper male protection. The scene at the Sussex proved it.

He ran an appraising glance over her and frowned. Her severe brown gown couldn't be drearier. Come to think of it, the nondescript grey cloak and black poke bonnet she wore to travel in were also exceedingly dowdy. To all intents and purposes, she dressed like a governess or lady's maid.

Christopher wanted to see her in something more elegant, lighter, perhaps the colour of sapphires to match her brilliant eyes. Something lacy and filmy that left little to the imagination. Something like Lady Delia, Garth's last fling, had worn when Christopher had dropped in on their love nest one afternoon.

The image of Sylvia Boisette's curvaceous form clothed in a wisp of silk stirred his blood.

Her small white teeth, with their adorable tiny space in the centre, bit into a petit-four. What would that moist, soft mouth feel like against his lips or on his…?

Bloody hell. He didn't need this. He pushed his plate away.

Her wanton behaviour yesterday and in Tunbridge Wells had his thoughts in the gutter. If she had stayed where he had left her, they wouldn't be in this fix. If she had dressed like a lady, the young lordling might not have been so ready with his insults and the landlord might have given her a room without question.

'Don't you have something smarter to wear?' he asked.

Blue heat flashed in her eyes. Quickly repressed, it hinted at higher passions beneath her cool distant beauty. His groin tightened. Mentally, he cursed.

'Why would I?' she asked. 'I plan to become a shopkeeper, not a courtesan.'

Her flat tone delivered a dash of cold water to his lust. He watched an expression of satisfaction dawn on her face. She intended to disgust him. What game was she playing?

He'd been billed enough for expensive clothes by the last woman in his life to know quality when he saw it. 'The mourning gown you wore to my uncle's funeral was well cut and in the height of fashion. Made from the finest silk, if I'm not mistaken.' He waved his glass in her general direction. 'I'm sure my uncle preferred you in something more attractive.'

Pain shadowed her eyes before she shuttered her gaze. 'That part of my life is over.'

He took a deep swallow of wine. 'Really? Then what were you doing at the Sussex Hotel?'

'Seeking a room for the night.'

'With Lord Albert, no doubt.'

Outwardly unruffled, she did not shrink from his gaze, but her hand clutched the locket at her throat. 'No.'

A low blow, he silently acknowledged, remembering the panic in her eyes when Lord Albert slobbered over her hand. Damn it, every time he thought about it, he wanted to throttle the snivelling fribble.

What the hell was the matter with him? He never let a woman distract him. Miss Boisette had caused him nothing but anxious moments. 'While we are on the subject, perhaps you would like to explain why you tipped me the double?'

'Tipped you the double?' She wrinkled her nose.

The urge to kiss away the furrow on her brow swept through him. He wanted to do more than that. Even with a frown, her incredible beauty numbed his mind and shortened his breath. His blood thickened. Never had a woman tempted him like this one.

He drew in a deep breath, crushing his desire. Dalliance with his uncle's ward or mistress—which he no longer believed—remained out of the question if he wanted to preserve a grain of family honour.

Hell. He needed to get rid of her and continue on his way to the Darbys'. He set his glass down, the chink loud in the quiet room. 'Come clean, Miss Boisette. Why did you not stay with your friend? You took money to go into business and within an hour of my leaving you, I find you at a common inn hanging on the arm of some young coxcomb.'

Arctic chill frosted her gaze. 'Are you implying that I took the money under false pretences?'

'I demand an explanation.'

'You have no right to demand anything. You brought me here against my will and if you try to touch me, I will scream bloody murder.'

It seemed he now had her full attention. This beautiful young woman, who behaved like a trollop one moment and an ice queen the next, needed a good shaking. 'Do you really think the Dorkins will pay any attention?'

Stark terror leaped into her eyes, bleakness invading their clear, cold depths like a plea for help. Fear hung in the air as thick and choking as smoke.

What did a woman like her have to fear from him? She had tossed more lures at him than a falconer to an ill-trained hawk. And he'd almost come to her fist, jessied and hooded.

Enough. He would do his duty and see her settled and he would see it done his way. Calmly, logically. The methods he used in his business dealings.

He poured a glass of wine from the decanter at his elbow and schooled his face into pleasant cheerfulness. 'I must apologise. My anger is directed at Lord Albert and that damn innkeeper.' Hell, the recollection caused his blood to simmer all over again. 'However, we did have an agreement, one you proposed and appear to have broken.'

She didn't speak, but stared at her empty plate as if trying to weave some new web of lies.

He pushed a plate of comfits in her direction. 'Here.'

A pathetic peace offering, yet it eased the palpable tension.

Sylvia gazed from the heaped pink-and-white sugared almonds on the blue dish to his face. Emerald fires burned deep in his hazel eyes, not the usual blaze of a lusty male, but a deep slow burn that fanned the embers in the pit of her own stomach to flame.

A tremor she could only identify as fear quivered in the region of her heart. Without him she was stranded. All her money, apart from the few coins in her reticule, had been left behind in Tunbridge Wells.

Trapped. A shiver shot up her spine. And he was right. She did owe him an explanation. She took a deep breath. 'My friend, Mary Jensen, moved her business to London.' She hoped he did not hear the hitch in her voice at her lie.

He frowned at his glass, then stared her straight in the eye. 'I thought she expected you?'

She sighed. Obviously, he had paid attention. 'There was some error in our communication. She left a forwarding address with the new tenant. The woman forgot to mail on my letters, therefore Mary did not know about your uncle's unexpected demise.'

His intense scrutiny made her shift in her seat. She had the strong sense he did not believe her.

'And?' he said.

She shrugged. 'I must now go to London.'

'You have her address?'

'I do.'

'What is it?'

'I don't see why—'

His mouth turned down and his eyes narrowed. 'I'm sure you don't. But you are mistaken if you think I am going to drop you off at a coaching house in the morning without knowing your proposed destination.'

'You agreed to drive me to Tunbridge Wells. Your obligation ends there.'

'I offered to drive you to the bosom of your friend and that is where my duty ends.'

The quiet emphasis in his voice made it clear he would not listen to further argument. She hesitated. It would do no harm to give him Mary's directions. Once she reached London, she would never see him again.

'Very well.' She dived into her reticule and handed him the dog-eared paper with Mary's new address.

He gazed at it silently for a moment. 'Dear God. The Seven Dials. Do you have any idea what sort of place that is?'

Her stomach plummeted. 'Not good, I assume.'

'I wouldn't worry if it were just not good, as you put it. It couldn't be worse. It houses London's worst slums and most dangerous criminals.'

'Mary Jensen is of a perfect respectability,' she flashed back. *Incroyable.* She'd lost her grip on her English.

'Not living in that neighborhood, she isn't.' He tossed the paper on the table next to a hunk of fruitcake.

His innuendoes wearied her; the whole day had tried her patience, and the strange, nerve-stretching awareness between them exhausted her most of all. She was an idiot for leaving Tunbridge Wells in his carriage. She would have been much better off at the damned Hare and Hounds.

'What does it matter? I am not of a respectableness enough for you or your most esteemed family. The sooner we make our own directions, the better, *n'est ce pas*?'

'Do not raise your voice to me, *mademoiselle*.'

'And do not dictate to me.'

She stood.

He followed suit with easy grace, looming over her, green pinpricks of anger dancing in his eyes. 'I would not have to dictate to you, if you had been more forthright in your dealings with me. It is my duty to see you safely established somewhere and I will not brook an argument.'

Golden in the firelight, he stood like a knight of old surrounded by the armour of righteousness. Trust him, her heart murmured with a little skip. Let him enfold you with his strength, urged her body with a delicious shiver. An urgent warning clamoured in her mind. *You are no better than your mother.*

'I do not accept your right to give me orders.'

He bowed. 'I suggest you go to bed. We will discuss what is to be done in the morning, when your nerves are less overset.'

She almost laughed in his face. Monsieur Jean must have lost his mind putting her in the hands of this dutiful and stuffy Evernden nephew.

'Nerves, Mr Evernden, are for pampered darlings with fathers and husbands to protect them while they lie about on *chaises* with vinaigrettes and hartshorn complaining of headaches. I don't have the luxury of nerves.' She headed for the door. 'We will certainly discuss this further *en route* to catch the mail in the morning.'

She turned in the doorway. 'We will need to be up at five. I hope that is not too early for you?'

His open mouth gave her satisfaction enough as she swept out of the room and up the stairs.

Chapter Five

Christopher paused on the front step of the inn and lit his cigar. The night air cooled his cheeks after the Bird in Hand's blazing fire and his argument with Miss Boisette. Abstracted, he ran a hand over the thick wooden door, the raised studs and black iron bands rough beneath his fingertips. Hard to imagine that the man who had built this door had died more than two centuries ago and the tree from which he carved it had probably grown for two centuries before that. Those were times of knights and lords and deeds of daring. What would those men think of this world now?

The faint haze of his smoky breath drifted in front of his face. He drew on his cigar and savoured the acrid burn on his tongue and the mellow aroma in his nostrils. He needed a walk to restore some sort of order to his body and his mind before he retired for the night.

He left the warm light of the inn and strode down the tree-arched lane, stretching muscles cramped from the journey. Amidst the sparse spring leaves of the canopy above his head, stars winked their steel-bright messages in a stygian sky.

A wooden stile broke a gap in the dense hedgerow and he leaned against its rail. The full moon hovered yellow, fat and lazy above the horizon. Scattered lights twinkled along the dark slash of river valley meandering through rolling meadows.

He'd wandered this countryside as a boy while quarantined from disease-ridden London and his family. They had visited him here at his grandparents' estate from time to time, but his father had insisted on residing in London.

He stared into the gloom, trying to identify boyhood haunts. He and Garth had ridden this country hard during school holidays. He grimaced. More often than not, Garth had been flogged for some of their more daring exploits, always taking the punishment for leading Christopher astray. He hadn't needed much leading. But deemed too sickly to receive his share of the blame, Garth had taken it for both of them. Garth never seemed to care, but he had ceased to spend much time at Hedly Hall once he went away to school and Christopher hadn't visited it in years. Too busy keeping on top of his business interests.

An owl hooted. Distant hooves beat the familiar rhythm of a gallop on the hard-packed earth. The drumming stopped, heralding a late-night visitor to the inn.

His mind flew back to Sylvia, the gorgeous vision of sensual womanhood he had seen in Dover, the frightened, but determined, girl at the Sussex Hotel. He smothered a curse. Stubborn woman. She had him out here pacing in the night air while she no doubt was tucked up in bed, dreaming of London, with a gown of the sheerest muslin covering every lithe inch of her. He grimaced. He didn't care what kind of gown she wore; he wanted to see it on her. He wanted to slide it from her alabaster skin the way she'd stripped off her gloves. He wanted what lay beneath.

His arousal, a low controlled thrumming during dinner, spiked with urgent need. What the hell was the matter with him? He never had any trouble controlling his base urges when confronted with members of the opposite sex. Not even the most famous of London's courtesans had heated his blood to the point he could think of nothing but slaking his lust inside her delicious body.

No matter how dull the attire covering her enticing curves, the longer he spent in her company, the more he wanted to explore her swells and hollows.

He groaned. He'd have more success knocking out Gentleman Jackson than battering his loins' demands into submission. Damn John Evernden for foisting the wench on him.

No one need know if she became his mistress. The idea lit in his mind like a beacon. In London the news would make the rounds in a heartbeat, but tucked away at his country house in Kent, their liaison would be discreet enough. No one would know he'd taken his uncle's ward under his protection.

He would know. And Garth would accuse him of hypocrisy the moment he guessed. He closed his eyes in silent contempt. Was he as bad as the rest of the Evernden men when it came to loose women?

Damn. There had been enough scandal in the Evernden family and he had sworn not to add to it.

He dropped the remains of his cigar, a smouldering red spark in the night, and ground it beneath his heel as if quenching the fire in his veins. If only it were that easy. He turned and strode for the inn.

What the hell should he do with her, then? The thought of a bordello chilled his blood. A lady's maid? A seamstress? Apparently, she had some talent in that direction.

Idiot. She was French. A married friend had complained bitterly about the cost of his French governess. If, as Christopher suspected, this friend in London proved to be a hum, why not palm her off on some country squire seeking to elevate the prospects of his hopeful brood?

Because he wanted her.

Hell fire. A wry smile twisted his lips at the way his mind bent towards the urgings of his body.

He rounded the bend. A lantern lit the sign of the Bird,

a clenched fist with only the head of a bright-eyed robin visible. The door lay open, but the parlour window was dark and blank.

What would Mrs Dorkin say if he requested a tub of cold water to be sent to his chamber? She'd likely think he'd run mad and predict his death from pneumonia.

Tension locked his spine and he rubbed the back of his neck. A good strong brandy before bed would relax him and take the edge off the want clawing at the heart of his resolve.

Maybe two.

A brown gelding lifted its head from the trough on the stable wall. A nice beast, perhaps a little long in the leg, it had been ridden hard judging from the steam rising from its flanks.

Christopher ducked his head beneath the lintel and made his way through a narrow passage to the back of the house and the dimly lit taproom. Behind the long bar, Jack Dorkin, jolly and fat on his wife's cooking, greeted him with a nod.

Dorkin put down a pewter tankard and his drying cloth. 'Something for you, Mr Evernden?'

'A brandy, please. Make it a double.'

Dorkin lifted a bottle and shook it. 'I'll have to go to the cellar,' he muttered. 'Won't be but a moment, sir.' He swung up a trapdoor in the floor and clattered down the steps.

Christopher leaned one arm on the battered oak bar. A couple of country labourers in traditional smocks, clay pipes clamped in whiskered jaws, clacked domino tiles in swift sure movements. An occasional chuckle or mutter indicated the state of play. A shepherd, his dog at his feet, nursed a tankard on the settle beside the red brick medieval hearth. Out of the corner of his eye, he caught a movement in the shadows at the far end of the bar. In a pool of light cast by an oil lamp, a square strong hand, the wrist covered by the cuff of dark green coat, lifted a mug. The horseman.

Christopher nodded. 'Good evening.'

The hand raised in greeting. 'The top of the evening to you too, sir.'

Irish by his brogue.

'That's a fine piece horseflesh you have there,' Christopher said.

'Aye, an' it is and all,' the man replied. He threw a coin on the counter. 'I'll be wishing you a good night, then.' He stood and, with a slight bow, placed his hat on his head and sauntered out of the bar. The flickering lamp by the door illuminated his rangy frame and lean jaw, then he was gone.

Where had he seen the man before? Christopher rarely forgot a face, but right at the moment he could not place this one.

'Here's your brandy, Mr Evernden,' Dorkin said, his cheeks puffing in and out. 'Sorry it took so long. I keeps me best stuff locked up. Can't trust the help these days, you know.'

'Who was that?' Christopher asked, his gaze fixed on the doorway.

'Dunno, sir. Just popped in on the off chance, like. I've never seen him afore.'

Christopher picked up the goblet. 'Cheers, Dorkin, and thank you.'

He wandered to the bench opposite the shepherd and stretched out his legs to the fire's warmth. He savoured the smooth amber liquid on his tongue.

Oh, yes, this was the best stuff all right. Definitely French and certainly an improvement over a cold bath, if not as effective.

A scuffling noise invaded Sylvia's consciousness. It couldn't possibly be time to rise. Her eyelids refused the order to open and she submerged into the opaque veil of sleep.

A sound like fingernails on glass tormented her ears. The maid must be scratching at the door to wake her. She had to get up. She must not miss the coach to London. She groaned.

Just a few minutes more, then she would open her eyes. She wriggled further beneath the warmth of the blankets.

Stupid. The inability to sleep after leaving Christopher Evernden in the dining room did not give her an excuse to lie in bed. He reminded her of a disapproving older brother, except nothing brotherly lingered in the depth of evergreen eyes flecked with brown. His steel-hard resolve to do his duty and his ingrained sense of honour pulled at her like the full moon on the ocean. Not to mention his handsome face.

An ache squeezed her heart and her breath hitched at the pain. Burrowing into the pillow, she shook her head in denial. No handsome face would lead her down the path to ruin and misery. No. She would not let another Evernden man break down her carefully constructed defences.

A sliding noise and a bang jolted her fully awake. She stared into the gloom. It wasn't morning. A pale square of light glimmered on the wall opposite the window; the rest of the room lay in deep shadow.

She turned over.

Oh, God! Outlined by moonlight, a head and shoulders filled the window frame.

Fingers of ice held her body immobile and squeezed her throat. She opened her mouth to scream. A faint croak emerged.

The dark shape dropped to the floor with a muffled thud. This had to be a dream. She swallowed what felt like gravel.

The shadow lunged at her. Shivers of dread clawed down her spine, breaking the frigid clasp of fear. She kicked the bedclothes aside. A heavy weight landed on her, driving the breath from her lungs, pinning her down. A warm callused hand covered her mouth and nose. She fought for air. The smell of tobacco filled her nostrils and she tasted salty sweat. She flailed her arms, kicked out at him. Her heart pounded in her ears.

Not again. This couldn't happen to her again.

Her lungs begged for air. Her head swam; darkness crept

to the edges of her vision. She flailed her arms. He grunted as her fist made contact in the region of his head. His weight shifted, his grip eased. She closed her teeth hard on the soft flesh of his thumb. Sweat and tobacco soured her tongue.

He cursed.

Triumph surged in her veins. She gulped at the sudden sweet rush of air and squirmed from beneath him.

'Don't touch me,' she cried. 'Get out.'

'I'm going,' he said, shaking his injured hand. 'An' like it or not, pet, you're coming with me.'

'No.'

She dived off the bed towards the door. Her elbow struck the bedpost and sent agonising tingles shooting to the tip of her little finger. Bent double, she clutched her arm to her chest.

'Help,' she screamed. '*À moi.*' Would no one come to her aid?

He raised his hand, his fist clenched around something black. She ducked.

The blow snapped her head back. A sharp pain, a flash of light, then sinking blackness rose up and swallowed her.

Christopher opened his eyes, his heart racing. What the hell? It had sounded like a woman's scream.

He groaned. It must have been a bad dream, either that or some lusty knave was hard at it with a red-faced maid. The sour thought only made his own fantasies of Sylvia more frustrating.

The mist of sleep and the fog of brandy slowly cleared. Good God. He'd lain down fully clothed. He'd clearly spent far too long with Dorkin and his finest French brandy before coming to bed.

A thud overhead sent him bolt upright.

Devil a bit. Miss Boisette must be pacing the floor.

More bumps. The hair on the back of his neck stirred, his skin prickled. It didn't sound like pacing. It sounded more like a battle. What the deuce was going on up there? He leaped off the bed, flung open the door and peered into the hallway.

A whispered curse from above directed his attention up the stairs. Caught in the dim glow from the lantern on the landing, a man stood rigid, ready to step down. In his arms, he carried something large and white like a bundle of sheets. A servant?

'Identify yourself,' Christopher ordered.

The man let his burden slide to the floor. A pair of slender legs and trailing blonde hair gleamed before they disappeared into the shadows.

Sylvia?

Christopher dashed up the stairs. The man swung a bag at his head. Sylvia's valise. Christopher ducked. He charged the man's gut with his shoulder.

His opponent grunted, stumbling backward. Christopher bunched his fists. Disadvantaged by the man's position above him, Christopher couldn't get a clear swing. The man flung himself forward. A sharp elbow jabbed Christopher in the ribs. Air rushed from his lungs. He doubled in pain. The man shoved him hard against the balustrade and hurtled down two flights of stairs. He crashed out through the front door, still clutching the bag.

Gasping, Christopher started after him.

Damn. He couldn't leave Sylvia. He turned and took the stairs two at a time to her side.

As still as death, she lay sprawled on the planked landing, her face pale and her lips bloodless in the lantern's flickering light.

Bile rose in his throat. Dead? He knelt and lifted her wrist. Her pulse beat strong and steady. He ran his hands over her limbs and her torso. Thank God, no blood.

He chafed her cold hands. 'Sylvia.'

She didn't move.

He pulled her nightgown down to cover her shapely calves and picked her up. Her head fell back, revealing her slender throat and a bruise behind her ear. Rage like molten metal surged through him. Damn the blackguard for striking a woman. If he ever got his hands on him, he'd kill the bastard.

He hesitated. He couldn't leave her here or take her to her own room in case the damned rogue came back. Instead, he carried her down to his chamber and laid her on the bed.

'Mr Evernden.' Dorkin's voice sounded shocked. 'What are you doing with that there young lady?'

'Damn it, Dorkin. Don't just stand there gawking. Miss Boisette is hurt. Fetch a doctor.'

'I'll get the missus,' Dorkin said. 'She'll know what's best. Mr Christopher, I never would have thought it of you.' Dorkin hurried off.

Christopher stared at his departing back. What the devil did he mean? He glanced down at the practically naked girl on his bed. Dorkin must think that he… Hell. Now he'd have some explaining to do.

He eased the counterpane from beneath her and pulled it up. He smoothed her hair back from her face. Unbound it had the texture of silk. He investigated the lump on her tender skin behind her ear.

The cur had struck her a vicious blow. A sick feeling washed over him. What kind of man would do that to a woman? Why had this man attacked her? Not just attacked, he'd tried to abduct her. He shook his head. Beautiful she might be, but people didn't go around stealing females because they were beyond-reason lovely. Not in this day and age, for God's sake. Unless some rogue thought Christopher would pay to get her back?

He enclosed her cold fingers in his hands, trying to warm them, his gaze on her pale face. Damn, she was exquisite. And he'd been right about the nightgown. He'd seen far too much of her beneath it. Her limbs were every bit as lovely as he had imagined and twice as tempting.

Need ripped through him like a torturer's knife pressed against his ballocks.

He cursed under his breath. He had to put a stop to this, and soon. In the meantime, he kept his gaze fixed on her face. Where the hell was Mrs Dorkin, anyway? Sylvia might die before she got here.

He felt her pulse again and sighed with relief to discover its steady rhythm. A rhythm that in no way matched the tumult of his own erratic heartbeat.

Hell's teeth, his racing heart had nothing to do with the scantily clad Sylvia and everything to do with his burning need to catch this criminal. He should be chasing the villain, not sitting here holding her hand.

Limp and white, her long slender fingers lay like a bird's broken wing in his large palm. The hand of a lady. Except that this lady was a courtesan's daughter.

'Now then, Mr Christopher Evernden, what's all this I hear?'

Thank God. Mrs Dorkin would know how to care for Sylvia. He moved aside to let her get to the bed.

Her face full of anxiety, Mrs Dorkin leaned over and peered down at the unconscious girl.

'Miss?' she said. 'Can you hear me?'

Sylvia drifted through thick grey fog.

A moan increased the pain in her head. She opened her eyes. A fuzzy moon-face hung over her. She shuddered. What did he want with her?

She put up her hands to ward him off. 'Don't touch me, you whoremaster,' she yelled. 'Get away from me, you pig.' She struck out with her fists.

'Lawks,' moon-face said.

'In English, Miss Boisette.'

Mr Evernden's voice.

What was he doing in her room? Why had he climbed through her window?

'You unholy bastard.' She tried to sit up. The room spun around her, nausea rose in her throat.

'Miss Boisette, speak English and for God's sake mind your language. You sound like a Paris trollop.'

French. They were speaking in French. She tried to get her mind working. Someone had filled it with treacle. Her temples throbbed.

A firm hand pressed her back against the pillows.

'Now don't you take on so, miss.'

It was Mrs Dorkin whose face hung over her in a shifting blur. Sylvia blinked the mist from her sight.

'You've had a nasty bump on the head, dear,' Mrs Dorkin murmured, smoothing her hair back. 'Pansy will be along in a minute with a compress. You lie nice and quiet and you'll be all right in no time.'

Sylvia gazed around the room. This was not her room. She stared past Mrs Dorkin at Christopher standing at the end of the bed. Another man hovered in the doorway behind him.

Christopher wore a shirt open at the throat and looked decidedly tousled. His expression held concern. What had he done to her? The last she remembered, they had been arguing at dinner.

'Why am I here?'

Christopher frowned. 'Someone tried to abduct you.'

'Someone? Who? Why?'

'I don't know. Did you not see who it was?'

A rough lilting voice came back to her, a growl close to her ear and full of menace. *And you're coming with me, pet.*

'He came in through the window. He spoke French with a strange accent,' she said.

Christopher leaned forward, his expression intent. 'What sort of accent?'

Sylvia shook her head. 'Hard to tell. He whispered.'

'Exactly what did he say?'

'He said I had to go with him.' Her limbs trembled as the fear rushed back.

Christopher's expression hardened. 'He got you halfway down the stairs. Luckily, I heard you cry out.'

She remembered the feel of his hand on her mouth, the taste of his skin on her tongue. She shuddered. 'He smokes cigars,' she said.

'How on earth could you possibly know that?' Suspicion darkened his eyes.

'He covered my mouth with his hand. I couldn't breathe, so I bit him. I tasted cigars.'

Admiration flickered in his eyes, replaced by worry. 'Good God, he might have killed you.'

Yes, she believed he might have. The man who had whispered in the dark was capable of anything, even murder. A shiver shook her at the recollection of his hands on her body. She had to leave here. He might return.

She pushed herself up on her elbow. An ache throbbed in her skull. She touched the back of her head and winced as her fingers encountered a tender lump. She closed her eyes, seeking relief.

'Now, now, miss, what did I say?' Mrs Dorkin said. 'You lie down. You've had a nasty shock. Mr Christopher, your questions must wait until later.'

'I must get up.' Her voice quavered, but she refused to acknowledge her weakness. 'I have to catch the stage to London.'

'Not today, you won't,' Mrs Dorkin pronounced. 'Ah, Pansy, there you are. Bring that bowl over here.'

The maid sidled around Christopher and set a bowl and towels on the bed next to Mrs Dorkin.

'Go on now, Mr Christopher,' Mrs Dorkin said. 'And you too, Dorkin. This young lady has had a nasty scare and a bad knock. I'll see to her head, and after some willow bark tea, she's going to sleep. Out you go. At once.'

Sylvia sent Christopher a look of appeal. 'I have to leave today. What about my trunk?'

A frown creasing his forehead, Christopher shook his head. 'Listen to Mrs Dorkin, Miss Boisette. Don't worry about your things, I'll look after them.'

He didn't wait for her to argue and Mrs Dorkin didn't listen to her protests.

Fatigue washed over Sylvia. As limp as the week-old lettuce she'd prized as a starving child running the streets of Paris, she sank back against the pillows and welcomed the cold compress Mrs Dorkin applied to her aching head.

Christopher took Dorkin outside and they scoured the perimeter of the inn, looking for signs of the intruder. Above the old kitchen at the back, the thatched roof sloped within three feet of the ground and Dorkin pointed out a pile of stones against the wall. 'He must have used them to climb up.'

Cold moonlight revealed broken thatch where the intruder must have stood to force open the second-floor window. Dorkin peered at Christopher. 'Very strange goin's on, sir. Why would anyone want to abduct the young lady?'

Since Christopher had asked himself the same question without an answer, he shook his head. 'I'm not sure.'

Most importantly, he didn't want a whole bunch of gossip about this. Travelling with a woman of less than savoury repute was bad enough; talk of tonight would just increase speculation. Christopher would come off just as badly as Miss Boisette and neither of them deserved it.

'I suspect it was a mistake,' Christopher said. 'Or someone thought to ransom her because she is travelling under my protection. I think it is best if we do not say anything to anyone else about this until I can speak further to Miss Boisette.'

Whatever Dorkin thought about the affair, he simply nodded his agreement, his close connections to the influential Everndens ensuring his loyal silence. With no particular expectation of finding anything, Christopher walked out to the lane. A black shape lay amidst the rough grass on the verge. He picked it up and turned the hat over in his hands.

There was nothing remarkable about the fairly common black felt hat worn by the lower orders. The man in the bar tonight had worn just such a hat. Christopher frowned. Had the man dropped it when he rode away or was he Sylvia's midnight visitor? If so, there remained the question of why? He tucked it under his arm and followed Dorkin into the inn.

Chapter Six

C hristopher gazed into the window of the most well-known dressmaker in Tunbridge Wells, taking in the lengths of brightly coloured muslins and satins and the assortment of gloves and hats and other more personal articles of ladies' apparel laid out before him. He tugged at his cravat.

He did not want to do this.

He had no choice. The damn rogue who attacked Sylvia had stolen every article of her clothing along with her bag and when Christopher had presented himself to the porter at the Sussex Hotel, the fool proudly announced he personally saw to putting the young lady's chest on the six o'clock coach. When Christopher upbraided him about the folly of sending the baggage without the owner, the man had shrugged and said the lady was very positive in her request. She could pick it up at the London office as soon as she arrived there. Meanwhile, Sylvia had nothing to wear but her nightgown.

Two ladies stepped around him and entered the establishment. The younger one slid him a curious glance.

Inwardly, Christopher cursed. He definitely didn't want to do this. Garth might take pleasure in overseeing his mistresses' adornment, but Christopher preferred to give them the money and send them shopping.

Hell and damnation. He'd spent the past two days doing nothing but things against his better judgement. Well, he'd damned well had enough of dancing to other people's tunes. Sylvia would travel to London under his escort and no argument. Last night was all the evidence he needed of the danger she faced travelling alone.

First, he'd buy her some clothes and then he would drop her off with this friend of hers. After that, he would wash his hands of the whole business and head back to Sussex as originally planned.

Perhaps a closed carriage would be a better mode of travel given the dreadful weather this year. He could leave his curricle at the Bird and take a post-chaise. He shook his head. Then he'd be left in London with no means of transportation. Bloody hell. She would just have to put up with it.

He squared his shoulders and strode into the cluttered shop. Manikins draped with swathes of cloth posed in front of shelves filled with fabrics of every hue. The two women ahead of him dithered over a tray of ribbons. Christopher flicked through a book of fashion plates on a side table and waited. One page pictured a blue gown with a modest, but attractive, neckline. He liked blue and it matched the colour of her eyes. Perfect.

He fixed the middle-aged dressmaker with a stern look. Rows of purple ruffles on her billowing lilac gown made her ample bosom all the more impressive.

She bade her other customers farewell and bustled to his side. 'How can I be of service, sir?'

'I want to buy a gown for my sister.'

On her way out of the door, the younger woman sniggered. Christopher ignored her.

'Yes, sir,' the smiling seamstress said.

The woman's knowing expression told him she did not believe a word. He narrowed his eyes and spoke firmly. 'My sister is having a birthday and I wish to buy her a gown, in blue, today.'

The woman frowned. 'It will have to be ready-made, sir.'

'Of course.'

The woman pulled a sheet of paper out from under the counter and stood with quill poised, looking at him. 'If you would provide her sizes, I will look and see what I have in stock.'

Sizes. God. He knew nothing about sizes. He took a stab at it. 'She's slender and petite.'

'Height?'

He held his hand at shoulder height. 'Her head comes to about here.'

'Waist?'

Christopher stared at her. 'Er…' He'd held her by the waist yesterday. He recalled the feel of her slender body under his fingers. He held his hands in a circle, not quite touching each other. 'Like this.'

'Eighteen inches, I should think,' the woman said, scratching on her paper.

'Chest?'

Christopher held himself steady, refusing to be put off, despite an overwhelming inclination to flee the store and forget the whole thing. How would a brother know that kind of thing? He wouldn't. He shook his head.

The woman tutted. She looked down at her own well-endowed figure. 'Like me?'

Perish the thought. 'Smaller. Quite a lot smaller.'

The woman crossed to a manikin and held her hands cupped in front of it. Christopher could tell that she had done this before. 'Like this?' she asked.

The shape of the woman's hands were nothing like the small upthrusting breasts beneath the nightgown he'd glimpsed in the small hours of this morning. He swallowed. 'Not so round.'

'Ah,' the woman said, her lips pursed. 'Lisette, dear. Do come out here a moment.'

A young woman in a stiff black gown cut high to the neck emerged from behind a yellow curtain beyond the counter. The shopkeeper swung her around by the shoulders to outline her figure's profile. She pulled the gown tight at the sides, revealing a pert and shapely figure.

'How about like this?'

He pushed the disturbing image of Sylvia's breasts, coupled with visions of her legs, her golden hair hanging to her waist, to one side. The girl was close enough to Sylvia to make no difference. 'Yes. About like her, perhaps a little more slender.'

The woman bobbed a curtsy. 'I'm sure we have something to your liking, sir. I'll be but a moment.'

Christopher approached a display cabinet and leaned against it, looking in. The case contained gloves and little lacy things. Soft and delicate things he imagined Sylvia wearing at night or beneath her gown. Filmy, clinging garments designed to hug soft feminine curves. Curves which felt so right in his arms. Curves he'd had no business touching and which were likely to disturb his mind and his body for a very long time.

Disgusted with the turn of his mind, he flung himself into a gilt chair jammed between stacks of cloth, his gaze fixed on the brightly coloured bales, refusing to think about Sylvia at all.

He didn't have long to wait for the woman to return. He stared at the froth of garments draped over her arms.

'I brought you a morning gown in blue-and-white muslin. Something for daywear, I think you said? I also took the liberty of bringing an evening gown, right for almost any function. This shade of rose is all the rage and truly lovely. No lady would be disappointed.'

He hesitated. Decisions never bothered him, but he had no idea what Sylvia liked. 'I'll take them both.'

The woman smiled. 'She is a lucky lady to have a generous…brother like you.'

He gritted his teeth at her impertinence, but leashed his temper. It didn't matter what she thought. 'I also need things to go under those, and a hat, gloves, you know the sort of thing.'

The woman's face lit up as if she'd been given a gift. 'Yes, sir,' she said. 'Might I suggest—'

'Just put it all together. Everything a lady will need for two days. I will come and collect them in half an hour, if it's not too much trouble.'

'No trouble at all, Mr Evernden,' the dressmaker said, rubbing her hands together.

He mentally cursed his stupidity. He'd lived not five miles from here during his youth—was it any wonder she knew him? She would also know he did not have a sister.

In the dark passage outside the parlour, Sylvia prepared herself to face Mr Evernden over luncheon. She smoothed her hair and swallowed a gasp when her fingers encountered the tender spot in her hairline behind her ear.

A shudder ripped through her. Who would want to abduct her in the middle of the night and steal all her clothes? The thought left her feeling shaky, unlike herself.

It seemed so peculiar. And now she found herself further indebted to Mr Evernden. She glanced down at the gown he had purchased for her. A fashionable high-waisted blue muslin with a generous amount of lace in the neckline and pretty puffed sleeves, it must have cost a fortune, it and the rest of the items he'd brought back from Tunbridge.

Spine straight, she pushed open the heavy oak door and stepped into the front parlour Mrs Dorkin reserved for her most favored guests.

Newspaper in hand, Mr Evernden rose to his feet and

bowed. 'Good afternoon, Miss Boisette. I hope you are feeling more the thing?'

The deep timbre of his voice and his concerned expression drove all thoughts from her mind, except how handsome and large he looked framed in the bow window. This man had saved her life last night. A fluttering warmth danced in her veins. 'Thank you. I feel much better.'

Afraid her eyes would give her away, she dropped her gaze to the table. 'My goodness.' A basket of bread, a cold ham and platters of fruits, cheeses and other delicacies lay spread out on the table in front of him.

His warm chuckle reverberated from his chest. 'I hope you are ravenous.' He gestured to the banquet. 'I certainly can't eat all this myself and Mrs Dorkin will be most put out if we do not do it justice.'

He went around the table and pulled out the chair for her. 'Please, sit down.'

The calm easy manner soothed her jangled nerves and, as she settled into the chair, the scent of his sandalwood cologne filled her senses. She risked a smile.

His eyes widened a fraction and a heat flickered in their green depths.

A fire ignited beneath her skin. Her pulse tripped and quickened. She felt warm and shivery all at once. She stared down at her hands folded in her lap and noticed their tremble. The blow to her head had affected her more than she thought.

He returned to his seat.

She wove her fingers together, stilling them. 'Thank you for purchasing this gown, Mr Evernden. I am sorry to put you to so much expense.'

His gaze travelled over her, appreciation in their depths. 'It certainly fits well enough and the colour matches your eyes.'

The urge to smile back, to simper like a schoolgirl, tugged

at her lips. She caught it and held it at bay. 'I would have preferred something a little less fashionable, but I do thank you.'

His mouth twisted in a wry smile and he raised a brow.
'There was little else to choose.'

She hadn't meant to hurt his feelings. 'It's a lovely colour.'

He grinned, cheerful and boyish. Her foolish heart
skipped a beat.

'I hope the other items were to your satisfaction?' he asked.

A laugh rose in her throat at his smug expression. Never
had a man charmed her like this. Razor-sharp claws of fear
tore at her stomach. Fear of her own weakness. She kept her
expression and smile cool. 'Yes, thank you.'

He cocked his head to one side as if puzzled, then
shrugged. 'Allow me to help you to a slice of ham.'

She unclenched her stiff fingers and passed him her plate.
'Thank you.'

On it, he placed a roll, some wafer-thin ham and three
asparagus spears, bright green against the white china.

'That is enough,' she murmured.

'You must keep up your strength after last night, Miss
Boisette.' He added a slice of chicken.

He returned her plate and filled his own.

They ate in a comfortable silence.

'May I pour you some coffee?' she asked.

'Please.' He pushed his cup and saucer towards her and she
filled it. The earthy aroma wafted up. It was as if they were a
married couple. A painful yearning ached in her chest. She
would never have a husband.

'You are very attached to your locket, Miss Boisette.' A
small jerk of his chin brought her to realise she clutched the
heart-shaped gold at her throat.

'It is the only thing I have left of my mother. The only thing
I brought to England from Paris.'

A muscle flicked in his lean jaw at the mention of her

origins and pain stabbed her heart. No gentleman would want to be reminded of her background.

After a mouthful of coffee, he placed his cup on the saucer and gave her a long steady stare. 'I'm afraid we must discuss last night. Do you have any idea why this man might want to abduct you?'

Nausea rolled in her stomach. The reason that had occurred to her was not something she wished to discuss with any man, particularly one as straitlaced as this one. 'I have no idea at all.'

'Did you recognise his voice? Can you describe anything about him?'

A hoarse low whisper echoed in her ears and a bitter taste touched her tongue. 'As I said before, he spoke French, but the accent was odd.' She shook her head and winced at the ache. 'He seemed familiar. Someone I've met.'

He stared at her, eyes narrowed, intent. 'Where?'

'I'm sorry, I can't remember.' The recollection of enveloping darkness rolled over her. She touched a hand to the lump behind her ear.

'Dorkin is of the opinion we should call in the local magistrate. I'm not so sure.'

The thought of the authorities made her shiver. Her blood froze the way it had when she had been a child on the streets in Paris at the sight of the National Guard. She strove to keep the panic from her voice. 'I prefer to leave for London immediately. There must be a later stage I can catch.'

He frowned. 'Quite honestly, I also would prefer not to become entangled in a lengthy enquiry. The circumstances of our travelling together are rather unfortunate. However, I cannot allow you to continue your journey by public transportation. After last night, surely you must see the danger?'

Unwelcome warmth glowed in her heart at the genuine concern in his eyes. She made one last-ditch attempt to stave him off. 'People travel quite safely that way every day, Mr

Evernden. Last night's events were perpetrated by some rogue trying to rob the inn. I was the unfortunate victim.'

He gave her a long searching look. 'I wish I felt sure it was a random act. I think I saw the fellow in the bar last night. He struck me as a man with a purpose.' Determination shone in his eyes and hardened the set of his jaw. 'Whatever the case, I will see you safely to London.'

Christopher eased his team around the tight turn on to White Lyon Street. He narrowly avoided a marauding band of sailors propositioning a group of tawdry trulls flashing their wares like exotic birds in the moulting season. Ragged men and women huddled in doorways. The dreary rookeries of London's East End crowded in on them.

He glanced at Miss Boisette's wooden expression. 'Your friend must have her business in a different part of town.'

'Yes, I expect so.' She sounded far from sure.

The weather had remained unusually fair and the drive had passed amicably. As they whiled away the time on the drive, he saw in her laughing replies hints of the sensuous woman who had teased him close to madness in Dover.

Strangely, his uncle seemed to have educated her more like a male friend than a female. She was well versed in the classics, Plato and Aristotle, and fond of the French philosopher Descartes. She had decided opinions on all of them.

Her fine mind would be wasted in a dress shop. She'd make a perfect companion with whom to spend the evening hours after mutually satisfying physical intimacy. The thought sliced through his idle musings. Had he lost his mind?

Awareness of her delightful feminine form scorched his hip. He shifted away and glanced around. Late afternoon lengthened the shadows between the buildings at an alarming rate. The district's evils were well known to him from his occasional business dealings here. He pulled up in front of a three-storey tenement house with peeling paint and an air of disreputable decay. A broken shutter hung from an upper storey. Filthy rags replaced glass here and there across the face of the building.

A frown creased her forehead. 'This is it?'

He nodded and signalled to a skinny youth with a shorn head and enormous ears slouched against the wall. 'Hold the bridle.'

The boy leaped forward.

Christopher climbed down. He gave the lad a stern glance. 'No funny business and I'll give you a penny.'

Red-rimmed assessing eyes stared back. The lad wiped his nose on a tattered sleeve. 'Right you are, sir.'

Christopher helped Sylvia down from the carriage and across the stinking kennel running with the day's effluence. She stared at the narrow door bearing the number they sought, took a deep breath and knocked. The sound echoed off the dank walls along the street.

Nerves of steel would avail her little in a place like this. Anger burned in his gullet. How could she possibly think of living here? It seemed too rank, too desperate for such a bright jewel. With half an eye on his carriage and the un-savoury youth at the team's heads, he drummed his fingers on his thigh.

The door opened a crack and a dirty face and two dark eyes peered out at them. Christopher didn't blame the occupant for caution in this neighborhood.

Sylvia took a small step back. She looked at the paper in her hand. 'Does Mary Jensen live here?'

'Aye.' The door widened to reveal a man in the rough garb of a labourer, his coal-dust-blackened face pierced by a pair of wary bloodshot eyes. The man's gaze ran over her, then took in Christopher and the carriage beyond. 'Who wants her?'

'My name is Sylvia Boisette. She used to be my governess.'

The man seemed slow to absorb the words, but finally he nodded. 'I'm her brother. Mary is sick in her bed.'

'I wonder if I might see her?'

The girl was persistent if nothing else. Christopher felt admiration well in his chest.

'Aye, ye best come in, then.' He glanced down at himself. 'You'll have to excuse my dirt, I just got in from work at the coal yard.'

An honest trade, at least. Christopher removed his hat and followed Sylvia into a dingy hall.

'This way,' Jensen said.

'Who is it, Bill?' a shrill voice called.

'No one,' he shouted back. 'Visitors for Mary.'

A woman, brown wisps poking out from beneath her cap, bobbed her head around a door along the passage. Her eyes widened at the sight of Sylvia and practically popped out of her head when she focused on Christopher. She joined them in the narrow corridor.

'This is my wife,' Jensen said.

'Lord have mercy,' Mrs Jensen said. 'You be that French girl she's always talking about. The one that was going to help her at the shop.'

'Yes, Sylvia Boisette,' Sylvia said.

Christopher heard relief in Sylvia's voice, but a chill of premonition told him that the worst was yet to come. No respectable woman would willingly live in this part of London. He couldn't leave Sylvia here. The thought hit him like a dunk in a horse trough on a cold day.

He placed a hand on her shoulder. 'I don't think this is such a good idea.'

She ducked out of reach.

'Who's that, then?' Mrs Jensen asked, with a nudge of her elbow. 'Your fancy man?'

'He drove me here.'

Christopher wanted to throttle Sylvia. She had dismissed him as if he was some sort of lackey, a coachman no less. Well she was about to find out that he considered himself a whole lot more.

'Mary's in the back room,' Jensen said.

He led the way into a cell of a room with flaking plaster walls, a truckle bed and a table beside it. On a narrow cot, a woman lay beneath the sheets, her skin like rice paper over blue veins. She opened her dark-circled eyes and slowly focused on the invaders of her cloister.

'She's on opium for the pain,' Jensen announced.

Sylvia sank to her knees beside the bed. 'Mary,' she said, her voice husky.

Christopher felt like a voyeur in this room of suffering. The familiar smell of illness, sickly sweet and vile, hung in the air and turned his mouth sour. 'I will wait for you outside, Miss Boisette. Don't be long.'

Questioning, Sylvia glanced up at him, tears hanging like bright diamonds on her lower lashes, her eyes deep pools of sorrow.

'I mean it, Miss Boisette. Ten minutes.' He headed for the front door and the fresh air of the street. Fresh. What a joke. Thick with smoke and the stink of rotting refuse, it was a slight improvement on a room full of death waiting to claim its own.

Damn it all. This time, Sylvia Boisette would do as he instructed. He didn't want to have to go back in there and haul her out.

Sylvia took Mary's frail hand in hers. 'What happened?' she asked gently. 'You never replied to my letters. When I went to Tunbridge Wells you had left.'

Mary's soft brown eyes closed for a moment. 'I'm sorry,' she whispered. 'I thought it was the ague at first. Before I knew it, I could scarcely crawl out of my bed.'

Sylvia pressed her palm to Mary's forehead. Hot and clammy to the touch, it told the story of her friend's suffering. Sadness filled her heart. 'Tell me what I must do to help you.'

Mary shook her head.

'It's a canker in her lungs,' her brother said from behind. 'Ain't nothing can be done, what we ain't already done.'

For all their poverty, the room seemed clean, the sheets smelling of soap, the floor swept. She glanced at Mary's sister-in-law. 'There must be something?'

'Mary's got a bit of money put by and we've been using that for the doctor and the medicines.' Mrs Jensen bit her lip. 'When that's gone, I'm not sure what we'll do.' With a glance at the woman on the bed, she lowered her voice. 'It may not be much longer, though.'

It seemed so unfair that someone as vital as Mary Jensen should be brought to such an end. Sorrow filled Sylvia's heart and tears choked her throat. She picked up the skeletal white hand and stroked it. 'You must get well,' she said, her voice thick. 'I'm relying on your skill with a needle. I have many new designs sketched out.'

'John Evernden is dead, then?' Mary whispered.

Sylvia nodded. 'A few days ago.'

'He left you well settled?'

If there was anything surer, Mary Jensen didn't need to hear about Sylvia's troubles. She smiled and indicated the door. 'His nephew.'

Mary frowned. 'Lord Stanford? I've heard bad things about that young man.'

A rush of tenderness filled her for a person who cared enough to worry about her at such a time. There had been few enough of those in her life. 'The younger brother. He's a good man.' He was, she realised. For all her annoyance at his interference, he had been kind and honourable.

A cough racked her friend's fragile form and Sylvia picked

up a glass of water from the small night table. She lifted Mary's head and helped her to drink.

Mary gave her a wan smile of thanks. 'I'm glad you're settled, then,' she said so softly Sylvia had to bend her head close. 'You don't belong here, Sylvia. There's too much sickness and squalor. Don't worry about me. Bill is a good man and takes care of me.'

'As good as I can,' Bill spoke gently.

Sylvia's heart gladdened at the thought that Mary had relatives to care for her. A family's love made all the difference at a time like this. But she and Mary had been such close friends; she did so hate to lose her.

Mary's eyes slid closed.

'Best leave her, miss,' Bill said. 'She tires easy. She'll talk about this visit for days, she will. In between the opium, like.'

The steady rise and fall of the thin chest beneath the covers seemed peaceful. Sylvia stood up and smiled at Mr Jensen. 'If you ever need anything, please let me know.' How? How could he let her know? She took a deep breath. 'Mr Evernden will know my whereabouts should you need to reach me.'

As soon as she settled her own affairs, she would see what she could do for Mary. She wiped her eyes on the heel of her hand.

'This way, miss,' Bill Jensen said.

Out in the ugly street, she stared back at the gaunt building. Poor Mary. And just when life had seemed so full of promise. How unkind the fates could be. In laying Mary low, they had twisted Sylvia's path until she could no longer see her way.

Up and down the grimy street full of shadows and dirt, her gaze sought answers. With nowhere to go, no plan, no future, confusion washed over her. She knew nothing of London. She would have to find somewhere to live, some means of earning a living.

She wiped her eyes on her handkerchief and straightened

her shoulders. She did not believe in fate. One made one's own destiny. And who knew, perhaps she would be able to come back and help her loyal friend.

Like a candle flame on a dark winter's night, Christopher guided her towards his carriage with gentle sympathy.

'Where now?' she asked, too tired to care.

'Now we go to Evernden Place on Mount Street,' he said and lifted her into the curricle.

Chapter Seven

The wall sconces remained unlit in his mother's upstairs withdrawing room. Christopher was not surprised to see his mother stretched out on a *chaise* asleep. She liked to nap before dinner and dance until dawn.

In repose, she looked younger than her forty and some summers. The gathering gloom gave her skin a fine and delicate appearance and her pale green gown showed off her still youthful figure.

'Mother,' he murmured.

Her eyes flew open and she sat up with a start, reaching to straighten her cap, a mere wisp of lace perched on silver-stranded blonde curls. 'Christopher, darling. What on earth are you doing back in town so soon?'

He strode to her side and carried her proffered hand to his lips. 'What?' he asked. 'Are you not pleased to see me?'

She waved her handkerchief at him. 'Naughty boy. Of course I am. I am merely surprised. You intended to visit friends, did you not? I did not look to see you for at least a fortnight.'

'Unfortunately, things did not turn out quite as expected,' he replied, unable to fully obliterate the wryness in his tone.

An expression of dismay crossed her face. 'Were things so

very bad at Cliff House? It just seemed so disrespectful for no one from the family to attend.'

Christopher sat down on the chair next to the *chaise*. 'Aunt Imogene and Uncle George put in an appearance.'

She pursed her lips. 'Oh, you poor dear. Now I'm sorry I asked you to go. It must have been simply dreadful.'

Dreadful didn't quite describe the past two days. Interesting, challenging, but as the face of Miss Sylvia Boisette intruded on his thoughts, he knew he would not have missed it for the world.

'It wasn't so bad. Aunt Imogene finally got the ormolu clock, so we've heard the last of it.'

'But why did you return home?'

His face heated under her intense scrutiny. She always knew when he was keeping something from her. He had better get this over with. 'Something happened.'

Her eyes lit with interest. 'You met someone?'

Christopher stemmed a groan. For the past few months, his mother had been trying to match him up with one suitable female after another. He'd been running the gauntlet of gently bred débutantes dressed in white at every function he attended. Hence his planned flight to the country. Unfortunately Miss Boisette and her problems had put it all out of mind.

'It is a little difficult to explain. You see, Uncle John left me with the care of his ward, Mademoiselle—'

'His ward?' his mother shrieked.

She never raised her voice except at Garth, and never in a shriek. Damn. 'Mother, you must listen. Uncle John left Miss Boisette in my care and I offered to drive her to a friend of hers in Tunbridge Wells.'

With a small sigh of relief, she raised a languorous hand to her temple. 'My word, child, you had me thinking you had brought that dreadful woman here.'

'Er…actually, I did.'

She sat bolt upright. 'You did what?'

He could not see a way to cushion the blow and readied himself for the peal she would ring over his head. 'I brought her to London with me.'

Twin spots of colour glowed on her cheeks. 'You brought his paramour to London?'

'Miss Boisette is downstairs in the drawing room.'

'Downstairs in my drawing room?'

Better she sound like a parrot than a banshee. 'Yes, Mother, that is what I have been trying to tell you. Her friend had left the Wells. I brought Miss Boisette here because she had nowhere else to go.'

His mother reached for his hand. 'Is it not enough for your brother to have no morals—now you, too? I always thought better of you, Christopher. You will oblige me by taking her back where she came from, at once.'

'I can't, Mother. The house is sold.'

'Surely there are places for women like her?' The corners of her mouth turned down as if she'd sucked on a lemon. 'Your father found them easily enough in his day. Take her to one of those.'

Christopher had never seen her so haughty or so heartless. 'She was Uncle John's ward.'

'Is that what she told you?'

The venom in her tone set his teeth on edge. He got up and strode to the window, staring into the street. It had been a mistake to bring Miss Boisette here. What with his father's behaviour in his last years and Garth's dissipated ways, how could he expect his mother to accept her? But he would not drop Sylvia off at some inn like so much rubbish.

He paced back to his seat and took his mother's hand in his. 'Mother, we cannot turn her out on to the street, no matter how much you dislike it. Uncle John left her in my care. If I take her to a hotel in London, surely word of it will be all over town in a day or so. You would not like that, would you?'

She shook her head doubtfully. 'Christopher, everyone knows about her. He brought her back from France and hid her away in that house of his. It doesn't matter what he called her, she was his mistress. Your father said so.'

The echo of his earlier misgivings hit a nerve. Sylvia had behaved disgracefully at Cliff House. Since then, her demeanour had been exemplary, but what if she treated his mother to a taste of her wantonness? He grimaced. 'She is less than half his age.'

His mother moaned and reached for her smelling salts on the table beside her. 'And that's what makes it so disgusting. Oh, Christopher, please. I can't bear to have another scandal in the family. How could you?'

Dash it all, he was making a pig's ear of turning his mother up sweet. 'I don't want a scandal either. That's why we have to find her a position as a governess as far away from London as possible.'

She pressed her handkerchief to her eyes as ever-ready tears welled up. 'A governess? You have run mad. I shall appeal to Garth. Lord only knows what he will say.'

Hell. He never fought with his mother. He'd seen her cry enough over his father and be driven to distraction by Garth. Gentle persuasion worked far better with her than harsh commands. Too bad his father hadn't discovered the secret.

Absently, he leaned forward and shifted the tea tray to sit dead centre on the rosewood table. 'I'm sorry, Mother, but you haven't met Miss Boisette and you are judging her without giving her a chance.' Much as he had himself, for God's sake. He glanced up at her. 'I'm not asking you to introduce her to the *ton*; I just want you to help her find a position. It doesn't have to be with one of your friends, just a decent family in need of a French governess.'

Lady Stanford gazed at him through watery blue eyes. 'I don't know anyone of that sort. What respectable family would allow a disreputable woman to educate their children?'

Mother had learned never to say no, she just found more difficulties. 'No one has to know anything about her past. As soon as she finds a position, she will leave. That is what you want, is it not?'

She pouted. 'I still don't see why we are responsible for this female.'

'I explained all that.'

Tears spilled over and coursed down her pale cheeks. 'Oh, Christopher, how could you?'

Reaching for every ounce of patience at his command, he rubbed his palms over his knees and prepared for battle. For one brief moment, his father had his sympathy.

Above the marble mantel, a portrait of a knight in a full-bottomed wig and shining ceremonial armour returned Sylvia's gaze with a half-smile. This Evernden ancestor must be from the last century. The way his green-flecked hazel eyes crinkled at the corners reminded her of Christopher.

Too tense to sit on one of the green-and-cream brocade sofas artfully arranged against the wainscoting, Sylvia circled the room inspecting the assorted bric-à-brac on elegant Sheraton tables. On the far wall hung the painting of a woman also from the last century. Powdered and rolled over her ears, her hair rose to startling proportions, topped off with white ostrich plumes. Sylvia vaguely remembered her mother dressing her hair that way.

'Extraordinary hairdo, ain't it?'

Sylvia jumped. She swung around to the man who spoke in such a contemptuous tone.

The word *satanic* leaped to her mind as she took in midnight-winging brows, a full mouth curled in a sneer and waving black hair. Inches taller, but of slighter build than Christopher, she guessed he must be Lord Stanford. The widening of his brown eyes told her she'd surprised him also.

'Stanford, at your service, madam,' he said with a gallant bow. He gestured to the portrait behind her. 'My mother, the dowager Lady Stanford.'

They had not been introduced, but she couldn't very well ignore him in his own home. 'Sylvia Boisette,' she replied.

Recognition flickered in his dark eyes. He raised an eyebrow.

'I'm waiting for Mr Evernden,' she explained.

An appraising glance ran from her head to her toes and seemed to see right through her clothes.

Hating the surge of heat in her face, she stiffened.

A rakish smile quirked one corner of his mouth. 'Well, good for Kit. Welcome to my abode, Miss Boisette.'

His home. She mistrusted the tenor of his scrutiny and the gleam in his dark, wicked eyes. She held herself aloof. 'Thank you.'

'And where is my younger brother? Hardly courteous of him to leave you kicking your heels here by yourself. Would you like some tea, or could I offer you something a little stronger after your journey? Wine, perhaps?'

Heavens, his deep lazy drawl sounded pleasing to the ear. 'No, thank you. Mr Evernden went to speak to Lady Stanford.'

The eyebrow shot up again. 'Bearding the lioness in her den, hmm. Christopher has more bottom than I.'

His lips twisted at her blank stare. 'Please, won't you be seated and make yourself comfortable?'

He placed her hand on his arm and led her to the sofa by the fireplace. She perched on its edge.

He lounged next to her, one long arm resting along the sofa's back, his hand inches from her shoulder.

She had tried to persuade Christopher not to bring her here, but he had refused to set her down at an inn. He had insisted she would be welcomed at Evernden Place and his mother would find a way to help her. The wolfish expression on the sinfully handsome face so close to her own reinforced her misgivings.

The silenced crackled with tension.

'It is a very pleasant house you have, Lord Stanford,' she managed.

'Thank you. What brings you to London, Miss Boisette?'

The steel beneath the lazy tone demanded an answer. Damn Christopher for leaving her alone. 'I intended to live in Tunbridge Wells, but unforeseen circumstances forced a change in my plans.'

'How very…unfortunate,' he murmured, staring at her mouth.

She winced at the sarcasm and the heated stare. His assumption rankled, but she had known how it would be the moment she had agreed to travel with Mr Evernden. 'I can assure you my presence here is wholly your brother's idea. I asked him to leave me at a coaching inn. I am quite capable of looking after my own affairs.'

Amusement glimmered in obsidian depths. 'How refreshing.'

She had the distinct impression this was some sort of game and she played the mouse to his cat. She touched the locket at her neck, seeking its comfort.

With the grace and menace of a panther, he rose to loom over her. 'I think I should go and see what is keeping my brother. I shall return in a moment.'

She nodded and watched him leave with an overpowering sense of relief.

Whistling softly, Garth mounted the stairs, knowing exactly where to find Christopher and his mother at this hour of the day. He paused in the doorway, a bitter taste in his mouth as he watched the affected fluttering of his mother's handkerchief and her pouting mouth, as she listened to the low voice of her adored younger son.

For once it seemed that Christopher had earned her wrath. It would do him good to receive the edge of her tongue until she found some reason to blame Garth for his brother's fall from grace. After all, Christopher was the beloved son, the one who looked like an Evernden and not a cuckoo in the nest.

To hell with the lot of them. He held the title whether his foolish fashion-plate of a mother liked it or not.

He sauntered into the room, stretching out his hand. 'Kit, I see you couldn't stay away. Who is the ravishing creature in the drawing room?'

Christopher's eyebrows snapped together and he gave Garth an intent look as they shook hands.

'Ravishing?' Lady Stanford cried. 'Christopher, you never said anything about ravishing. How can I help find a governess position for someone with her reputation who is ravishing to boot?'

'A governess, eh? What a waste,' Garth mused. 'She didn't strike me as that sort.'

Christopher glared at him. 'You don't know anything about her.'

Garth shrugged.

'Is she really beautiful?' Lady Stanford asked.

'Stunning,' Garth replied.

Christopher glowered.

'That settles it,' Lady Stanford said, swinging her feet onto the floor with a rustle of skirts. 'I will have nothing to do with her. I don't care what you say, Christopher, I can do nothing to help the girl. Send her away at once.'

The idiot must really be smitten if he thought to foist his ladybird off on Mother. Fascinating. 'If Christopher wants to invite Miss Boisette to stay here in *my* house, I am sure I have no objection. And if he feels obligated to find her a position as a governess, then I believe we should do everything we can to assist.'

Lady Stanford wrung her hands, but Christopher's expression lightened and he clapped Garth on the shoulder. 'Thank you. You won't regret it. Despite her unfortunate…er…background, she is truly unexceptionable. You will have no reason to find fault with her manners, I promise you.'

He swung around to clasp his mother's hands. 'Mother, I'm sure you will be able to help her if you would just put your mind to it.'

'Since Garth insists,' his mother said with a sniff, 'there is no more to be said. As he says, it is his house now.'

Garth ignored the slightly baleful stare that accompanied the words. His mother's borderline insults no longer troubled him. While she never quite came out and spoke her mind, her dislike always simmered below the surface. As a child, he'd been mystified by her cold disapproval. As an adult, he'd seen right through her hypocrisy. Christopher, on the other hand, seemed oblivious to underlying tension filling the Evernden household. Garth could only imagine his brother's resentment if he ever discovered the truth.

A chill ran down his spine. He shrugged it off. He didn't give a tinker's damn.

For now, Miss Boisette would provide an entertaining diversion. A cat among the pigeons. Or was she a pigeon for the cat? He almost licked his lips. She would relieve his boredom, annoy the hell out of his mother and he might even get a rise out of even-tempered Christopher.

'Miss Boisette is very welcome to stay here as long as she wishes,' Garth said.

Christopher strode towards the door. He halted in the doorway and glanced at his mother. 'I will bring her to meet you at once.'

Lady Stanford patted her hair. 'I'm sure I look a perfect fright. I really must tidy myself.'

'You needn't bother,' Christopher said with a grin. 'You always look beautiful.'

Garth swallowed a cutting remark as his mother simpered. She wasn't worth the effort.

'Thank you, dearest,' Lady Stanford said. 'However, I am sure she would like to freshen up after her journey. Have Merreck take her to a chamber on the fourth floor. I will see her in the drawing room in one hour.'

Christopher frowned. 'The fourth floor?'

His mother raised a haughty brow. 'A governess, Christopher, not family.'

Garth silenced a chuckle at Christopher's obvious displeasure. What had the lad expected? That his uncle's paramour would be treated like a long-lost cousin? Even Christopher couldn't be that naïve. 'Best trust Mother in issues of protocol, old chap.'

Christopher grimaced and strode out.

Garth strolled to his mother's side and kissed her hand, barely grazing her white skin. He glanced into her clouded blue eyes with a laconic smile. As usual, she fretted about her darling younger son. Had she ever looked that anxious about himself? He kept his expression bland. 'So, our Kit is finally breaking the rules. And what a sublime creature she is, to be sure.'

'Oh, never say so, Garth. You can't be serious. Tell me the truth now—is she really lovely?'

'Devastating.' He sank into the chair beside her.

'As head of the family, you must do something, Garth. You must put a stop to it, not encourage him in this madness. He says John left her in his care. But to bring her here… Think of the scandal if people should learn of it.'

Always the scandal, always afraid what others would say. And it had rubbed off on to Christopher, poor idiot. Anyone would think Mother had walked with the angels all her life. He allowed himself an ironic smile. 'As to that, my dearest mama, my advice is to let things run their course.'

Lady Stanford pouted her pretty lips. 'I never thought Christopher would turn out like you.'

He curled his lip and inclined his head a small degree. 'Thank you, my dear.'

Her cautious glance gave him a modicum of satisfaction. Since he now held the purse strings, she occasionally realised just how obliged to him she was.

'Christopher,' he said, 'is too sensible to embroil himself with someone so far beneath him in any serious way. Don't worry, he will come to his senses.' He smiled wickedly. 'I intend to give him a little help. I find myself quite charmed by her.'

'Not you, too,' she cried.

Did she have to be so obtuse? 'The worst thing you can do is try to set Christopher against her. The more you oppose it, the more likely he will be to dig in his heels. You know how stubborn he is.'

'Just like his father.' She sighed. 'Well, if you truly think so.'

Just like his father. She said it so innocently, so sweetly, and buried the knife a little deeper. As usual he shrugged it off. 'I do. Someone of her ilk is bound to give him a disgust of her in short order. You know how particular he is in his notions of propriety. And perhaps I can provide some assistance.' He looked forward to it.

Thoughtfully, she gazed at him. 'I suppose so. I am relying on your help, Garth.'

If it suited Mother to believe he was helping her, he saw no reason to object. He had his own game to play and the thought of toying with this particular morsel pleased him exceedingly.

He took her hand and patted it. 'Always your willing servant, *dearest* Mama.'

Sylvia unpacked her few belongings in the sort of room one would give to a poor relation or an upstairs servant. In addition to the bed, it provided a wardrobe, a washstand and mirror and a writing desk. Dull cream-painted walls and a small window looking out on a noisy London street made it a far cry from her apartments at Cliff House. She pushed the past firmly back where it belonged.

Sighing, she dropped her bonnet on the bed. She poured cold water in the white china bowl on the washstand and washed her face and hands. A glance in the mirror showed her that the day had taken a toll on her hair. She repinned it in a severe bun, an appropriate hairstyle for a governess. Her new life.

Tomorrow, she would seek her lost trunk at the coaching office at the George in Southwark where the Tunbridge Wells coaches arrived in London. On the short journey from the Jensens', Christopher had suggested she consider applying for a governess position. Taken aback at first, the more she thought about it, the more viable it seemed. Certainly, opening a dressmaking business with only the few guineas from the sale of Cliff House and without the help of a skilled seam-stress was out of the question. Working in an attic or basement as an unskilled needlewoman held little allure. Unless there was no other option.

A governess. Her eyes stared curiously back at her from the glass. She knew too few children to know if she had the patience or the skill, but surely it could not be too difficult? It was certainly a respectable occupation. Take it, embrace it, no matter the cost to her pride, her mind encouraged. If she could find a suitable position with a wealthy family, she would save all her earnings and open a dress shop some time in the future.

She strolled to the window and looked down into the busy street. There were numbers of people going about their business in the early evening: carters, fruit sellers, flower girls, and rich folks beneath umbrellas. A well-dressed boy skipped through puddles on the pavement, trailed by a woman in sombre grey. His governess? It did not look so bad.

Other people, shabby and aimless, wandered down the

street. A man in a long black coat and a black hat pulled down low leaned against the lamppost on the distant corner. He looked oddly familiar, but every street corner in London seemed to attract loitering males and beggars like the bedraggled old woman hunched against the railings opposite. Sylvia shivered. She would not become that woman.

A knock on the door broke her thoughts and she hurried to open it.

'Are you ready?' Christopher asked, flashing her the charming smile that sent her heart beating a little too fast.

She nodded and forced a smile. Everything depended on her interview with Lady Stanford. Sylvia had been the object of enough disapproving glances during her life with Monsieur Jean to know not to take anything for granted. A recollection of the instant assumptions in Lord Stanford's dark eyes reminded her to be cautious.

Once more, she wished Christopher had not bought quite such a fashionable gown. Her own clothes would have presented a much better appearance for someone seeking work.

She rested her hand on Christopher's arm and he led her downstairs.

The dowager Lady Stanford, with her oldest son standing behind her, sat in state on a sofa in the same drawing room where Sylvia had waited earlier. She instantly recognised Lady Stanford as the woman in the portrait, even without the elaborate wig. The blush of youth captured by the artist had long since faded, but she remained a handsome woman dressed in the first stare of fashion in a Pomona crepe morning gown over a white satin slip from beneath which matching green slippers peeped. The cashmere shawl covering her shoulders must have cost a fortune.

An intense desire to make a good impression swept over Sylvia in a wave, but the dowager's frigid expression chilled her hopes. She resisted the urge to turn tail and run. She needed this woman's assistance. She would endure anything if it provided her with the means of becoming independent. She kept her expression remote and curtsied deeply on Christopher's introduction.

'I am so sorry to hear of your misfortune, Miss Boisette.' Lady Stanford's cold tone disheartened Sylvia further.

By misfortune, did she mean John Evernden's death or the loss of her trunk? Sylvia looked to Christopher for some explanation, but Lady Stanford waved a wisp of lace and continued. 'I understand from Christopher that the friend you were relying on to help you is ill and you would like me to help you find a place with a suitable family.'

No doubt the ill luck referred to Sylvia's presence. She maintained her calm expression. 'Yes, my lady, if it pleases you. I am skilled in watercolours and drawing. I speak fluent French.'

A wry expression twisted Lady Stanford's face. 'I am glad my husband's brother provided you with such a good education.'

Despite her quaking limbs, Sylvia forced herself to speak calmly. 'Mr Evernden was exceedingly generous.'

The words sounded dreadful and Lady Stanford's face froze into a mask of indifference.

Sylvia winced at the upward slant of Lord Stanford's mouth.

His lazy drawl broke the stiff silence. 'Miss Boisette, allow me to seat you.' He sauntered to her side, took her hand in gallant style and led her to the sofa opposite his mother.

He lounged next to her, his long legs brushing her skirts. Christopher frowned at his brother.

Lord Stanford glanced across at Lady Stanford. 'Mother, it is good of you to offer Miss Boisette your assistance. It is certainly not something where I could be of any value.'

Lady Stanford's expression became horrified and she twisted her handkerchief around her fingers. 'Good heavens. I should think not indeed. Just imagine the reaction of any of our acquaintances if you were to recommend Miss Boisette to them.'

Christopher's face darkened and he glared at his brother. 'No one suggested he would.'

Lady Stanford gave a long-suffering sigh and forced a stiff little smile. 'Since Christopher is so insistent, I will do what I can. To be frank, I know very few matrons with young children, Miss Boisette.'

Sylvia glanced at Christopher. Her heart squeezed painfully at the discomfort in his eyes. When he said nothing, her stomach dropped to the floor. She should never have let him persuade her to come here.

His earlier kindness had lulled her into thinking he no longer held her in contempt. She began to reconstruct the wall of ice around her heart, her defence against a world that despised her. 'I do not wish to put you to any trouble, my lady. I believe I might easily find a position through advertisements in the newspapers.'

'It's no trouble at all, is it, Mother?' Christopher said.

Lady Stanford sighed again. 'Of course not.'

Sylvia didn't believe a word of it and nor did Lord Stanford from his sardonic smile. He seemed entertained by the discord permeating the room.

'Thank you, Mother,' Christopher said, sitting beside Lady Stanford. 'I know Miss Boisette is grateful for any help you can provide.'

Sylvia gritted her teeth. She would be grateful if the promised position materialised; until then all she could do was hide her resentment at Lady Stanford's disapproval. 'Indeed,' she said.

'Well, now that's settled,' Lady Stanford said. 'Christopher, I do hope you will accompany Garth and me to Covent Garden tonight. Mr Macready is quite the latest rage. I know you hadn't planned to go, but Garth never stays until the end and I would so appreciate your company on the drive home.' She smiled expectantly.

Christopher nodded, a trifle unwillingly, Sylvia thought. 'As you wish.'

Lady Stanford, it seemed, used a mixture of delicate nerves and guilt to get her way. By now, Christopher must thoroughly regret bringing Sylvia to meet his mother.

'Perhaps Miss Boisette could accompany us?' Christopher said, his expression brightening. 'I am sure you would enjoy the play.'

His open smile sent Sylvia's heart leaping into her throat. He wanted her to go with them. Against her will, a glow of joy melted a brick in the chilly wall around her heart.

Covent Garden. An unlooked-for courtesy. For a moment, Sylvia imagined attending one of London's fashionable playhouses in the rose-silk gown Christopher had purchased until she caught the horrified expression on Lady Stanford's face.

She packed ice into the chink. 'No indeed, Mr Evernden. Your acquaintances would think it very odd for a woman seeking a place as a governess to attend the theatre as your guest.'

Not to mention her disreputable background. That thought raced across Lady Stanford's face.

Christopher's mouth thinned to a straight line. Disappointment that his mother was right? Lord Stanford engaged himself in removing a piece of lint from his sleeve. Embarrassment charged the air.

Her face blank, Sylvia dared them to utter what was on their minds.

A deep chuckle from Lord Stanford broke the uncomfortable silence. 'I don't know about the rest of you,' he drawled, 'but I am sorely in need of my supper.'

'And so unusual of you to join us, Stanford dear,' the dowager said, with a downward curve to her mouth.

'I would not miss it for the world,' he replied with a small bow. 'After all, it is not every day we have such a charming guest for dinner.' His hooded gaze left Sylvia with the impression she was the main course.

She acknowledged his supposed compliment with a stiff nod.

Lady Stanford's expression would have soured a bowl of cream.

Giving his brother a sharp stare, Christopher rose and strode to Sylvia's side. 'Good Lord, yes. You must be ravenous after all the travelling today, Miss Boisette.' He took her hand and brought her to her feet. 'Allow me to escort you into the dining room.'

'Mother,' Lord Stanford said, rising and holding out his arm.

Christopher gave Sylvia a little grimace as they followed Lord Stanford and his very proper mother.

Unsure of his meaning, she felt only relief at surviving the interview, if not in good order, at least with her dignity intact.

Chapter Eight

W hat better way could she spend an evening than hemming
a handkerchief in the Everndens' drawing room? Sylvia stifled
a yawn and set another small stitch in the fine white lawn.

The theatre would have been better. She forced the thought
aside. She had no reason to envy the Everndens their evening
and she needed this time to get her thoughts in order after the
sinking of her well-laid plans by poor Mary's illness. Having
found herself in uncharted waters, she needed to set a new
course. The governess idea might well provide a welcome haven.

In the meantime, to counteract her feeling of obligation to
the grudging Lady Stanford, she had offered to make herself
useful during her stay. She had begun right away by fetching
Lady Stanford's shawl from the drawing room when she complained of a draught.

Christopher had encouraged her with a nod, Lady Stanford
had seemed a little less frigid and Lord Stanford had raised a
cynical brow. So here she sat, usefully employed on one of
Lady Stanford's indispensable scraps of lace.

A clock in the hall chimed the hour into a silent house. Ten
o'clock. Preferring not to hear about the play, she folded the
needlework and placed it in the basket beside her chair.

The door swung open. She started, her heart picking up speed.

In full evening dress, Lord Stanford loomed in the doorway. A quizzical smile leavened his chiselled features. 'Miss Boisette, did I startle you? I was not sure I would find you still downstairs.'

He probably thought she should scuttle off to bed like an upstairs maid. She wished she had, given that everything about this man smacked of danger. Unlike his younger brother, who wore his sense of honour on his fair and open countenance, Lord Stanford hid his thoughts behind a mask of cynicism. 'I did not expect you back so soon,' she said.

He chuckled. 'Oh, I left during the first intermission. The house was sadly lacking in interesting company. I thought I might find more amusement here.'

Dread clenched her stomach. 'You flatter me. I can assure you I am not in the habit of amusing gentlemen and I am just about to retire.' She rose to her feet.

As solid as any door, he leaned a shoulder against the doorjamb. 'Come now, Miss Boisette, I'm certain I detected a distinct unwillingness on my brother's part to leave such delightful company at home. You have been travelling together, have you not?'

Sylvia kept her expression aloof and her gaze steady on the wickedly handsome untrustworthy face. 'Lord Stanford, you are quite mistaken. Mr Evernden simply undertook to escort me to my destination.'

His gaze lingered on her mouth, before rising to her eyes. 'To a friend who seems as elusive as fog, Miss Boisette. Or do I call you *mademoiselle*?' he murmured.

The dread clawed its way up into her throat. She stepped forward, meaning to pass him, but he didn't move. She stopped two steps away. 'My friend's illness was as much a surprise to me as it was to your brother. Now, if you will excuse me…'

He reached out and put one finger under her chin. His dark

gaze raked her face. 'Unbelievable,' he muttered. 'You are exquisite. But you know that, don't you? You are quite wasted on my brother. He is far too strict in his notions to appreciate your undeniable charms.'

She held her ground, resisting the temptation to slap his smiling mouth. 'At least your brother is a gentleman, my lord.' An honourable gentleman. She bit back the words, fearing to push him too far.

He laughed. 'So, you've got claws too. I like spirited women.'

She swallowed a gasp, meeting his gaze with a silent stare.

His lips curled. 'Oh yes, Kit is definitely a gentleman.' He made it sound like an insult. 'You know, I could offer you a much better arrangement than ever my brother would. I have an exceedingly well-appointed house in Blackheath and you would find me most generous. You would lack for nothing now, or later when we go our separate ways.'

Warmth stole up her neck and into her face at his callous assumption that she was available to the highest bidder. She kept her hands relaxed at her sides. She needed Lady Stanford's help to find a position and it wasn't the first time she had been forced to swallow her pride.

Look to the future and survive the present. In a respectable position, a situation where no one knew her history, she would not be subject to this kind of humiliation.

She kept her smile cool. 'I thank you for your offer, my lord, but I am not in the market for a protector. I have other irons in the fire.'

He regarded her silently for a moment. When he spoke, his soft tone held a warning. 'You're a hard little piece, ain't you. You know, Miss Boisette, I would not want to see my brother embroiled in any sort of…difficulty.'

Sylvia blinked. If it wasn't so out of character, she might suspect him of trying to protect his sibling. Or had Christopher, suspecting her growing attraction, sent his brother to warn her off? An unexpected pang caught at her heart. 'I acknowledge my debt to your brother and I certainly would not dream of diverting him from his familial duty.'

A dark brow flicked up and he nodded. 'Even if you are not interested in him, Miss Boisette, I am sure you have noticed his interest in you. Whether by accident or by design, it is a problem I would rather avoid. I hope you will not repay his kindness by putting him under some further obligation.' He flashed a charming smile.

She bit back a heated retort and smiled sweetly. 'He has fulfilled all of his obligations, my lord.'

'I'm pleased to hear it.' He placed one languid white hand on the doorframe, blocking her passage. 'If you change your mind about my offer, you will let me know, won't you?'

She lifted her chin. 'Highly unlikely, my lord.'

Lord Stanford eased away from the door to let her pass. 'Too bad,' he drawled. 'But I'm glad we had this little chat and understand each other.'

She understood very well. She had just been told to keep her unworthy claws out of his precious brother. Her foolish heart ached for something she had known all along she did not deserve. Pride straightened her spine. 'I too prefer frankness, Lord Stanford.'

She cast him a careless smile on her way past and swept through the door. She barely avoided colliding with Christopher. He looked from her to Lord Stanford and frowned.

'Back already?' Lord Stanford asked.

His gaze fixed on Sylvia, Christopher nodded. 'I have some documents to sign. My man of business wanted them first thing in the morning.'

'Quite the businessman these days,' Stanford said, a cutting edge to his tone.

Christopher shrugged. 'I thought you were going to White's tonight?'

'Indeed I am. I came home to change and found Miss Boisette alone with her needlework. I became so entertained by our conversation I quite forgot the time.'

Christopher's expression darkened. 'I see.'

Sylvia stared at him. Just what did he did see? That his brother had spent the last fifteen minutes warning her off? Or that the dissipated rake had offered her a *carte blanche*? To her annoyance, fire burned her cheeks. She wasn't the one who should be blushing—it was his horrid brother.

Tears prickled the backs of her eyes. What on earth was wrong with her? It didn't matter a damn what either of them thought of her. She ducked her head. 'If you will excuse me, gentlemen. I am going to my room.'

Lord Stanford bowed elegantly. 'Goodnight, Miss Boisette.'

Christopher hesitated as if he wanted to say something. Whatever it was, Sylvia could not stay to hear it. One more insult and she might really cry. She brushed past him.

'Goodnight, *mademoiselle*,' Christopher said to her retreating back.

The ironic note in his voice almost caused her to turn back. Men. They were all the same. She held her back straight and marched up the stairs.

'I see you managed to pry yourself free of the clinging vine.' Garth's words echoed up the stairs.

'Damn you, Garth, but you're an insulting cur to our mother.'

'So I am, dear boy.' His sardonic laughter rang out as Sylvia reached the landing. She shivered. Bitterness seemed to hang over Lord Stanford like a shadow.

Over the past week, Sylvia had run errands for the fragile Lady Stanford to the best of her ability. Lady Stanford had generously said she wasn't sure what she would do without Sylvia's help when she left. But there was no doubt about it, Sylvia would be leaving.

Today, she had promised to return a novel to Hookham's on Bond Street. After receiving directions to the famous lending library from the haughty butler, she put on the grey merino and brown pelisse she'd taken to wearing since the return of her trunk. Since her only bonnet had been stolen, she wore the high-crowned, blue confection decorated with pink rosebuds purchased by Christopher in Tunbridge Wells.

Outside, a fine drizzle slicked the streets and coated everything with damp soot. A little nervous about her first expedition in London, she stepped out smartly.

Around her, horse-drawn equipages crowded the road. Coalmen and other tradesmen filed by in a variety of creaking and rumbling wagons. Barouches trundled sedately over the cobbles and young bloods perched in their sporting curricles turned their heads to stare at her over high shirt points. She avoided their gazes.

Shouts, horses' hooves on cobblestones, whistles and catcalls added up to an almost unbearable din. Unpleasant and unnameable smells invaded the smoky air, mitigated only by the scent of cinnamon wafting from a cheeky lass selling sticky buns and the floral perfumes worn by the well-dressed ladies she passed. The noise and the dirt reminded her too much of her childhood in Paris for comfort.

Cliff House and her hitherto secluded existence seemed hundreds of miles away. She prayed for a position with a family who resided in the country.

In Hookham's, she returned Lady Stanford's novel, collected the one on order, then spent a happy hour feasting on the vast selection of books on the floor-to-ceiling shelves. When she emerged into the street, the rain had ceased and Bond Street thronged with gentlemen and ladies sauntering along the pavement. They browsed the shop windows and chatted with acquaintances, their stylish attire and carefully coiffed hair proclaiming their wealth and status.

Sylvia studied the dressmakers' displays as she strolled along. The array of gowns and bonnets dazzled her with their variety of fabrics and styles. An unusually fashioned morning gown in green sarsenet trimmed with points of white satin caught her attention. How cleverly the fabric had been cut on the bias. With a regretful sigh, she stored the idea away and picked up her pace.

A black town carriage drew up at the curb's edge beside her. A footman jumped down and blocked her path.

Jolted out of her reverie, she stepped to one side.

'Your carriage, miss?' He nudged her towards the open door.

She shook her head. 'You are mistaken.'

He put out an arm. 'There's a gentleman friend of yours inside.'

Christopher?

She peered through the open door. A man with a hat pulled low and a muffler over his face sat in the shadows.

The footman took her arm. 'In you go, miss.'

Hot pinpricks flashed across her back. She jerked her arm out of his reach. 'This is not my carriage.' She turned to push past him.

His portly body blocked her. He thrust her back towards the lowered steps.

Her throat dried. 'Take your hands off me.'

Heart hammering, she glanced around for aid. No one appeared to notice. She clutched the string of her reticule, heavy with her borrowed book, and judged the distance to his head. If she hit him hard enough and ran, even in hampering skirts, she'd easily outdistance such a fat man. She stepped closer. Her heart picked up speed.

Garth waited for a hackney to drive by, then stepped off the curb, tossing a penny to the street sweeper who cleared him a path.

Damn, but Madame Eglantine had been in fine fettle last night. He grinned to himself at the recollection.

A couple of servants arguing on the footpath caught his idle glance. The woman looked ready to assail the fat fellow. He drew in a sharp breath. What the hell was Miss Boisette doing on Bond Street brawling with a footman? This young woman collected admirers, the way he collected snuffboxes. He strode towards them.

Miss Boisette's expression turned to relief, her colour rushing back in a flood. Perhaps he would make one of her collection after all. The already pleasant morning had just improved by leaps and bounds.

He composed his expression in a bored smile. 'Miss Boisette, is aught amiss?'

The lackey mumbled something and retreated. He clambered on to the box of the nearby carriage. Its occupant slammed the door shut and the coach forced its way into the traffic.

Garth stared after it. 'What the deuce is going on?'

'He offered me a ride.' Her voice shook. Clearly she remained upset, despite her outward calmness.

'Someone you know?'

Distress once more clouded her expression. 'A case of mistaken identity, I believe.' She sounded too uncertain for him to believe her, the cheating little baggage. She must think him a fool. No one would mistake that face of hers for another.

He toyed with the idea of chasing the carriage down and getting to the truth. Rot it. It would put a damper on his plans. There was a team of bays he wanted going on the block today at Tattersalls. If he didn't beat the rush, he'd lose them.

She gazed up at him. Never had he seen such intensely blue eyes. He flicked a glance over her and imagined her naked. His blood stirred.

No wonder Christopher wanted to hang on to her. Garth chewed on the inside of his cheek. Christopher had better watch his step with this one or she'd have him leg-shackled before he blinked. Not a chance. His brother was far too sensible. In fact, no fun at all. Perhaps this young lady would enjoy a bit of sport. If so, Garth was more the man for the job.

He held out his arm. 'Come, I will see you home.'

Still trembling inside, Sylvia took Lord Stanford's arm. While the speculative expression on his face caused an unpleasant flutter in her stomach, she felt safer with him than with the man in the carriage. Had it really been a mistake, as she first thought, or did it have something to do with the man at the inn? Surely not.

Slowly her heartbeat returned to normal and she felt calm enough to glance at her escort. Dressed in his evening clothes from the night before, the dissolute young lord had definitely not slept at home. In her youth, she'd seen too many men leaving at dawn in their evening clothes to question where he'd been.

Lord Stanford shot hera penetrating glance. 'What on earth *are* you doing out here alone, Miss Boisette?'

A fair question, considering. 'I returned a library book to Hookham's for your mother.'

'You should not go out alone.'

'I could hardly ask a maid to go with me.'

'Why not?'

She stared at him. Did he think she was not aware that her position in his home was under sufferance? The servants certainly knew it. 'I'm not exactly a guest.'

His frown deepened, but he did not take issue with her statement. He glanced down the street in the direction the coach had disappeared. 'Tell me who he was.'

She gave him a cold glance. 'The man was a stranger.'

'Then you should not have stopped to speak to him.'

This was beyond all. Now he was accusing her of wrongdoing. 'Lord Stanford, I had no intention of getting into that carriage, *je vous assure*; I was never more pleased to see anyone in my whole life as when you arrived just now.'

The expression in his dark eyes warmed. 'I beg your pardon, Miss Boisette, I believe I mistook the matter. Come, a truce. Whoever the blackguard was, he is a coward. We will not give him another thought.'

If only it were that easy.

With only Sylvia for company at lunch, Lady Stanford toyed with the food on her plate. When she signalled to the footman to take it away, Sylvia noticed she had barely touched the roasted breast of pheasant or the aspic.

'Miss Boisette,' Lady Stanford said, while the footman poured coffee, 'I have some good news for you. I meant to tell Christopher, but he left so precipitously this morning, he didn't give me the opportunity.' She paused and frowned as if puzzled. 'Ah, well. A friend of mine knows of a family looking for a governess.'

At last. Now Sylvia could get on with her life. She put down her knife and fork. 'That is good news.'

'Yes. The family lives in Wiltshire and they are in London for a short stay. Apparently, they have sought a governess without success for quite some time. It seems as though I have hit on the perfect solution. Mrs Elston will come for tea at four this afternoon and interview you.' She beamed. 'Now, what do you think of that?'

'My lady, I cannot express enough my appreciation for your help. I will do my best to make a good impression on Mrs Elston.'

Lady Stanford pursed her lips. 'I sincerely hope you will.'

The murmur of men's voices, interrupted by shouts of triumph or groans of despair, rumbled around White's gaming room. Across the green baize table from Christopher, Garth scribbled on a scrap of paper and dropped it on top of the pile of guineas. 'I'll raise you a pony.'

The dim light from the lantern above their heads did nothing to deaden the reckless glitter in Garth's eyes. He seemed to be well on the way to half seas over.

A trifle warm himself, Christopher had drunk only half the quantity Garth had imbibed in the past two hours. Damn Garth for an idiot to bet another hundred on the single queen in his hand when she wasn't even trumps.

He raised his eyebrows at the crumpled vowel. 'Under the hatches again?'

Garth shrugged. 'Is my note not good enough for you?'

Christopher gritted his teeth at the sarcasm. 'Of course it is.'

His own hand wasn't very good, but it would take the trick. His facility with numbers never let him down, no matter how much he imbibed, and he never relied on blind luck. Something Garth ought to know by now.

'I need a drink.' Garth signalled to a passing waiter for another bottle. 'No mistake, though, she's a diamond of the first water,' he said, picking up their earlier conversation on the subject of Mademoiselle Boisette.

They'd been around this topic once. 'Leave well enough alone.'

'But a governess.' Mock pain edged Garth's tone. 'What a waste of delicious womanhood.'

'It's what she wants.'

'It's what she says she wants. Women never say what they mean.'

Christopher felt the hackles rise on the back of his neck. A hot rush of something unpleasant closed his throat. He forced his words past it. 'What the hell are you talking about?'

One side of Garth's mouth curled in a sneer. 'Women. They are all the same. You just have to find the key to unlock the gate. Usually jewels, or money.' He chuckled.

'I don't much like your sense of humour.'

Garth flashed him a grin. 'I thought we'd agreed never to argue over the fairer sex. They aren't worth it.'

They had. Years ago, when they had come to blows over the milkmaid at their grandmother's house. They'd agreed to let the woman choose and she'd decided on the older, far more experienced Garth. They'd never competed for a female again. Until now. The thought didn't sit well in Christopher's stomach. 'Then stay away from Miss Boisette.'

'Bloody hell, don't be such a dog in the manger. You don't want her, therefore she's fair game.'

Want was far too weak a word to describe the insistent throb low in his groin each time he saw or thought about her. 'She wants to be a governess.' Now he sounded like a sulky schoolboy denied a treat. He tossed off his brandy, then stared at his glass. Damn. At this rate he'd be under the table before the end of the evening.

'You're a damned fool.' Garth threw an impatient glance at the money on the table. 'Are you in or not?'

Christopher wanted to be inside Sylvia's slender body. Buried to the hilt in her hot, sweet flesh. He pushed one hundred guineas into the pile. 'I'm in.'

Garth scrawled on another slip of paper with a flourish. 'Two hundred.' He flicked the paper on to the growing pile.

Christopher stared at it. The raving idiot.

Garth leaned forward. 'If you think I'm going to let an Incomparable hie off to be a drudge in Wiltshire with a parcel of brats instead of warming my bed, you are more of a bloody fool than I thought.'

It was all Christopher could do to stop from reaching out and choking Garth with his bare hands. His brother would love that. 'She's not interested. She's as cold as a mountain stream.'

The waiter arrived with a bottle of brandy, filled both glasses and set the bottle at Garth's elbow.

With a deep sigh of contentment, Garth leaned back. 'Now that's where you are wrong.' He raised his glass in a toast, then took a deep swig. 'Take it from an expert. There's a hot spring beneath the frigid waters waiting for a man to dive in. Haven't you seen that smile?'

Rarely. A vivid image of her performance at Cliff House filled his mind, the teasing way she removed her gloves, her tempting smile with its fascinating tiny fault. The same smile she had bestowed on Garth a week ago, after the theater.

The thought of Sylvia with Garth sent sparks of anger chasing through his veins. He snapped his cards face down on the table. 'You bastard. If you go anywhere near her, I'll murder you.'

Garth's inscrutable gaze rose from contemplating the dregs of brandy in the bottom of his glass. His sneer deepened. 'Do you really think you can?'

Probably not. Garth was a crack shot and an expert duellist, but Christopher, with his greater bulk, might have a chance at his own sport, boxing. He glared across at his brother. Tension crackled across the table, palpable in the thick air.

Two men playing chess across the aisle from them perked up in their deep armchairs. An argument always attracted a crowd.

Christopher lowered his voice. 'Don't think I won't. Stay away from her.'

'Don't let that angelic face fool you. If you want her, take her. Otherwise, get off the pot,' Garth said crudely. He gestured at Christopher's cards. 'Your play.'

Garth deserved to lose. Christopher closed the fanned cards. 'Your trick.'

A frown on his face, Garth reached for the discarded hand.

Lurching to his feet, Christopher nudged the table. Cards and guineas and promises to pay tumbled to the floor.

Garth glared at him. 'Don't play me for an ass, brother.'

Christopher bowed. 'I wouldn't dare now, would I? I'll see you later.'

Garth slanted him a wry look. 'Not if I see you first.' He reached for the brandy bottle. 'I'll give you one day and then it's open season.'

The desire to plant his knuckles in Garth's leering face made Christopher clench his fists. He took a deep breath to steady himself, nodded and sauntered off to find his hat and coat. He needed to talk to Miss Boisette about her smile.

Tonight.

Chapter Nine

'Come in,' Sylvia called out at the rap on her chamber door. At last, the scullery maid with her supper. The only sure way to prevent another encounter with Lord Stanford. She hastened to clear the clutter from the writing desk.

'Good evening, Miss Boisette.'

She jerked around, hand at her throat.

Christopher. Why now, after avoiding her all week? 'Mr Evernden. I'm sorry, I thought you were Lucy with the tea tray.'

His shoulders spanned the doorway of her small chamber. 'I am sorry to disappoint.' The corners of his eyes crinkled as a charming smile curved his lips, the reserve of the past few days replaced by an expression of warm appreciation.

Awareness of his maleness, his aura of controlled strength, unfurled in a strangely pleasant flitter in her stomach. Warmth rushed up her body to heat her face. She retreated. 'It is no disappointment. Indeed, I had wanted to seek your advice.'

'Good. I wanted to talk to you.' He strolled to the bed and with a sigh slouched back against the headboard. His weight dipped into the cream cotton bedspread as he hitched up one long leg.

Her breath caught in her throat. He looked so comfortable, so right, on her bed. The last place she ever expected to see him. The flitter turned into the wild beating of a bird trying to escape.

He grinned. 'Won't you sit down?' He seemed unusually relaxed.

The straight-backed wooden chair at the writing desk offered safety and distance. After turning it to face him, she perched on its edge.

'I expected to find you in the drawing room,' he said. 'I hope we haven't made you feel so unwelcome you feel obliged to hide up here in the evening.'

Unable to voice her real reason, she avoided his frank gaze and gestured to the bedside table. 'I borrowed a book from Hookham's and hoped to finish it before I leave.'

'You are leaving, then?' His voice held regret.

She clenched her hands in her lap. 'I have been offered a position.'

He nodded. 'So I understand.'

The quiet murmur and calm expression gave her courage to go on. 'The family lives in Wiltshire. There are four children, all rather young. I'm not sure it is exactly what I had hoped for and yet Lady Stanford is convinced it is the best offer I am likely to receive, given my lack of experience.'

The candle beside the bed bronzed the plains and valleys of his angled face and flickered in his eyes as he shot her a quizzical look. 'You are asking my opinion?'

A tremor shook her hands and she fingered her locket. 'It sounds foolish to hesitate, I know.' She attempted a bright smile. 'My only other option is to visit a friend in Paris.' She'd written to Denise, but she hated the thought of returning to France. 'I'm sure your mother is right. It is the best solution.'

His voice lowered, thickened. 'There is another option.'

She'd half-expected this, half-dreaded the thought of refusing him. Her hands trembled. Unable to bear the tension of waiting for the words she despaired to hear, she rose and went to the window. Lamps twinkled along the street like diamonds on a necklace. 'What option?'

The bed squeaked, then a wall of heat shimmered at her back. His hands, large, warm, dropped to her shoulders. His face, reflected ghostly in the glass, bent close to her cheek. 'Stay with me.' His breath tickled her ear.

At least he had the courage to ask for what he wanted. She could say nothing. Since the moment they had met, she'd denied and resisted his pull. She turned in his arms. Brandy scented his breath and mingled with sandalwood and musky male, a heady combination.

For long moments, she savoured the feel of him close, the correct words refusing to form in her mind, let alone on her tongue. 'I must not,' she forced out.

His gaze lowered to her mouth and his head angled down. 'You must not or you do not want to?'

She stared at his full, sensual lips, glimpsed the dappled forest green of his eyes. Oh, she wanted, but not what he had to offer. He'd splintered the wall of ice around her heart, exposing it, vulnerable and raw, to his power to wound.

The heartbreak in her mother's eyes grazed her memory. 'I think it is best if you leave.' The words tore her in two.

'Don't think,' he murmured and captured her mouth with his.

The warm, moist touch of his lips branded her mouth. Shock waves of shivering heat tore through her chest and settled deep in the pit of her stomach.

Drowning in her blood's molten heat, she clung to his solid form, melted against his hard body, her arms inching around his neck without permission. A hard thigh pressed between her legs and she angled her hips into it. Urgent need pulsed deep in her core.

His heart hammered against her chest. She yearned to open to him, to trust him. Insidious need had softened her heart and weakened her will. He had slipped past her guard.

Her lips parted and his tongue teased at the corners, plundered her mouth, drove her to a need so great, she arched her back. His hands ran over her shoulders and down her spine, lighting fires of longing. Her body cried yes in sly encouragement.

A small sound escaped her throat.

He cupped her buttocks and pulled her hard against the ridge of his arousal with a soft groan.

By all the saints, he wanted her, Christopher acknowledged. She haunted his dreams. Warm and soft in his arms, she felt right, perfect in fact.

Damn Garth and his hints. Had she yielded to him? The thought crashed over him like cold surf. He broke the kiss and closed his eyes against the demands of his body. If he didn't stop now, he'd take her right here, under his mother's roof, and be damned.

Breath rasping in his throat, he grasped her shoulders and stepped back. Her beautiful blue eyes, hazy with passion, stared up at him; her lips rosy and moist from his kiss called him back. He would not share her. 'I have a small house in Kent, less than a day's drive from town. We can live there. I can stay at Grillon's when I have business in London.'

Sorrow shadowed her face and her gaze dropped to the floor.

'What?' he asked.

A brittle laugh broke the silence 'I thank you for your flattering offer, but I find I must decline.'

She made it sound as though he'd handed her a bouquet of poisonous weeds. Clearly, he'd missed something along the way. Damn the brandy he'd drunk. He recalled Garth's mocking words. She must want more. 'You will find me generous and, when we part, I promise you will never have to worry about money again.'

'No. Thank you.'

The flat-out rejection hurt more than he wanted to acknowledge. 'It can't be worse than playing nursemaid to a pack of unruly brats.'

She raised a brow. 'I disagree.'

An impression of tears in her crystalline eye panicked him. He never panicked. Damn drinking too much and damn her. One moment she played the Jezebel, the next her repertoire consisted of untouchable ice maiden. He didn't like either role.

'Oh, come on. We both know you are no gently bred female straight from the schoolroom.'

She averted her gaze. 'I am not interested.'

Suspicion roiled through his gut. Garth had been just a little too smug. The demon leaped out of the abyss in his mind and into his mouth. 'If you are seeking a man with a title, I can assure you my brother's no green 'un to be taken in by that lovely face of yours.'

Her head jerked around. Shock, dismay and something far worse mirrored in her gaze. Guilt.

Hemmed in by the small chamber, he paced around the foot of the bed, logic slipping beyond the grip of his hazy mind.

She shrank back as he swung around to face her.

'Don't give me that innocent look,' he said. 'I saw your true colours in Dover. And I saw the way you smiled at my brother, while all I see are cold stares.'

Her face became wooden, her eyes remote. He'd hit a nerve.

With shock, Sylvia heard the slur in his words and saw the way he rocked on his feet. He was drunk. She'd been so pleased to see him, she hadn't noticed. She swallowed. Men in their cups were hard to manage. Strong and heavy and mean.

He rubbed a hand over his chin. 'Sylvia. Don't hold out for Garth.' His tone held a warning. 'He knows I have first option.'

She gasped. They'd bargained for her between them. She eased around him and pulled open the door. 'I want neither of you and you, sir, are sotted. You will oblige me by leaving immediately.'

He stared at her, stark disbelief in his face, then his lip curled in a sneer. 'Oh, so now you play the prim and proper lady again.' He laughed, low and bitter. 'Well, let me tell you, *mademoiselle*, don't hold out for marriage. Even Garth knows better than that.'

Lord Stanford's proposal sprang into her mind and heat scalded her cheeks. Men only wanted beautiful women for one thing, and when they were satisfied they cast them aside.

How had she ever thought she could trust Christopher? Her throat burned with unshed tears; tremors shook her body. 'Get out. I have no more interest in you than I have in your brother.'

His eyes narrowed. 'I don't know what game you are playing, but the sooner you find yourself a place away from this family, the better for all of us. I knew what you were the moment I set eyes on you.'

Her heart bled from his unjust words, but she would not let him see how he had wounded her. Shattered pride would not allow it. 'Oh, and what is that?'

'A trollop.'

Bloodless, her heart shrank into a cold hard lump. The need to fight back, to wound him in return, straightened her spine. 'And Lord Stanford is exceptionally generous, I'm told, and very charming.'

A shadow darkened his eyes from green to brown. 'Then I wish you good luck.' He walked past her and closed the door with a violent softness.

It was the worst day of her life. First the incident with the carriage, then the awful Elston woman had offered her hard work for little pay and now Christopher had shown exactly what he thought of her. He hadn't wanted to kiss her; he had done it to prove she was the same as her mother. And she was. Just as weak and wanting.

Damn him to hell. Sylvia buried her face in her pillow and sobbed. And damn Mrs Elston and damn Lord Stanford. To the devil with them all. She dashed away the hot tears running down her face.

Merde. She would not turn herself into a drudge for a

woman she could only describe as a harridan for the sake of respectability.

In her dreams, she had seen a different life, a comfortable home, laughing children, a man who would smile at her over his newspaper each morning with love and respect in his eyes. That dream would never be hers. She'd always known it. No decent man would marry her knowing her background and the sordid truth of her life in Paris.

Christopher Evernden and respectability were out of her reach.

…the sooner you find yourself a place away from this family, the better for all of us. Wasn't this what she wanted in the first place? To disgust him, so he would let her go? Then why this hollow sensation of loss? She rolled over on her back and stared at the sloping ceiling. Surely she had not expected him to be different? A pang twisted her heart. How foolish. How weak. She had actually started to trust him. Now she must get as far from him as possible.

She'd take up Denise's offer and join her in Paris. First thing in the morning she'd leave for the coast.

Christopher pressed his shaking fingers against his thumping temple and cursed the brandy he had drunk after leaving Sylvia last night. Self-disgust gnawed at his entrails.

He strode across the library to the fireplace and pulled the bell again. Where the bloody hell was Sylvia? It didn't take this long to find someone in this damned town house. At well past noon, she should be up and downstairs. It was bad enough that he had to face her to apologise without hanging around thinking about it.

'Kit, old chap,' Garth said, breezing in and picking up a newspaper. He glanced at the headlines as he spoke. 'If you want to make Darbys' place by nightfall, shouldn't you be on your way?'

In his black riding coat, skintight buff riding breeches and wearing his usual cynical expression, Garth epitomised the noble English rake about town.

Christopher nodded, then flinched at the pain the movement caused inside his skull.

Garth slouched into an armchair by the fireplace and turned to the racing page. 'Well?'

He didn't need Garth's sharp eyes focussed on him. He'd never hear the last of it if Garth learned what ten kinds of idiot he'd been last night. He glared at Garth. 'Well what?'

'Why are you still hanging about here?'

All he wanted to do was apologise to Sylvia and get out of London. The hurt in her eyes had floated before his face from the moment he'd opened his eyes, like an accusing Banquo's ghost. Shakespeare certainly knew how to portray a guilty conscience.

And why the hell was Garth so interested in his movements? For months, Garth hadn't spent any time in Mount Street, until this week. It all came back to the same thing. Miss Boisette. He glowered. 'I need to speak to Miss Boisette before I leave.'

Garth looked up from his paper. 'Actually, I rather wanted to talk to you about that young lady. Something rather untoward happened yesterday.'

Untoward? Bloody hell. She'd told Garth about his behaviour last night. Christopher strode to the window and looked out. Bright daylight burned red-hot needles into the backs of his eyes. His brother's flailing tongue could hardly make him feel any worse than he did, but he deserved it.

'Yes,' Garth continued, 'she really shouldn't be out on the streets on her own. She's far too lovely for her own safety.'

Christopher swung around and grabbed at the curtain as a wave of giddiness made the room pitch worse than a galleon in a hurricane. He took a deep breath to steady himself. 'What are you talking about?'

Frowning, Garth eyed him up and down. 'Are you all right, Kit?'

Oh God, not more brotherly concern. 'Yes. It's just a headache.'

A slow smile spread over Garth's face. 'You young idiot, you're jug-bitten.'

'What about Miss Boisette?'

Garth tossed the newspaper on the table beside him and stretched out his long legs. 'It was the oddest thing. A footman was pressing her to get into a carriage when I came along.'

'Whose carriage?'

'I didn't see the man inside, though she said there was one.'

The hairs on the back of his neck rose. Surely this couldn't have anything to do with the earlier attempt to abduct her? Could it? 'A case of mistaken identity?'

Garth looked unconvinced. 'She said so, but the lackey was pressing her pretty hard, I thought, and she looked terrified.'

'Why didn't you mention this last night?'

'I forgot.'

'Bloody hell. It can't be a coincidence.'

Garth shot a piercing glance from under his brows. ''Fess up.'

'It's not the first time there has been an attempt to abduct her. Someone tried to kidnap her from the Bird in Hand the night we stayed there.'

Garth's eyebrows almost disappeared into his hairline. 'Something you failed to mention.'

'I thought it was a random attack. Some Mohawk looking for a ransom.'

'Who knew you were there?'

'That's just it, no one as far as I know.' Christopher strode to the chair opposite Garth and dropped into it. 'Unless we were followed from Tunbridge Wells. There was some god-awful dandy at the Sussex Hotel. I just didn't think anything of it.' Mentally, Christopher reviewed the scene in Tunbridge

Wells. He'd been so embarrassed; he'd put it out of his mind. He groaned.

'What?'

'There was another man in the lobby that day, a dingy fellow in the shadows behind her. A man very like the stranger at the bar in the Bird in Hand later that evening. He could have followed us. I didn't recall seeing him at the Sussex until right now.'

'No real reason to, I suppose.' Garth frowned. 'Who would want to kidnap a poverty-stricken female like Sylvia Boisette?'

Christopher raised his gaze to meet Garth's puzzled expression. 'Uncle John said she is the daughter of an English duke by a Parisian prostitute. He'd been trying to prove her claim.'

Garth whistled through his teeth. 'Which duke? Not one of the Prince's brothers, I hope?'

'He didn't provide the name. But it doesn't make any sense that he would want to harm Sylvia. Half the nobility have by-blows scattered around England. What difference would one from Paris make?'

Garth stilled. After a moment's hesitation, he shook his head. 'There's been some public mutterings about the morals of the nobility since the French Revolution, especially Prinny. It's not had much of an effect. The only duke I know who might have anything to lose is Huntingdon. He's supporting the introduction of a bill against prostitution.'

'How would you know? I didn't think you cared for politics.'

Garth brushed the question away with an impatient gesture. 'Huntingdon has all the passion of a crusader. I heard him speak in the House a few weeks ago. The man positively frothed at the mouth.'

The radicals would certainly have a field day if Sylvia proved to be the daughter of such a moralistic Tory, but she had been explicit in her uninterest about her father.

Christopher frowned. Where the hell was she?

'Mr Evernden.' The butler hovered in the doorway, offering a silver tray with his nose so elevated he might have been holding a week-old chamber pot. 'The young person is not in the house, sir. One of the footmen recalls seeing her depart early this morning. I found these on the hall table.'

'Depart?' Christopher asked. A nasty sinking sensation invaded his sensitive gut.

'How early?' Garth asked.

'About five, my lord.' Merreck placed the tray on a green marble-topped table.

Suppressing an oath, Christopher retrieved the note addressed to him in fine neat script and left the one to his mother on the tray. 'Thank you, that will be all.' He waited until the man left before opening the sealed, plain white paper.

He read the few terse words and recalled the pain in her expression when she'd showed him the door last night. A strange sense of loss squeezed his chest. How sweetly her body had melded to his until he'd allowed jealousy of Garth to cloud his reason. He'd driven her away.

If she wanted to go to Paris that was her prerogative, provided she was safe. Every instinct told him she wasn't.

Garth stared at the paper. 'For Satan's sake, Kit. What does it say?'

'She's left for France.'

Christopher passed the note to Garth, who grimaced when he finished reading. 'I can't say I blame her for not wanting to work for the Elston woman. She's a cheese-paring hag of a female by all accounts. But why France? There are plenty of others in need of a governess.'

Now the truth of what he had done had to come out. His stomach roiling, he rested his chin on his fist. 'I as good as called her a whore.' And that probably wasn't the worst of it, but it was all he was prepared to admit.

'Oh.' Garth sat silent for a moment. 'That would do it.'

He didn't need Garth's sarcasm to tell him he'd fumbled things. She was gone and that was all there was to it. She hadn't deserved what he'd said to her. She'd tried her best to behave like a respectable female, but she attracted trouble like jam lured wasps. She'd almost been abducted, not once, apparently, but twice.

'You are really smitten, aren't you?' Garth's question interrupted his train of thought.

He must be as transparent as glass. He tucked the note into his breast pocket. He thought about how much he liked her and swallowed. 'Aye.' His voice was strangely thick and gruff. His throat burned.

Garth grinned. 'Then you had better fetch her back. Get her out of your system.'

He forced himself to recognise the truth. 'It's you she wants.'

Garth raised a brow. 'Then she wouldn't have run away. Don't you know anything about women?'

'Obviously not. I stormed into her room last night and practically took her right then and there without a kiss-your-hand or by-your-leave. Then I told her she was dirt beneath *my* feet.'

Sympathy flashed in Garth's normally cynical eyes.

He didn't need sympathy. He wanted to hit something, someone, anyone, before the anger at himself exploded.

'Look, Kit,' Garth said and Christopher forced himself to listen, 'the only way to get her off your mind and out of your overactive conscience is to follow her and get her to listen to reason.'

For once Garth made sense. At least he'd be able to apologise. He would convince her to let him escort her to her destination. Or perhaps bring her back to London—and Garth. Anything to ensure her settled securely. After all, that was Uncle John's wish. 'Perhaps you are right.'

'I know I am. You can offer her far more than she'd ever get as a governess.'

Christopher's gut twisted. 'Or you could.'

After a sharp stare, Garth nodded. 'Before you leave, I'll get my man to mix you up a tonic for that head of yours. He has this amazing recipe. It really works. I should know, I drink the vile stuff every day.'

Everything suddenly seemed clear. If he left right away, he might stop her at Dover before she caught a packet to Calais and Mother would not know of her departure. When she returned, she could still take the Elston position or he'd make some other arrangement. He pocketed the note to his mother. 'I'll do it.'

'Right, come upstairs and I'll have him prepare it.'

'What?'

'The tonic.'

'To hell with that. I've got to get my horses put to.'

Chapter Ten

The sound of each shaky breath filled Sylvia's ears. Her heart knocked against her ribs. The pistol in the gloved hand of the hatchet-faced man on the carriage seat opposite remained unwavering, pointed at her chest. She licked her dry lips. 'Where are you taking me?'

He had introduced himself as Seamus Rafter when he swooped down and threw her in his coach outside the Lion d'Or. After that, he'd refused to say another word. He'd snatched her up on the way to catch the early *diligence* to Paris. She had instantly recalled him from the Sussex Hotel. Worse, she'd remembered his voice. He was the man who'd crept into her bedroom.

'You'll see soon enough, colleen.'

She jumped at the sound of his harsh voice in the confined space. Irish, then, not French. That was the reason for his strange lilting accent. 'What do you want with me? I demand you return me to Calais.'

His slate-grey eyes gazed unblinking back at her face. It was all she could do not to shudder. A lump welled up in her throat and prickles burned the backs of her eyes. Years of iron control threatened to desert her. She swallowed her tears. She would not let him see her fear.

As the carriage turned off the main road on to a lane, it rocked and bounced worse than the Channel packet crossing from Dover. Her heart picked up speed until breathing became a chore. She clung to the handstrap for what felt like hours. When the carriage slowed and then halted, she wasn't sure she wanted the journey to end. Rafter gripped her wrist and hauled her down the carriage steps. He pulled her tight to his bony body. He smelled of stale cigars and sweat.

She tore at the hand around her upper arm. 'Let me go.'

Impervious to her struggles, Rafter propelled her along a weed-infested path towards a dilapidated grey stone mansion covered in ivy.

Sharpened by the harsh sunlight, his angular profile revealed nothing of his thoughts. Grey eyes as cold as polished steel stared straight ahead. When she dragged her feet, he simply tightened his grip around her shoulders and lifted her from the ground.

'Put me down,' she gasped, his hard squeeze crushing her ribs.

The house loomed closer. Paint peeled from the brown front door beneath the crumbling portico. She did not want to go in there. Her heart beat so hard it drowned out the sound of his steps on the flagstones.

The door swung open at his push. He hustled her inside, down a dark, narrow hallway and into a gloomy room.

'Why are we here?' she asked again, more to hear the sound of her voice than in expectation of an answer.

He released her arm and closed the door behind them.

Adjusting to the dim light, she stared around the room. Red velvet curtains fully covered the windows, gilt sofas with red upholstery stood against dark green walls illuminated by candles in three mirrored wall sconces. A sickening surge of familiarity washed through her. The gaudy furnishings were shabby and worn, the edges of the curtains frayed. Her stomach lurched. It seemed horribly familiar. 'What is this place?' She hauled in a shuddering breath. 'I demand an answer.'

Light eyes observed her with cold uninterest and his thin lips curled up in a sneer. He sauntered to the bell beside the fireplace and gave it a swift tug. It clanged in the nether regions of the old house like a call to the dead.

Sylvia eyed the door. If she could reach it before he did, she could be gone before anyone arrived.

'Don't try it, colleen.'

She glared at him. 'What do you want with me?'

'Nothing.'

She shuddered at the menace in his harsh indifference.

A frowsy, full-bosomed woman with red hair waddled in. Sylvia clutched at her throat, all thoughts driven from her mind.

Madame Gilbert beamed, her full rouged lips parting in a simpering smile, her fat cheeks all but obliterating her beady, brown eyes. 'Why, *mon petit chou*. You do remember me. I am flattered.'

Sylvia swung around to Rafter. 'Why here?'

He leaned against the mantel, his lean face dispassionate. 'It's where you belong.'

'No.' She forced the croak from her dry throat.

Monsieur Jean had rescued her more than ten years ago, but she had never forgotten the groping, pawing hands, the pain, the bitter shame. Nor had she forgotten how Madame Gilbert paraded her before an old gentleman one evening. Young as she was, she had known what he wanted. Dread ate at her soul.

'Now, now, little one,' Madame Gilbert murmured, reaching out to touch her shoulder.

Sylvia's skin crawled. She pushed the pudgy hand away, her eyes on the door. She had to get out of here.

'You owe me, girl,' Madame Gilbert rasped. 'All those

years I kept your mother when she was sick—she barely earned enough to pay for her own food, let alone yours. You will pay your debt, pretty one.'

The cloying scent of attar of roses over the smell of unwashed flesh and stale breath strummed at chords of remembrance. As the obese *madame* closed in on her, all the old terrors returned, the helplessness, the suffocating fear of being caught in a passageway or in her mother's room. Sylvia stumbled back until the backs of her legs came in contact with the edge of a sofa.

Trapped.

Madame Gilbert's beringed, damp fingers tipped Sylvia's face to the light.

She shuddered at the clammy touch on her skin. Bile filled her throat and threatened to choke her. Her worst nightmare had become reality.

Damn them. How dare they do this to her? A rush of hot anger released her numb mind. She jerked her head away. 'Don't touch me, *cochon*.'

Madame Gilbert's smile broadened. 'Magnificent. You are everything you promised to be all those years ago.' She turned her head and spoke to Rafter. 'You tell Milor', she'll be better than her mother. His secret will be safe.'

Rafter grunted. 'Watch your tongue, *madame*. You say too much.'

Milor'? Secret? Sylvia gazed from one to the other.

'Your father wants you back where you belong. Your mother was a whore. It is your destiny,' Madame Gilbert said.

The room rocked. In all these years, she had never heard from her father. She sank on to the sofa. 'My father wants this?'

'You've said enough, old woman. If you say another word, the bargain will be broken and you will be dead.' The Irishman did not raise his voice, but the threat hung heavy in the dingy room.

Madame Gilbert cackled. 'It's all right, *mon ami*. All will be well now I have *mon petit chou* again.'

'*Salope.*' Sylvia spat the word at the vile woman who had somehow reached out from her past to claim her.

Madame Gilbert grinned. 'I see your command of French is as good as ever it was.'

She had reverted to the language of her childhood, curses and all. In those days she had fought for her right to survive. 'I am not staying.' She stood up and pushed past the *madame*'s solid wall of flesh.

'Temper, temper,' Madame Gilbert said. 'My gentlemen like a bit of fire in my girls.' She winked. 'But I demand obedience.'

She ran her hand down Sylvia's cheek. 'So soft and fine. I wonder who will pay the highest price to be first with you?'

Heat flamed in her face and she looked away.

Madame Gilbert's eyes narrowed. 'Your mother did protect you, did she not?'

Sylvia faced her interrogator. 'I know well enough what trade you ply.'

Madame Gilbert grimaced and shrugged, her voluptuous breasts jiggling in her low neckline. 'Then you know what is expected.'

Sylvia tamped down her rising panic. She must not show weakness. 'I will not do this. I'll scream. I'll tell them you kidnapped me. You cannot force me.'

Rafter moved towards the door, a speculative expression on his face. 'You have your hands full, *madame*.'

The vast body shook as she chuckled. She stroked Sylvia's cheek. 'Fight all you want, little one. They will love it.'

A shudder racked her from head to toe. 'Don't touch me.'

'Ah, but not the first time,' Madame Gilbert crooned. 'The first time you will be gloriously accommodating, for you must learn.'

'I'll leave you to your business,' the Irishman said. 'I will come tomorrow for the paper in accordance with our agreement.' His expression hardened. 'Do not forget. It must be here when I return or it will go poorly with you. My patience is exhausted.'

Panic shortened Sylvia's breath. '*Monsieur*, do not leave me here. I have no intention of embarrassing my father. I will disappear. I will never speak his name.' She stretched out her hands to him.

The man paused, his hand on the door handle. He did not turn around. 'You know his name then, colleen?' He pulled open the door.

The terrible finality in his tone plunged her stomach to the floor. If only Monsieur Jean had not told her of his suspicions at the last, begged her to seek him out despite her objections, then she would not have made such a mistake. Frantic, she shook her head. 'No. I do not.'

Too late. The click of the latch behind him was the slam of a prison door.

She swung around and glared at Madame Gilbert. 'I have friends. They will look for me.'

The *madame* pulled the bell. 'The young Englishman you ran away from perhaps, *chérie*? You left him. He will not want you back after you have been here.' Her piggy eyes narrowed. 'Was it he who took what was mine to sell? If he comes near you, he is a dead man. There is no love for the English in this part of France.'

How did Madame Gilbert know so much about her? Rafter must have told her. He'd been following her, watching her.

She shuddered. And Madame Gilbert was right. She would get no help from the Everndens. No doubt Christopher was celebrating her departure. 'I have other friends.'

'Don't lie to me. Your so-called guardian is dead and the woman you hoped to live with is dying. There is no one.'

There was Denise. 'You are wrong.'

Madame Gilbert pulled an envelope from her pocket. 'Perhaps you are thinking of this?' Madame Gilbert waved her letter to Denise. Her last hope.

Sylvia failed to contain her gasp of disappointment as all hope of rescue fled. 'You have no right interfering with my mail.'

Madame Gilbert shook her head. 'Ah, *mon petit chou*, now there is only me.'

Her teeth wanted to chatter in tune with her trembling body. She clenched her jaw. She might be alone. But she was not helpless against an old and weak woman.

She edged towards the door. 'You cannot keep me here against my will.'

The *madame* raised a brow, her leering smile unwavering. She lowered her bulk onto the nearest sofa with a wheezy sigh. 'You think not, *chérie*?'

With a swift pull, Sylvia jerked open the door and stepped into the hallway. Broad and squat, his nose flattened and a jagged white scar across one swarthy cheek, a man with a straggling beard blocked her path. A leering toad. She stopped short.

'Alphonse,' Madame Gilbert said, 'meet Sylvie, our newest acquisition. She is not to go anywhere without my permission.'

Alphonse grunted and barred her path with one thick arm.

Sylvia glared down at him. 'Let me pass, oaf.'

He grinned.

She pushed at his arm and he shoved her backwards into the room. She stumbled, but managed to prevent herself from falling.

'Sit down, Sylvie,' Madame commanded.

'No.'

Alphonse lumbered forward and thrust her into a chair, then returned to his post in the hallway.

A smug smile slithered across the *madame*'s face. 'That's better. You will soon learn.'

Sylvia swung her head around at a noise at the door. Her heart lurched. Alphonse returning?

Instead, a hunched and wrinkled woman in a black maid's uniform pushed her way in. 'Gi' over, ye great lummox.'

'Jeannie?' Sylvia gasped.

The maid cocked her head sideways and peered up at Sylvia from beneath bushy grey brows. 'Aye. I heard you were back.'

Hope sprang in Sylvia's heart. The dour Scotswoman had stayed with Sylvia's mother through thick and thin, despite her Calvinistic disapproval of her mistress's lifestyle. 'You are still here?'

'Aye, Miss Sylvie. I always knew you'd return. Bad blood always proves true.'

Jeannie meant she had her father's blood. An old and well-remembered refrain.

Beyond Alphonse, two other women lurked in the shadowed corridor, their eyes curious, their faces painted. Not girls she recognised from the old days. No help there.

Madame Gilbert waved towards the door. 'Jeannie will show you to your room. The other girls will be along shortly to help you prepare.'

The words and smile threatened. Sylvia shook her head.

'I will ask Alphonse to carry you up, if you insist,' Madame Gilbert said.

The gloating glance from the dwarf-like Alphonse crushed the thought of resistance. Jeannie beckoned with a sly little smile. In despair, Sylvia followed her out of the door and up the stairs, aware of Alphonse's gaze at every step she took.

Jeannie led her to a chamber. Light struggling through a grimy window festooned with red velvet curtains revealed a straight-backed chair in one corner and a wardrobe in another, the whole dominated by a bed covered by white silky sheets.

The old woman pointed to the bed. 'Sit there and wait for *madame*. It's na more than ye deserve, let me tell ye.'

Tears blurred Sylvia's vision at the triumph in the old

woman's tone. 'Why are you being so cruel? You used to be my friend. You loved my mother.'

Jeannie shuffled to the bed and turned back the sheet. 'That I did. More than my own life. I stayed with her in this heathen country until the day she died. Never a word of complaint from the poor wee lassie. Aye, nor of blame.' Her mouth turned down. ''Twas your fault, ye and the no-good man who stole her from her family, then got her with child and abandoned her.'

Jeannie twisted her head sideways on her hunched shoulders to look up at Sylvia. 'I hate ye both. And so shall ye both be punished.'

Sylvia recoiled from her venomous expression. 'You hate my father, yet you help him.'

'I've never helped him. I told Madame Gilbert he'd pay. And he did. He bled freely, just like my sainted mistress coughing up her lungs and bleeding and bleeding, till I couldna' wipe the blood from her lips fast enough.'

Jeannie's wrinkled face twisted into a mask of hate. 'Then the war got so bad, even Rafter could no' get in or out of Paris. Niver mind that the Irish sided with France. After that, there was no money for food or medicine.'

Sylvia sank on to the bed, sickened as she imagined her mother unable to work at all and with no money to pay the doctor.

'Oh, aye,' Jeannie said, her watery eyes gazing into the distance at the scenes playing out in her head. 'I stole and I even tried whoring, but with my face and form I never got naught but pennies from drunks and sailors.'

Regret, dark and painful, crushed Sylvia's soul. She should have stayed. 'But why do you hate me, Jeannie? What did I ever do to hurt you or my mother?'

'If she'd have never bore you, he'd never have left her. I know it.'

'That is hardly my fault.'

Jeannie's gnarled hands shook. She twisted them in her apron and glared at Sylvia. 'You selfish little bitch. You left her to die with niver a thought for her who bore ye and fed ye and kept ye by the toils of her body. You left her when she needed you most. Dying she was. Your beautiful little body could have kept her alive.'

The bitterness in the old woman's tone struck Sylvia like a blow. Jeannie had expected her, a child of eleven, to provide for her mother. And, Sylvia realised with shock, she would have if her mother hadn't sent her away.

She sank down on the bed. The sheet clenched in her fingers felt slippery and cold, like the tears on her cheeks when she learned what her mother and Monsieur Jean had done that long-ago day. She gazed at Jeannie, desperate to be believed. 'I didn't want to go. I didn't want to leave her. I missed her so much.'

A sob broke free. She swallowed the lump in her throat. 'Monsieur Jean was kind and generous, but I would have given up my life to stay with *maman* to the end.' Husky and raw with emotion, her voice broke. 'She was all I had. I loved her.'

Puzzlement in her tired eyes, Jeannie stared, then sank to perch next to her. 'D'ye mean John Evernden forced you to leave with him?'

Sylvia cast her mind back. 'He never said we were leaving. She sent us for pastries. The carriage just kept going and going, further and further. Then he put me under a blanket in the coach. It was a game, he said, hide and seek from the bad soldiers. I must have fallen asleep. When I awoke we were in England. They tricked me. He told me I would never see *maman* again.'

Tears glazed Jeannie's eyes and she swiped at them. 'Aye. She was that set on saving you. But she pined away after. I couldna' forgive ye. My poor sweet lady that was so beautiful, so sweet and loving, and they all left her to die.'

Scalding tears trickled down Sylvia's cheeks. She envisaged her mother's last days, saw again the face that had become vague and misty over the years, only a faint likeness in her locket to remind her. The memories sharpened to vivid pictures of blonde hair, sallow skin and unhealthy flushed cheeks. Dark circles outlined luminous blue eyes full of pain and soul-deep hurt. Jeannie was right. Sylvia should have stayed.

She placed an arm around Jeannie's bony shoulders. 'I'm so sorry. Thank you for taking care of her. I know she loved you just as much as you loved her.'

Jeannie pulled a handkerchief from her apron pocket and blew her nose. 'Aye. She did. I didna' tell her where the extra money came from to feed the two of you. 'Twas between me, the *madame* and the Irishman. She never would have let me take money from that bastard. She loved him, y'see, and she wouldna' listen to reason.'

Jeannie dabbed at her eyes. 'They were so happy when they first came to France. I thought he loved her too. Then the troubles started. All the nobles left Paris. A message came from the old duke for him to come home, but he wouldna' accept your mither. They couldna' make up their minds.'

The old maid wrung her hands. 'Then it was almost too late. The embassy closed and British soldiers were sent to take us all to a boat, her and the duke. We got separated from him in the confusion. He got to the boat, we didna'. Rafter was a soldier then. He brought us to Madame Gilbert's to hide.'

Rafter? Suspicion uncoiled like a loathsome snake in Sylvia's stomach. 'Rafter brought you to Madame Gilbert's?'

Lost in the past, Jeannie stared into the distance. 'We waited and we waited, but he niver came back. But we had to eat. Your mither was two months gone with you and, in the end, Madame Gilbert gave her no choice but to work. All the old friends were gone from Paris, or had lost their heads, ye ken. After you were born, you had to be fed. Rafter came back to see his old friend Madame Gilbert a few months after your birth with the news the Duke wasna' interested in your mither. I decided your father would pay. I found the paper that Marguerite said proved who you were tucked away with her trinkets. I gave it to Madame Gilbert.' Her face lit with a smile of triumph. 'For a while things were easier, he sent money to keep us in France. He'd do anything to keep the both of ye a secret, Rafter said.'

Sylvia froze. She placed a hand on Jeannie's arm, jerking the old woman back into the present. 'Wait a minute. Are you saying there really is proof I'm his daughter?'

'Aye. But Marguerite wouldna' use it. If he didna' want her, then she said she didna' care, not for herself. So I took it to pay him back. I niver dared tell her what I'd done, even when she discovered it gone that day when Evernden took ye.'

Sylvia got up and went to the window. Outside the day was bright, the sky blue, while inside this dreadful house everything seemed dark and twisted. 'What did the paper say?'

The old woman slumped and shook her grizzled head. 'I canna read. But they came home one day giggling like naughty children with the paper. They must have known then that she was with child.' Jeannie's claw-like hands clenched. 'Everything was a game to them in those days. A game against his father.'

Sylvia's mind whirled. All those years Monsieur Jean had sought proof, and it was here all the time. 'Why did my father deny us all these years?'

Sorrow crumpled Jeannie's wizened face. 'I don't know, lassie. I just dinna' ken. I suppose he didna' love her as she did him.' Her old eyes filled with tears again. 'You look just like her. Ah, I'm right sorry, lass. I should never have told them about John Evernden whisking ye off. It fair makes my heart weep to see such loveliness wasted. It's inner beauty what counts. She had it and now I see it in you too.'

With a heart aching so much she thought it would break, Sylvia hugged Jeannie's bony body close. 'My father should not have abandoned her and nor should I.'

'Dear God,' the old woman moaned. 'What have I done?'

Footsteps and female voices sounded on the stairs. They jumped apart.

'That's Madame Gilbert,' Jeannie said, wiping her eyes. 'And the other girls, coming to settle you in.'

The sounds drew close and Jeannie stood. 'I must go. I'll help ye if I can, Sylvie, with my last breath, so I will.'

The door opened. Madame Gilbert waddled in with what looked like a bottle of medicine. Three girls in tawdry, revealing gowns, their eyes bright and hard and distant, followed her in.

'That will be all, Jeannie,' the Madame said, her smile treacle-sweet. 'You can leave Sylvie to us.'

Christopher felt an utter idiot lurking in a hedge like some peeping Tom. The rented hack flicked its tail at the flies on its sweating, dun-brown flanks. He'd pushed the nag hard to catch up to the travelling carriage containing Sylvia and her escort after he caught sight of the blue bonnet he'd bought in Tunbridge Wells. It had passed him on his way in to a Calais inn in search of her.

Cradling the horse's nose to keep it silent and still, he peered through the hedge. The dusty black coach turned around in the narrow lane outside the unremarkable house. Large and square, it had tangled bushes encroaching on the path to the front door. Weeds infested what must once have been a rose garden, while ancient ivy clung to the grey stonework, draping the upper windows. It appeared to be the kind of country house a gentleman might own, if it weren't so neglected. Yet for all its apparent state of disrepair, the ruts in the lane indicated frequent visitors.

Into this house Sylvia had waltzed, encircled within the protective embrace of the Irishman from the Bird. A friend or a lover? A pang pierced his chest. He didn't want to believe it.

Damnation. Was he about to make a fool of himself over a strumpet, a beauty who tempted him against all his principles? He'd only wanted her because he couldn't have her. Lust. Nothing more.

Yet he wanted her still.

He cursed. Perhaps she'd plotted with this man to blackmail the Evernden family. In that case, why had she left without the rest of the money Christopher had promised her?

While he stood here wondering like a besotted fool, matters of business awaited him in London, important matters she'd driven from his mind. He'd wasted enough time over a woman who had so quickly found another protector. He mounted and brought the horse's head around.

A door slammed.

He glanced over his shoulder.

The Irishman sauntered down the steps and out of the front gate. Alone. A smile curved his thin lips. He set what looked like a brand-new hat on his head at a jaunty angle. With a brief word to the coachman, he climbed inside.

The hairs on the back of Christopher's neck prickled. Despite all his logic, something about this felt wrong. He had to know if Sylvia and this man meant trouble for him and his family. He had to know Sylvia was all right.

He edged the horse deeper into the hedge's shadow and watched the coach rumble and sway down the lane. Nothing about the house revealed Sylvia's purpose in coming here. If it was an assignation, why had the man left so soon?

He recalled the farm labourer hoeing a field a mile or so down the lane. He would know who owned the house. Careful to keep out of view of the windows for the first few yards, Christopher retraced his tracks to where the lone man toiled, his hoe swinging in rhythmic arcs. The peasant looked up when Christopher drew close. He leaned on his implement and touched a hand to his forelock. The lines in his weathered face deepened as he squinted up.

'Who owns these lands?' Christopher asked, with a sweep of his arm.

'Today, milor'?'

Christopher frowned. 'What do you mean?'

A grin revealed rotting teeth and further creased the labourer's crumpled face. 'They used to belong to le Duc de Verendelle, then they belonged to the peasants, then to Bonaparte. Now?' He spread his arms wide. 'I don't know. I just do what I have always done, milor'.'

Christopher understood the man's confusion. Since Bonaparte's departure for St Helena, the government of France under Louis XVIII had yet to organise itself. Lands were still being parcelled out to their former owners. 'Then the land does not belong to those who occupy *la grande maison*?' He nodded back in the direction of the house.

The grin widened, black eyes twinkled. 'No, milor'. Though it is true that many a furrow is ploughed there. They do not work the land.'

'Speak plainly, man.'

'Why, milor', 'tis a bordello. Only *les filles de joie* live there now.' He grimaced. 'Though I have only heard tell of it. It is not for the likes of me. Only men like the mayor and rich merchants can pay their prices. And men like you, milor'.' The leathery face leered up at him.

Prostitutes? Christopher's mind reeled. He couldn't imagine it. A vision of the day he met her flashed into his mind. If that was the true Sylvia, then he could picture it very well. A cold hand seemed to fist in his chest. He was a stupid fool to follow her like some callow youth.

He flicked a *sou* to the peasant and, not wishing to arouse suspicion, he continued in the same direction as before. As he rode, he cast his mind over her entrance into the house. The Irishman had held her tight against him. She appeared willing enough.

Damn her to hell. He needed to know, to hear that this was what she wanted from her own lips.

He doubled back and once more observed the house from the shelter of the hedge on the other side of the lane.

Blank-eyed, the shade-covered windows stared back at him. He tied the horse to a hazel tree and circled the house. At the back, he discovered a stable from which the sounds of at least one horse emanated. Smoke drifted from a chimney on the low wing jutting at right angles from the main house. Probably the kitchen.

None of the back windows were open. Fresh air seemed unpopular in this establishment. Apart from breaking a window, he did not see any way in.

Hell fire. If the old peasant told the truth and it was a brothel, who more likely to seek its services than a hot-blooded gentleman? He jogged back to his mount. Pulling the horse behind him, he marched boldly up to the front door and rang the bell.

The man who answered his summons barely reached his chest, but the aggression in his stance and the brutality in his pugnacious face marked him for a bruiser. 'Yes?'

Christopher raised a haughty eyebrow in true Garth style.

The glowering gnome raked Christopher with an appraising look, then pushed the door wide. 'Welcome, *monsieur*. Tie your horse to the post and come in. May I take your coat and hat?'

'I'll keep them, thank you.' He retained a firm grip on his cane. The sword hidden within might be needed. The swaggering ox ushered him into a murky parlour. 'I will tell *madame* you are here.'

Christopher strolled to a shabby couch and made himself comfortable. He grimaced at the filthy furnishings. They had certainly seen better days.

The *madame*, a red-haired, gargantuan woman of indeterminate age, bustled in.

He maintained his nonchalant expression as her avaricious eyes took in his dress, his jewellery and his physique. He resisted the temptation to tug at his cravat.

He obviously passed muster, because she smiled coquettishly. 'I am Madame Gilbert. How can we be of service to you, *monsieur*?'

He waved a languid hand. 'I was told you have some of the best women this side of Paris. I find myself in need of some female company.'

'You were informed correctly, *monsieur*. Most of my girls used to work in Paris before the troubles and well know the taste of aristos. Do you have any preferences? They are all excellent, clean and experienced in all the arts. The *vice Anglais*, if you desire?'

Christopher kept his expression bland at the mention of an aberration favoured by Englishmen who had developed a taste for the birch switch at public school. He had never gone away to school.

'I prefer blondes,' he said. 'Slim and young.'

The *madame* nodded and waddled out.

Christopher leaned back against the sofa and forced himself to appear nonchalant as he imagined Sylvia's surprise, or anger. Hell, perhaps this wasn't such a good idea.

A hunched-up witch of a servant arrived with wine. Christopher refused it. He needed his wits about him and he had no faith in the cleanliness of the down-at-heel place. She departed, muttering under her breath.

Two buxom females slouched into the room followed by the *madame*, her eyes greedy.

'This is Berthé,' the woman announced, pointing to the one with rouged lips and straw-coloured hair. She wore a tawdry red velvet gown that skimmed her nipples and knees.

'And this is Yvette.' A slighter and younger version of Berthé with light brown hair and brown eyes had on a black lacy corset and filmy yellow skirt. The women flaunted their attributes and batted their eyelashes. Worn and tired, neither of them were Sylvia.

He shook his head at the fat woman. 'Nice enough in their way. But I want something fresher, more innocent in appearance, younger.'

Avaricious eyes gleamed from between rolls of fat. 'A virgin, *monsieur*?'

'A virgin would be a special treat,' he replied, trying to hide his disgust. 'But younger, smaller and…' he curled his lip as his gaze ran over the two women who postured before him '…a true blonde.'

The woman licked her red lips. 'If I had such a girl, she would be very expensive.'

Christopher pulled out a handful of gold. 'But, *madame*,' he said in an icy voice, 'do not presume to think to cheat me.' His hand moved suggestively to the cane at his side. 'I am as accomplished with one sword as I am with the other.'

She eyed his crotch and then his swordstick. She nodded as if coming to a decision. 'I have a girl who might suit you. I would as soon let you be her first as some fat merchant. You will teach her well, I think.'

'If I'm to be her tutor, perhaps you should pay me?'

Her fat face reddened.

Christopher put up a placating hand and smiled. 'I jest, *madame*.'

'Ah, a jest,' she said. 'So English to jest about business.' A suspicious expression crossed her face. 'Your name, *monsieur*?'

'Lord Albert, at your service.' He inclined his head. The name of the obnoxious dandy had jumped into his mind and the woman seemed satisfied. Christopher breathed a sigh of relief when she didn't ask for his calling card.

The pudgy hands slapped together. 'Yvette, go. Berthé, make sure *mon petit chou* is ready for milor'.'

'Surely the gentleman would prefer a more experienced woman?' Berthé said in surly tones.

The *madame* glared. 'Do as I tell you.'

With dragging steps, Berthé left the room. Jealous rivalry amongst whores seemed ludicrous.

'Where is she?' Christopher asked. 'Am I to approve of her first?'

'This one is special. You will see. But first we must conclude our business.'

The exorbitant price to which he agreed seemed all the worse since he strongly suspected he wouldn't get his money's worth. Deep in his heart, he wouldn't believe Sylvia had stooped to this.

Cane swinging, he followed the wheezing *madame* out to the dingy hall and up the staircase.

At the end of the second-floor passage she flung open a door and ushered him in.

Christopher froze at the sight of the naked woman on the bed.

Chapter Eleven

The scene, lit by one candle on a rickety nightstand, burned indelibly into his mind. The wanton Sylvia of his dreams waiting for him, naked, creamy skin on a silky white sheet, slender legs sprawled wide.

Each slow breath lifted her tawny-tipped perfect breasts. Fascinated, he imagined them hardening, responding to his tongue, peaking beneath his palms. A mental image of his hands on her body tingled his fingers and his gaze followed the lines of her tiny waist, the flare of her gently curved thighs crested by the fine, pale blonde curls of her mound and the hint of what lay beneath.

Roses perfumed the air. A vision of loveliness filled his gaze. He didn't want to believe she was here, waiting for him like this, but she was truly lovely and completely irresistible, when he had done nothing but imagine her like this for days.

His loins grew hard and heavy with need. Hunger ached deep in his bones. Never had he felt such driving, urgent need. He slipped out of his coat and waistcoat and pulled his shirt free of his waistband. One taste and he'd leave. He dragged off his shirt and stared at Sylvia.

Her eyes remained closed.

The abbess caught his questioning glance. 'A little

laudanum laced with cantharides,' she whispered. 'You will find her most grateful for your gift.' She gestured at Christopher's groin, where his erection strained against the tight fabric of his pantaloons.

Drugged? Was she then not here of her own free will? He needed to get rid of the *madame* to find out.

His body burned to lie down beside her, to cover her, flesh to flesh, to feel her heat against his skin, explore her depths, join with her. Ruthlessly, he stamped out the fire. He bit back a groan and glared at the *madame*. 'I don't want an audience.'

Regret twisted her mouth. 'Too bad.' She wagged a finger. 'Teach her well, milor'. If she gives you trouble, call me and she will be punished. She is a wilful girl, but she will learn.'

The thought of Sylvia servicing men to this woman's command dampened his ardour. He stared pointedly at the door, hiding his revulsion, and she waddled out.

He listened to her heavy tread on the stairs. Certain she had gone, he placed a chair against the door in case she returned and set his swordstick alongside.

Forcing himself not to look at the tempting sight on the bed, he pulled the sheet from its foot up to her neck. He shook her shoulder. 'Sylvia. Wake up.'

After several repeated shakings, her eyelids fluttered open. She stared at him without comprehension, then smiled the blindingly beautiful smile he had seen at Dover and once for Garth.

'Christopher,' she murmured huskily, her French accent more pronounced than usual.

The pulse in his groin beat a wild tattoo at the sultry sound of his name on her lips.

Languidly, she snaked out a hand, reaching for him. The sheet slipped, revealing the rise of her breasts. Her fingertips dragged across his naked chest. 'Ummm. Soft,' she murmured. 'I wondered if you had hair there.' She giggled.

He shuddered on an indrawn breath. How much of the

sultry seduction in her gaze was Sylvia and how much the drugs? She'd tormented him like this once before, in Dover. Clearly she wanted him and not for the first time.

Her gaze slid from his chest to his face like a hot caress. A frown furrowed her brow. Confusion darkened her eyes. 'Please. I need…'

Beneath the sheet, her hands caressed her body, over her breast, hardening her nipples to points against the sheer fabric. A flush blossomed on her delicate cheeks and travelled down her neck. Perspiration pearled on her upper lip and forehead. A picture of blatant sensuality.

Hard and ready, his blood a river of fire, he reached for the sheet, aching once more to fully feast his gaze on her glorious, slender body. He'd imagined this so often in his mind, he could taste her sweet flesh. He bit back a curse and stopped.

'Christopher,' she moaned. 'Help me.' She shifted restlessly.

There was only one thing that would ease her. Only a cur would take advantage of the situation. 'They've given you drugs,' he rasped in a last-ditch battle for control.

With a moan deep in her throat, she arched towards him, rose up and wrapped her arms around his waist, then drew back with a gasp. 'So hot. I want…'

He closed his eyes. The torment of denial ached in every nerve. His chest shuddered on a breath. 'Where are your clothes?'

He flung open the wardrobe in the far corner of the room. A blue creation, like those the girls downstairs had worn, tumbled out. Useless. What had they done with the clothes she arrived in? He tried the lid of the press at the end of the bed. Padlocked. Damn them.

Again she stretched out her slender white arms. 'I want you to hold me,' she murmured, her accented voice husky.

His erection jerked to full attention at the raw need in her voice. He hauled in a deep breath, seeking control. He had to get her dressed and away, then he'd find a way to help her recover. He laid the flimsy garment on the bed—even with his coat over the top, it wouldn't cover much, but it was better than nothing.

Forcing a snake into a stocking presented an easier task than squeezing the wiggling Sylvia into the snug garment. While he pulled the gown over her head, she pressed her slim length against his body, begging for his help.

Once he had her vaguely inside it, he rolled her on to her stomach and knelt astride her. Pinned beneath his thighs, she moaned and struggled to turn over, her legs grazing the insides of his thighs. His breath hitched. The fires in his blood raged higher. Fingers trembling, he worked at the strings of the ridiculous froth of blue.

'Lie still and let me lace you.'

She lifted her hips and circled her plump *derrière* against him. 'I don't want a dress. I want you.'

Sweet agony. Desire built to raging proportion, a flaming conflagration, pushing him to the edges of reason, where lust warred for supremacy. His blood pulsed and his breath rasped in his ears. He hung to sanity by a thread. Sweat rolled off his forehead and down his cheek. With a groan he pressed her back to the bed with his knee.

She arched her back, her gaze desperate when she looked over her shoulder. 'Christopher. Can't you…? I need…you.'

The appeal in her eyes snapped the rope of hard-fought resistance. The pressure of her hips at his groin poured sweet agony through every nerve. She wanted this. Nay, she needed it, desperately. And God help him, so did he.

He groaned and pressed a kiss to her nape. She shivered. He cupped her cheek with a hand that looked large and tanned on her pale complexion. Her soft skin burned his flesh. She turned her fiery mouth to kiss his palm. A lightning jolt of pleasure shot through his body. He hardened to rock.

She sighed. 'Love me, Christopher.'

When had an invitation ever been this sweet? He fumbled with the buttons and pushed his pantaloons over his hips. Stiff and pulsing, he pushed against her silken thigh. A glorious sensation.

She moaned her pleasure and her desire. Gently, with one hand under her stomach, he lifted her. The other cupped the swollen flesh of her. She rubbed against his palm, hot and moist. Ready for him.

Sweet heaven. It felt so good.

'Sylvia,' he whispered. 'Tell me you want me to do this.'

She whimpered.

'Sylvia, please. Tell me.'

'Yes,' she said. 'Oh yes.'

He massaged the delicate, hot female folds, slid a finger along her swollen heated cleft. She shuddered and moaned. His fingers sought her tiny nub of pleasure, circled and pressed. God, she was sweet and hot and slick with dew for him. He stroked her rhythmically, preparing her for his entry.

She cried out, shuddered and collapsed beneath him.

He almost howled his frustration. The cantharides had made her so ready, she had climaxed from his touch.

She lay still and limp beneath him. With a savage curse at the hell of unsatisfied lust, he hung above her, his chest heaving, and waited for his body to accept his will.

After what seemed like minutes of agony, he refastened his pantaloon over his rigid protesting flesh and scrambled back into his shirt and waistcoat. God knew how long it would take to cease its rampant demand for satisfaction, but cease it would. Once free of the slavery of the drug, she would remember this and then she would surely hate him for humbling her. He swallowed his regret. Better she hate him, than remain under this roof. What if it happened again? Bloody hell. They had to leave before the drugs took hold again, before he did something he would regret.

Regret? A wry smile twisted his lips. He regretted not having her. He took a deep breath and returned to the task of dressing her.

The chair scraped across the carpet.

He jerked his head around. The hunchback maid glowered at him from the doorway. In her hand, a wicked kitchen knife glinted. 'Get away from her, before I cut your balls off.'

Christopher glanced at his cane beside the chair. The maid stood between him and it, waving the knife. A trick to get more money? 'I paid my gold to your mistress. Get out.'

The old eyes raked his body. *'Cochon.'*

A hot flush rushed to his face at her scornful sneer.

Her gaze darted to the inert figure on the bed, her expression softening with sorrow. 'What filthy perversion are you forcing on her?'

'I haven't touched her.'

'Liar. You've had her. Bastard.'

She would understand the effects of the aphrodisiac, be aware that, without a climax, Sylvia would be all over him, trying to ease the effects of the drug. He deliberately kept his tone cool, all the while watching the knife. 'I caressed her and she came.'

The maid stole closer to the bedside, gazing down at Sylvia, while her knife pointed at the mismatched buttons of his pantaloons and his still-evident arousal. 'Poor little Sylvie. Damn all men. Taking, that's all you know.'

Her sorrow seemed genuine. Hope flickered in his breast. 'If you are any kind of friend to her, you'll help me. I need to get her away.' He gestured to the blue gown. 'There's nothing for her to wear but this.'

The old woman's eyes narrowed on his face. 'What is your name, *monsieur*?'

He hesitated. Instinct told him to trust the old Scot. 'Christopher Evernden.'

'I've heared of ye. I'm Jeannie. I served her mither. Are you her protector?'

'Her guardian. I am responsible for her safety.' And up to the moment, he'd made a damned fine mess of it.

Jeannie visibly relaxed. 'Sylvie trusts you. But it is too late. *Madame*, even now, arranges the move back to Paris. After today she will be rich.'

Christopher swallowed sour bile. He would have no hope of rescuing Sylvia from a Paris brothel. But rich? 'I didn't pay that much for the privilege of having her.'

With a short hard laugh, she laid a gentle hand on Sylvia's shoulder. ''Tis not you who makes *madame* rich, but her *cochon* of a father, the Duke. He paid *madame* to keep the mother, and now the daughter is back, he'll pay a fortune to keep her here too.'

'Why?'

She shrugged. 'He always has.'

What father would want to force his child, even an illegitimate one, into so abhorrent a trade when he could simply pay her off? 'It makes no sense.'

She smiled slyly. 'There's proof he's her father.'

A bastard daughter had no rights, and unless one was royal, the ignominy was better kept hidden by the child as well as the parent. 'It makes no difference.'

Her expression hardened. 'It does, else why would he pay all those years?' She made a cutting gesture across her throat and rolled her eyes. 'My poor Marguerite died after a journey from hell.'

She hobbled to the window and pulled back the curtain, letting in a long shaft of dusty light to reveal the filthy bed hangings and shabby furniture in squalid starkness. Christopher grimaced.

With light outlining her crooked form, she continued in a soft regretful voice, 'The *madame* blackmailed the Duke for years, threatening to expose him to the world. Madame Gilbert used to laugh about it behind Marguerite's back.'

'Why did the *madame* let Sylvia go in the first place?'

She dropped the curtain and swung around.

Christopher blinked, adjusting his vision to the candlelight.

'Your uncle came for the child the day before we fled Paris,' she said. 'Someone had a grudge against the *madame*. We left in such haste, she did not discover the child missing until we departed.'

With halting steps, she wandered to the bed and gazed down on the still-sleeping Sylvia. 'We hid here, barely making a living and with no means to contact the Duke during the war with England.'

She lifted her sad brown gaze to meet his. 'Until a year ago. The noble pig sent his Irishman. He almost killed *madame* for letting the girl go to England.' Jeannie's glance shifted to Christopher. 'He promised to pay a fortune for the paper. The *madame* insisted he bring Sylvia back as part of the price. The hard-eyed Irish boggert found her and brought her back.' A smile of triumph curved her corrugated lips. 'But they don't have the paper. I stole it back, to buy my way to Scotland.'

Bitterness turned the smile to a wry grimace. 'Rafter'll kill Sylvie if he learns it's missing. The scandal, if it gets out, will ruin the Duke.' Her face crumpled. 'I'll have to give it to him. I'll no have the bairn killed.'

Bile churned in his gut. What sort of man would do this to his child? 'Who is this Duke?'

Jeannie shook her head and stared at Sylvia. 'The secret is the only thing keepin' her alive.'

Clearly, the old woman believed it, and it really didn't matter. 'You have to help me get her away from here.'

Jeannie shivered. '*Madame* will punish me if she found out I helped you.'

Christopher stifled his impatience. One cry from this

woman and the game would be up. He gave her an encouraging smile. 'No one will know if we act quickly.'

Sylvia flung out an arm and Jeannie tenderly replaced the sheet. She put her knife on the table and prowled around the room.

Christopher judged the distance to the knife. It would be an easy thing to snatch it up and turn the tables on the old woman. But the noise might alert Madame Gilbert or, worse yet, the doorkeeper. He held himself ready in case Jeannie decided to betray him.

'Are ye not just like her father? Will ye throw her to the dogs when you tire of her?' Jeannie muttered.

Christopher winced. He had just about done that already. He'd been prepared to see her enslaved to some ghastly matron with a brood of spoiled children just to get rid of her. He squared his shoulders. 'I give you my word, I will care for her for the rest of her life. She will do nothing that is not of her own free will. I swear it on my honour.'

Jeannie stopped her restless walking and gazed into his eyes.

Sylvia moaned and Christopher glanced at her. Please God, she wasn't going to start that again.

'Her father broke his word of honour to Marguerite.' She stared hard at Christopher. 'I think you are different. You are like your uncle. If only Marguerite had loved him instead of being blinded by the glory of her precious Duke. The lying divil.' She drew in a deep breath. 'I will help you.'

Dare he trust her? Something told him he should. 'Help me finish dressing her.'

He rolled Sylvia on her stomach, trying to ignore the expanse of beautiful back above the lacy gown as the old maid worked. She tugged on the laces. 'How will ye get out of here? There is nae much time afore they come to tell ye your time is up.'

'The way I came in, I presume.'

The old woman straightened. She pulled something from her pocket with a smug smile. A small iron key. 'Then ye'll be needing this.' Quickly she unlocked the press to reveal Sylvia's clothes.

He rolled his eyes. 'Why didn't you say anything before?'

Jeannie shrugged.

'Never mind. Help me get her out of this costume and into her own gown.'

'There's no time. *Madame* will return soon. We must pull her gown over the top.'

The old woman was right. He held Sylvia up and the maid dropped the gown over her head. Between them they got her into her shoes and pulled her to her feet.

Jeannie shook Sylvia. 'Wake up, little one. You must leave here.'

Sylvia opened her eyes. She smiled and hugged the bent old shoulders. 'Jeannie. I never thought I would see you again.'

Christopher frowned at the thought of what might happen to Jeannie when they left. 'If I can get to my horse, you could come with us.'

Regret filled Jeannie's expression. 'I'll just keep ye back. And besides, you will have to fight Alphonse to leave here. They must not know I helped you.'

Alphonse, the dwarf doorman. Christopher knew the type, fists like iron and a head to match, a street fighter. His sword-stick would be of no use in close quarters. He needed a pistol. He just hadn't thought to bring one.

He strode to the window. The room overlooked a weedy patch of garden at the back of the house. 'What lies below this room?'

Her brow wrinkled. 'The kitchen.'

'Who works there?'

'Only me.'

He pushed open the window and stuck his head out. Ivy

grew around this window, just as it had at the front of the house. A thick stem clung to the wall just below the ledge. A nearby lead rainwater pipe went from the roof to the ground. Many a time he had followed Garth out of their bedroom window at their grandparents' country house on some mad adventure or other. Why not now? As long as Sylvia held on and provided the pipe and the ivy held both of their weights, it should be easy. 'We'll climb down.'

Jeannie pushed him aside and leaned out. 'Ye'll fall for sure.'

'No. I won't.' Hurriedly, aware of time passing, he stripped the sheets off the bed and knotted them together. He tied one end to the leg of the sturdy four-poster. 'We'll use this to slow our descent,' he said at Jeannie's questioning look.

Sylvia giggled. 'What are you two doing?'

He repressed the vision of two broken bodies at the mercy of Madame Gilbert and Alphonse. 'Jeannie, remake the bed when we are gone and close the window. It might keep them confused for a while.'

She nodded, then glanced at Sylvia leaning against the wall with a dreamy expression on her face. 'She canna climb down.'

'I have a solution to that.' Using Jeannie's discarded knife, he rent the pillowcase into strips.

Sylvia smiled mistily as he tied her wrists. He placed her arms around his neck and she leaned against him, nuzzling below his ear. Cold shivers of hot pleasure ripped through his body. He hardened.

Hell. She had no idea what she was doing. It meant nothing. He picked her up. She wrapped her legs around his hips. God, it felt so damn good.

He tossed his cane out of the window into a rosemary bush, then perched on the windowsill. Grasping the knotted sheet, he swung his legs out. Sylvia slipped from his waist and hung like a dead weight, apparently asleep. As long as she didn't fight him, he could hold her. He twisted the sheet around one arm, and leaned out. The muscles in his back screamed as he stretched across the distance. There. He had it. He scrabbled with his fingertips, then gripped the drainpipe. Using the ivy as a ladder, he clambered down.

As his feet touched *terra firma*, he let go a long breath. Swiftly, he lowered the sleeping Sylvia to the ground, behind a rosemary bush, then glanced up, seeking signs of pursuit. Instead, Jeannie stuck her grizzled head out of the window and beckoned him closer.

Blast. She should be closing the window and hiding the evidence.

Gesturing to her to hurry, he ran beneath the window.

'There's an abandoned farmhouse off the Calais road, if ye need a place to rest,' she whispered. 'About ten miles on.'

He waved his thanks.

She glanced over her shoulder. 'Wait a moment.'

Damn it. They did not have time for this.

She disappeared for an instant then returned with a bundle, which she dropped down to him. His driving coat and hat. He bowed his thanks and she pulled in the sheet and closed the casement.

He collected his sword and took a quick look at the sleeping Sylvia. Quiet for the moment, at least. He crept to the front of the house. His heart sank. While his horse was happily chomping on the weeds by the front door, Alphonse stood a few feet away on the portico, smoking a pipe, the pungent tabacco drifting on the breeze.

He cursed silently. There was no help for it, he would have to walk and he would have to carry Sylvia.

He ran back, and gathered her into his arms, and ran for the back gate. Rusty and half off its hinges, it creaked open at a nudge. With a quick glance at the house, he dashed across the lane and through a gap in the hedge. According to his reckoning, they were about twenty miles from the outskirts of

Calais. The hue and cry would start the moment the *madame* realised her customer had not emerged satisfied and sated by her exquisite new girl. At most, he had an hour before they discovered him missing.

The rough terrain alongside the lane slowed his progress to a crawl. Sweat trickled down his back. Some thirty minutes later, he set Sylvia down on the ground and took stock of the distance he'd covered. A mile?

He glanced around. Too damned bad he hadn't been able to retrieve his horse. They would have been back to Calais and on the next packet to Dover long before dark. At this pace, so close to the lane, they risked imminent discovery. He had to cut across country.

Sylvia moaned as he picked her up.

Bloody hell. When she woke, he would have to contend with her needs again. *Don't think about it.* His body howled a protest.

Chapter Twelve

The rhythmic jolt of Sylvia's body matched the steady drumbeat in her ear. She inhaled the spicy scent of sandal-wood and shaving soap and heated man. One particular man.

She opened her eyes. The world tilted, then righted.

Against a backdrop of grey sky, a firm stubble-lined jaw appeared inches from her gaze. A trickle of moisture coursed from his temple, over his cheek and down the strong column of his neck into his collar.

Christopher. A snaking desire to follow the trail of moisture with her tongue stilled her heart.

With a slight grunt deep in his chest, his strong arms flexed around her waist and beneath her knees, shifting her weight. Why was he carrying her?

An urge to press her lips against his warm skin flashed, torrid, through her body.

He stumbled and his grip tightened, squeezing the air from her lungs.

'Ouch,' she gasped and pushed at his shoulder.

'Damn it. Hold still.'

Gripping her, he sank to his knees and lowered her on to the prickly grass. Brown flecked with green stared into her eyes.

'How do you feel?' His chest rose and fell in time to his harsh breathing.

Confused, Sylvia stared across an open field, trees in the distance a dark shadow against a horizon of black clouds edged with gold. The last thing she remembered was arriving in Calais. 'Where am I?'

'Still too close to Madame Gilbert's, I'm afraid.'

What did he mean? She tried to stand up. Her head spun and dry heaves wrenched her stomach. Bent double, she crouched on the grass, clutching at the rough stalks. She must have *mal de mer*.

'Are you all right?' he asked.

She would never be all right again.

A comforting pressure squeezed her shoulder. 'It's the drugs, I expect.'

Miserable and weak, she made no sense of his words, but the dizziness eased and she looked up into his concerned face. 'Drugs?'

'The *madame* drugged you.' His voice sounded strained.

What was he talking about? She glanced around. 'What are you doing here?' Where was here?

His stiffened. 'I might ask you the same question.'

Flashes of recollection tumbled through her mind. Rafter, Madame Gilbert. Oh God, she was going to throw up.

She retched, her empty stomach aching.

He held her hair back from her shoulders and patted her back. 'Relax. You'll feel better soon.'

A picture of Christopher, rippling muscles outlined in flickering candlelight, danced through her mind. 'What have I done?' she moaned.

'You haven't done anything.'

As the nausea subsided, she managed to sit up.

'Are you feeling better?' he asked and handed her a handkerchief.

She wiped her face and her eyes. 'Why are you here?'

His jaw tightened and he looked off into the distance. 'You left in rather a hurry. I followed you, to make sure you were all right. When I saw you with that man, I wasn't sure what to think.'

'I… Rafter. He forced me to go with him.'

He leaned forward and peeled a damp strand of hair from her forehead. 'I know.'

The fleeting touch of his fingers brought back other memories. Warm hands on her body, doing things, pleasurable, wonderful things. Shame swallowed her whole. She turned her face away, staring at the clods of earth and matted grass. 'How you must despise me.'

Fingers gripped her chin, warm and strong. He turned her face towards him. 'You have no reason to be ashamed. They drugged you. You could not help what happened.'

She remembered how she had clung to him. 'But you—'

He shook his head. 'I did not take advantage of you, Sylvia. Much as I wanted to. Jeannie saw to that.'

'Jeannie was there?'

He nodded.

In spite of what little she remembered of her wantonness, his hand touching her in intimate places and the terrible overpowering need followed by hot waves of pleasure, she believed him. He'd never once lied to her. 'I'm so ashamed.'

'You must not be. That wasn't you back there.'

Her heart tumbled over. She trusted him. A strange and wonderful feeling. 'Thank you,' she whispered.

The corners of his eyes crinkled as he smiled down at her. 'Do you think you can walk? We have a long way to go.'

She took stock of her body. Her stomach felt as hollow as a drum, her mouth dry and sour. 'I'm hungry and thirsty.'

With a gentle hand under her arm, he helped her to her feet.

'Water we can do something about quite soon, but food will have to wait.' He brushed the dirt from his knees.

She gave a shaky laugh. 'Water would be welcome.'

'There's a stream over there.' He pointed in the direction of a stand of trees, willows and larches and long grass. 'You can drink and rest, but not for long, I fear.'

Unable to do more than lean on his arm and force her feet to move, she followed his lead. A small stream meandered through the field and she knelt on the bank and scooped up the clear water in her hands. Cold and pure, it settled her stomach. Her head began to clear. She washed her face and hands, but with nothing to tie or pin her hair, she had to leave it loose.

When she had drunk her fill, he led her to the shade of a small larch. Grateful for the respite, she leaned against the rough bark. Small insects darted around her head and she batted them away. She felt safe with Christopher. Safe and secure.

He leaned his forearm against the tree above her head and scanned the horizon.

'Do you expect Madame Gilbert to leap out of the bushes?' she asked.

He threw her an irritated glance. 'No. But your Irishman might.'

A cold rock landed in her stomach, driving away the peace. 'He is not my Irishman.'

His lip curled. 'Maybe not. But he'd like to be.'

Nothing could be further from the truth, but who would believe a woman like her? Not true. She wasn't like those women. *Your mother was*, the little voice of doubt whispered, *so why not you?* She squeezed her eyes against the fear she'd carried for years.

'When did you eat last?' His breath grazed her ear and sent a delicious shimmer to the depths of her feminine core and ignited her blood. Her mind whirled away.

The drugs must still hold her in their lascivious grip. She fought her wicked desires.

'When?' he asked again.

'When what?' He spoke of food. She blinked to clear her thoughts. 'This morning. Early. I was to catch the first *diligence* to Paris.'

'We have hours to go before we reach Calais and an inn. Do you think you can last?'

He looked so handsome, so fierce, like a chivalrous knight determined to protect his lady. The kind of man she had dreamed of as a child, until she realised that no honourable man would ever want someone of her birth.

'How did you get here?' she asked.

'On horseback. The damned horse is nicely locked up in the *madame*'s stable by now.'

'How far to Calais?'

'Fifteen or more miles. Maybe less straight across country.'

Fifteen miles? Lethargy invaded her limbs and she slid down the tree to the leafy ground. 'I don't think I can walk that far.'

His jaw thrust forward and green fire blazed in his eyes. 'We have to move on, even if I have to carry you every step of the way. I'm damned if I am going to risk them catching up with us.'

The thought of Madame Gilbert spurred her on. She stretched out her hands and he pulled her to her feet. 'Let us go.'

Clumps of coarse long grass ambushed her legs; pebbles stabbed the soles of her feet through her shoes, while ahead of her Christopher, in his serviceable riding boots, set a gruelling pace. Every now and then, she had to half-run not to fall behind. Sweat trickled down her back beneath a gown that seemed too tight. It constricted every breath she took.

Each time the memory of the darkened room flashed through her mind, a hot flush accompanied a horrible sinking sensation in her stomach.

Forget about it. He does not blame you.

* * *

Hours had passed since they'd first stopped to drink. Whenever they crossed a stream, they swallowed another mouthful or two of clear water.

They kept to the strip-farmed fields and, where possible, small stands of trees. They crossed lanes only when they were sure they were clear of other travellers. They avoided farms and other signs of habitation.

Night drew in. Sylvia's feet and thighs ached and burned. All her years of long walks on the Kentish downs had given her endurance, but she doubted her ability to continue much further. Hunger gnawed at her insides.

As if he had read her mind, Christopher ceased walking. 'We have to find somewhere to rest for the night. Even if there is a moon later, it might be difficult to find our way. If I am right, we should be close to the main road between Calais and Paris.'

Legs, leaden only moments ago, felt light and airy at the thought of food and a soft feather bed. 'Is there an inn nearby, do you think?'

He frowned. 'We dare not risk it and unfortunately I gave all of my gold for…'

The strange tone in his voice gave her pause, then the truth slapped her in the face. He'd spent his money to buy her.

Shame writhed in her stomach. She took a deep breath. What was inherited was over. 'We have to eat something.'

'Not until we reach Calais and I can pawn my watch.'

'Then what do you suggest we do now?'

'We will look for a barn, some sort of shelter, where we can spend the night.'

She stared into the dusk. 'A barn will mean a farmhouse.' Saliva filled her mouth. 'And hens, and eggs.'

Christopher shook his head. 'I told you, I don't have any money. And besides, I am hoping for something unoccupied.'

A growl rumbled in her stomach. There was more than

one way to relieve a farmer of his produce, only Christopher Evernden wouldn't know about that. He had never starved in his life.

'Come on, then,' she said. 'Let's find this barn of yours.'

'I think I saw smoke up ahead,' he said, keeping pace at her side, a large comforting presence in the dusk.

Less than a mile later, lights flickered ahead of them. Its round oasthouse like a church spire, a stone farmhouse sat at the end of a dirt track. A wall enclosed the single-storey building and the barn.

'Devil take it,' Christopher murmured. 'The barn is too close to the farmhouse. We'll have to move on.'

Not when she could smell cooking. She picked up her skirts and began to run.

Christopher grabbed her arm. 'Where are you going?'

'To the farm. They will have food.'

'I told you, I don't have any money.'

She grinned. 'I hadn't planned to pay for it.'

A heavy silence greeted her words. His expression turned frosty.

She pushed her hair back from her face. 'Whether you come with me or not, I am going to get something to eat.' She tugged her arm from his hand and trotted towards the twinkling yellow lights. His heavy breathing and booted steps followed her.

A cockerel crowed and dogs barked as they neared the farmyard. Close up, the high stone walls made the farm look impregnable. A wooden gate gave access to the courtyard.

'You go to the front door and keep them talking, while I go around the back to the kitchen. Act like a stupid Englishman, speak dreadful French and ask for directions,' she whispered.

'I won't let you do this.' His voice cut through the night in a low rumble.

Carefully, she eased off her shoes with her toes. 'I cannot walk to Calais on an empty stomach.'

'I do not want to finish my days in a French prison.'

She grinned, snatched up her shoes and darted away. 'Then you had better hurry up and knock on the door or they'll catch me and I'll tell them you put me up to it.'

He groaned. 'You little witch.'

The stones and dirt, cold and rough under her feet, reminded her of her childhood. She'd often gone barefoot in the cobbled Paris streets, wandering the markets looking for scraps. Ordure had trickled along the kennels in the centre of the medieval alleys. They built to foul torrents whenever it rained. Soldiers and revolutionaries had loitered on every street corner on the look-out for aristos. She'd been full of bravado in those days, a skilful shadow, and she'd fed them all when business was bad, her and Mother and Jeannie. Anything, her mother had said, was better than Sylvia working on her back.

Dropping her shoes by the gate, she inhaled the scent of hay and manure and musty earth, wholesome country smells. Whatever she risked, she would never go back to that old sordid life.

The gate opened without protest. Squares of warm light from a ground-floor window revealed a well-swept dirt yard. No sign of the dog. Carefully feeling ahead with her bare toes before trusting her weight on her foot, she eased along the wall in the murky shadows. Her heart thundered in her ears. It was a long time since she'd felt such a nervous thrill. She reached the window and risked a peek through the open casement.

An apple-cheeked woman picked up a ladle from the heavy plank table running the length of the room. She bustled to the hearth and lifted the lid of a black cauldron suspended over the fire. A wonderful aroma floated out of the window. Rabbit stew. Sylvia swallowed her saliva.

The dog barked frantically. But at the front, not the back.

'Who is it?' the farmer's wife shouted above the yelps.

A sigh of relief escaped Sylvia. Christopher had followed her instructions.

A man shouted something from beyond the kitchen.

'I'm coming, I'm coming,' the woman called back and slammed the lid down on the hearth. 'Men,' she muttered. 'Can never do anything.' She stomped out of the kitchen.

Her breath held, Sylvia tiptoed to the back door and lifted the latch. It opened without a sound. She crept inside and left it ajar.

'*Oui, monsieur,*' the woman said in the distance. 'Yes. *À droite*. To the right.'

Christopher's deep voice said something indistinct.

'*Non,*' the woman shouted, as if at a deaf person. '*À droite*. That way.'

A ginger cat leaped from a chair seat and shot under the table. Sylvia's heart jumped into her throat.

Steady. The front door seemed to be at the other end of the house. She had time. She picked up the cloth the woman had used to lift the cauldron lid. Glancing around, she noticed a door to the right. The pantry. She nipped in and laid the cloth on the flagstone floor. She rescued a round of cheese from a shelf and half-a-dozen rolls from a bin.

Her hard breaths rasped in the small, dark room. *Hurry.* She placed the cheese and the rolls on the cloth, lifted the four corners to the centre and tied them. She darted back into the kitchen.

'Calais, it is zat way.' The woman sounded angry.

No time. The stew smelled wonderful. Her stomach growled. Sylvia couldn't resist. She snatched up the ladle and scooped up a mouthful of bubbling stew, blowing hard. With one eye on the door, she sipped the delicious gravy. She hooked out a lump of meat with her forefinger and thumb.

'*Oui, oui, monsieur*, zat way.' The door banged shut and

two grumbling voices headed her way. A big black dog raced into the kitchen, its nails rattling on the stones.

Sylvia shoved the meat in her mouth and dashed for the door. The cat hissed and spat, claws slashing her bare ankle.

'*Sacré,*' she mouthed.

Her stomach tight, she slipped through the open door and forced herself to close it without a sound.

The dog snarled and snuffled through the gap at the floor.

Wings on her bare heels, she flew across the courtyard and out of the gate. She grabbed her shoes and bolted.

A black shape rose up in front of her. She stifled a scream with her fist.

Christopher caught her by the shoulders. 'Watch out.'

'What in God's name are you doing down there?' she whispered, her heart pounding. 'Did you fall?'

'No,' he said. He took the bundle. 'Let's go before they miss this.' He sounded thoroughly peeved. 'You, madam, are a hussy.'

And that surprised him?

A carefree laugh bubbled in up her throat.

Sylvia sighed with satisfaction and leaned back on her elbows. 'I'm full.'

The abandoned barn stood alongside the crumbling ruins of a farmhouse, destroyed in the war, Christopher had thought. He hadn't been at all surprised to find it. They had climbed a shaky ladder with missing rungs to the loft and agreed it would make a good hideout.

Christopher discovered a leaky wooden bucket beneath a pile of old straw and lugged water from a nearby pond. They'd washed their hands and faces before sitting down to eat.

The remains of the bread and cheese lay on the gleaming white square of cloth. Poking pale shiny fingers through the opening high in the gable end and the chinks in the rotting roof, the moon served as their candle.

Christopher leaned over and flicked a straw out of her loose hair. 'I'm glad you are satisfied. Perhaps now we can get some sleep. But first I want to check to see exactly where we are.'

'Do you think we are in any danger of discovery?'

He rose to his feet, ducking his head beneath the great wooden beams. 'I certainly hope not. I'd like to have a better sense of what lies around us, though. We could have two lots of people after our blood now.'

He meant the farmer as well as Rafter. 'They had plenty of food. They won't miss it.'

'Perhaps not.' His voice echoed around the dark cavern of a barn. 'However, I don't care for stealing.'

No doubt he thought she did. Well, what else could she expect? 'I will send them money when we get back to England.'

He strode to the ladder. 'I left them a note saying as much.'

So that was what he had been doing on his knees by the gate. She tossed him a grin. 'The Right Honourable Christopher Evernden promises to pay for five rolls and a round of cheese.' She didn't mention the mouthful of stew.

'Something like that.'

She lay back in the scratchy straw and stared at a star between the roof planks. 'Then everything is right with the world.'

He chuckled. 'You are overly optimistic.'

A feeling of well-being washed through her. She had felt safe the moment she had opened her eyes and saw Christopher in the field beyond Madame Gilbert's house of ill repute. Her heart swelled. She would trust him with her life. And as long as he never knew how she felt, where was the harm? 'Why should I not? We have tricked the *madame*, we have food in our belly, and tomorrow we will be in Calais.' She closed her eyes and stretched her arms above her head.

At his sharp breath she looked up.

'I'll be back in a while.' His voice sounded gruff.

She sat up as the top of his head disappeared below the

edge of the loft. Now what maggot did the stuffy Englishman have in his head? Still angry with her for stealing no doubt.

She was what she was.

With the thought came a new sense of freedom.

No one expected her to be perfect, or good or respectable. She had imposed those strictures on herself and look where it had got her. Right back where she had started. There was no use in pretending anything any longer.

No sense at all.

And another thing, she was tired of not being able to breathe properly. Whatever the garment was under her gown, it had to go. She struggled out of her gown, then worked at the laces down her back. Short and slippery, the strange shift barely covered anything. She managed to free the laces from the first few hooks, then her fingers encountered a knot.

Blast. She would have to wait for Christopher to untie it for her. She glanced around the loft. The floor was scattered with the remains of old hay and straw, but if she gathered them together, they might provide more comfort than hard bare boards. She set to work pushing the straw into a heap against the wall. Dust flew up around her. She sneezed.

Persevering, she soon had a rough sort of bed. Now, if she covered it with his driving coat…

'What in thunder are you doing?'

She swung around. 'Christopher.'

'For goodness' sake, be quiet. We are not three feet from the road. You could spit on it from here. I saw lights and the sounds of a carriage passing. With you crashing around like a maddened cow, I'm surprised they didn't come to see what was amiss.'

'I certainly wasn't crashing around. I was trying to make a bed.'

He stared at the heap of straw in the corner, then gazed back at her. 'Why aren't you wearing your gown?'

'Because,' she said as if he were a simpleton, 'this thing is so tight I can't breathe. And why am I wearing it anyway?'

He swallowed audibly. 'There was nothing else in that room for you to wear. Jeannie found your clothes by the time I had already dressed you.'

'You dressed me?'

'Yes.'

Flickers of memory came back to her. Him bending over her. Delicious sensations ripping through her body in an endless tide of pleasure. Distant pleasure, unreal, unfocused, part of her, yet far away.

And through it all, he'd remained honourable.

Her heart turned a somersault. She smiled and turned her shoulder. 'It seems to be knotted. Do you think you can release it?'

'If you wish.'

'I do.'

He stepped over the top of the ladder, bending to avoid the low beams.

Warm fingers brushed her skin. Tingles skittered across her back. Her insides tightened like an overtuned violin, reminding her of the delicious feelings he'd created in the dark bedroom at Madame Gilbert's. The desire she'd been ignoring for days unfurled deep in her body, wicked and urgent.

She bit her bottom lip, hard. Anything to take her mind off the sensation of his hands on her flesh.

After a few moments of fumbling, he cursed. 'Give me a moment.' He picked up his cane and pulled out a sliver of flashing blade.

Seconds later, the strings lay at her feet and she clutched the scrap of fabric against her chest.

'I'll leave you to change,' he muttered and stomped off down the ladder.

Always the English gentleman, just like his uncle. And she

owed him more than she could ever repay in a lifetime. Freedom from Madame Gilbert.

She let the gown fall to her feet.

His head popped back up, his face all shadows and moonlit angles. 'Damn,' he said and dropped out of sight as she stared open-mouthed.

'I'm sorry,' he called out, his voice hoarse. 'I came back to ask you to let me know when you are ready.'

He wanted her.

It had only been a moment, captured in moonbeams, but the hunger burning in his eyes had been unmistakable.

Her heart soared. The only thing she had to offer in repayment for her rescue, she'd gladly give.

Chapter Thirteen

'Sylvia. Miss Boisette?' His whisper echoed around the barn.

Her heart tumbled over. 'Yes.'

'Are you ready?'

She shivered. 'Yes.'

With her back turned to the ladder and one edge of his driving coat tucked close around her, she held her breath and listened to his steps. The rustle of cloth, a faint huff and a thump drew pictures in her mind as he removed his coat and boots. Pictures of Greek statues.

The driving coat beneath her pulled tight as he lay down beside her.

She turned over and touched his arm. 'Christopher?'

'Go to sleep.'

How did one do this? The only man she had ever talked to in any meaningful way was his uncle. 'I'm cold.'

He sighed, a long exhausted exhale of breath, and sat up. His shirt gleamed white and a heavy weight landed on her shoulders. 'Here, have my coat.'

So much for seduction. Perhaps she'd imagined what she saw in his eyes and he didn't want her at all. Some time during the long day, her cold wall of pride had melted. Without its protection, pain pierced her heart. A prickling sensation burned the backs of her eyes. She muffled a sniff.

His body tensed. 'What is the matter?'

'You don't want to make love to me because you despise me. That's it, isn't it?'

He groaned. 'Sylvia, don't do this. Not again.'

'Again?'

'It is the drug they gave you.' His voice thickened. 'It makes you wanton and I won't take advantage of you in this condition.'

Joy filled every corner of her mind, like beautiful music, dispelling her fears. Christopher would never deliberately harm her. She ran her hand across his cheek, along a jaw rough with a day's growth of beard, dragged her hand over his warm lips.

He captured her hand and pushed it away. 'Stop.' He rose to his knees. 'I'll sleep below.'

'Christopher, this has nothing to do with the drugs.' She flung back the driving coat, baring herself to his gaze. 'It is you who makes me this way.'

In utter silence, he gazed down on her. Not a breath.

'Hell fire,' he whispered and swept her up in his arms. The earthy, hay-scented smell of him filled her nose, his strong, encircling arms crushed her against his hard body. His lips, warm and moist, brushed against hers, a note of deep yearning rumbled up from his chest and she melted against him.

He raised his head and nuzzled her neck. 'I have never seen a woman as beautiful or as courageous as you,' he murmured into her hair.

Her hands ached to touch him. She ran her fingers through his hair, across his back, down his shoulders. She had never touched a man like this. He was granite heated by the sun, solid, stable; her fingertips wanted to explore every inch of him.

He drew her close and recaptured her lips. His kiss was soft and warm and gentle. She opened to his questing tongue, revelling in the hard wall of him pressed to her breasts.

He sat up. She almost cried out in disappointment until she saw him pull his shirt over his head. Within moments he had discarded his breeches and was as naked as she, his long body hard and warm. He fondled her breasts with a roughened palm. 'Beautiful,' he whispered.

He kissed her again and she pressed into him.

He nudged his knee between hers and she stiffened, suddenly afraid, harsh memories intruding. 'Will it hurt?'

'Then you haven't…?'

She turned her face away. Of course he'd thought the worst.

He touched her shoulder. 'I'm sorry. I thought—'

'The customers grabbed at me. One of them caught me on the stairs, up against the wall, he squeezed me so hard, I had bruises everywhere. He almost…' She gulped in a breath. 'I kicked him between the legs. That's what Mother told me to do. But I knew what went on, what they did, and how the women hated it.'

'Sylvia, what they did was not making love.' Raw pain filled his voice and he enfolded her in a gentle embrace. 'And that man, to try to attack a child… Ah, sweet, to betray the trust…to harm such delicate beauty… The foul cur.'

'I have feared men ever since.'

'My sweet Sylvia, I promise it will not hurt more than you can bear.' He breathed warm air against her throat. 'Trust me.'

'I do.' Her voice caught. 'I can't quite believe it, but I do.'

He ran his hands down her back, over her ribs. Touching, feeling, teasing his fingers, leaving heat and chills in their wake. Fire and ice. His reverential exploration tortured her quivering skin. He grazed his thumb across her nipple and tweaked the sensitive bud until she cried out with wanting. His hand roamed across her stomach and his fingers played with the curls between her thighs.

Pleasure tightened to breaking point. Yet still he touched her gently with hands and mouth and tongue until she thought she would die if he did not take her to some far-off peak. She whimpered, a soft noise in the back of her throat.

A deep groan rumbled in his chest and sent the world spinning around her as she sensed the depths of his desire. Her hands found his slim hips, and the hard muscles of his round firm buttocks. She dug her fingers into him, wanting, needing him closer. His heart beat strong and loud in time to her own.

He lifted himself and hung above her. He pressed his knee between her thighs and she opened to him. He lay between her legs, his hard member pressed hot against her inner thigh.

He slid one finger inside her. Intrusive, yet wave after wave of sensuous pleasure rippled through her.

He stared into her face, concern rampant in his moonlit expression.

'Tell me, Sylvia,' he said, his voice harsh with need. 'Tell me you want me. Now. Like this.'

She wanted him so much, she would die if she waited any longer. 'Yes. Now.'

He sighed, a rush of warm breath in her ear. Her body shivered in anticipation.

He eased forward, pressing against her, sliding into her, a small pause, one swift thrust, a small stab of pain and he filled her, hard, hot and delicious.

'All right?' he whispered in her ear.

'Yes,' she managed on a sigh, and she heard his sigh of relief.

'Hold on, darling.' His back muscles bunched and flexed beneath her hands as he drove forward yet again.

He filled her.

Her body stretched, adjusted to his heat and size. A thrill tightened every nerve as he moved inside her, with her. Heat suffused her. His strokes were slow and sensuous. Each fraction of movement driving her need to a higher notch of unfulfilled desire.

'You like this, my darling?' he asked in tender concern.

'Oh, yes.'

He thrust harder, deeper, his intensity a promise of fulfilment. She lifted her hips to meet him. 'Yes.'

All she was resided in their joining of the place where his flesh became at one with hers. She was him, his pleasure mingled with hers, his flesh throbbing within her. Yet she wanted something just out of reach.

She lifted her legs high around his waist and raised her hips to meet his powerful thrust, to receive him deep inside her.

'Sylvia,' he moaned. 'You're making me come.'

He held still for a moment, trembling with effort, the muscles in his muscular back and arms taut and slick with sweat. She arched her back, encouraging him.

He reached between their bodies and circled his thumb on her nub of pleasure. 'Now, Sylvia. Come to me, now,' he said, commanding and desperate all at once, pleasure and sweet pain in his voice.

Delicious waves rolled through her, peaking with crests of excitement. She crashed through the barrier that held her earthbound and soared with him.

She felt him shudder and pull away. Gasping, he spilled his seed on her stomach. Moments later, he rolled on his side and pulled her close.

She floated to earth. Heat radiated out from her core, leaving her limp, sated and strangely triumphant, as if she had achieved some great feat. She was delightfully weary.

'Ah, sweeting, you amaze me,' he murmured and kissed her eyelids, her lips, her throat.

Somehow she managed to drape her arms around his neck and kiss his shoulder, inhaling his scent as if she could somehow keep something of him inside her.

'A moment,' he said and leaned over to wipe her stomach with the edge of his coat. When he lay back, she snuggled into his welcoming arm, her cheek against his thundering chest.

She would remember this for the rest of her life. She would always have this memory of him, of them, no matter what came to pass. She nuzzled his damp flesh. 'Thank you.'

He squeezed her tight, then pulled his driving coat over the pair of them.

A smile tugged at her lips; always considerate. She drifted on a soft cloud of contented tiredness.

A sound, furtive and out of place, brought Christopher alert, the scent of woman and old straw pleasant in his nostrils.

He lay still, breath held, listening. It came again. Muffled footsteps. An animal chomping. The ring of a bridle and bit, indicating at least one horse.

Someone had arrived below while they slept. He cursed softly. He should have kept guard, not slept the night away in dreamless bliss.

Sylvia stirred in the crook of his elbow, but did not wake. Her hair, guinea bright in a shaft of sunlight piercing the ancient roof, lay in wild disarray across his naked chest. Visible beneath the dirty straw, the silver head of his swordstick lay just out of reach. He eased his arm out from beneath her head.

Careful to make no sound, he pushed to his feet, picked up his swordstick, releasing the blade, and tiptoed to the window. The road twisted away from the barn, empty in both directions. Whoever lurked below, they had apparently not brought reinforcements.

He stared at his pile of clothes. Idiot. At least he could have put his shirt on before falling asleep. Hopefully it was a local farmer stopping to rest his horse, and not Alphonse or the Irishman who had discovered their refuge.

He crept towards the opening where the ladder poked

through. At any moment, someone might stick a head up through the floor. Christopher wanted to be ready.

Sleepy and warm, Sylvia couldn't believe her eyes. Christopher, standing as still as a statue, staring down into the barn. Strong, well-formed calves and thighs sprinkled with dark, crisp hair, a heavier thatch circling his male member and running in a line up his ridged stomach. The early morning light cast the muscles of his chest and arms into sculpted bronze. Glorious in his nakedness, he was quite the most beautiful thing she had ever seen. Tingles tightened her breasts and she lifted her gaze to his intent expression. She smiled.

He must have sensed her gaze, because he glanced at her, frowned and shook his head, then pointed down the hole.

Someone was down there? Dread filled her heart. They had found them after all. It was all her fault. If she had not stopped to rob the farm, they would never have spent the night here. They would have kept on going to Calais.

She got to her knees, grabbed up her gown and slipped it silently over her head. She rose to her feet, staring at Christopher, waiting for a signal, some sign of what to do next.

He pressed his fingers to his lips and lowered himself to lie flat on the floor.

Her mouth dried. Never had she seen a man laid out naked like a banquet. Her gaze lingered on round firm buttocks and lean flanks, drifted up his narrow waist to his broad shoulders. Beneath his dark coats and quiet demeanour, Christopher was one very beautiful male. And she wanted to taste him. All over.

Had she run mad? This was definitely the wrong time to discover her salacious side.

She drew in a deep steady breath and crept across the floor to lie down at his side, peering into the darkness below, the only patch of light directly below the open hatch to their loft.

She opened her mouth. He shook his head.

Then she heard the snorting chewing sounds of an animal

that must have attracted his attention. An animal enjoying breakfast? The thought made her stomach rumble. It might just be a cow who had wandered in and found the old hay. Another sound. Shuffling footsteps.

'Ach. I was sure I'd find them here, wee horsy,' a voice muttered.

Sylvia giggled and rose to her feet.

Christopher jumped up and slammed his hand over her mouth.

She tore his fingers lose. 'It's Jeannie,' she breathed in his ear. She rose to her feet and prepared to go down the ladder.

He grabbed her forearm. 'Let me go first,' he whispered. 'She may not be alone.'

She swallowed a laugh and gazed pointedly down his length.

He coloured and headed for his clothes. With his back to her, he slipped his breeches over his muscled thighs and hid his gorgeous rump from her view. The muscles in his arms and shoulders rippled as he reached down for his shirt.

She narrowed her eyes. If there was someone else down there, they had come for her, not him. She could not let him be harmed.

Sucking in a breath, she grasped the top of the ladder, and placed one foot on the ladder.

'Sylvia.' Christopher's frantic whisper echoed off the ancient beams.

She frowned and put a finger to her lips. 'Wait here,' she mouthed and climbed down.

'Oh, thank God,' Jeannie said, twisting her neck to look up at her. 'Rafter is expected at the whorehouse at any moment. There will be hell to pay when they see the horses are missing.'

Sylvia closed her eyes in thanks. Jeannie would come with them. And Sylvia would care for her, as she had been unable to care for her mother. The thought eased a little of the hollow place in her heart. 'Christopher, she's alone,' she called up. She turned to Jeannie. 'How ever did you find us?'

'I mentioned this place to yon gentleman of yourn. I hoped to find ye here. Alphonse scoured the land around the house last night when they discovered ye were gone, but *madame* would not send him further afield until the Irishman came.'

Sword in hand, Christopher scrambled down the ladder. He glared at Jeannie. 'Did you tell them where to find us?'

Jeannie drew herself to her full height and stared at his waistcoat. 'Of course I didna'. I told them I thought you would continue on to Paris, to your friend. The *madame* is going to kill me when she finds out what I did.'

Christopher wasn't looking at her, he was looking behind her at the horses at the manger. 'My God. You brought both horses.'

Jeannie's face broke into a grin. 'That, too. Alphonse isna' going to be happy. It will sure slow him down.'

Christopher slid his blade back into its sheath. 'Well done, Jeannie. Come on, then, we best make haste for Calais.'

'Aye,' Jeannie said. 'We'll need to hurry. Yon Irishman is due back at the house this morn, and he's nae gonna be pleased, I think. An' he'll soon realise ye didna' take the Paris road. Now there's a man I dinna want to face when he's fashed.'

The thought of an angry Rafter sent a shudder down Sylvia's spine.

Jeannie's fingers dug into Sylvia's waist as Alphonse's ancient nag ambled along the road. Christopher dropped back to her side. 'Can you go any faster?'

Sylvia glanced over her shoulder at Jeannie's terrified face. 'No. We are doing our best.'

'We will miss the last packet to Dover if we don't hurry. I don't want to be in Calais when Rafter arrives.'

Nor did she, but they'd been forced to take a circuitous route to the coast, not daring to risk the main highway. How long would it be before Rafter realised he'd been sent on a wild goose chase? Probably not long enough.

'Leave me, Miss Sylvia,' Jeannie croaked.

Sylvia shook her head. She had lost too many people in her life. She would lose Christopher when they returned to England, but she would not lose Jeannie.

Hours later, they clattered into the town, their horses' hooves echoing off the silent, cobbled streets. She recognised the inn she'd slept in a few days ago. They were almost safe.

A stable-boy dawdled from somewhere at the back to retrieve their horses. Christopher's weariness showed in his slumped shoulders as he dismounted, but his hands were strong and firm around her waist when he lifted her down, before he assisted Jeannie out of the saddle.

Poor Jeannie looked as if she had been out in a violent storm. Thin strands of grey hair hung around her face and she'd lost her cap. Sylvia put a hand to her own stringy hair. She probably looked worse after her romp in the hay.

In low tones, Christopher arranged for the stabling of the horses. Though his posture indicated confidence, Sylvia saw the concern in his eyes as he spoke to the groom.

He strode back to her and Jeannie at the stable door. 'We've missed the last boat tonight. I'm going to see if I can find a local fisherman to take us across. If you ladies wouldn't mind waiting in the parlour, I will return as soon as may be.'

Sylvia caught his arm. 'Is it safe to stay here? What if Rafter should come?'

Christopher frowned. 'I'll rent a private room for you and Jeannie. Stay in it and stay out of sight. That's all I can do.'

He put a hand to his pocket. 'Blast. I haven't a penny to my name.'

'Perhaps we should take shelter in the barn?' She sent him a saucy smile.

'God, no. My credit is good enough and, if not, there's

always my watch.' He caught her look and grinned. 'Hussy. Wait here while I make the arrangements.'

He strode into the inn.

Sylvia rubbed her chilled hands together. 'We won't be long now, Jeannie.'

The hunted expression in Jeannie's eyes cut her to the quick and she gave the old woman a hug. 'Hold on. Everything will be well, I promise.'

A moment or two later Christopher returned with a thin little innkeeper trotting behind.

'This way, ladies,' the skinny man said with a bow low enough for the Queen, despite their dishevelled appearance. Clearly, Christopher had paved the way well. Sylvia inclined her head, hooked Jeannie's arm in her own and followed the innkeeper.

The private parlour at the back of the inn welcomed them with a warm fire and bright candles.

'What can I get for you, *mesdames*?' the innkeeper asked.

Jeannie and Sylvia looked at each other. 'A nice cup of tea,' they chorused and laughed.

'Ah, *les anglaises et le thé*,' he murmured and bowed himself out.

When Christopher entered the empty taproom, his hopes of finding a ship's captain plummeted.

'No fishermen tonight?' he asked the boy behind the bar washing glasses.

'It is late, *monsieur*,' the pot-boy said. 'All the local men are all down at the waterfront where the women are.' He winked lewdly. 'We cater to a different clientele and they left on this afternoon's packet. You are the only guests tonight.'

'If I needed to find a man with a boat, where would I go?'

'At the Sign of the Mermaid most likely, *monsieur*. Can I get you something to drink?'

The days were such a blur, he couldn't remember the last time he'd had a tankard of ale. He swallowed the dust in his throat. He didn't have time. He had to get the women to safety before Rafter came up with them. 'No, thank you. Just give me directions to the Mermaid.'

The pot-boy did so and, intent on getting there before everyone was too drunk to sail, he hurried to the door. A pair of broad shoulders clad in black blocked his path.

'Kit. Finally I run you to earth.'

Christopher reeled back. 'Garth. Bloody hell. What the devil are you doing here?'

Garth's dark eyebrow flicked up. 'Nice greeting, I must say. I'm looking for you, of course. I thought I'd better make sure you were all right.' He frowned. 'Except when I got here, it was as if you had disappeared into thin air.' His usual devil-may-care expression turned grave. 'You are all right, aren't you? You look a bit pale.'

For Garth to notice that kind of detail meant he looked a perfect scarecrow. 'I'm passable.'

Garth stared at him. 'You've been involved in some sort of scrape without me to get you out of trouble. Devil a bit.'

Christopher gave a shout of laughter. 'Doing it a bit too brown, brother. It's usually the other way around. I'll tell you all about it later. Right now, I have to get Sylvia and her maid back to England.' A thought occurred to him. 'You didn't by any chance sail over in the *Witch* did you?'

Garth grinned. 'I did. Thought you might need her and knew you'd never think of taking her yourself.'

Christopher stiffened. 'Why would I? She belongs to you now.'

Garth clapped him on the shoulder. 'You know how I feel about that. We always shared her when Father was alive. You're just too damned stiff-necked to accept anything from me.'

Christopher raised a hand. It was an old argument and the wrong occasion. 'The thing is, she's here. Can we get off tonight?'

'I'll have to ask Porter.'

'If anyone can do it, he can,' Christopher said.

'Right,' Garth replied with a nod and a big grin. 'Let's ask him.'

Chapter Fourteen

Luxurious indeed. Glowing from her sponge bath, Sylvia wandered around the *Sea Witch*'s well-appointed stateroom. So well appointed she'd found a nightgown to fit her in the sea chest, and, best of all, a sailor had brought jugs of hot water for bathing. Over Jeannie's protests that she ought to help, Sylvia had sent the poor old woman to bed. This luxury she needed no help to enjoy.

Absent-mindedly, she pulled a comb through her wet hair as she investigated the room. The polished mahogany fittings with brass hinges and handles gleamed in the swinging lamp-light. An ivory-backed hairbrush rested in a cunning rack on the dressing table fixed to the wall. She picked it up and turned it over. Everything had a place and everything was small and neat, like a doll's house. Except the bed.

The blatant, opulent monstrosity had a midnight-blue canopy and pale blue satin sheets embroidered in gold with the Stanford crest. 'I'll join you in a while,' Christopher had said before he left her to bathe. Expectation blazed in his eyes and her heart had quickened.

After she had bedded him willingly, he assumed she was his. Sadly, she was. Her body was his, but had she given him her heart? She wasn't sure. But she would not become his plaything, to be discarded at will. The thought of waiting for that dreadful day tore a hole in her chest. Better to get it over with before she became too attached.

She set the hairbrush back in its place and continued her roaming. This was Lord Stanford's room, she guessed. Or rather the room where he entertained his ladies. Fleetingly, she wondered where he would sleep tonight.

A cosy armchair behind the door looked inviting. Tucking her bare feet up under the hem of her gown, she curled up in it. She glanced at the bed again. Whatever would she would say to Christopher when he returned?

Anticipation simmered in her blood like water over hot coals. She wanted him. Just once more, she promised herself. Back in England, back to reality, she would insist they go their separate ways. Tonight would be their last together.

She turned her head at the sound of the opening door and smiled as Christopher entered. He had also bathed and was wearing a short blue-silk dressing gown. His or Lord Stanford's. Not that it mattered. His attention focused on the bed and she caught his disappointed expression in the dressing-table mirror when he saw it was vacant.

She laughed and opened her arms to him. 'I was waiting for you.'

In three short strides, he reached her and knelt at her side. 'You look beautiful,' he whispered. For a moment his large, warm hands cupped her cheeks and he brushed his lips against her mouth, a seductive invitation. She parted her lips.

'Ah, not yet,' he murmured against her mouth, his breath moist against her skin. 'This time we use the bed.' He picked up a strand of her hair and ran it across his palm. 'I love your hair down. Like spun gold, yet soft as silk.'

She ran her fingertips across his jaw. 'You shaved.'

'Mmm. Garth lent me his gear.'

'You talked to your brother about us?'

'A little.'

'And?'

'Garth doesn't judge.'

Sylvia's gaze wandered to the bed. Of course Garth didn't judge.

'Come, sweet.' Christopher's soft tone turned husky. She'd never heard him sound so intense. He caught her up in his arms.

Spicy cologne filled her nostrils. 'Mmm,' she hummed against his neck. His indrawn hiss of breath in response set up a drumming in her pulse.

Without effort, he carried her to their own blue ocean of desire. Triumph gushed through her. For this brief moment he belonged to her.

Later, as she lay in his arms, sated, languid and content, she clung to the sense of belonging. If they could only stay here, rocked by the gentle motion of the waves, like innocent babes.

Her fingers traced the sculpted muscles of his arms and chest, circling its flat nipples and raking through the smattering of light brown curls.

'Mmm,' he murmured and she smiled and gave his shoulder a gentle nip.

She wanted to remember for ever the way he looked and tasted and felt beneath her hands. She placed her palm against the strong firm line of his jaw.

He turned his head and kissed the inside of her wrist. From beneath his lashes, he glanced down at her, emerald fire in forest green. He smiled. Open, frank and youthful. The rare smile he seemed to save exclusively for her and for Garth, his brother.

He petted her hair where it lay over her breast. 'Pretty.'

'Why did you come chasing after me?' she asked. 'I assumed you would be happy to see me gone.' Her breath seemed to catch in her throat as she waited for the answer.

He looked puzzled. 'It was my duty. My uncle charged me with the responsibility of making sure you were settled.'

The reply didn't surprise her, but it sounded cold, unfeeling, and a chill ran over her skin as if a stray gust of sea breeze had found its way into their cosy nest.

She let go a little sigh, desperately trying not to mind. She could not expect him to feel as she did. While her parentage might be as noble as his, her bastardy put her beyond the pale.

His large warm hand closed around hers and she realised she had clutched at her locket. She glanced up and found him watching her.

'What did I say?' he asked.

'Nothing. I was thinking how lucky I was that it was you who…' Her face grew hot. Yet the time for blushes had long passed. She was a woman in truth. A well-bedded one. She chuckled. 'That it was you who came first to Madame Gilbert's. I just wish I remembered more about what happened.'

His shaft hardened against her thigh. Her own centre pulsed in reply. Interesting. Thoughts and words seemed just as sensual as touches. Something she had not learned as a child.

'I would sooner forget,' he growled.

She gasped. Hot prickles stabbed at the back of her nose and eyes; she sniffed to clear them away.

He tipped her chin with his clenched fist. 'Tears, Sylvia?'

'No, of course not.'

'Well, you might not remember all that happened, but it was torture for me. There you were, one of creation's most beautiful creatures, laid out like a dream, and you had no inkling of who was in the room.'

Others had said she was beautiful. She'd heard it all her life, with admiration or with envy, but never had it touched a chord in her heart as it did now. She wanted to throw her arms around him, bury her face in his neck, to ask him to keep her close for ever.

She couldn't. She didn't have the right to ask him to ruin his life, to bring his mother's wrath down on his head, to be excluded from his world.

'Why didn't you also take your pleasure?' She knew different words for the act of copulation, crude, disgusting words used by the whores. But what she and Christopher had done together was so much more. Blissful.

'I could have been anyone,' he said. 'Even though you said my name. How could I take advantage of a woman suffering under the influence of drugs?'

'Some men would have,' she murmured.

'They might,' he replied. His voice sounded harsh, as if just thinking about it made him angry.

'Then why not, when it was you I wanted?'

He drew in a deep breath and rolled on his side to face her, one heavy thigh splayed across hers. He picked up a lock of her hair and stroked the ends around the swell of her breast.

Suddenly she couldn't breathe. A thrum started low in her belly. A tickle between her thighs made her squirm.

'You are very responsive,' he murmured, leaning over to lick the tightly furled bud at the peak, before swirling the lock of hair around the other breast.

She swallowed. 'Why not, Christopher? I want to know.'

'Single-minded female.'

She bashed his shoulder with her fist. Not hard. Enough so he would know she meant business.

He sighed. 'Because it would have been wrong.' He bent his head and kissed the tip of her nose. 'To be honest, I almost succumbed. You were so ready, you did not give me time to get inside you before you came. But I was glad. I never would have forgiven myself for taking advantage of someone who could not say no.'

She traced his mouth with a fingertip, loving the fullness at the bottom and the fine sculpted upper lip. He caught her finger between his teeth, nibbled it, then sucked it into his hot mouth.

Desire jolted deep in her core. She rocked her hip against his thigh, felt the sweet promise of pleasure. 'Are you always so dutiful, so noble?'

He grimaced and let her finger go. 'You make it sound like a fault.'

'Oh, no. Pardon me if I seemed rude. I am surprised, that is all, and pleased, naturally. Most men, men like your brother, Garth, for instance, never give a thought to what is right or good for a woman. I must thank you for that. After my experience as a child, I very much feared that I could never let a man get close, let alone touch me. I am grateful.'

He stared at her. 'How do you do that?'

'I'm sorry, I do not understand what you mean?'

'You unman me. These things you say, they choke me up inside.'

'Is that bad?'

'Yes. Just accept the fact that any man with honour would not have taken advantage of your situation.'

'But, Christopher, you don't understand. Because it was you, I would not have minded had you taken your ease.'

He rolled on his back. 'Women,' he muttered. 'There's no understanding them at all. If you were to tie my hands and take me whether I wished it or no, do you think I would like it?'

She gazed at his erection, proud and stiff, then peeped at his frowning face, with a hesitant smile. 'I am not so sure you would not.'

'Sylvia, this is serious. Honourable men do not do that sort of thing.'

'I am sorry if I insulted your honour,' she whispered. 'It is just that I have never met anyone like you before.'

'There,' he said, his voice husky, 'you are doing it again.'

Perhaps he was right. That only if they were equal partners would the loving be right. Yearning for the contact he'd broken, her hand wandered his magnificent body. As it slid down the flat plane of his stomach, she encountered his turgid hardness. He sucked in a short breath. His stomach ridged with hard muscle. She stilled. 'Oh.'

'Don't stop,' he said. There was agony in his tone.

With a tentative fingertip, she touched him. He took her hand in his. 'Like this,' he said, moving her grasping fingers in swift hard strokes. She glanced at his face and saw abandonment to pleasure.

She'd learned some things from listening to the *filles de joie* growing up. Perhaps now would be her only chance to try them. 'How about this?' She squeezed him and his breath hissed between clenched teeth.

'Oh, yes.'

She bent her head and kissed the tip and found it silken and smooth, then raised her head to gauge his reaction.

'Sweetheart, don't stop now,' he begged.

She opened her mouth and took all of him in. Hard, hot, male musk and salt on her tongue. He filled her mouth. She cupped him in her other hand. So soft.

'Gently, girl,' he groaned. 'God, yes. That's it.'

She licked his smooth hardness, turning her head to savour the length of him with her tongue. He grew thicker in her mouth. It was an instrument of pleasure. Her pleasure. It was now her joy to pleasure him, however he desired. She tightened her grip around his rigid length.

He groaned, and threw his head back, eyes squeezed shut in the agony of ecstasy. He looked so beautiful she wanted to cry. He raised his head and caught her smiling at him. He grasped her shoulders and rolled her on to her back.

'I have to be inside you,' he said. He hung above her, his

gaze fixed on hers. 'This is what you want, isn't it? Me inside you.' The fierceness of his tone frightened her for a moment. Then she saw his need to please her.

'Yes, Christopher. I want you. Just you and no one else. Not ever.'

'My girl. My lovely Sylvia.'

He pressed his hard male member against her opening. His eyes never leaving her face, he drove his hips forward. Pleasure rippled through her in growing waves and his pleased expression told her he delighted in her arousal.

With each slow stroke in, she lifted her hips to meet him. The feel of his groin hard against her was sweet grinding torture after sliding pleasure. She lifted her legs around his waist and he probed deeper yet. He filled her, tightening the knot of need, stretching her nerves to breaking point. And yet she did not break. She soared and flew on a gale of pleasurable sensation.

She cried out. Begged for the final flight to the stars.

'Yes, sweet. Soon,' he gasped. 'Hold on to me, stay with me, darling.'

He lowered his head to her breasts and laved each one with gentle strokes of his tongue that sent her mindless. Then he suckled. The cords that held her together were so tight, so fine, they thrummed in wild vibration. She shuddered.

His rhythm changed, harder, swifter, deeper. She could barely breathe, but still she matched him stroke for stroke.

The strands unravelled. Nerve endings shattered in a thousand points of light. She called his name. Somewhere inside her, she heard Christopher's groan of male triumph and her body surrendered to a river of hot bliss melting her bones.

She lay beneath him, smelling him, salt and sweat and musky man, feeling him stroke her hair, kiss her breasts, her lips, and listening to his soft murmured praise until she fell asleep. He was hers.

* * *

'Wake up, sleepy head.' Christopher's warm breath in her ear sent a shivery thrill to her core.

Stretching, full of contentment, she opened her eyes and smiled at a fully clothed Christopher.

A grin of pride beamed from Christopher's beloved, stubble-hazed face. 'We're here.'

'Here?'

'Dover.'

The word had the ring of a death knell, the ending to their interlude.

He took her hand and pressed it to his warm lips. He turned it over and, starting with her palm, trailed tantalising kisses up the delicate inside of her arm to its crook.

Her limbs turned to melted butter. She sighed and wiggled with pleasure beneath the covers. 'You are up early.'

He waggled his eyebrows. 'Definitely up.'

'I don't mean that,' she said, but couldn't resist a peek.

He chuckled. 'Garth has disembarked already, but I didn't want to wake you. You've been through hell these past few days.'

She sat up. Grey light from the window showed a new day. The ship barely rocked.

She flung back the covers. 'Goodness, I'm sorry to keep everyone waiting.'

Fire blazed in his hazel eyes as his gazed travelled her naked length. He leaned forward and kissed the rise of her breast.

Sun-gilded hair tickled her skin. She ran her fingers through the silky waves. 'Are you sure you want me to get up?'

A groan rolled up from his chest. He raised his head and looked down at her with a rueful grin. 'No, I don't. Unfortunately, Captain Porter has to get the *Sea Witch* berthed further down the coast. So, milady, you needs must arise.'

Placing her palms either side of his wonderful face, his lean cheeks rough against her palms, she kissed him soundly on the lips. Sandalwood and soap filled her nose. She loved the male smell of him. Clean and musky at the same time. She licked his bottom lip. 'Then you must leave and send Jeannie to help me dress.'

He chuckled. 'Then you must let me go.'

A sweet pang squeezed her heart. She never wanted to let him go. Moisture blurred her sight. She gave a shaky laugh and released him.

His expression turned serious, his eyes the colour of mysterious northern forests. 'Don't worry. I will take care of everything.'

She nodded, unable to speak for tears. What a mix, happiness that she'd found him, tears of losses to come. She flashed him a brilliant smile and hoped he didn't notice.

With a last yearning glance, he got to his feet and strode for the door. 'Do you think you can be ready in half an hour?'

'If you want me to be,' she murmured with an eyebrow raised.

'Sylvia,' he said, his warning voice full of laughter. 'Be good.'

If she was good, she wouldn't be here.

A half-hour later, she and Jeannie met him up on the gleaming mahogany-and-brass-fitted deck of the *Sea Witch*. She raised her eyes to the white cliffs guarding the English Channel. Somewhere up there, Cliff House clung to its rocky perch. The house where she had grown up and learned the truth about her life.

Captain Porter touched his hat. 'Mr Evernden, a pleasure to have you on board again.' A knowing look crossed his face as his gaze rested on her. 'Ma'am.'

Inwardly, she squirmed. He knew, of course, what they'd done, what she was.

Christopher's protective hand touched the hollow of her back and he moved closer, claiming her. She relaxed.

'Thank you, Red,' Christopher said.

'Yes, sir. Good day.'

With Christopher's help she and Jeannie clambered into the small boat waiting to take them to the post-chaise at the dockside, where a yellow liveried post-boy sprang to attention and opened the door.

Once inside, Sylvia snuggled against Christopher, his strong arm around her shoulders pressing her into his hard wall of chest. It was as if all her childish dreams of a noble knight who would rescue her from the dragon of her fears had come true.

Jeannie, on the other side of the carriage, smiled and nodded.

Life suddenly seemed unbearably wonderful. Dare she hold on to it?

After a leisurely lunch at Cobham and several short stops to change horses, the chaise came to a stop outside a curving terrace of Palladian town houses. Sylvia frowned. This was not London.

'Why are we stopping here?' she asked.

'This is Blackheath. You are spending the night here.'

The house, fronted by a wrought-iron fence, looked over a green open space on the other side of the street.

'Surely we can reach London in another hour or so?'

Embarrassment filled his expression and he glanced at Jeannie. 'I thought you wouldn't mind staying here. It belongs to Garth. He doesn't actually live here, he…well, it's where he lives some of the time.'

Disappointment emptied her heart. 'It's where he keeps his mistress,' she uttered, her tone flat.

She couldn't help her reaction. For some foolish reason, a glimmer of hope had sprung to life that there really might be more than this in her future.

Christopher opened the door. 'Since there is no one living here at the moment, Garth is loaning it to us until we make other arrangements.'

Of course she couldn't return to his mother's house. Not now they were lovers. She forced calmness into her voice. 'I see.'

'Rafter won't have a clue where to find you. If we go into town, there's the risk of him ferreting you out. He'll expect us to go to London.'

Christopher was carving out her future as surely as if it were set in stone and this the final lettering in the block.

The thought of parting with him tugged at her newly discovered heart. Why not accept? She could stay with him for a while, a month, a year. They'd make some happy memories together.

A nagging doubt, a memory of her mother, skittered across her mind like a spider scuttling out of a dark corner. She pushed it aside. If she wanted him, this was her only option.

With Jeannie trailing behind her, she alighted and followed Christopher up the two steps and in through the front door held open by the butler.

They were obviously expected.

On the outside, the town house looked unremarkable. Inside told a different story. Appalled, Sylvia gazed at the opulent marble staircase with its Turkey runner. Marble and plaster statues of Greek gods and goddesses filled elegant niches; paintings of nude women adorned the walls. Frolicking nymphs leered down from the ceiling.

Disappointment washed through her and extinguished her hopes. She was a fool to expect something less garish, more genteel. After all she had become her mother.

It suddenly seemed difficult to breathe.

'If you would step in to the drawing room, Mr Evernden, I'll arrange for tea,' the butler said.

'No tea for me, thank you, Bates,' Christopher said.

She followed Christopher into the drawing room, while Jeannie disappeared into the nether regions of the house with Bates. A sense of unreality numbed her.

She glanced around the room, at the rose-coloured walls and gilt furniture, at the satisfied expression on Christopher's face.

'At least Delia didn't get started on this room,' he said.

'Delia?'

'Garth's last lady. She had a thing about decorating. The entrance hall was her handiwork. It was as far as she got before she was handed her *congé*.'

The ease with which he accepted the departure of a woman who had made this place her home sent a chill down Sylvia's spine. 'Oh.'

'Eventually, we will go to my house in Kent. I haven't been there since my grandmother left it to me, so it will take a couple of days to make it ready for us. This will be perfect until then.'

'Perfect.' Her lips felt stiff.

He pulled her into his arms and pressed his lips against hers, firm and warm and so tempting. He ran his fingers through her hair and deepened the kiss.

The feel of him, his large body hard against her, his passion, his heat, his strength, drove her thoughts and fears into the far reaches of her mind. She melted into him. She wanted this with him.

She reached up and curled her hand around his strong column of neck, arching into him. She nibbled at his lower lip, felt his desire rise, a hard ridge of arousal pressed against her stomach.

Desire flooded her, rushing through her veins in hot rivers. She ground her hips against him and revelled in his sharp indrawn breath.

She never imagined wanting a man like this. It went against everything she thought she knew about herself, everything she believed.

He groaned and pulled away. 'I'll be back first thing tomorrow.'

Panic gripped her. 'You aren't staying?'

'I have business requiring my attention, people relying on me.'

She couldn't stay in this place without him. 'Don't go.'

She hated the begging note in her voice. 'Or take me with you.'

He smiled down at her and gave her a squeeze. 'I can't. My ships can't sail until I sign the manifest, and I have nowhere to take you in London except a hotel, and it would be too easy to find you.'

Pain pierced her heart. It was starting already. Him leaving her for his other world. His real world. A world to which she could never belong. 'Can you not go tomorrow?'

'I wish I could.' He nuzzled her neck, sending a delicious shiver all the way to her core. 'But I have already delayed this sailing by several days. We will start to lose our crew.'

Releasing her, he took her hands. 'Come, sit with me a moment.' He led her to the sofa and drew her down, his arm around her shoulder. 'Everything will be all right, you will see.'

She desperately wanted to believe him, but the spider crawled out of the dark and completed a web of doubt in her mind. Doubt about Christopher and, worst of all, about herself. She sought escape. 'What if Rafter comes looking for me again? Perhaps it would be better if I disappeared, went somewhere alone.'

His mouth flattened. 'Where else can you go where you will be safe? Not to London or France. This is the perfect solution.' He tipped her chin with one finger and gazed into her eyes. 'Don't you want to be with me?'

Every particle in her body and her heart said yes, but her mind knew better. 'How long must I remain in hiding?'

His expression darkened. He sighed. 'I don't really have the time to discuss this now. Bates will see to your needs until I get back. You don't have to worry, he's very discreet.'

He would have to be. She drew in a breath. Without Christopher to tempt her, to overcome her reason, she would be able to think. Perhaps it was better if he left. She fought the tears threatening to spill over and nodded.

He smiled and kissed her forehead. 'That's better. Rest now. You've been through a lot. We will talk tomorrow.'

She flung her arms around his neck, abandoning her lips to the pleasure of his for an all-too-brief moment.

Tomorrow she might not be here.

Unease churned in Christopher's gut as he took his hat and coat from the imperturbable Bates. Beneath Sylvia's impassioned kiss, he'd sensed tension.

Fear of her father? He stepped outside. Not fear, she was too full of courage for that, yet he sensed a brittleness, like a delicate vessel ready to break at a touch, the way she'd been the first day he had met her at Cliff House.

Something prodded him to turn back.

Bates raised his brows.

'Please see that Miss Boisette has everything she needs.' Christopher flicked the man one of the guineas he'd borrowed from Garth.

'As you wish, sir.'

A tension gripped him. Twice now she'd tipped him the double. He didn't want to risk her leaving again. 'Bates, I would prefer it if Miss Boisette did not leave the house. Not for any reason.'

The door hesitated in its swing. A frown puckered Bates's forehead, then smoothed. 'As you wish, Mr Evernden.'

Christopher turned and strode to the waiting post-chaise.

Chapter Fifteen

Light blazed from every window at the Mount Street house. A carriage disgorged a couple in evening attire. Christopher frowned. It seemed that Mother had gone all out for this birthday party. Damn lucky he'd remembered once he arrived in town. His brain still wasn't working right. Anxiety about Sylvia had haunted him all the way to London and through most of his meeting with his man of business. Something about his leavetaking felt wrong.

With a roll of his shoulders, he handed his rumpled driving coat to the butler on his way past. He headed for the stairs. Garth cast a laconic glance at him through the open drawing-room door, then looked pointedly at his watch. Things really had gone to hell if Garth needed to remind him about the time.

Studiously ignoring Reeves's darkling glances and tongue-clickings over the state of his raiment, he bathed, shaved and changed at breakneck speed and went downstairs. He joined a bored-looking Garth.

'I didn't think you'd leave her,' Garth murmured out of the side of his mouth.

His sly wink added to Christopher's sense of unease. 'I must have more control than you.'

Garth laughed.

'Christopher, darling.'

His mother bore down on him like a frigate about to deliver a broadside. He gave Garth a don't-you-dare-say-a-word stare and went to greet her.

'Here you are at last, dear,' Lady Stanford announced, clearly in high spirits and her best looks. 'I was beginning to think you had forgotten.'

Somehow she made him feel guilty even when he wasn't. Perhaps Garth was right to be so offhand. 'I'm sorry I'm late. I was delayed on the road.'

'Blackheath, wasn't it?' Garth put in with a grin.

His mother fluttered her handkerchief in question.

'It doesn't matter where,' Christopher said.

'No, indeed,' his mother said. 'You are here now and that is what is important.' In a swirl of silk and a waft of lavender, she sailed away to greet the Molesbys. Even from here Christopher could hear Aunt Imogene protesting about the rudeness of the hackney driver who had brought them from their friend's house in Golden Square and grossly overcharged them.

Over her shoulder, George Molesby raised an eyebrow. Christopher could guess the question on his mind. Sylvia. Damn the man. Still, he was glad to have his mother's attention diverted. He glowered at Garth. 'Can't you be serious for a moment?'

Garth's brow shot up, but a smile lurked in his eyes. 'Apparently not.'

Christopher took a good look at him. 'You're foxed.'

'Not yet,' Garth replied with utter good cheer. 'Soon, I hope.'

The gentlemen gathered around their ladies, who reclined on sofas or perched on chairs. The butler circulated with glasses of madeira.

Garth stepped forward and raised his glass. 'To Mother.'

'Lady Stanford,' the company chorused.

With a gracious incline of her head, Mother accepted their good wishes. It warmed Christopher's heart to see her so happy, something that had not occurred when their father lived. Christopher's earlier irritation dissipated.

He grinned when he saw Garth's thunderstruck expression as first one guest, then another presented a gift: handkerchiefs from the Molesbys, a miniature from Lord Angleforth, her latest flirt, some perfume from one of the other couples. Garth had obviously only just realised gifts were expected.

Christopher took pity on him and sauntered to his side. 'I bought something from both of us when I first learned she planned this party.' It seemed like aeons ago. Before he had gone chasing off to Dover, when his life had been ordered and organised and totally in his control. Strangely he didn't miss it at all.

'I'm in your debt again,' Garth muttered under his breath. 'I will pay you back.'

Christopher slapped him on his broad shoulder. 'Indeed you will.'

He pulled a slender red velvet pouch from his pocket and placed it in his mother's lap. 'From your sons.' She squealed and fumbled with the ribbon around its throat.

A general gasp greeted the glittering diamond-and-emerald bracelet as it spilled into her hand.

'Gad, young Kit. Where'd you get the ready for a piece like that?' Garth asked.

'Investments.' Christopher couldn't keep the pride out of his voice. It might not be quite the thing for a noble gentleman, but his head for business had its uses.

'I'll have to take some advice from you.'

The respect in Garth's face gave him a deep sense of satisfaction. 'Any time, brother.'

'Dinner is served, my lord,' the butler announced and opened the double doors to the dining room.

'Looks like we are on parade, old chap,' Garth murmured. 'Who has she got you tied to this evening?'

Christopher groaned. 'The old Fanshawe trout.'

'Hah. Well, as head of the family, I've got Mama.' He didn't sound any more pleased than Christopher. Whatever lay between Garth and their mother, it ran deep and always left Christopher with a vague sadness.

But as always, they presented a united front and turned to their respective duties. It was not until dinner was over and the ladies had withdrawn, leaving the gentlemen to their port and cigars, that Christopher contrived a quiet moment alone with Garth on the dining-room balcony. While the other men lingered at the table over their wine, they ignited their cigars in the comfortable dark.

'So, did you get your little ladybird all nicely set up?' Garth asked, blowing a ring of smoke at the sky.

It sounded so bloody tawdry. 'Miss Boisette is not my ladybird.'

'You could have fooled me, dear boy. The *Sea Witch* practically keeled over after you went to the stateroom, not to mention the cries of delight. There I was, thinking of you enjoying yourself.'

Palms moist and cheeks heated, he held off from strangling Garth. 'Take a damper. I'll have her out of your house in a day or so.'

'What a bloody hypocrite you are.' Deceptively lazy, the mocking tone lashed Christopher in a place he had not known was sensitive. 'She's a lovely armful. Keep her there as long as you want.'

'The house is too close to London and, with all the traffic buzzing down to visit Princess Charlotte, someone is sure to recognise me.'

The cigar glowed in the dark and Garth leaned one elbow on the balustrade. 'The truth now. What is this all about? What happened in France?'

'I don't think I should discuss it. It's bad enough that I'm embroiled in it. It seems Miss Boisette has powerful enemies.'

'Her father?'

'Likely. Anyway, I am taking her to my house in Kent, just as soon as I can make the necessary arrangements with my man of business.'

A low whistle emanated from the dark. 'You're inviting a scandal. Even I wouldn't install a woman like that in a family home.'

The hot rush of anger in defence of Sylvia surprised him. 'She's not *a woman like that*.'

'Good God. Have you lost your mind? She was Uncle John's paramour. Everyone said so.'

'I can assure you, she was no such thing.' He tossed his cigar on the stone floor and ground it out with his heel. 'I'm taking her out of sight for a while.'

'Take it from one who really knows women,' Garth said with a harsh laugh, 'she'll bleed you dry and move on to the next victim. Don't risk your precious reputation for a tumble in the hay.'

Christopher glanced over his shoulder. 'Sylvia would never do that.'

'You are a fool if you think so.'

'Your cynicism is ill founded.' Christopher reached for the door handle. He knew Sylvia, and she was nothing like the women Garth favoured. Just a few more hours, his business finished, and he would be back in her welcoming arms. 'What is more,' Christopher said. 'I don't give a damn what you or anyone thinks.'

The realisation burst like champagne bubbles in his blood, lifting him to dizzying happiness. He strode out of the room and left Garth to think whatever he pleased.

Sylvia pulled back the rose-coloured damask curtain from the window. The fading daylight revealed only a sky threatening rain, a few passers-by on the pavement beyond the wrought-iron railings and the open common, where a small boy attempted to fly a yellow kite. No sign of Christopher.

With a sigh, she dropped the curtain and strode to the fireplace. A swift tug on the bell brought the butler within moments. She pressed her lips together, quelling the urge to say something cutting about him lurking outside the door.

Since it was Christopher who had earned her wrath, he would hear her opinions, not his instrument. 'Tea, please, Bates.'

'Yes, miss. Cook has prepared an early dinner for you. It is set out in the dining room, if you would care to partake?'

The thought of food nauseated her already churning stomach. Where was Christopher? She wanted to advise him of her decision to leave for Harrogate immediately.

The answer had come to her at dawn. She would not stay here or anywhere else as his mistress, always anticipating her *congé*. She'd steel herself and make the break, right away, before she became accustomed to having him near. No one would ever look for her in a so unfashionably remote northern watering place.

The butler remained in the doorway, awaiting her answer. If her plan was to be successful, she didn't need to faint from lack of nourishment. 'Thank you. Something light would be most welcome.'

She followed him into the dining room. This household's idea of a light repast exceeded expectations. A silver tureen filled the centre of the round walnut table. On the sideboard, several meat pies were set out along with a roast fowl, a large bowl of fruit and an assortment of cheeses and breads. Sparkling silverware on the white linen cloth, adjacent and intimate, waited for two people.

'Are you expecting Mr Evernden?' she asked.

The butler's expression remained wooden. 'The table is always set for two. Lord Stanford's orders, miss.'

She winced, stung by the butler's assumption she was the

same as all the other females who inhabited this house under Lord Stanford's protection. What else would he think, since she had arrived here on Christopher's arm? She clenched her jaw. She had to leave here while she still had a shred of self-esteem.

He pulled out one of the Sheraton chairs. 'Please be seated.'

He filled the bowl in front of her with cream of mushroom soup. The delicate, delicious aroma filled her nostrils. He set a slice of wild pigeon pie on a plate beside it. When she refused his offer of burgundy, he filled her goblet with water.

'Will there be anything else, miss?'

'Just the tea, please.'

He bowed and left her in solitary state.

The soup was delicious, hot and creamy with a peppery tang. Lord Stanford employed an excellent chef for his *filles de joie*. Everything in this house was of the finest quality. He treated his women well. No doubt Christopher would follow his example. Her heart squeezed.

One mouthful of soup and her appetite fled. She poked at the pie with her fork, suddenly indecisive. This elegant existence would be hers with Christopher. A strange twist of fate had brought them together. Perhaps she should not fight it.

But she had always sworn she would not make her mother's mistakes. If only he would offer more. Marriage? How could she ask him to stoop to her level? In the end, he would hate her and abandon her.

No. She had made the right decision. She had to disappear from his life. She would control her own destiny.

But would Christopher let her go right at this moment?

She set the fork down. Her heart ached too much to allow food to pass down her throat.

Behind her, the door opened with a creak.

'Leave the tea on the sideboard. I'll help myself,' she said.

An amused chuckle made her swivel in her seat. 'Lord Stanford.'

Hands raised and a wicked smile on his lips, he bowed. 'Sorry. No tea.'

'I beg your pardon. I thought you were the butler.'

'Really? I told Weston this jacket fit me not at all well.'

She couldn't resist a smile at his barb against one of London's most fashionable tailors.

As lithe as a predator on the hunt, he sauntered to the sideboard and poured himself a glass of red wine. He spoke casually over his shoulder. 'No Kit today?'

'Mr Evernden has not yet returned. He had some business in town.'

A dark eyebrow winged up as he turned to face her. 'Mr Evernden, is it?' The appraising gaze that travelled from the top of her head to her bosom expressed his opinion. Once more, she felt the heat of embarrassment in her face and fought to remain calm.

'I am expecting your brother soon, my lord.'

'Please, call me Garth.'

He slid into the other chair. Beneath the table, his knee touched hers and she jerked away.

His mouth curled in a sardonic smile. 'I expected him to dash straight back here to your welcoming arms last night. I can't think why he would stay in town.'

He was trying to bedevil her for some reason. Beneath his insouciance, he seemed to care about his brother. But did he care enough to try to extract him from an unfortunate alliance? 'He is making arrangements for us.'

'Us?' For once, his face reflected his serious tone of voice. 'Just what sort of arrangements are you expecting, Miss Boisette?'

It took all her self-control not to throw his suspicions back in his face. Instead she curved her lips in a smile. 'Your brother is an honourable man. I am sure he will provide everything I ask.'

'And what will you request?'

She cocked her head to one side, tapping a finger against her lips. His eyes followed the movement. 'A very permanent arrangement, I think.'

His eyes darkened and his brows drew together. 'Christopher is not such a fool.'

This man despised her.

'Your tea, miss.' The butler had entered silently.

Garth rose to his feet, towering over her. 'Miss Boisette will take it in the rose room. And,' he said, leaning close and murmuring into her ear, 'then you will tell me everything.'

This might be her only chance for escape. She rose to her feet and placed a trembling hand on his arm. She allowed him to escort her into the drawing room.

They chatted idly as the butler set the tea tray on the table in front of the sofa. Sylvia kept up a flow of bright chatter, anything to hide the rapid beating of her heart as she prepared to play her role in what she hoped was the final scene.

'No interruptions, Bates,' Garth said.

Her stomach tightened.

The butler bowed and closed the door behind him.

Seated next to her on the sofa, Garth laid one arm along the back. With only a slight tremor in her hand, she poured tea for herself. She recalled the first time she had played this part with Christopher. She hadn't felt nearly so nervous. Despite his sternness, he hadn't frightened her. This man emanated darkness.

Garth twisted the stem of his wineglass in long strong fingers, gazing into the depths of the ruby liquid as if it were a crystal ball. She had never seen him quite so serious.

'Now, Miss Boisette. Tell me your story.'

Sylvia assembled her thoughts. 'I don't know how much Christopher, Mr Evernden, told you about my…my history.'

He sent her a sharp glance. 'He told me enough. I know you

are in some kind of danger from your father, who is not interested in claiming parentage. I also know that you have my brother firmly in your toils.' He hesitated, pausing as if to select his words with care. 'Christopher is not like me, Miss Boisette. He led a sheltered life as a boy. Practically cloistered.' Garth's lips twisted in a mirthless smile. 'He's no fool, but he's always been too softhearted when it comes to a sad story.'

The chill, so recently gone from her heart, spread through her chest. His suspicions wounded far more than she expected. Even this unmitigated rake realised a woman with her past didn't deserve an honourable man like Christopher. He was right.

She took a deep breath and slanted him a glance through her lashes. 'How *much* do you want to rescue your brother?'

A slow, lazy smile curved his lips. His arm dropped from the sofa back and slid around her shoulders. 'How *much* would it cost and what else would I get in return?' He trailed a finger suggestively up her neck, along her jaw and brushed across her lips. His warm breath tickled her ear. A predator on the prowl.

Emptiness engulfed her. Christopher would never forgive her for this piece of work.

She leaned back and turned on a brilliant smile.

Garth drew in a sharp breath.

'One hundred guineas,' she said. 'And you get the satisfaction of knowing your brother is out of my toils.'

The easy, confident smile disappeared. 'I would offer you much more to stay here with me.' He stared at her mouth and leaned forward. His voice thickened. 'Jewels, clothes, whatever you desire.' The scent of his cologne, acid lemon mingled with musty bay, stifled her.

She forced herself not to flee the room. The fine line between coquette and harlot might drive him past the bounds of reason. A man with lust on his mind rarely behaved rationally, as she knew to her cost. Pinpricks raced down her spine.

The teacup her only barrier against his overpowering

presence, she smiled. 'I don't think Mr Evernden would appreciate that.'

He shrugged. 'No, he wouldn't. It would be a pity to waste your talents, however.'

She sipped thoughtfully. 'I prefer not to become a bone of contention between two brothers who seem fond of each other.'

His lips thinned. 'That's awfully kind of you, *mademoiselle*.'

He took the cup from her hand, set it on the table and drew her to her feet. He placed his hands on her shoulders, hot and heavy, a weight almost too great to suffer. She held her ground and stared boldly into his intent, dark eyes.

'Christopher is a good man,' he said. 'Far better than I could ever hope to be. I suspect he'll give you his heart if you want it. Don't trample it in the dirt, if this is only about money.'

How long would she keep his heart before he tired of her? She couldn't bear to find out.

Keeping her voice flat and distant, she selected her words with care. 'Your brother feels obligated to provide for me. Like his uncle, he seeks to secrete me away like an unpleasant truth, to hide my scandalous past in case it besmirches the good name of Evernden. I prefer to go my own way.'

Doubt filled his expression.

Desperate, she played the last card in her hand. 'If you help me, I will disappear from his life. Otherwise, I shall do my utmost to convince him to marry me and I promise you I will lead my life as I see fit. Quiet isolation and discretion are not words in my vocabulary.'

The lines beside his mouth deepened. 'By God, you're a cold-hearted bitch.' A wolfish grin lit his face and he pulled her hard against him, breast to chest. He forced her chin up with his fist. 'I thought you were a scheming little slut when I saw you first. You certainly have Christopher fooled and I almost let him convince me otherwise. But truth will out, Miss Boisette. Your true colours are revealed.'

She allowed a sultry smile to dawn on her lips. 'And will you pay me to haul down my colours?'

He moistened his lips. 'I might be persuaded.'

'I have one request.'

'And that is?'

'That you say nothing about our arrangement to Christopher until I am long gone.'

A chuckle rumbled in his chest and vibrated through her. 'One kiss and you shall have your money and be on your way.'

He lowered his mouth to hers. Lemon and bay, the scent of betrayal.

Bile rose in her throat. She couldn't do it. She couldn't kiss Christopher's brother. She ducked his seeking mouth.

'What the devil is going on?'

They jerked apart.

Shaken, Sylvia turned to face the door and Christopher.

As bright with truth and honour as his brother was dark with deceit, he stared at them. Broad and solid. She wanted to fold herself within his strong arms. She cringed at the hurt in his eyes as he looked from one to the other.

With an awkward laugh, Garth raised his hands in a helpless gesture of appeal. 'Sorry.'

'Damn you, Garth. I'll see you in the study. First I want a word with Miss Boisette.'

Rigid, he glared at Garth, who sauntered out. He turned his smouldering gaze on Sylvia. 'Damn him. He's incorrigible. I'll make him apologise if I have to call him out.'

Mentally, Sylvia winced. 'I—'

'Never mind him now. I'll deal with him.' He strode to her side and took her hand in his, gentle and kind, warm and strong. The creases at the corners of his eyes begged for her touch. Control almost escaped her.

He guided her to sit and rubbed his thumb over her knuckles. Heat trailed from his touch all the way to her core.

Her breasts tightened. She wanted to feel his hands on her body, his lips against her mouth. It was too late.

'Everything is arranged,' he said. 'I will take you to Kent the day after tomorrow.'

It took all her will-power to speak. 'I'm not going to Kent.'

His eyes widened. 'Don't be a fool. If Rafter discovers your whereabouts, he might do more than spirit you away to some ghastly brothel. You really don't have a choice.'

The choice lingered in the study. Her heart ached. 'I have plans of my own.'

His hazel eyes blazed, then his face hardened. 'I won't let you face Rafter or your father alone. Be realistic, Sylvia. You can't do this without help and you're penniless. Or have you forgotten that I have been keeping you for weeks?'

She was stung and heat rose to her cheeks. He'd turned something beautiful into a tawdry exchange of money for human flesh. 'I have the money from the sale of Cliff House.'

'There was no money. It was all mine, along with the gold I paid for you at Madame Gilbert's.'

She sagged into the sofa back, the size of her indebtedness weighing heavy on her shoulders. And she intended to repay him with a lie.

Anger at being forced into a corner sharpened her tongue. 'I will not continue as your dependant. I have my own life to live.'

He scrubbed at the back of his neck. 'Frankly, whether you wish it or not, it is my duty to my uncle to protect you.'

Desperate, she clung hard to her decision. She kept her voice flat and cold. 'Damn your duty, Christopher Evernden.'

When Garth told him what she had done, Christopher would recall this conversation and he would despise her. The thought of parting on such bad terms tore at her soul. Hot prickles burned behind her eyes and clogged the back of her throat.

Swallowing hard, she rose to her feet and, too cowardly to

face him, glanced out of the window at grey clouds scudding across a watery blue sky. 'My mind is made up.' She strode out of the room and dashed up the stairs.

His angry words followed her. 'Damn it, Sylvia. You will be ready to leave two days from now.'

She slammed the door of her room and turned the key.

Christopher clenched his fists. He didn't know who he wanted to strangle first. Sylvia for her stubborn refusal to let him look after her, or Garth.

A picture of Garth with his hands on Sylvia rose up to choke him. Garth had frightened her. That was why she was behaving so strangely. Well, that was one problem he would resolve.

As Christopher entered the study, Garth leaned back in the chair behind his desk and lifted his booted feet on to one corner of the battered oak. He waved his glass towards the decanter in front of him. 'Brandy, Kit?'

'No. And you shouldn't be drinking, either, since you will be driving your curricle back to town tonight.'

Garth grinned. 'I drive better when I'm foxed, sobersides.'

'That's nonsense and don't change the subject. What the deuce were you doing with Sylvia?'

'Ah. The beautiful Miss Boisette.' He raised his glass in a silent salute.

What the hell was the matter with him? He'd always been wild, but never suicidal. 'Well?'

'A momentary lapse, Kit. An aberrant feeling of affection that I don't believe was returned.'

'You don't believe it was returned?' A red haze filled his vision. 'She was fighting you off, you idiot. Are you so foxed you can't tell the difference between one of your whores and a decent woman?'

Garth sneered. 'Are you?'

Garth must be sotted. It was the only possible explanation. Christopher stamped on his urge to smash his brother in the mouth. 'You drunken, lecherous bugger. I'll talk to you when you sober up.'

'You may wait a very long time.'

Unable to contain his fury, Christopher swept Garth's feet off the desk.

Garth lurched forward and spilled his brandy in his lap as his feet hit the floor. He cursed.

Christopher grabbed his coat front and, nose to nose, glared into his brother's sullen eyes. 'I'll only tell you this once. If you get within three feet of Sylvia again, I will call you out and I will kill you.'

Garth knocked Christopher's hands away and staggered to his feet, his lip curled in a snarl. 'You don't have a chance in hell.'

The stupid arrogant bugger. 'Try me.'

Garth's cynical sneer shifted to haughty. For a moment, Christopher thought Garth would take the challenge, then he laughed. The hard-edged sound was as unlike Garth as anything he could imagine. 'Not today, little brother. You have as much on your hands as you can manage.' He slumped back into his seat. He looked as if he wanted to say more.

Christopher scowled. 'Wait here and I will drive you back to London.'

Anxiety gnawing at his gut as he thought about the possibility of Rafter finding Sylvia, he took the stairs two at a time. Damn it, she would go to Kent.

He knocked on her chamber door.

'Who is it?'

Her voice sounded husky and thick. He winced. Was she crying in there? A pang tightened his chest. He was doing this for her own good. 'It's me. Christopher.'

'Go away.'

Not an auspicious response. He stared at the closed door. 'We need to finish our conversation.'

Silence.

He knocked again. 'Garth is an idiot. He is foxed. I am taking him back to town so you need not concern yourself about him any longer.'

'As you wish.' A sort of hopelessness filled her voice.

He wanted to hold her in his arms, comfort her, feel the silk of her hair against his cheek. 'I'll come tomorrow. Be packed and ready to leave.'

'I am not going.'

Christopher rattled the door handle. 'You are being unreasonable.' He eyed the doorframe. He could easily break the lock, if he thought it would do any good. 'Very well. We'll talk tomorrow.'

Besides, he'd have plenty of time on the drive to Kent to convince Sylvia he was right.

The door remained firmly closed and he regarded it with regret. He'd hoped to stay the night, but had he no intention of sleeping on the sofa like an out-of-favour husband. Besides, he needed to ensure Garth got safely back to London and he still had to finalise things with his man of business before he left for an extended stay in the country.

There would be many other nights in their future. But by God, he hated to leave.

On the other side of the door, Sylvia pressed her forehead against the cool wood. It was the closest she could come to Christopher without opening it. She willed herself not to throw the door open, not to fling herself at his feet, not to beg forgiveness.

Swift and light, his tread descended the stairs. She forced herself not to call him back. The sound of male voices in the hall and the sharp click of the front door closing released her from her trance. She would never see him again.

Heavy-hearted, she moved away from the door. The stiff leather pouch in the centre of the bed dinted the blue counterpane. Bates had delivered it while Christopher wrangled with Garth in the study. She picked it up. It weighed heavy on her palm. One hundred guineas—it felt like thirty pieces of silver. Her price for betrayal. Blood money. Somehow, some day, she would repay Lord Stanford every penny. Perhaps that would wash away her guilt.

Dispirited, she turned to the task at hand. She sat down at the delicately inlaid rosewood escritoire. The cold little note she had written lay on its polished surface.

Thank you, it said. Not, I'll die a little every day I don't see your beloved face.

I wish you future happiness, it said. Not, I hope that in some corner of your heart you will always remember me.

Goodbye, it said. Not, I'll miss your touch all the days of my life.

Cordially yours, it said. Not, *Je t'aime, je t'aime, je t'aime.*

Sylvia folded the note precisely, careful to ensure that none of her foolish tears marred its pristine surface. Slowly, lovingly, she wrote his name, *Christopher Evernden.*

Je t'aime, her heart replied.

Resolute, she propped it up against the glass inkwell where he would be sure to see it when he came the next day.

Chapter Sixteen

In the chill blast of the early morning air, Sylvia hugged the cloak she had found in the bedroom wardrobe tighter around her shoulders, then quietly pulled the side door of the town house closed behind her. Bates had left it unbolted just as he promised.

Her quick steps tapped on the flagstones as she made her way past the front of the house to the street. The iron gate, cold under her hand, swung open silently on well-oiled hinges. Grey clouds blushed rosy in the eastern sky. The air smelled of wet grass and the first coal fires of the day.

Also as promised by Bates on behalf of his master, a post-chaise waited at the curb. Sylvia forced herself to concentrate on the future, not the past, and definitely not on Christopher's likely reaction when he returned to find her gone.

Up at the second-storey window, Jeannie's pale face peered through the glass. Sylvia had given Jeannie enough funds to take her to her relatives in Glasgow, promising to send for her once she found a home for them both.

Taking a deep breath, Sylvia climbed into the carriage.

Anticipation hummed in Christopher's veins on his way into Evernden Place. It had taken him all morning to finalise his business; this afternoon he'd kicked his heels in Doctor's

Commons for hours. He couldn't wait to get back to Blackheath and Sylvia. Why the hell had it taken him this long to decide?

He dashed past the butler, who had opened the door for him, and made for the stairs.

'Excuse me, Mr Evernden.'

Christopher swung around, knowing he had a grin on his face and not giving a damn. 'Yes, Merreck?'

'Lady Stanford asked to see you the moment you returned. She is waiting in the drawing room.'

Mother. Damnation. He'd hoped to avoid her. She was not going to be pleased at his decision. His hand strayed to the breast pocket wherein nestled a small velvet-covered box and a special licence. A pang of the old guilt stirred in his chest. He didn't want to be yet another disappointment in her life. What with his father's temper and Garth's dissolute lifestyle, she hadn't had an easy time of it. Surely when she realised this was right for him, she would come around? No matter what anyone thought, he was going to ask Sylvia for her hand in marriage.

At least Garth wouldn't turn his back. Some of his warmth dissipated as he recalled Garth's hands on Sylvia and his mocking comments. He pushed his unease aside. Garth would be surprised to know it was the sight of him mauling Sylvia that had finally tipped the scales. Unable to stand the thought of another man touching her, Christopher had known exactly how to solve the problem.

His grin broadened at the thought of her happiness. God. His happiness too.

Squaring his shoulders, he strode to the drawing room and found Mother reclined on the sofa idly turning the pages of the *Ladies' Magazine*. He raised her hand and pressed a brief kiss to her knuckles. 'Mother. You were looking for me?'

She fluttered her handkerchief and the scent of lavender wafted around him. 'Christopher, darling. Where have you been all day?'

'I had urgent business matters in need of attention.'

'You are taking me to Lady Wallace's tonight, are you not?'

Wallace's rout. Damn. He'd forgotten all about it. 'I'm sorry. Something came up. I have to go out of town.'

She pouted. 'You're becoming just like Garth. You never have time for me any more.'

He grinned. 'Mother, you don't need me to escort you. You always end up abandoning me for one of your many admirers before the end of the evening.'

Her face brightened and her handkerchief stilled. 'I'll send a note around to Angleforth. He's always most obliging.'

'Good grief, Angleforth? He's nothing but a dashed Bond Street beau. And he's becoming far too marked in his attentions.'

'Your language, Christopher, is quite deplorable. The Marquess of Angleforth is one of my oldest and most faithful friends.' A pretty pink suffused her cheeks and Christopher hid his smile.

He dropped into the chair next to her. 'Mother, you do want me to be happy, don't you?'

A surprised expression met his change of topic. 'Of course. I want the best for both of my sons.'

'If I were to become involved with a person you weren't entirely pleased with, would you cast me off?' Coward. He should have said marry.

Wide-eyed, she sat up, her air of languor disappearing. 'Oh, Christopher. What can you mean?'

'You wouldn't, would you?'

Silent for a moment, she stared at him. 'If it's about that female…'

He frowned. 'Mother.'

She sighed and leaned back against the damask cushions. 'You are far too precious for me to deny you my company. But I would strongly advise you to proceed with care. The *ton* is unforgiving. No one knows that as well as I.'

A faraway expression crossed her face and Christopher was not sure what to make of it. She must mean Garth. He didn't want this day spoiled by recriminations about his brother. He would tell her of his own plans later, when it was too late for arguments. He got up. 'I have to go.'

'Think before you act, darling,' she murmured. 'Mistakes remain with you for the rest of your life.'

Half-forgotten memories tugged at his consciousness, bitter words and harsh voices. 'As with you and my father?' The words were out before he thought about them.

A glaze of tears softened her blue eyes and provided the answer. He left her to her regrets and her memories.

When he entered his chamber, he found Reeves laying out his evening wear. Still sour about being left behind on Christopher's last two excursions, the valet went about his duties in heavy silence. Christopher ignored him. His mood was far too high to be pulled down by Reeves's sulks and, as the valet assisted him to dress, he made no attempt to close the breach. He wanted to reach Blackheath for dinner.

Dressed and ready, Christopher claimed his hat from Reeves's outstretched hand.

'Mr Christopher.' Reeves glanced pointedly at his driving coat draped across the bed.

'I don't need it.' Then he softened at the misery etched on Reeves's face. The man couldn't help it. He'd spend most of his employed life worrying about Christopher. They all had since he had suffered one debilitating illness after another as a child. They seemed to forget he now stood six feet in his stocking feet and had gone several rounds with Gentleman Jackson at his boxing saloon.

'I'm not driving my curricle, so I won't need a coat.'

Reeves's expression lightened. 'Yes, sir.' Christopher picked up his discarded jacket, fished out the ring and licence and relocated them into the breast pocket of the one he wore.

Glad to be on his way, he whipped open the door. 'Don't wait up for me.'

He ignored Reeves's huff of disapproval.

Cold, soot-scented rain dampened Sylvia's cheeks and trickled down her neck. She shivered.

A smart town carriage clipped by at a fast pace. The horses' hooves rang on the wet cobbles as the wheels fractured the lamplit puddles and scattered them in showers of yellow diamonds.

Across the street, wrought-iron gates bearing a coat of arms of two fearsome-looking boars on an azure ground guarded the Duke of Huntingdon's mansion. A circular drive beyond the gate allowed for carriages to pull off the street. It was three times as big as the Evernden house on Mount Street.

The decision to confront her father with his crimes had seemed simple enough in Blackheath. Now, with rain running down her face and standing against the railing of the garden in the centre of the square, her feet felt as cold figuratively as they were literally.

She didn't belong here.

She had lost her right to belong anywhere because of the heartless and selfish man who lived in that great house. If she wanted to sleep at night, she needed to tell him what he had done to the woman who had loved him until the day she died.

A heavy weight rapped against her knee reminding her of the pistol she'd filched from Garth's study. Along with a deep breath, it bolstered her courage and before she could talk herself into running away, she darted across the road. A footman, the ducal badge on his navy coat and an expression as blank as the waiting front door, emerged from the gatehouse at her tug on the bell. He pushed back the pedestrian entrance in the huge gates.

Wordlessly, he opened his large black umbrella and

escorted Sylvia to the massive front door. Rain drummed on the taut fabric. Dogs barked somewhere at the back of the house. A *frisson* of fear shimmered in her stomach. If any of them knew who she was, they'd set those dogs on her.

Beneath a lamplit columned portico fine enough to make a Greek god proud, he rang the bell and stepped back smartly.

As she clutched her cloak close to a throat as dry as three-day-old bread, her staccato heartbeat filled her ears. She suddenly felt like the child she'd been the day she had landed on England's shores, insignificant and out of her depth.

The door swung back and a middle-aged butler surveyed her from crown to heels. His expression changed from supercilious to puzzled. 'Yes, miss?'

'Miss Boisette, to see Lord Huntingdon,' she managed with barely a quaver.

'His Grace is not at home.'

Liar. She'd seen him arrive an hour ago.

The great wooden door swung ponderously closed. Sylvia thrust her foot in the gap. Pain shot through her toes, but she held her ground.

The butler peered down, then opened the door enough to allow his large silver-buckled shoe through the gap, ready to crush her foot like an earwig.

Sylvia shoved at the door. Off balance, the butler staggered back.

'It is to the Duke's advantage to see me,' she said.

'I told you. His Grace isn't receiving callers.'

'He'll see me,' she said with icy determination. 'Here's my calling card.' She dropped her mother's locket into his outstretched palm.

Indecision hovered in the butler's expression. Taking advantage of his momentary loss of aplomb, Sylvia pushed her way into the cavernous, circular entrance hall. On the floor, black-and-white marble tiles encircled the Huntingdon coat of arms. A double staircase swept up both sides of the hall to meet at an arched balcony beneath a portrait depicting medieval knights and their ladies.

'Look, miss. You can't just barge in here. His Grace is dining *en famille*. No one can see him.'

A wry smile curved her lips. Who better to join his cosy family evening than his daughter? 'Take him the locket. He'll see me.'

Apparently overborne by her confidence, he gestured to an upright gilt chair against the wall. 'Wait there.'

He disappeared down a corridor.

Either he intended to fetch reinforcements or in a moment or two she would face her father. As the minutes ticked away, Sylvia's tremors turned into earthquakes. Her mind emptied second by second. Each carefully rehearsed word froze beneath the hard lump in her throat, pressed down by the smell of beeswax and old money, as if the weight of every ancestor rested on her chest.

She leaped out of the chair when the butler returned. She was ready to leave.

'Follow me, miss.'

Her heart drummed with such force she felt sure the butler must hear it. She swallowed and nodded.

They traversed the chequerboard marble and entered a dark passageway beneath one of the staircases. She followed him into a small room with a warm fire. He gestured to the sofa in front of it. 'Wait here, miss. His Grace will attend you shortly.'

The overstuffed sofa in front of the hearth looked comfortable, a walnut console stood beside the window holding an assortment of brandy and wine and at the other end of the room sat a huge desk. An untidy pile of newspapers occupied one end of the desk, a pipe rack the other. Behind it stood a glassed-in bookcase. The Duke's private study, his inner sanctum, bared to her curious gaze.

She moved around the room as if by touching its contents she could breathe some life into the vague and shadowy figure from her past. Her father.

Nothing about the room seemed threatening. A couple of pictures of horses and hounds hung on the panelled walls. A portrait of a rather haughty lady with a child on her knee graced the wall above the hearth. The Duchess?

An ordinary study.

Drawn to the warmth of the fire, Sylvia sat down to wait. She touched her throat, stilled, then remembered. She'd given the locket to the butler.

A clock chimed nine somewhere outside. Feet scurried back and forth in the passageway beyond the door, the rattle of dishes indicating the progression of dinner. His Grace apparently intended for her to wait until after dessert.

She slipped her damp cloak from her shoulders and sat back, hands in her lap. Another hour or two in a lifetime of waiting to set eyes on him made little difference.

The door opened. Expectations bowstring tight, Sylvia looked up.

'Well, well. 'Tis a wet night to be out wandering the streets of London, to be sure, colleen.'

Rafter.

Her heart sank and she dragged the pistol from her pocket.

'You better know how to use that,' he said.

'Gone? What do you mean, gone?'

Christopher knew he was shouting at Bates, but he didn't care. The idiot. He had told him categorically that she wasn't to leave the house. Damn it all. Surely she understood the risk?

With so little money, where would she go? He closed his eyes as he imagined her wandering the highways and byways of England. Or worse yet, the streets of London. Why the hell hadn't he told her what he was going to do before he left? Because he hadn't known it himself.

He took a deep breath and got hold of his temper. She wouldn't be alone. She would have taken Jeannie. 'She took her maid, of course.'

'No, sir.'

'Blast.' His mind churning, Christopher sat down on the hall chair. 'Does the maid know where she went?'

'She says not, sir. She's all set to leave for Scotland. I'm to take her to the stage in the morning. His lordship's orders.'

Suspicion stirred in his gut. 'Garth's here?'

'In the study, sir. The young lady left this for you.'

Christopher stared at the small white square of paper. She'd left him another damned note.

He breathed a sigh of relief. Now he would know where she'd gone. 'Why the hell didn't you say so right away?'

He snatched it up and read it through.

Nothing. He felt his jaw tighten. Not a bloody word about where she was going. Just goodbye and good fortune. And thank you. He felt like a flag deprived of breeze, deflated and limp. She hadn't cared for him one jot.

And Garth was here. He narrowed his eyes, remembering the scene he had interrupted. This was Garth's fault. He'd scared her away with his lecherous pawing.

'Send Jeannie to the study,' he said, marching down the hall. For once Garth would pay for his idiocy.

The door crashed against the wall and Garth raised his head slowly. He had that stupid, distant expression of a man in his cups. 'Hello, Kit, old boy. Drink?'

'You lousy, rotten bastard.' Christopher lunged across the room and hauled Garth to his feet by his shirtfront. He raised his fist.

Garth made no move to defend himself. Guilt shadowed his eyes.

'Blackguard,' Christopher said. 'You know where she is.' Disgusted, he shoved him away.

Garth staggered back and landed in the seat. He made a feeble attempt to straighten his cravat. 'I don't. I gave her the money to go.'

Christopher couldn't think or breathe. A cold numbness enveloped him. 'You gave her money?' His stomach crashed to the floor, leaving him nauseous. She'd taken money from Garth. For what? His fists clenched.

A small china bowl on the shelf at eye level filled his vision. He picked it up and flung it at Garth's head.

Garth ducked. The bowl hit the wall with a crash. He brushed the dusting of porcelain shards from his shoulders. 'I never did like that bowl.'

'You gave her money?' Christopher wouldn't believe it. His heart felt like the ornament, shattered in a million pieces. But he had to know. He had to let Garth give him the *coup de grâce*. 'For services rendered, no doubt.'

Garth's expression turned wary. 'No. I paid her to leave you alone. She's a scheming little bitch. She planned to wed you. She as good as admitted she planned to have a fine time at your expense. I wouldn't have believed it if she hadn't told me herself.'

The contents in the pocket over his heart burned a hole in his chest. His throat filled, clogged with a solid lump. He took a long slow breath, blinking away the hot sensation behind his eyes. He hauled in a shaky breath. 'What the hell happened?'

Garth shrugged. 'I asked her how much she wanted to buy her off.'

He had to know. Had to hear it. 'How much was I worth?'

'A hundred guineas.'

The world seemed to stop spinning. He felt empty. He hadn't for a moment thought she wanted money. It didn't make any sense. Hell, he could have bought her off the day after the will was read. He'd been taken for a fool. A short laugh scraped his throat raw. He'd been ready to marry her, a girl from the stews, the daughter of a prostitute, a bastard.

Somehow he'd been bewitched by her beautiful face and luscious body. But by God, he wished Garth hadn't spoiled the dream. It took a moment, but finally he managed to speak. He kept his voice flat. 'You had no right to interfere.'

'Head of the family. Duty and all that.'

'Utter rot.'

They turned towards the opening door.

Jeannie, more bowed than ever, crept into the room. She had a firm grip on the butler's sleeve and a dog-eared paper clutched in her hand.

She glowered at Garth from beneath her bushy brows, then twisted her neck to look up at Christopher, holding out the scrap of parchment. 'She niver told me what she planned to do or I would have given her this.' She twisted her neck to glare up at Bates. 'All right, cully. Tell 'em where she's gone.'

Bates sputtered and pulled his arm out of her clawed fingers.

She wiped her eyes on her sleeve. 'Mr Evernden, I'm that worried about my wee lass.'

Chapter Seventeen

The pistol in Rafter's hand waggled and Sylvia stepped back as a fair-haired man, with distinguished grey at his temples and vivid blue eyes snapping anger, strode into the room. He halted in front of the desk and leaned against it.

This must be the Duke of Huntingdon, her father. An ache spread through her chest, so painful her ribs hurt when she drew breath. Her mother had adored this man. She had died, knowing he didn't care one snap of his fingers for her.

He couldn't be more duke-like. Regal and straight shouldered, his demeanour spoke of privilege and command, but his mottled red complexion warned of a volatile temper or some disorder of the blood. She'd waited all her life to look him in the eye. She took a deep steadying breath.

Rafter tightened his grasp on her arm. She winced.

The Duke swept back his black evening coat and set his hands on his hips. 'What is going on here, Rafter?'

'This woman pushed her way in, demanding to see you, your Grace. Bradford came and got me instead.'

'I heard a shot,' the Duke said.

'Yes, your Grace. She fired at me.'

Trust Rafter to tell only half the story. Sylvia glared at him. 'He grabbed at the gun and it went off.'

The Duke turned his haughty gaze on her. 'When I ask you a question, young woman, you will answer. Until then, be silent.'

Damn his arrogance. This was not the civilised conversation she had envisaged holding with him, the one where she held the gun.

'Your Grace,' Rafter said in dulcet tones, 'allow me to introduce Mademoiselle Sylvia Boisette.'

Sylvia forced herself not to curtsy. Instead, she acknowledged the introduction with a slight nod.

Huntingdon's cheeks turned a darker shade of red. 'Good God. What the hell is she doing here? I am surrounded by incompetence. I thought you said you could handle this problem.'

That was all she was to him, a problem to be swept under the carpet liked so much unwanted dust, or locked in the closet like a skeleton. She shivered. The truth of that thought came closer to reality than she cared to admit. She kept her gaze locked on his face. 'I came here to talk to you.'

The Duke seemed nonplussed. 'Damn it all, Rafter. You told me I'd heard the last of her. How much more will it take to be rid of you?' He curled his lip in distaste. 'Between you and your mother, you'll see me ruined.'

His scornful words and expression gouged into Sylvia's soul like the claws of a raging beast. 'Do you have any idea what my mother suffered when you abandoned her?'

A flash of pain flickered in his eyes, then his expression hardened. 'Give her what she wants, but get rid of her, Rafter. This is the last time I give her money and to hell with the consequences.'

What was he talking about? She'd never asked him for a penny and never would. 'I don't want your money. I want an apology for what you did to me and my mother.'

Scarlet-faced, he jerked his gaze to her. 'Apology?' The word choked him. 'Apologise to a woman who's been bleeding me dry for years? A woman who sells herself to the highest bidder just like her mother did? Never.'

Damn his arrogance. Her mother had given up her pride and her body so this man's child could survive. '*Cochon!* She had no choice because you never came back, you heartless cur.'

'I'm afraid we have another little problem, your Grace,' Rafter said.

Huntingdon stilled. 'What now?'

'This little ladybird has a friend. A Mr Evernden has taken her under his wing.'

Heat branded Sylvia's cheeks. Rafter had turned something beautiful into filth.

Huntingdon shrugged. 'Pay him off. Anything. Surely he'll see reason.' He glowered. 'Warn him of the trouble it could cause for him and his family. God knows I've seen enough of it.'

'Ah, your Grace,' Rafter said, his hoarse voice full of warm congratulation, 'that's the way of it. Threaten them into submission.'

The Duke brushed Rafter's words away with a sharp gesture. 'I don't care what it costs, get her and her false claims out of England. Buy Evernden's silence.'

Outrage boiled in her blood. She hated her father for what he had done to her mother. Now he wanted to do the same to her and make Christopher his accomplice.

She looked longingly at Rafter's weapon, the one he'd pulled from his pocket after hers fired harmlessly into the wall. She wanted to put a bullet in the Duke of Huntingdon so badly she pictured the blood staining the pristine white of his shirtfront. She'd hang to feel the satisfaction it would bring.

Sylvia wrenched her arm from Rafter's grip. Ignoring the pistol aimed at her back, she crossed the thick patterned rug and glared into Huntingdon's face. 'Leave Christopher Evernden out of this game of yours. He has nothing to do with you or my mother. As far as I am concerned, I don't want to remember I have you for a father.'

His blue eyes blazed anger. 'You are no daughter of mine.'

'Liar. Why are you trying so hard to get rid of me, then?'

The Duke recoiled as if struck. 'Don't play me for a fool, my girl.' He lowered his voice. 'Look. I've paid you more than enough to set up your own establishment in Paris, much as the thought disgusts me. You've got what you want. Now go away and leave me in peace.'

Nothing he said made any sense.

Rafter crossed to her side, grinning like some insane Celtic pixie. For once, his usually implacable grey eyes danced with unholy amusement.

'I don't think it's going to be that easy, your Grace.'

The rain had eased into a fine drizzle. Moving swiftly through the garden at the back of Huntingdon's house, Christopher slipped and slid on sodden grass. He cursed the wet creeping up his legs from where he had landed in the shrubbery when he had jumped down from the back wall. He ducked as an ornamental willow slapped wet fingers in his face.

'Bugger,' Garth mumbled.

Christopher glanced behind him.

The light of a wall lantern caught Garth hopping on one foot. Deep barks issued from the back of a building the waft of manure and hay identified as the mews.

'Quiet,' Christopher whispered, wishing he'd made him stay behind. 'They will set the dogs on us.'

They skirted the patch of light spilling out on to the drive and strode up the alley beside the house as if they belonged there. At the side door, Garth grasped Christopher's shoulder. 'What if she's not here? We are going to look like a pair of fools.'

Christopher shook him off. 'Bates said she asked for a carriage to bring her here.' He had no doubts. He knew her only too well. She went after what she wanted with solid determination and she was in danger.

Christopher pulled his pistol from his pocket and pushed the door open.

A footman leaped up from his seat beside the door. 'You can't come in here…' He fell silent at the sight of Christopher's weapon aimed at his chest.

'Tie him up,' Christopher said to Garth.

With the footman's neckcloth as a rope and his handkerchief as a gag, Garth bound the servant to his chair.

'Which way now?' Christopher asked.

Duelling pistol in hand, Garth jerked his head towards the passageway. 'The formal rooms are that way. Lord knows where we'll find the Duke.'

They crept along the hall. A bustling figure, the butler by his dress, almost ran headlong into them. 'What the deuce?'

'Just the man we need.' Christopher pressed his pistol against the man's neck. 'One sound and you are a dead man, understand?'

The butler nodded.

'Where is his Grace?' Christopher muttered.

'In his study with Mr Rafter and a woman,' the butler croaked.

Now they were getting somewhere. He swung the man around and grasped his shoulder. 'Lead the way.'

The door opened unannounced. The butler, framed in the doorway, opened and closed his mouth like a landed carp.

'Get out,' Huntingdon said.

The butler lurched forward.

The room filled with broad shoulders and simmering male rage. Christopher shoved the butler aside and aimed his pistol at Huntingdon's chest. Garth stumbled towards Rafter.

Cold metal, hard and unforgiving, nudged Sylvia's temple.

Garth halted in his tracks.

'As I was saying, your Grace,' Rafter said.

Sylvia caught Christopher's glance in hers. No emerald fire, no smile, just a cool stare. Garth had told him, of course, and now he scorned her. She steeled herself to bear his hatred despite her longing to throw herself at his feet, tell him what she had said to Garth wasn't true. She must not. For his sake. She held her head high.

'Who the devil are you? And what are you doing in my house?' the Duke asked.

Garth flashed a charming smile and bowed with courtly grace as if this were some chance meeting in the park, or a morning call. 'Stanford, at your service, your Grace. We met at Lady Elphinstone's last month, you might recall. This is my brother, Christopher Evernden.' He raised an eyebrow at Rafter. 'I don't believe we've met.'

Rafter gave him a sharp nod. 'Seamus Rafter.'

Sylvia blinked as Garth swayed on his feet. Good heavens, he was his usual three sheets to the wind.

Stunned silence filled the room while the men took stock of each other. The fire popped. Everyone jumped except Rafter.

The Duke scrubbed a hand over his chin. 'Will someone tell me why you are invading my house?'

'I should have thought that was obvious, your Grace,' Christopher said. 'We are here to make sure no *more* harm comes to Miss Boisette.'

The protective words and the anger in his voice draped Sylvia like a warm blanket for all his impassive expression. He should not have come here, but even so her heart swelled with joy.

Then, at the thought of what could happen to him as a result, her mouth dried. 'Thank you, Mr Evernden, Lord Stanford, but I believe the Duke and I were about to come to a mutually satisfactory arrangement.'

Christopher's gaze flicked to Garth. 'Another one?'

Heat scalded her face. She couldn't blame him for his

thoughts. The rage she glimpsed in his eyes seemed to twist the knife that resided in her chest. Clearly she'd burned her bridges.

Turning to Huntingdon, she forced herself to continue. 'Mr Evernden is an innocent bystander caught in your web. Let him go.'

Rafter chuckled. 'Too bad he didn't think of that earlier. Now, if you don't want the young lady dead at your feet, you *gentlemen* will drop your weapons.'

Christopher cursed and let his pistol fall.

Rafter narrowed his gaze on Garth. 'And you.'

Garth tossed his on the sofa. 'Now what, Kit?'

Everyone swung around as the door opened and a fresh-faced youth of about thirteen strolled in. His brilliant blue eyes immediately settled on Huntingdon. 'Are you coming, Father? I have set the chess board up in the library.' His voice faltered as he caught sight of Rafter's pistol. 'What is it, Papa? Who are these men? Shall I call the footmen?'

'Welcome to the play, Lord Basingstoke,' Rafter said with a grin. 'It's the final act.'

The lad frowned. 'Rafter, what is going on?'

'Allow me to do the introductions,' Garth cut in.

Sylvia gaped at him. He was definitely in his cups.

'This is your half-sister, Sylvia.' Garth nodded at the others as he went round the room. 'Mr Rafter you know. Behind your father is my brother, Christopher Evernden, and I am Stanford. Sylvia, this is your brother, David Woods, the Earl of Basingstoke. Oh, and shrinking in the corner over there is your butler.' He grinned with obvious delight at his own humor.

'Stow it, Garth,' Christopher muttered.

The young earl frowned at Sylvia. 'I don't have a sister.'

'Oh, but indeed you do, my lord,' Rafter said with smug satisfaction.

'Silence, Rafter,' Huntingdon roared. 'I'll not have my

personal business bandied about in this fashion.' He pulled at his cravat, his complexion heightened with a nasty purple tinge.

Sylvia pulled her arm free of Rafter's hand. She didn't want to do this any more. Too many people had become involved in this confrontation with her father. 'There is nothing more to discuss. Give me your word you will not follow me and nothing spoken of tonight will leave this room.'

'You think I can trust a blackmailer?' the Duke asked.

'I don't understand,' the young Basingstoke said.

'You are right, David,' Huntingdon said. 'You don't understand. She's not your sister, no matter what she says. Please leave this to me to sort out.'

'No one is going anywhere,' Rafter said, menace clinging to him like creeping sea fog. He shifted his weapon's aim to the boy. The lad's jaw dropped as Rafter continued. 'It's time your son knows what kind of a bastard you really are, your Grace. Or is it the other way around?'

Clearly distressed, Sylvia rubbed at her temple.

There was a red mark where Rafter had dug the metal barrel against her delicate skin. Christopher wanted to ram the pistol down Rafter's throat and make him swallow it.

'No,' the Duke's voice choked out in a whisper. He clutched at his chest, pushed Rafter aside and collapsed on the sofa.

David crouched beside his father, fingers fumbling at his neckcloth.

Garth stiffened to attention, his wide-eyed gaze fixed on Rafter. 'Dear God, no.'

Rafter's chilling laugh rippled around the room. He drew himself up straight, like a soldier on parade, and glanced in contempt at the Duke's anguished expression. 'It's time, your Grace.'

Sylvia knelt at Huntingdon's side and chafed his hands. 'Stop talking riddles. Someone send for a doctor. This man needs medical attention.'

Christopher couldn't believe it. She should be strangling Huntingdon, not helping him. He deserved to die.

Garth went to the console by the window and poured a snifter of brandy. He returned and handed it to Sylvia. 'Give him this.'

Sylvia coaxed the glass into Huntingdon's hand and guided the glass to his mouth. He took a swallow and gradually his colour reduced and his breathing became less ragged.

'Look out,' Garth cried.

Out of the corner of his eye, Christopher caught Rafter's swift movement. Too late. Rafter pressed the muzzle of his gun against the boy's neck while Garth stared at the lad as if he'd seen a ghost.

'Papa!' The boy's voice cracked with panic.

Christopher started forward, then stopped. Rafter would pull the trigger before he could knock the gun away.

'Let him go,' the Duke gasped. 'He's an innocent.'

Rafter shook his head. 'Wrong. He needs to know. Either you tell him the truth or he dies.'

'What truth?' Huntingdon asked.

'The truth about her mother,' Rafter said, malicious glee on his face.

Twin spots of colour stained Sylvia's cheeks. Her obvious distress sliced Christopher's heart. There was no need for this cruelty. 'The game is up, Rafter. If harm comes to Miss Boisette, I'll make sure you both pay.'

'It's not Miss Boisette, is it, your Grace?' Rafter tightened his finger on the trigger.

'Don't hurt my son.'

'It's all up to you.'

'You'll ruin us all,' Huntingdon whispered.

'You've run out of time,' Rafter said.

'All right. All right. Damn you. So I was married to her mother. It doesn't make any difference.'

Christopher glanced at Sylvia. Her expression was full of disbelief and shock and desperate hope.

A rush of gladness filled his veins.

'She's not my daughter.' The Duke's voice rose in a desperate plea. 'Tell them, Rafter. She's De Foucheville's.' His expression filled with anguish. 'God damn him for a whoring bastard and Marguerite for going to him.'

'It doesn't matter who sired her,' Christopher said. 'If you were married to her mother, she's your child.'

'Without a doubt,' Garth muttered.

What the hell had got into Garth? Christopher gave him a hard stare that told him to keep silent.

'For God's sake, Rafter,' Huntingdon pleaded, 'think what you are doing.'

Rafter sneered at Sylvia. 'You'd never believe it to look at him now, but your father and the Vicomte De Foucheville risked their lives for months, helping other aristos like them to leave France during the Terrors. Proper hero, he was.'

'Dear God,' Huntingdon said in a hoarse whisper, tears standing in his eyes as he stared into the past. 'De Foucheville got the poor sods out of Paris, then I took them to the coast and waiting fishing boats.'

'Then the Jacobins turned into rabid dogs,' Rafter said with a smirk. 'The Ambassador insisted that all the English leave. Your father had just arrived from the coast and sent me to collect your mother, while he reported in at the Embassy.'

The Duke bowed his head. 'It was hell. Women and children begging us to take them. We had to leave so many behind. It wasn't until we were on board that I discovered Marguerite missing.' He glared at Rafter. 'If I had known she hadn't boarded with the rest of the women, I would have gone back for her. I begged the captain to turn around. Later, when he returned to England, Rafter told me she had preferred to stay with De Foucheville.'

Huntingdon raised his head, his expression filled with dark hatred. 'Damn him. I thought he was my friend. And Marguerite. I never thought she'd betray me. Curse the pair of them.'

'No,' Sylvia said, standing up. 'De Foucheville was my mother's friend, nothing more. He tried to help her escape to England. He was arrested before he could get her out of Paris. Someone betrayed him.'

Rafter grinned. 'That would be me.'

The Duke swallowed. 'You said she was his mistress. That she was expecting his child. I loved her. I would have taken her, child or no, but you said she refused to come.'

'That I did, your Grace,' Rafter said. 'And I told her that you regretted marrying her and didn't want her any more.' Rafter shook his head. 'De Foucheville almost got her out and spoilt my plans. I had to turn him in.'

The Duke lunged at Rafter, halting only when Rafter tightened his grip on the boy. 'You betrayed De Foucheville?' He swore. 'Half the *émigrés* in England owe their lives to him.'

'Believe me, I regretted his death. I admired his courage. He had to die.'

'Because he got my wife with child? I never wanted that.'

'You fool.' Rafter pointed at Sylvia. 'Look at her. De Foucheville was as dark as a blackamoor. She's fair like her mother and you. She has your eyes. De Foucheville never touched Marguerite. He was your loyal friend to the last breath of his life. She is the child of your loins.'

Christopher's mind reeled. Rafter was like a puppet-master, manipulating lives for some dark purpose of his own.

A tentative smile on his lips, David glanced from his father to Sylvia. 'She's my sister?'

'Aye, spalpeen,' Rafter said with a firm nod, the boy tight to his side. 'That she is. Your father's legitimate child, born in wedlock. Just as he's always known.'

'Oh, God,' the Duke said, his eyes wild. 'What have I

done? I never meant them any harm. I believed Rafter.' He looked at the disapproving faces surrounding him, his eyes desperate and pleading. 'There's no proof of any of this.'

Christopher clenched his jaw at the sight of Sylvia's wounded expression. Damn him for being so stiff-necked.

'There's a room full of people who have just heard you admit you married her mother, Huntingdon.' Christopher couldn't bring himself to honour the man with his title. He pulled the document from his breast pocket. 'And this, I believe, is the missing proof.' Garth looked over his shoulder as he unfolded the note Jeannie had given him. The writing was blurred, but it had the signature of a Protestant cleric and the avowal that William Woods had married one Marguerite Seaton.

'But why the last name Boisette?' Garth asked.

'To hide her from the Jacobites,' Rafter said. 'Basingstoke, as he was then, was well known to the authorities.'

'Boisette,' Garth said. 'Little forest. A clumsy play on words, I presume.'

Sylvia pressed her hand to her mouth. 'It is the name my mother used in Paris.'

The Duke groaned. 'Madame Gilbert has been milking me dry for years with that document. Then *she* started sending letters.' He nodded at Sylvia.

Sylvia gasped. 'I did no such thing.'

'They are all there in that drawer.' Huntingdon jerked his chin at the desk. 'She wanted a king's ransom to set up a brothel in Paris, to follow in her mother's footsteps.'

'No,' Sylvia cried out.

'Ah, your Grace,' Rafter put in, 'did ye never wonder how your trusted Irish factotum managed to buy a grand estate in Ireland and raise the best horseflesh this side of Arabia?'

'What?'

'It was never your wife or your daughter. 'Twas me that

had most of your money once Evernden's uncle took the girl from Paris.'

'Papa, I don't understand.' David's eyes grew round. 'If she is my sister, why doesn't she live with us?'

'He just doesn't understand,' Garth murmured in Christopher's ear.

'Understand what?'

A wry smile twisted Garth's mouth.

'The reason is, my young buck,' Rafter said, 'if anyone ever learned the truth, there would be no heir and possibly no dukedom either. Right, your Grace?'

Bloody hell. Christopher had been so busy thinking about what all this meant for Sylvia, it hadn't dawned on him that if the Duke's second marriage was bigamous, therefore not valid, Sylvia became a legitimate daughter, and young David became a bastard, leaving the Duke with no heir at all. His revelation must have shown on his face.

'Exactly,' Garth said.

What the hell was wrong with Garth? He looked green about the gills. Any moment now, he would cast up his accounts. Christopher had never seen him look so strange.

Christopher concentrated on Rafter. Somehow they were going to have to put him out of action and Garth didn't look as if he'd be much help.

Rafter puffed with pride as the Duke crumbled into the sofa cushions, suddenly spineless. Huntingdon buried his face in his hands.

For some dire purpose, Rafter had deliberately set out to destroy the Duke, inch by painful inch.

Desperation ravaging his face, Huntingdon looked up at his tormentor. 'Don't do this, please.'

Rafter moved so he could look directly down into Huntingdon's eyes. 'I planned to reveal all this when your daughter was back in the brothel, a *bona fide* whore, used by every man in Paris. Unfortunately, the Right Honourable high-and-mighty Mr Evernden here has been nothing but a thorn in my flesh. Still, he did the job just as well as any other client of Madame Gilbert's, didn't you, mate?'

Christopher swore violently, but repressed the desire to smash his fist into Rafter's smiling face. He couldn't risk the life of the youth glued to Rafter's side. Christopher wouldn't let another innocent be harmed by this madman.

Forcing David to bend with him, Rafter thrust his face into the Duke's. 'How does it feel? Your wife died of the pox, your daughter is a whore and your son is a disinherited bastard.'

David gasped.

The Duke groaned. 'Why did you do this to me? First my wife and now my son. You've taken everything.'

'Why?' Rafter howled with glee. 'The sins of the father shall be visited upon the children. I did to you what your father did to me and mine.'

Sylvia sank to her knees and grasped Huntingdon's hand. She inched nearer to Rafter. Christopher frowned. What the hell was she doing so close to the lunatic? Her eyes brightened, she peeped from under her lashes at the pistol, then sent a quick glance at Christopher. Tension radiated from her body. He felt its vibration in his own.

Bloody hell. She was going to knock the man over or do something equally rash. But what other choice did they have? He tensed, ready to spring and gave her a slight nod of acknowledgement. He was ready.

Sylvia threw herself up and back and knocked the pistol away from David. Christopher snatched the gun out of Rafter's hand.

The Irishman backed away and raised his hands. 'Do your worst, Evernden. I've done mine.'

Eyes full of pain, Sylvia stared down at Huntingdon as he hugged his son close to his chest, his shoulders shaking with suppressed sobs. Anguish formed a shield around her stiff body and Christopher feared she might shatter if he spoke one word.

He reached out and touched her arm. She thrust his hand away, her eyes glittering bright. 'I don't care about all this.' She swung her arm wide. 'I hate you. I always have. Keep your precious heir. I'll not tell anyone the truth. I'm leaving.'

Plain Mr David No-Name, with set jaw and tears drying on his downless cheeks, pulled himself out of his father's arms. 'It doesn't work that way, my lady.'

Chapter Eighteen

A glimmer of hope lifted Huntingdon's expression. 'If that is what she wants, perhaps it is for the best. No one regrets what happened more than I, but to ruin so many lives… Think of your mother, son.'

David's young face flushed. 'Think of the dishonour.'

Huntingdon's tongue flickered over his lips and he glanced at Sylvia. 'I never meant Marguerite or her daughter any harm. I truly loved her. When Rafter told me you wanted to be a courtesan like your mother, I let anger rule my head. I was wrong. I promise to do my duty by you.'

Pain filled Sylvia's eyes; it cut into Christopher like a whip.

Hades. What a dilemma. In one fell blow the Duke had lost his heir, his whole future, but for the man to let his own daughter sacrifice herself was pitiful. He wanted to take Huntingdon by the throat and force him to apologise.

He clenched his fists at his sides. Sylvia had made it clear she would not welcome his interference.

David drew himself up straight, his child's face mirroring his father's earlier haughty expression. 'No, Father. You taught me better. I will not dishonour my name…' he swallowed '…your name, by adding further crimes to Rafter's misdeeds against my half-sister. She has her place and I have mine.'

'Well said,' Christopher murmured.

At Christopher's side, Garth looked as sick as a horse. 'The devil is in it now,' he muttered. 'Such bloody nobility and he's no more than a stripling. I'm going to lose my dinner.'

'The boy is right, your Grace,' Christopher said, his tone impartial. 'No matter how you try, you can never keep this hidden.'

'I'll make sure of it,' Rafter gloated.

'Silence,' Huntingdon and Christopher said in unison.

Sylvia frowned at Rafter. 'Why are you doing this now? You've made your fortune in blackmail.'

Rafter dropped on to the sofa across from Huntingdon, his weather-beaten face arrogant and insolent. 'Because the old duke forced all the tenants off his land in Ireland, so he could raise fecking sheep.' He curled his lip. 'My family lived on that fine estate, but I wanted more and went off for a soldier. When I came back, cock o' the walk at having made me way up through the ranks, the jingle of gold in me pocket, they were gone.'

His hands curled into fists on his knees, the sinews in his wrists corded tight. 'Not even the foundation of the old house remained to show where they had lived for generations, working the land for the betterment of Huntingdons. Nothing but grass and sheep.'

Seemingly unable to bear to look at the Duke any more, he gazed into the flames in the hearth. His voice dropped to a roughened whisper. 'Oh, I found them in Dublin, all right. Me da was dead of a broken heart. Me mother lay dying in a stinking hovel on the charity of her relatives and me little sister was selling her body for pennies.'

He drew a shaking hand across his eyes. 'That's why.'

Nothing but the ticking clock and the hiss of the fire filled the silence.

As angry as Christopher felt at Rafter's use of Sylvia to gain revenge, he couldn't prevent a surge of pity for the fellow's agony. Sylvia's eyes reflected a similar sympathy. Of all people, she should not feel sympathy.

'I knew nothing of this,' Huntingdon said, his voice hoarse. 'My father did it without my knowledge.'

Turning, Rafter straightened and arrowed a glance at the Duke. 'It was your obligation to know what happened to your people. Just as it was your responsibility to protect your wife and child. But ye left it to someone else. And it was not done.'

Huntingdon wrung his papery hands. 'If you had just told me—'

'You dashed off to France like the divil was after you. And he was.' He gave a sharp laugh. 'I'm satisfied. You'll get no more heirs off your old duchess, even if you marry her now, and your whore of a daughter is restored to the family, while your son wallows in bastardy.'

Garth drew in a sharp breath. He looked like he'd been cut to the quick.

But something about the story did not make sense. Christopher racked his brain for an elusive memory somewhere on the fringes of his mind. Slouched in his seat, Rafter's eyes shifted from Christopher's direct gaze.

Drawing herself to her full height, Sylvia fixed Rafter with a haughty stare, so like her half-brother's just moments before Christopher couldn't doubt their relationship. 'I won't be party to this revenge of yours.'

'You don't actually have a choice,' Garth muttered. 'Whether you like it or not, his second marriage is bigamous.' His mouth twisted in a bitter smile. 'Under the law, a man has to recognise another man's child born to his wife. Your half-brother has no claim to the dukedom. There is no heir.'

Young David stood unflinching beneath Garth's harsh words and stared his fate bravely in the face. Christopher could only admire his courage.

Sylvia reached out a hand to the lad. 'You've been bred and trained for this all your life. Surely something can be done?'

How could she be so selfless? She was the legitimate daughter of a duke, entitled to all of the privileges and rights that went with it. A cold fist bunched in Christopher's stomach as he realised the full implications of her new status. She was so high above him, so close to royalty, he normally wouldn't even be invited to the same functions, let alone be permitted to marry her.

A black pit opened up in front of him.

He shook the thought away. This was not about him, or Sylvia, this was about truth and justice. And by God, he would see justice done.

Rafter shifted on the sofa. His gaze devoured the duke's son as if the destruction of the boy satisfied some primal hunger. At thirteen, the innocent youth didn't fully comprehend the face of evil.

Whereas Sylvia had never had the chance to be truly innocent. Rafter and the Duke had seen to that. Christopher tasted ashes in his mouth. David was roughly the same age now as Sylvia had been when John Evernden had rescued her from a horrific future in the brothel.

The recollection clicked into place like tumblers in a well-oiled lock. 'What was the date of your mother's death, Lady Sylvia?' Christopher asked.

Rafter jerked in his seat.

Sylvia stared at Christopher as if he was mad. She blinked and shook her head as if trying to make sense of his question.

Christopher raised his voice. 'When did she die?'

'What does it matter?' Rafter shouted. 'Die she did. In the pain and agony of the pox. A whore.'

Sylvia recoiled, her face as white as parchment.

'Shut him up,' Christopher said savagely to Garth.

Garth, foiling Rafter's attempts to bite him, shoved his handkerchief in the Irishman's mouth.

The Duke, slumped in the chair, his skin as grey as the ashes in the hearth, raised his head. 'I heard from Rafter that she died in March 1805. I had married again the previous February, thinking she must be dead by then. I had heard nothing for years. My God. My poor Marguerite. I never wanted that for her. Never.' He covered his face with his hands. 'When Rafter brought the news that the marriage was invalid, I didn't know what to do. Cover it up, Rafter said. No one would know. I... When she—' he pointed at Sylvia '—started to blackmail me, I thought it served her right.'

Christopher kept his voice calm. 'Sylvia, think. This is important. Jeannie told us the date of your mother's death. It was three months after you left Paris. When was that?'

'I arrived in England in—'

Rafter struggled to his feet and threw himself at Sylvia.

Without thinking, Christopher shielded her with his back. He lifted her out of Rafter's path by her shoulders. Her sweet body pressed against his chest. Her rapidly beating heart matched the banging of his own. She softened, her warmth pulled to him, her lips curved in a smile as she glanced up at him. He forced himself to pretend it wasn't happening, this instant arousal between them.

Garth seized Rafter by the throat and flung him back on to the sofa.

Christopher set Sylvia down at arm's length, ignoring the overwhelming desire to hold her close, to shelter her from this room of raging storms. He locked her sapphire gaze with his. 'When?'

Comprehension sparked in her expression. 'It was the winter of 1804—January, I think.'

'Then she died before my parents were married,' David cried. Face flushed red, he leapt at Rafter, fists flying. 'You lied.'

Garth restrained David in a gentle hold. 'Relax, lad. He'll get his dues soon enough.'

The relief flooding Huntingdon's face told Christopher all he needed to know. Christopher rejoiced in Sylvia's good fortune, even as his own situation solidified with all the ugly twists of a churchyard gargoyle.

The legitimate daughter of a duke, an heiress, a beautiful, desirable woman with her pick of the most eligible bachelors of the *ton*, would never choose the second son of a baron. Nor would he expect it. Loss emptied his chest and left a hollow space.

He'd have to admit to ruining her and do the honourable thing and ask for her hand. For one blissful moment, he imagined Huntingdon accepting his offer, then despair rolled over him. If Huntingdon didn't laugh in his face, the old Duke would probably challenge him to a duel.

All he had ever offered her was a *carte blanche*. And now, right after he learned she was legitimate, he was going to offer her marriage. How bloody ironic. She'd never believe he'd already decided he didn't care about the misfortune of her birth. Not now.

He straightened his shoulders. No matter what, he'd do his duty.

'A Mr Christopher Evernden to see you, your Grace,' announced the Huntingdon butler.

Christopher. At last. After four long weeks since they'd seen each other, Sylvia couldn't prevent a smile from curving her lips or the rush of pleasure at the sound of his name. She threw her embroidery to one side and surged to her feet.

She caught the Duchess's raised eyebrows and subsided onto the sofa. Lady Huntingdon, with her tight bun and unusually severe style of dress for a member of the *ton*, had proved to be a welcoming angel to her long-lost stepdaughter.

The Duchess had accepted Huntingdon's explanation about his daughter's sudden emergence from an isolated convent in the French Alps. There had been stranger tales of lost family members during the French Revolution and the wars that followed.

The Duchess had thrown herself into the business of bringing Sylvia out with an energy that seemed to surprise even the Duke. Sylvia had begun to love her stepmother and she adored her half-brother, David. She'd even learned to forgive her father as she learned of the lengths to which Rafter had gone to destroy his belief in her mother.

Christopher paused in the doorway, his gaze sweeping the room and meeting hers. His forest-green eyes contained the haunted quality of a lonely mountain glen, all dark shadows. Had he missed her as much as she had missed him?

Not a hair out of place and his black coat and white cravat impeccably neat, he looked paler than when she had seen him last, thin and hollow-cheeked. She recognised his expression, reserved caution, the way it had been at the reading of Monsieur Jean's will. But she had seen the other side of him since then—anger, recklessness, passion, tenderness. All the things she had grown to love in him.

Christopher bowed low. 'Your Grace. Lady Sylvia.'

In the weeks since Rafter had made his dreadful revelations, this was the first time Christopher had called. She smiled and held out her hand. 'How lovely to see you, Mr Evernden.'

He took it. His touch was fleeting, hesitant. 'I'm glad to find you well, Lady Sylvia.'

'All the better for seeing you,' Sylvia said.

Christopher glanced at the Duchess, who watched him with bright, expectant eyes in her severe countenance. 'I wonder if I might ask Lady Sylvia to take a turn around the square with me, your Grace?'

She inclined her head. 'Of course, Mr Evernden. One of the footmen will accompany you.'

Sylvia tamped down her impatience. This need for constant

attendance sparked her impatience at regular intervals, but she tried to accept it with good grace.

Her heart fluttered with anticipation. How clever of Christopher to think of it. Walking with a footman a few steps behind would give them more privacy than her stepmother's drawing room and she had so much to tell him.

She hastened to her chamber to fetch her shawl and hat. By the time she got downstairs, Christopher held his hat and gloves in his hand.

He placed her hand on his arm and they stepped out into the street and crossed the road to the small deserted park in the centre of the elegant square. Sylvia glanced up at the grey sky. No doubt the intermittent rain had kept the nursemaids and governesses indoors today.

Silently, they strolled beneath the overhanging branches and between the flowerbeds full of daisies and roses.

Sylvia revelled in Christopher's closeness, the heat of his body at her side, the firm strength of his arm beneath her fingers, and yet she sensed a distance in him.

'I'm so glad you came today,' she said. 'So much has happened these past few weeks. My head is spinning. You can't imagine. I have been introduced to so many people I can't remember them all.' She laughed. 'To tell you the truth, I am not sure if I am on my head or my heels, but I missed you.'

'I didn't get back into town until yesterday. I came as soon as I received your note.'

Disapproval coloured his tone, as if sending him a note were somehow improper.

'I met Lord Stanford at Almack's and he mentioned you would be back this week. I wanted to talk to you.'

'Well, here I am.'

There was brusqueness in his tone, a subtle impatience she had never heard before.

She stopped and turned, staring into his eyes, trying to see behind the greens and browns gazing back at her. 'What is wrong?'

His expression remained polite, formal, as if they were strangers. 'Nothing is wrong. I just didn't expect to receive a note requiring my presence, that is all.'

A dreadful sense of impending doom ran like a cold snake down the back of her neck and into her stomach. 'If I hadn't sent you a note, would you have come to see me at all?'

He shrugged and gestured that they should continue walking. He matched his steps to hers.

Fear sharpened her tone. 'Would you?'

'Lady Sylvia, I am sure you have realised by now that you are far above my touch. You are moving in circles to which I could never aspire.' He paused as if he were searching for words.

She glanced up at him from beneath the brim of her hat. His gaze was fixed on the distance, his mouth a thin straight line. 'I think it would be better if you do not contact me again.'

Her breath caught in her throat. It was as if someone had placed something heavy on her chest, a rock, or a mountain. Hot tears choked her throat. No wonder he hadn't been to see her. Here she was, assuming she was respectable enough for him at last, when all the time he wanted nothing to do with her.

Fool. He had never spoken of love. He had wanted her and she had given herself to him with all the abandon of a whore. He was telling her he had had his fill. And now, just like her mother, she would humble herself before him because she couldn't help it. Because she loved him. 'Why?'

At the centre of the park, four wrought-iron benches sat in military square formation. In front of them, an ornamental fountain played gentle water-tunes to a pool of reeds and water lilies.

'Please be seated, Lady Sylvia,' he said.

Boiling temper erupted from deep inside her. Rage at her own foolish heart. Anger at her belief in him and at his coldness when she needed his warmth. She plumped down on to the seat and glared up at him. 'Lady Sylvia this and Lady Sylvia that. Are you so impressed with titles then, Mr Evernden? And is it still not good enough for you? Or is it because you know the truth about my mother?'

A flash of pain glittered like splintered glass in his eyes. He glanced away. 'You are talking nonsense.' His tone was harsh. 'My business demands a great deal of my time. In fact, I do not know how much longer I will be in England, since I have business interests abroad.'

A muscle flickered in his jaw, then he lowered himself to sit beside her. He flicked at a speck of dust on his boot with his glove. 'Your father has great plans for you, Lady Sylvia. He has an opportunity to make up for all the years he lost because of Rafter and his schemes. You should be happy.' His words were rational, his tone gentle, persuasive and patently false.

Aware of the rapid beating of her heart, Sylvia took slow, deep breaths. She'd controlled this pain before, this urge to cry hot tears. She'd been hurt many times by careless cruelty. But not like this, her heart cried.

He didn't love her.

It wasn't a mountain on her chest, squeezing out every bit of hope and joy she'd ever known, it was a whole continent.

She kept her gaze fixed on the footman, who gazed with blank concentration at a nearby rhododendron bush. Hands behind his back, he rocked on his heels and kept a wary eye on them. But for his presence, Sylvia might have thrown herself at Christopher, kissed him and taunted him to tell her that he didn't want her. It had worked last time.

She felt her need for him with every fibre of her being each time he glanced her way. Like the yearning note of a violin, it thrummed sensuously in the air between them, calling. Sickened by her weakness, she turned her face away.

'And what about you, Mr Evernden? Are you happy?'

'Of course.'

Two of the smallest words in the world, they were rapier-sharp and accurate in the precision with which he used them.

Anger, fear and pain all disappeared at their cruel incision.

An icy calm filled her. A cold emptiness chilled her blood, her limbs and her sliced-to-ribbons heart. She had too much pride to let him see the effect of his carefully delivered *coup de grâce*.

She schooled her face into calm indifference. 'Thank you for coming to visit me today, Mr Evernden.' She rose to her feet. 'I appreciate you taking the time, since you obviously have so many more important matters demanding your attention. Now, if you will excuse me, I believe I have an imminent appointment with the *modiste*.'

Careful to avoid allowing her skirts to brush against any part of him and with a bare nod in his direction, she swept past him and strolled home, a home as meaningless as a prison.

Sylvia craned her neck to see around the gentlemen who hemmed her into the corner of Lady Dunfield's glittering ballroom. She had hoped Christopher would attend this last major ball of London's Season before everyone departed for the summer. It was two in the morning and no sign of him yet. Why would tonight be any different? She hadn't seen him once in all these weeks since he'd called on her.

She had no pride left, she realised sadly. Each morning she got up, hoping that today she would see him, and that his eyes would reveal his feelings and prove her heart wasn't broken, even if his lips would not speak the words. That, in spite of what he had said, in his heart he loved her.

Each night, she went to bed and cried into her pillow. Before she had met Christopher Evernden, she had never cried. She dragged her mind from the memory of his beloved face to the eager young fop murmuring in her ear.

'Allow me to fetch you some lemonade, Lady Sylvia,' Colonel Nettle said.

Sylvia nodded, squinting against the dazzle of diamonds and staring past the flurry of pinks and lemons and whites of the débutantes swirling on the arms of their black-coated escorts in the last waltz of the night.

Lord Banbury on her left said something and Sylvia nodded absently as Lord Stanford, a full head taller than most of the men around him, threaded his way around the room. It wasn't so much that others blocked his path, he just seemed to be taking a highly circuitous route. The reason became clear as he hauled on the shoulder of a footman carrying a tray of drinks and nearly pulled the man over. Stanford was a positive drunkard and nothing like his brother.

She wanted to go home.

'Will you, Lady Sylvia?' Lord Banbury sounded insistent.

'Yes,' she said to be rid of him.

'Wonderful. I will call for you tomorrow at half-past four.'

Sylvia turned her full attention to the pimply Viscount. He was at least twenty-five, but from her observation of him at the dizzying number of balls and routs she had attended these past few weeks, he behaved more like an emerging adolescent. 'What?'

He pouted. 'You weren't listening. But you said you'd come. I'm driving you to the park tomorrow. You said yes.'

Sylvia took pity on him. It wasn't his fault he wasn't Christopher, that he didn't have hazel eyes with emerald fire in their depths or an intellect like a steel trap. 'Of course. But you will have to excuse me, I need to speak to my mother.'

'You lucky dog, Banbury,' Marchant said, a wisp of a man who had stepped on her toes twice during the cotillion. 'The Snow Queen never drives with anyone. She won't even waltz. We should try to distract her more often.'

A ripple of male ridicule lapped against her back at

Banbury's discomfort. God, they were such a shallow lot. Sylvia walked towards her stepmother as swiftly as she could in her slender-fitting blue silk ballgown and matching slippers.

Broad shoulders collided with her and their owner turned to apologise.

'Good evening, my lady.'

Garth. *Merde.* She didn't want to speak to him. 'Excuse me, Lord Stanford,' she said and glided away.

He kept pace with her. 'Still the same cold-hearted bitch, I see,' he said low in her ear. 'I would have thought driving my brother out of England would have been enough to warm even your chilly little heart.'

The words penetrated her haze of misery. 'He's leaving the country soon?'

Garth's smile was a sardonic sneer. 'People in your exalted world don't hear much about the damage they do to the little people, do they?'

He referred to Rafter, no doubt. 'What about Christopher?'

He raised a slashing dark brow.

Heat climbed into her face. 'Mr Evernden, I mean.'

'He's taken your father at his word. He's leaving for America. You'll never have to suffer the embarrassment of his presence again.'

She recoiled at his venomous tone. 'My father?'

'Just so. At the request of the Duke and to avoid you further distress at the sight of lowly, unwanted Christopher, he sets sail on the *Free Spirit* out of Dover. She casts off at noon on Saturday. I can't imagine what he ever saw in a hardened cow like you, for all your beauty.'

With a flourish, he executed an unsteady bow. 'You, dear lady, will be happy to know you got your way. He's leaving England.'

As he strode away, several female heads turned to watch the dark and dangerous rake's progress. His imperceptible roll spoke volumes about his state of inebriation.

Christopher was leaving.

For a moment, Sylvia felt strangely dizzy. A hollow sinking sensation swirled in her stomach. It clawed its way into her chest and filled her mind with darkness. A rushing sound filled her ears. *Oh, God. Don't let me faint. Not here.*

'Are you all right, Lady Sylvia?' Nettle, with her lemonade, hovered at her elbow.

She took slow deep breaths. Christopher had never spoken of love. Never had he indicated anything beyond passion during their brief time together. She had convinced herself his omission was unintentional. Now she had her answer. She must have been mad to think anything else.

The wall of ice that had protected her all her life did nothing to shield her from the ache where her heart had once resided. Carelessly ripped out and discarded by a man who cared nothing for her, it lay crushed at her feet. She was just like her mother, waiting for a lover who would never return.

Incroyable. She was not her mother. She knew better.

She glanced at Nettle's anxious expression and gave a shaky laugh 'Yes. Thank you. I just…' Her eyes burned and she choked on her words. 'Excuse me,' she murmured and followed Garth into the card room.

'Goodbye, Kit.'

Dover's white cliffs towered above Christopher's head and seagulls screamed abuse at the stiff breeze supporting them aloft. He hunched into the collar of his thick woollen coat.

Dover. It seemed as if some of the most portentous moments in his life were somehow connected to this dirty port. He released his grip on the rail and turned to grasp Garth's outstretched hand.

'Look after yourself, brother.' Garth's voice hoarsened with unspoken emotion.

It wasn't like Garth to be so serious, so grave, almost lost.

Christopher blinked away the mist blurring his brother and the clean lines of the *Free Spirit*. 'I'll miss you too. Take care of Mother. I know she acts as if she favours me over you, but if you'd be a little kinder to her, Garth, you and she might rub along better. I talked to her about it too. Yesterday.'

Garth took a step back, his mouth open. 'You did what?'

Christopher shrugged. 'I told her she could be a little less hard on you.'

'And what did she say to that, pray?'

She'd closed up like an oyster protecting a sharp grain of irritation. 'She changed the subject.'

Garth blinked. 'Kit…' His gaze dropped to the deck. He cleared his throat, tugged at his cravat. 'Kit, there's something you need to know.'

'What?'

'The devil. It's not really my secret to reveal, but, damn it it all, you are the only one who doesn't seem to realise…'

Never had Christopher seen Garth speechless. 'Spit it out, before you choke, or the ship sets sail.'

'I'm not an Evernden.'

Garth had something loose in his attic. The drink was finally ruining his mind. Christopher put a hand on his shoulder, prepared to suggest he visit a doctor.

'I'm not Father's seed,' Garth bit out. 'Mother…made a mistake. I'm sorry.'

The deck pitched beneath Christopher's feet, yet the sea remained calm. 'My God. That's why you acted so oddly at the Duke's. But why apologise to me?'

'You're not thinking, Kit. You should have been the heir. You are Father's first-born.'

'Bloody hell.' The realisation hit him like a hammer between the eyes.

Garth stared over the rail. 'I hope you aren't going to hate me, the way Father did. The way Mother does.'

'You numbskull. Is that why you've been such an idiot all these years? Look around you. I have everything I could possibly want.' Everything except Sylvia, and a minor title wouldn't have helped him in that quarter.

'Thank you, Kit. You don't know how much that means.' Garth's voice sounded hoarse.

'Please,' Christopher said, 'do something for me. Try to get along with Mother until I return?'

'God,' Garth drawled, suddenly his old insouciant self, 'Mother's hooks are so deep into Angleforth, she wouldn't notice if I dropped dead tomorrow.'

Christopher laughed just as Garth had wanted. He shook his head. 'She'd notice.'

'I wish you weren't going.'

'I'll be back before you know it. Five years is not so long.'

'Yes,' Garth choked out. 'It bloody well is.'

Christopher found himself crushed in Garth's bear-like hug, his nose pressed into the rough wool of his brother's coat. He squeezed back and patted Garth's shoulder. They parted and gazed past each other with embarrassed grins and watery eyes.

A bell rang. Whistles sounded. The ship strained against its creaking ropes as if anxious to be underway.

Christopher rubbed his chilled hands together and nodded to the waiting tender. 'If you don't go soon, you'll be on your way to America.'

'I wish.'

'Come with me.'

A cynical smile twisted Garth's mouth. 'Sounds too much like hard work.'

They walked together to the gangway where a boat waited to row Garth to shore. One last link, a flimsy wooden boat soon to sever the tie with England. Tarry-pigtailed sailors shouted back and forth at the capstan and released the hawsers holding the ship at anchor.

'I saw her,' Garth said, stepping through the gap in the rail.

His breath caught. He didn't have to ask who Garth meant. 'Don't,' he managed.

A strange rueful grin on his lips, Garth hesitated a moment before he plunged down the ladder, nodding at the sailor waiting, oars at the ready. A few strong pulls took him to shore, where his long stride carried him swiftly along the dock, past the sailors and fishermen and past the blowsy fishwives who followed his broad-shouldered figure with longing glances.

The *Free Spirit* slipped her moorings and eased out of her berth.

Christopher walked to the stern, keeping his gaze fixed on Garth's back, now just a black speck, until he could no longer discern him from the rest of the teeming ant-like masses scurrying along the shoreline.

Returning to the rail, he kept his gaze fixed on land, determined to see the last of England before he went below to his stateroom.

It was an over-luxurious apartment for a merchantman, but this was his ship. He glanced around with pride at the gleaming decks and smartly turned-out crew. He acknowledged the captain's salute with a nod. He lacked the sense of excitement he'd once felt for this ship, yet his pride remained—after all, it belonged to him.

He returned his attention to the horizon. The wind picked up and the ship heeled over, making every yard of canvas count. The sun escaped the confines of billowing grey-and-silver clouds, making steely waves shimmer like pirate's treasure. Far off, the cliffs gleamed like brilliant sails, the ancient walls of Dover Castle a turreted crow's nest against the skyline. The great ship of England was departing, leaving him alone on an insignificant wooden platform, marooned in a vast ocean, perhaps never to see it again.

The clouds returned to gobble great bites out of the light

and the coast became a faint smudge in the distance above sluggish grey-green water.

Somewhere along that smudge he had first set eyes on Sylvia. She had been so solitary at his uncle's funeral. Alone, but bright and hard-edged like a polished jewel. It wasn't until he'd looked deep beneath the glittering facets that he'd found the fire of her soul. But once found, there was no forgetting its heat.

As the ship drew further from shore, he realised no distance would be far enough to allow him to forget. He struck the rail with his fist. Shockwaves vibrated up his arm and jarred the hollow emptiness in his chest. He clenched his jaw. Nothing, not even sheer physical strength, could change what had happened.

He took a deep breath and forced himself to calmness. Sylvia deserved better. The Duke had put it succinctly the morning Christopher had gone to make his offer of marriage. All her life, she had been deprived of the privileges of her birth. It was Huntingdon's avowed intention to restore everything Rafter had stolen from her.

Everything. Including a brilliant marriage.

Forced to agree with Huntingdon, he hadn't flinched when the Duke had suggested it might be better if Christopher left London. He was a distraction and a possible cause of gossip. He'd made his plans to leave for America the same day.

Hell. He had always wanted to go to the New World. It was a land where men stood or fell by their own abilities, their wits, their physical strength, not by who their father was, or the order of their emergence from the womb.

His cabin was filled with books about the new country he was about to embrace. They would keep his mind off his regrets. He turned away from the sight of land.

A lone figure, slight, windblown, leaned against the mast.

Sylvia? Strands of gold hair lashed her rosy cheeks. Her bright blue gaze held steady on his face.

Half-expecting to find some kind of mystical sea beast had enchanted him, he gazed around the ship. He was dreaming, only now he was doing it in the daytime.

He shook his head to clear his vision. But this was no mirage. This was a living breathing Sylvia.

She braced one hand against the mast and cocked her head in question.

What the hell had she done? If word got out, she'd be ruined. His feet seemed glued in place.

Despite Garth's assurances, Sylvia hadn't been completely convinced Christopher would be happy to see her. At the sight of his shocked face, the deck began to crumble beneath her feet.

'What the hell are you doing here?' he shouted against the wind.

She forced herself to remain still, not to throw herself against his broad chest and beg him to let her stay. 'I'm going to America.'

He strode across the deck and grasped her shoulders, his eyes full of green fury. 'What are you talking about?'

She took a deep breath and flung herself trustingly over the edge of the precipice of her pride. 'I love you and I'm coming with you.'

Stark horror filled his expression. 'You can't.'

She was in a headlong fall and Christopher hadn't made a move to catch her. 'You don't have to marry me,' she gabbled. 'I'll leave whenever you get tired of me. But I won't spend my life waiting.'

He shook his head.

Oh, God. He was going to let her shatter in a million pieces at his feet.

He pushed his hair out of his eyes. 'You have to go back.'

Sharp rocks of despair rushed up to meet her. He didn't want her. He really didn't.

She began to pull away.

He caught her hand. 'Your father. He's only just found you. He'll be devastated.'

This was about them, her and Christopher. 'He knows. He doesn't like it, but he understands. Christopher, please.'

His lashes swept down, blocking his thoughts, deep lines etching the sides of his mouth.

The ship rolled and bucked beneath her feet; the sound of the wind reverberated like thunder in the sails and hummed in the rigging. Her hair whipped at her face, salty and damp. Each second crawled like an hour, while she waited for his denial.

He opened his eyes. Powerful yearning and fierce possessiveness burned deep in their gleaming emerald depths. 'Sylvia. My love.'

He pulled her tight against his warm, hard body. He bent his head and found her mouth with his. Crushed in his arms, his heart beating steadily against her chest, the pure delight in his voice ringing in her ears, her fear faded like sea mist.

She floated to the ground as light as thistledown, caught firmly in his arms.

'Oh, God,' he whispered against her mouth. 'I love you so much. I thought I'd come back and find you married to a bloody marquess or an earl.'

He tilted her chin until he could look into her eyes. 'You're absolutely sure about this?' Anxiety roughened his voice.

She didn't try to hide the tears of joy blurring her sight. She nodded.

His hand came up and freed her hair from its pins. It swirled around them, a shimmering veil of gold. 'I love you.' His mouth covered hers with infinite tenderness.

A boom thundered overhead and they looked up.

A red flare streaked above them. 'What the devil…?' Christopher muttered.

'*Sea Witch* on the port bow, sir,' the captain called.

Sylvia laughed at the ludicrous expression of surprise on Christopher's face when they went to the rail.

'How the hell did Garth get my mother on that ship?'

Sylvia felt the heat rise in her cheeks and looked down at the deck. Now he would know they were all in the plot.

'Bloody hell. And your father and brother. They're all on the *Witch*.'

Sylvia peeped over the rail at the madly waving crowd on the deck of Garth's yacht and waved back. A string of coloured flags climbed the mast.

'Message from the *Sea Witch*, sir.'

'Well?' Christopher said, his mouth quirking at the corners.

'It says "marry the girl", sir.'

Christopher fumbled at his neck, pulling at his neckcloth. Braced against the ship's rail, Sylvia held her breath, suddenly unsure. He pulled free a chain and opened the clasp. A gold circle encrusted with diamonds and sapphires lay on his palm. Christopher took her hand and went down on one knee.

'My lady, would you do me the very great honour of becoming my wife?'

A huge burning lump blocked her throat and made her eyes water.

He gripped her hand. 'Sylvia,' he said. 'For God's sake. Will you?'

'Yes.' She laughed through her tears. 'Oh, yes. I will.'

He leaped up, slipped the ring on her finger and crushed her to his chest.

'Sir,' the captain said. They turned to face him. He wore a huge grin and beside him stood a parson with a bible in his hand.

'Garth managed to find a cleric who wanted to travel to America,' Sylvia explained at his look of amazement.

More rockets burst overhead. Christopher glanced over the rail at the upturned faces of the expectant, but distant, bridal party and raised a questioning brow.

'Shall I begin, sir?' the parson asked.

Christopher encircled Sylvia in the warmth of his strong arms and his chuckle reverberated through her body.

'What the hell are you waiting for, man? Begin. Time is wasting and we've some catching up to do.'

* * * * *

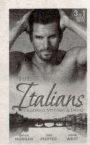

> 'A fresh new voice in romantic fiction'
> —*Marie Claire*

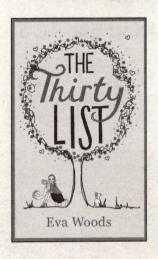

Everyone has one.
That list.
The things you were *supposed* to do before you turn thirty.

Jobless, broke and getting a divorce, Rachel isn't exactly living up to her own expectations. And moving into grumpy single dad Patrick's box room is just the soggy icing on top of her dreaded thirtieth birthday cake.

Eternal list-maker Rachel has a plan—an all-new set of challenges to help her get over her divorce and out into the world again—from tango dancing to sushi making to stand-up comedy.

But, as Patrick helps her cross off each task, Rachel faces something even harder: learning to live—and love—without a checklist.